Herrick's Lie

Book 2 of The Neath Trilogy

By

T.M. Blanchet

A Tiny Fox Press Book

Library of Congress Control Number: 2022949976
ISBN: 978-1-946501-49-3

Tiny Fox Press LLC
North Port, FL

*For Bert Roens,
Elisha Atkins,
and Elizabeth Atkins*

Prologue

Salem Village, Massachusetts Bay Colony
December 1692

After the summer and autumn had vanished into snow, after the trials had ended, after the bodies had been cut from the gallows at Proctor's Ledge and left to freeze in the ground, Salem Village Deputy-Sheriff George Herrick "most humbly" submitted a petition to the village court and council.

The proceedings were brief. Herrick's head dipped in deference as he awaited the decision from the row of stone-faced, black-robed men sitting behind the wooden table. Birds twittered in the rafters above. When the pronouncement came, it was delivered in a nasally voice by one of the seated men: "The petition is denied."

Herrick's head snapped up. "Denied? On what grounds?"

"On the grounds that the court sees fit to render it so. You have been paid your wages, Deputy. And yet you beseech this court now for still more?"

He straightened his hat. "Aye, I have been paid. But those wages, Your Honors, were established before this…wickedness descended upon us. Before my duties expanded far beyond their original designs."

"The wickedness of which you speak has burdened all of us, it is true," the magistrate replied. "Do you mean to say you now grow tired of serving your king and country?"

"I do not, and I shall not," Herrick huffed, lifting his chin. "I ask only for fair compensation. As all those here know, I have been bred a gentleman and not much used to work. And yet I have spent these many months toiling, morning and night. Transporting and examining the guilty. Leading them to the very scaffolding from which they hung by the neck. All for the good of our fair village."

"Aye," agreed the magistrate in the center of the row. Thin gray hair curled against his shoulders. "Indeed, you have proved more eager than most to expose the devils in our midst. You yourself were listed as plaintiff in several of those indictments, were you not?"

"I was," Herrick nodded. "I say not that the accusations were unfounded. I say only that my duties as a participant in these hallowed proceedings have not yet been fairly compensated. Surely the court must—"

"Your service to the village is appreciated, Deputy. And your petition has been heard. Heard, and denied." The man handed a sheet of paper to a clerk, who in turn passed it to Herrick. Then he called out, "Next petitioner."

"But Your Honors!" Herrick sputtered. "Have I not done all that you ask, and more still? Have I not done God's work?"

"Next petitioner," the magistrate said again, his voice booming in the empty air.

It was plain for all assembled to see: The cause was lost.

George Herrick spun on his boot heel and stormed from the building, bursting onto the cold street with a stream of curses spewing from his lips. White flakes swirled, blinding his vision. Fury burned in his chest. Did they not understand the sacrifices he had made? The professionalism he had shown? How could they all, to a man, be so ungrateful for his service to the good people of Salem?

He did not, at first, notice the figures in the road ahead, masked as phantoms in the snowfall. By the time he saw them, recognized them, they had surrounded him in a circle.

"A brisk morning, is it not, Deputy?" one in the group commented, stepping closer. Her tone was pleasant. Suspiciously so.

Herrick's face hardened. "Begone," he said. "I'll have no quarrel with the likes of you today."

He counted three—no, four—women, and two men. Flakes continued to fall around them, rendering the street as silent as a grave.

"What brings you out on such a blustery day, good Sir?" another asked. This one was tall, almost as tall as he, with bright skin, apple cheeks, and a pert nose. One might even call her beautiful. One might. George Herrick would not. The woman stepped forward and, without seeking permission, pulled the crumpled paper from his hands and cast her eyes upon it. "It would seem our Mr. Herrick has brought a petition for the court."

The gathered group murmured.

He turned left, then right, only to find that the intruders blocked any route of escape from this ridiculous interrogation. "And what business is it of yours, woman?" he spat.

She continued as if he had not spoken. "Tell us, Deputy, of what do you protest? By our count, you have dragged twenty-five innocent souls to their deaths in these past months. I would think it was they who had more grounds for complaint."

"Innocent, you say?"

She smiled serenely. "I do say, yes. And I have cause of which to know."

"The courts have said otherwise," he retorted. "I do only my job. And you wish to fault me now for doing it well?"

No one in the circle responded. That silence, more than their words, stabbed a needle of foreboding into his chest.

"Begone," he said again. "You know not of which you speak."

"On the contrary, good Sir. We understand much. And I think you, too, are beginning to understand. Are you not?"

He didn't answer.

"For months, these farcical proceedings have continued," she said, holding his gaze. "Accusations based on nothing more than whispered, foolish falsehoods. One after the other. And you knew, even as you helped to perpetuate it, that it was wrong."

"I knew of no such—"

"You knew!" the woman interrupted, her eyes narrow. "You can lie to your townspeople, and you can lie to yourself. But you cannot, dear Deputy, lie to us. Has that not yet become clear?"

Herrick swallowed past the growing drought in his mouth.

"You have killed them," she continued. "By your own actions, you have condemned your neighbors. Worse still, you have shackled them, and starved them, and tortured them. You have stolen the very breath from their lungs with heavy stones and twisted ropes. And now, at the end of it all, your primary concern is that—" She paused, glancing at the paper in her hand. "Is that you were not paid enough to do so?"

The winter wind had cracked his lips; he licked them and felt the sting.

"The court has denied your petition, I see," she said, skimming the words on the page. "They have decreed that you, George Herrick, have earned enough. And we decree the same." She stepped forward and the others followed, tightening the circle around him. "Your time for earning, for taking, is past. Now the time has come to pay."

"Pay?" Herrick scoffed, though his face betrayed a bald fear. "What exactly would you have me pay, woman?"

"Only what you owe," she answered.

Around him, the others spoke in unison, echoing her words in a melodic hum: "Only what you owe."

Panic mounting, he spun in a circle, looking frantically from face to face. When he finally spoke the word that had been clogging his throat, it escaped in a hiss: "Witches!"

A flutter of laughter spread through the assembled group.

The curly-haired woman tilted her head and smiled. "Yes, Deputy Herrick," she said. "For once, you are right about that. It is most amusing, it is not? To think of all the time you've spent searching for witches. Yet in the end, it is the witches who find you." She leaned ever closer, until her breath fell like acrid steam against his face. "And soon, good Sir, you will wish we had not."

One

The Neath
Present Day

Herrick's End was just the beginning.

Which made no sense, of course. The word "end" was right there in the name. But that was how things seemed to go in the Neath, sometimes. Most of the time. Highs were lows, strangers were saviors, the unimaginable was imagined. And ends didn't even know enough to stay where they belonged.

This was not, generally speaking, a good sign. Everybody's heard of happy endings. Happy beginnings? Not so much.

In hindsight, Ollie supposed he should have known the balloon would pop. He was used to disappointments, after all. Unhappy endings *and* beginnings. And middles, and three-quarters-of-the-way-throughs. But he had been floating in pure helium happiness for months, now. It was a feeling as unfamiliar to him as—well, as any other kind of happiness, really. He should have realized that balloons can only fly so high before they hit a ceiling fan, or a seagull's beak, or the spiky tip of a stalactite hanging from a cavern wall. All it takes is one tiny hole to send the whole thing spurting and whirling and falling back down to earth in an embarrassing, flaccid spiral.

Like most unexpected blows to euphoria, this one came while he was looking the other way. Looking at her, specifically. Then again, he always seemed to be looking at her. Who could blame him? Tera was, quite simply, perfection in human form. If they were back on the Brickside, or what he used to know as the "real world," he would have called her his girlfriend. He would have said the word as often as possible, sneaking it into casual conversation with cashiers and dentists and guys selling roasted peanuts from pushcarts. "Have you met my girlfriend?" Or, "These are delicious! I'll bring some home for my girlfriend." And maybe: "I have a cavity? Oh, no. I wonder if my girlfriend has cavities, too?"

But Ollie Delgato was not on the Brickside. Not anymore. Instead, he was trapped miles below and a world away, in a place where words like "girlfriend" were less common. Down here in the Neath, they used words like "trog" (noun: a furry, round mammal with a platypus-like beak and a penchant for snacks), and "glog" (noun: a barrel used to store vast quantities of fizzing, fermented liquid), and "snog" (verb: that thing you do with your girlfriend after consuming vast quantities of fizzing, fermented liquid), and lots of other words that, only a few months ago, would have sounded as foreign to him as hieroglyphics. Which is saying something, since hieroglyphics didn't technically make any sound at all.

It was only supposed to be a quick visit—day or two, max. But one day had turned into many more, thanks to an unexpected and definitely unwelcome stint in a terrifying prison tower, a.k.a. the aforementioned Herrick's End. Ollie eventually made it out in one piece, thanks to Tera—then ran smack dab into an even worse quandary when his lungs had adjusted to the underground oxygen levels. Once that happened, it was game over. If he wanted to breathe, he had to do it down here. And Ollie found that he was pretty attached to breathing. Thus, his new and permanent residence in a weirdly enormous cave.

Weirder still, Ollie didn't even mind.

His life on the Brickside had been decent enough. Not spectacular, to be sure, but comfortable. He had been a fourth-generation Italian in Boston's most Italian neighborhood, the

North End, with a reliable (if dull) job at Bonfiglio's Caffe and a reliable (if dull) future planned in medical imaging after a stint at Bunker Hill Community College. There was even a scholarship with his name on it, somewhere up there, though of course he'd never use it now. A gift, unopened. *Unfulfilled potential,* his mother would have called it. Part of him was glad she wasn't alive to witness the waste.

His former social life, likewise, was not what anyone would have called vibrant. After his mom had died of breast cancer, he'd taken her spot at the neighborhood old timers' weekly Bingo game. He'd muddled through the days trying not to eat pastries while simultaneously serving them to others for a living. Though he'd struggled to make friends, he did get along well enough with his coworkers and the other members of his weight-loss support group, Lighter Tomorrows. He'd even had his own small apartment and an ever-expanding collection of video games. For better or for worse, everyone on Hanover Street had known his name.

Ollie had loved his city—its manageable size, its history, and its famously no-bullshit attitude. He loved St. Anthony's Feast, holiday lights along Commonwealth Avenue, the Gardner's atrium greenery, and the smell of old books at the Brattle. He'd loved the rattling rumble of the T, the constant and reassuring wail of sirens in Longwood, and the undeniable electricity in the air during home games. Unlike most locals, he didn't even mind the annual tsunami of college students in the fall, or the swirl of nor-easters in January. He was a Boston boy, right down to the strands of his DNA. Ollie had never met an R he couldn't drop.

But none of that had mattered, in the end. If Tera was here, in the Neath, then here was where he wanted to be…even if "here" was a sometimes dangerous, always peculiar grotto filled with things like phosphorescent worms, clairvoyant witches, fights-to-the-death, supersonic chairlift rides, 350-year-old men, rickety bridges, one-eyed cellmates, and more than a few mystifying magical potions. Very little about his former, powdered-sugar life in the North End had prepared him for any of that.

It wasn't all bad. Some of the locals were actually pretty great, and Ollie had already made more friends in the Neath than he'd ever had back at home. A few enemies, too. He supposed that was unavoidable, given the unsavory things he'd had to do to help himself and his new compadres escape the tower and overthrow the regime that had made too many suffer for too long.

In the months since, Ollie had spent his days admiring his girlfriend, eating with his girlfriend, kissing his girlfriend (did he mention he had a girlfriend?), and earning his keep. He even ran a support group of his own, not unlike the one he used to attend in the North End—though his new "Lighter Tomorrows" focused on lifting the spirits of abuse victims rather than trimming waistlines. Life could not have been better. And it would, he imagined, continue in that perpetual state of bliss forever.

"Two up!"

"Hmm?" Ollie straightened.

Ajanta was staring at him with her hands on her hips. "Two up!" she barked again, gesturing at the line of customers in front of their stall. "Are you going to help, or what?"

"Right. Sorry." He lifted his elbows from the counter and reached for the wooden scoop. He and Ajanta ran the food stall together. That technically made them business partners, he supposed, though she was more like the older, wiser mentor and he was more like the younger and perpetually distracted hired help. The sign out front read "Ollanta's" in a cutesy combination of their two names. They mostly served rhizers, the Neath's main crop, which grew in bountiful varieties in the cavern's deep-earth soil. Despite their many visual differences—blue and pink, round and tubular, smooth and spiky—each and every rhizer nonetheless tasted like a bland, white potato. There was just no getting around it. So, Ollie and Ajanta used Indian and Italian seasonings, and their mutual love of food, to try to spice things up a bit. So far, it had worked; the line outside Ollanta's often stretched around the market docks and all the way back to dry land.

"This might surprise you, young man, but you're not here to make googly eyes at the ladies all day," Ajanta added, her Indian accent making the words march.

"Sorry," Ollie muttered again. But he wasn't sorry. Not even a little bit. As he scooped oily rhizers into waiting customers' hands, he stole another look. Tera was there, two docks over, doing the hustle thing she always did. Working her contacts. Making connections. At the moment, she was talking to a small man in front of a merchandise stall. Convincing him of something, no doubt. Tera Martinez was so clever she could talk a Red Sox fan into wearing a Yankees hat. She could make a real-estate deal on a sandcastle—and get the signatures before high tide. She could do anything she wanted, be anything she wanted, and have anything she wanted. And amazingly, she seemed to want him. He reminded himself, again, that he didn't deserve her. That he was the luckiest overweight, sandy-haired, ghostly pale, rhizer-scooping guy in this underworld cave or the next.

"Ollie!"

"Right, right! Sorry!"

He resumed ladling and serving as Ajanta handled the money. All the while, his eyes continued to follow Tera on her meandering path around the docks. It wasn't until she had approached the third person in ten minutes—a woman with wiry hair wearing the standard Neath off-white jumpsuit—that his brow began to furrow. What, exactly, was Tera up to out there? She seemed to be asking each person a series of questions. And all of them, in turn, had shaken their heads, held up their hands, and finally walked away.

He chewed his lip, considering the possibilities. Tera hadn't mentioned any kind of problem to him. In her day job, she worked as a crow-boat driver, ferrying passengers around to the various Neath islands with the help of her eight-foot-tall (and somewhat grouchy) crow, Mrs. Paget. The two of them were often gone for long stretches. But Tera was also an aspiring painter and portraitist, with hopes to open her own art stall. Was that what she was doing now? Inquiring about rents and space?

The market's colorful flags flapped in the air above her head as Tera maneuvered through the crowds, balanced on the ever-shifting floating docks, and made her way to yet another person with her questions. All around them, vendors hawked their products—buckets, bowls, headlamps, rudimentary furniture, fabrics, and an endless array of grotesque foodstuffs—and shouted to entice passersby. Like the others Tera had questioned, this woman shook her head and shrugged her shoulders before wandering off.

As he watched, Ollie couldn't help but notice that Tera looked pained. Confused. And worried. The sight was strange enough to lift the hairs on his neck. No circumstance was too daunting for his

Tera. No challenge was too great. So why, then, did she suddenly look like a tax evader at an IRS audit?

His unease turned to queasiness. Finally, he dropped the scoop. "Hey, Aja, you mind if I kick off a little early?" he asked. "I've got...a thing. To do."

She sighed but didn't look surprised. Ajanta had been a mother figure to Tera when he met them, and now, he supposed, she was a mother figure to him, too. A much needed one, as it turned out. His own mother had been dead for a little over a year, and Ollie was still drifting in a steady and confusing current of mourning. "Fine," she said. Her long braid swayed when she shook her head. "But make sure you're here on time tomorrow."

"Of course!" he said. "Thank you!"

"And be careful!"

"I will!" Ollie bolted before she could change her mind. He darted left and right, dodging the sauntering shoppers and the stall keepers peddling their wares.

"Mix and mettle!" shouted someone nearby.

"Hardball hatties!" called another. "Two for nine!"

A woman grabbed his elbow as he passed. "Whole nestie for you?" she asked, waving a bowlful of wriggling, wet, feathered creatures under his nose. They smelled like old parmesan. Ollie coughed, tugged his arm away, and kept moving.

He towered above them all. That was one thing that had stayed consistent during his transformation to Neath life: Aboveground or below it, Ollie was always the biggest person in any crowd. Not only in height, but also in the generous rolls of flesh that wrapped his midsection like pre-baked pretzel dough. He used to hate his body. Some days, he still did. He used to go to support groups and weight-loss meetings to try to change himself, and to surround himself with others who could relate. Mostly, though, he used to hide—from the mirror, and from the world.

Then came Tera. Incredibly, she seemed to love every part of him, even the parts he detested. She painted portraits of him— portraits that glowed with obvious affection. She seemed happy, even proud, to slip her arm through his, no matter where they happened to be. She wanted to be near him. To watch him. To touch him. Ollie still didn't understand it, and he probably never would. All he knew for sure was that for the first time in his life, he was done hiding. He was free. He was just...himself. And it felt shockingly good.

Finally, he rounded a corner and caught sight of her again. She had her back to him, talking to a bearded man near a display of sharpened shovels. The conversation seemed intense.

Ollie approached from behind. She was like a tiny, delicious package: five-foot-one, or maybe two, with an unmistakable swirl of purple hair at the top of her head. Her hands waved in the air as she spoke. Grinning, he stepped behind her and began to wrap his arms around her waist.

"Surprise!" he said.

Or at least, that's what he had planned to say. But he got only as far as "Sur—" before his feet left the ground. With the swiftness of a ninja, Tera had spun, thrust out her arms, and swept his legs. The next thing he knew, Ollie had hit the dock hard enough to make water splash up through the slats. He groaned. Opening his eyes, he saw only the glowing blue ceiling of the cavern above him. And then he saw Tera's face, peering down into his own. Two of Tera's faces, actually. Three? They spun around each other in a hazy square dance of head trauma.

"Ollie? Krite, what the hell are you doing?"

He blinked, then groaned again. The three faces coalesced into one. His favorite face. Warm brown eyes. Cinnamon skin. Mouth opened into an oval of surprise.

Ollie smiled dumbly.

"You know this guy?" the bearded man asked Tera.

"Yeah, I do."

He grunted. "Then you'd think he'd know better than to sneak up behind you."

"Yes, you would think that," Tera replied, staring down at Ollie with one eyebrow raised. She held out a hand. Though half his size, she still somehow managed to hoist him effortlessly off the damp dock.

"I'm okay," Ollie said, struggling to his feet.

"Sorry about that, Babe," she said. "You can't sneak up on a girl like that."

"I wanted to surprise you," he said, rubbing his neck.

The bearded man chuckled.

"Ollie, meet Yasgar. Yasgar, Ollie."

The two men grunted at each other.

"Yasgar was just helping me with...some questions."

"Questions about what?" Ollie asked.

Tera opened her mouth to answer, then closed it again. For a moment, no one spoke.

Yasgar looked from one to the other. "I'm gonna get going, T," he said, jerking his thumb.

"Okay, thanks. I'll see you later."

"Sorry I couldn't help," he added. Then he turned to Ollie with a smirk. "Nice to meet you, man. I hope those bruises heal up quick."

Ollie flashed him a pinched, false smile. He watched Yasgar wander away before spinning to face her.

"Tera, what's going on?"

Her head tipped to the left. "Don't tell me you're turning into the jealous type."

"Don't be ridiculous. I'm worried about you."

At this, she looked amused. That didn't surprise Ollie, considering that she was usually the one worrying about him—with good reason. Still, this was different. Or seemed to be different, anyway. "You've been...distracted," he said. "Somewhere else, even when you're here. And now you're walking all over the market, talking to everyone. Looking upset."

"It's nothing," Tera said. She was lying, badly. And since Ollie imagined she was probably as good at lying as she was at everything else, he had to assume that meant that she wanted him to know she was lying. That she wanted him to pull the truth out of her. And he was happy to do it. If the truth was hurting her, he would pull it out and stomp it and burn it like a goddamn vampire in the sun.

"Please," he said, shrinking his massive frame down to her level. Lifting her chin with one finger to look straight into her eyes. "Let me help."

Tera returned his gaze, unwavering. She seemed to be considering something. Finally, she gave a slow nod. "All right."

"All right?"

"Follow me," she said.

"Where?" he asked, though the question was just a formality. He would have followed her anywhere.

Tera sighed, again. "There's something I have to show you."

The balloon hit something sharp then, in that moment, though he had no way of knowing that the deflation had begun. That his solid, colorful orb of joy had just sprung its first leak. Like most things in life, the change was invisible, and inevitable. And like most things in the Neath, it was probably going to splutter and spin its way through ten kinds of awful before ever landing anywhere near happiness again.

Two

Tera led Ollie to the end of a far dock where her boat was waiting. Mrs. Paget, as always, perched in the back. At their arrival, the giant crow stood and stretched her wings.

"Hello, miss lovely," Tera said, jumping on board and rumpling the bird's black, feathery head.

Ollie was more cautious. He and Mrs. Paget had developed a truce of sorts back when Tera had needed their help. Now that the crisis had passed, they had resumed a polite arrangement: Ollie agreed to welcome the outlandishly huge, beady-eyed creature into his daily life, and Mrs. Paget, theoretically, agreed to suppress her natural inclination to peck out his vital organs.

"Where are we going?" he asked.

"A little field trip," Tera answered, untying the rope from the dock's post and climbing onto Mrs. Paget's back. She snapped the reins and the crow spread her wings and flapped, thrusting the small boat forward into the dark green water. As always, the sight gave Ollie an unnerving flash into his previous life: The Neath's crow boats were freakish reflections of Brickside's Swan Boats, which ferried tourists around the lagoon in Boston's beautiful Public Garden. There, the water was blue, and sparkling, and scattered with friendly ducks. Here, the water was brackish, lit only from cave luminescence, and obscured God-only-knew what kind of distinctly *un*friendly creatures lurking below.

The noise of the market faded quickly behind them as they moved away from the shoreline. Ollie stood and leaned against the railing, gazing out into the vast grotto that had become his unlikely home.

Fog touched everything: the lake, the islands, the comings-and-goings of the busy inhabitants as they scuttled over bridges and hills. Ollie had once called these people victims, though Tera had been quick to correct him. The people of the Neath were *survivors*, she explained. Most, like her, had chosen to come to this underground sanctuary for a better, safer life. Aboveground, they had been victimized and abused, often by the same people who were supposed to be protecting and loving them.

Many had come only after other efforts had failed: efforts at relocating, or changing their names, or trying to leave their past behind them. Some had learned the hard way that restraining orders usually managed to restrain very little, and in fact often inflamed abusers into ever-more threatening acts. For these people, the Brickside had become a place of fear, uncertainty, and constant running. Danger was always around the corner. And it only took a quick scan of the headlines—and the obituaries—to learn what the eventual outcome might be.

Here, in the Neath, they could be free. Happy. Living among people who understood their pain. That was why this place had been created hundreds of years ago, as a refuge for those who had nowhere else to turn. An underground oasis of protection.

Somewhere along the line, though, things had changed. Ollie's eyes slid to his right as the tower loomed into view: Herrick's End. Monstrous and decrepit, even from a distance, the prison was a later addition to the Neath. How much later, Ollie couldn't say. According to legend, the witches—no strangers to abuse and persecution—had created the Neath. But it was the humans—no strangers to screwing things up—who had created Herrick's End.

The prison had been home to unimaginable tortures, horrific living conditions, and brutal fighting contests, all overseen by a Warden who had been happy to prey on anyone—even children—to maintain his stranglehold on power. This went on for years, until Ollie himself landed in Herrick's End ("due to an unfortunate mix-up," as he now liked to say) and started a chain of events that had changed the place for good. Or so he hoped.

Ollie shivered and turned his eyes away, letting them land on the gentle slopes of Blackstone Park as the boat passed. The former Warden was there, now: Ollie could just barely make out the man's seated, perfectly still figure in the throne-like chair on the hill. Ollie and Tera had tricked him, trapped him, and left him to suffer his frozen-in-time fate. Now, there was no more torture at Herrick's End. Reforms were in place, and their friend Leonard had been installed as the new, kindlier Superintendent of Operations.

But tempers still rumbled within the prison walls. Not everyone was happy about the changes. And the Warden, it was said, was starting to twitch in his chair. One person claimed to have seen his fingers curl. Was the spell wearing off? If the Warden did somehow manage to free himself, or if his grumbling former minions decided to take matters in their own hands, what would happen then?

Ollie had asked himself that question dozens of times, but never seemed to be able to ponder it out loud. Mostly because he was afraid of the answer.

With a shiver, he turned his back on the park view and asked Tera, "How far are we going?"

"Not far," she said, smiling down at him from the bird's back.

Another unhelpful reply. Ollie heaved a deep breath and settled into one of the boat's bench seats. He didn't like any of this. Not her evasiveness, not the shadow of trouble, and especially not this impromptu field trip. He didn't want to go on any trips. All he wanted to do was curl up with Tera in their cozy little cottage, pan-fry blindfish over the fire, and watch the world pass by the windows. Well, window, singular. And in truth, very few people ever passed by. Still, was a little simplicity and peace too much to ask?

Mrs. Paget continued to flap her wings in a steady, powerful rhythm. Water lapped against the sides of the hull. The boat passed several islands he didn't recognize and eventually entered a marshy area, thick with reedy stalks. He might have called them cattails, except for the fact that the brown, soft tubes at the top of each stem seemed to be expanding and shrinking. In and out, up and down, like crinkling, upholstered accordions. He could also swear he heard them emitting some kind of melodious sound.

"Are those things...singing?"

"Hmm?" Tera followed his gaze to the fat reeds. "Oh, yeah. Those are hummingtails. Pretty, huh?"

He nodded, dazed. The music was hypnotic. Not toe-tapping, exactly; more like a colony of bees had suddenly decided to buzz in perfect unison and harmony.

Moments later, the boat slid up onto a sandy shore. The hummingtails' music faded into the background as Mrs. Paget stopped flapping and tucked her wings into her sides.

"You wait here, okay?" Tera told her, sliding off the animal's large back. "We won't be long."

The crow shimmied her feathers and settled in. Ollie watched her warily, keeping his distance as he followed Tera off the boat and onto the sand.

She gave him a reassuring smile. "You up for a little climbing?"

"Sure," he replied, mostly because that was always how he replied when Tera asked him to do something. He didn't tell her that prior to coming here, his idea of "a little climbing" was standing on the bottom shelf to reach the top of the storage closet at Bonfiglio's Caffe. Rooting around for bakery boxes, maybe. Or year-old coffee filters. But that was not, he was fairly sure, what Tera had in mind.

They walked for several minutes in comfortable silence, passing coppery mounds of stalagmites and patches of moss along the ground. Thick mist swirled and concealed most of their surroundings. Above their heads, the domed ceiling of the cavern crawled with thousands of wormwalkers, all of which emitted their usual electric-blue glow. It felt, as always, like wandering through the interior of a gigantic, psychedelic snow globe. Minus the snow. Ollie knew they had reached their destination when he looked up to see a man in a blue jumpsuit standing behind a podium.

The podium itself was laughably tiny, teetering on the uneven ground. The man appeared not to notice.

"How many for entry?" he asked, sounding stern. Like most Neath residents, the attendant wore a miner's light on his head and a tool belt around his waist. Various and sundry gadgets hung from the belt's holes.

Ollie looked left, right, and straight ahead. He saw nothing except a solid rock wall.

"Two," Tera answered.

"Very good," the man said, checking a box on a paper in front of him. That simple act caused the petite, wobbly podium to tip forward; the man reached out, caught it, and pulled it back into an upright position. Then he peered at each of them through a pair of glasses, also absurdly small. His big eyeballs dwarfed the frames, making Ollie wonder how much of the man's vision was actually being corrected. "Tickets?"

"Yes, right here," said Tera, rooting around in her jumpsuit's pockets. She found two pieces of paper and handed them to the attendant. He examined each carefully for what seemed like a very long time. Finally satisfied, he tucked them into an orange, crinkly envelope that hung around his neck.

"No feeding, no touching," he said to Tera.

"Right," she nodded.

Ollie looked from one to the other in bewilderment. No feeding or touching *what?*

Then the attendant looked at Ollie. "No feeding, no touching," he repeated.

"Yeah, okay, got it," Ollie said, lifting a hand.

The man's wide forehead wrinkled as he examined them both. Finally, he said: "Proceed!" The word came down like a decree: forceful and loud.

"Proceed where?" Ollie muttered. He saw nothing but a strange, bulgy-eyed man, a woefully undersized podium, a surrounding thicket of calcium lumps, and a sheer rock wall. And fog. Lots and lots of fog.

Tera shushed him and thanked the attendant. Then she pulled Ollie forward to the wall. It was impossibly high and steep, disappearing up into the haze. No door, no path, no signs.

"See those?" Tera asked, pointing to a spot to her left. Ollie approached it and saw a rusted bit of metal piping, shaped a bit like a drawer pull, protruding out from the rock. "It's a rung," she explained. "For climbing. See? They go all the way up."

Ollie's throat went suddenly dry. "Oh, you meant...actual climbing? Like, rock climbing?"

"Just for a little bit," she said. Her foot tapped his. "Not far, I promise."

"Right," he said, attempting a shrug. "It's cool. I can climb. I mean, I've climbed before."

Tera, of course, wasn't fooled. "It's easy, I promise," she said.

Of course it was easy—for her. Everything was easy for Tera. Navigating, conversing, surviving. Being kind. Being beautiful.

Ollie pushed up his sleeves. "Should I go first, or...?"

"I'll go first," she said. He could have sworn he saw a grin flash across her features before she turned to face the wall.

As Ollie watched, Tera hoisted herself up onto the first two rungs: feet on one, hands on the other. Then she started to climb.

He followed her example, embarrassed to feel his heart hammering inside his chest. He had climbed ladders before, hadn't he? This was no different. Up and up and up they went, one rusty iron bar at a time. Ollie stared straight ahead at the rock wall, just inches from his nose, with occasional glances up at Tera's feet. His hands began to sweat. He told himself not to look down...and then did anyway.

As the ground moved further and further away, Ollie's breath came in shortened gasps. How much weight could these rungs hold? Had they ever been tested? Had anyone as big as him ever climbed them before? He had lost a few pounds since coming down to the Neath, but he was still—and probably always would be—a big guy. Too big, perhaps, to be clinging to the side of a cliff, one clumsy slip away from a sudden and fatal plunge to the ground. Hell, the way things were looking from up here, he'd probably be lucky to hit the ground. More likely, he'd land smack-dab in the center of a pointed stalagmite like a shish-kebabbed hunk of steak.

His biceps ached. His thoughts jumped and shifted. Ollie had just moved on to panicky worry about his pet trog—*who would take care of Meatball if he died? Who would give him his bedtime snack? And his morning brush?*—when he noticed a change above him. Lifting his head, he saw Tera...disappear. First her arms and head, then her lower half, and finally, her feet.

"Almost there!" he heard her call. "You're doing great. Just a few more!"

Huffing and puffing, Ollie pulled himself up the last few rungs. When he got there, he realized that Tera had crawled inside a hole in the rock wall. With one final grunt, he followed, landing in an ungraceful heap beside her.

"See? That wasn't so bad," she said, clapping his back.

"Mmm," he said noncommittally. They were in a cramped crevice, not even big enough to stand in. He pushed himself into a sitting position and tried not to look to his left, at the yawning, vast expanse of nothingness. And the long, long drop below it. "Isn't this where they found the Dead Sea Scrolls?"

She jerked a thumb. "No, that was over on the next wall."

He gave her a withering look and she shrugged, smirking.

"Tera, what the hell are we doing up here?"

"It's not much further, I promise. Just down the tunnel, there."

He followed her pointing finger. The tunnel was dark, as tunnels tend to be. It was also narrow, and tight. Like the slow strangle of a blood-pressure cuff. Like the chute they push the cows through right before they slaughter them.

He swallowed. "Oh. Wow. It's so...small."

"I know," she said. "I'm sorry. It's just that this is the only way to get there."

"To get where?"

She sighed. "It's hard to explain. It's one of those things you just have to see."

"Oh, I don't know," he countered. "You're really good at explaining."

"Ollie, do you trust me?"

"Of course, I do."

"Have I steered you wrong before?"

"No."

"I swear, it's not far."

"But will I—"

"Yes, you will fit," she interrupted.

His face flushed red. "Are you—"

"Yes," Tera interrupted again, resting her hand on his cheek. "I am sure."

She smiled at him then, and the terror receded somewhat. Tera's lips, plump and pink and curled up to form tiny dimples, tended to have that effect.

"All right, then," he said. "Let's go."

She nodded and spun, crawling into the shadowy burrow. Ollie took a deep, calming breath and followed. The tunnel smelled damp and slightly metallic, like socks left to dry on a stove. His fingers, he noticed, were stained red from the rust on the climbing rungs. At first, Ollie heard nothing but the echoed shuffling sounds of their hands and knees as they fumbled along. Then, he heard something else. A rumbling kind of noise.

Voices.

"Almost there," Tera called over her shoulder. She rounded a bend ahead of him. By the time he reached her, she had entered a new, much larger space, and was standing on her feet.

Ollie ducked his head through the tight opening and joined her. When he stood at full height, he realized that they had entered a room, of sorts. A semi-circular, concave room. Down near the ground, people reclined in long seats, which seemed to be made of stone. Maybe twenty people altogether, relaxed and happy. Pointing, Chatting, Enjoying themselves.

And in the air around them, he saw birds.

No.

Ollie squinted and took a step forward. Not birds. They were huge, flying insects, mostly white, gray, and coral. And fuzzy. They swooped and flapped and spun in the air over the heads of the reclining people, who watched the show with obvious delight.

"Are those butterflies?" he asked in a whisper.

"Moths," she corrected. "Mirrormoths, they're called."

Ollie grimaced. "Are they... Is it safe?"

"Oh yes, perfectly safe," Tera said confidently. As though everything in this twisted underground labyrinth was perfectly safe. As though singing swamp reeds, crow-powered boats, and moths the size of baseball mitts were the most normal things in the world.

"Come on, let's find some seats," Tera said, nudging him forward.

Ollie complied. Dodging the flight paths of the insects, they found two vacant, built-in "recliners" on the ground and settled in. No one else took much notice of them. Moments later, Ollie found himself staring up at a mesmerizing scene of color and motion. It reminded him of a school trip he had taken to the science museum's planetarium, where he had leaned back in his chair and watched the galaxies unfold above his head in mind-boggling beauty.

"Push over," Tera said. She left her seat and moved into his, pressing her body into the sliver of space.

He startled, as always, at the feel of her: the wonderful warmth that swept through him whenever she was near. It was like a hit of nitrous oxide that left him delirious and dizzy and happy to have his teeth drilled. He was all too aware, suddenly, of his sweaty skin. His unwashed hair. The splatters of grease from Ollanta's, still soaked into his jumpsuit. If Tera noticed any of those things, she didn't say.

"Pretty cool, huh?" she asked. She was looking up, but he was looking at her.

"Amazing," Ollie agreed. He leaned in for a kiss.

Tera turned just in time to meet her lips to his. They lingered there, disappearing into a private utopia, until she pushed him away playfully. "Pay attention," she said with faux sternness, pointing up.

"Fine, fine," Ollie said. He tore his gaze from her face and tipped back his head. "So, it's like a show? People buy a ticket and climb that whole wall to see...moths?"

"Well, no. Not exactly." Tera smiled. "We're not here to see the moths. Well, we are, but not just them. We're here to see what's *on* them."

"On them?" he repeated. He saw flapping wings, spindly legs dangling below fat bodies, and feathery antennae probing the air. And colors. Lots of colors. At first, he had only noticed the white, gray, and slightly apricot tones. But now that he looked closer, he could make out distinct patterns on the moths' wings. No two were alike. Browns and yellows, stripes and circles.

Ollie squinted. Then he sat up straighter. "They're pictures!" he said, pointing. One particularly large moth circled over their seats, giving him a close look at its wings. He saw...a face? Yes, definitely a face. A *person's* face. Not like a drawing—more like a crisp photograph, etched with mind-boggling detail. The flapping motion blurred the image slightly, but he could still make out two blue eyes, a smiling mouth, and even a baseball hat. All somehow reproduced with startling clarity onto the flickering, feathery scales.

Seconds later, it flitted away, and Ollie twisted his head to take in the closest darting insect to his right. This one was mostly reddish with silvery white lines. No...wait. The red blotches were bricks, and the thinner white lines were mortar. Interspersed with the occasional dark window, and a door. The moth's wings depicted a building of some kind. A brick building.

As quickly as it had appeared, the moth with the brick-building wings flew out of sight. Seconds later, Ollie spotted one flashing the image of a baby stroller. The expensive kind, with fat tires and a couple of cup holders. Next to that one, he saw another image of a person—a man, this time, with a scarf wrapped around his neck and sunglasses on his nose. Next to that, Ollie saw a German shepherd, tongue lolling. Then, a kid on a bike. Then, a squirrel on the trunk of a tree.

"The detail!" he breathed. "It's...incredible!"

"People call them Mirrormoths because they reflect what they see," Tera explained. "Like taking a picture. And then sort of...developing it onto their skin. Well, scales. Wings. Whatever."

He asked the most obvious question: "But...how?"

"I'm not sure."

Ollie stared again at the images flapping overhead. One after another, he saw them, popping in and out like an old-fashioned slide show: Brunette man, frowning. Another gray squirrel, then another. Bus, spewing exhaust. Blonde woman, clutching a backpack. Bare branches. Cement sidewalk. Small white cart—sausage cart?

He knew this place, this world. He recognized it all. These were scenes from his old life. Ollie felt a sudden tightness in his chest. He hadn't realized how much he had missed it—all of the extraordinarily mundane beauty—until it was right there in front of him again.

Tears stung his eyes unexpectedly. To mask them, he protested, "But they can't be reflecting what they see. Those things aren't even down here. They're showing pictures from the Brickside. How do they do that?"

Tera pointed to the ceiling. "See those holes?"

He nodded.

"The Mirrormoths burrow up, through the earth. They're farming oxygen."

"They're *what?*"

"They get oxygen from the Brickside and bring it back down here. Kind of like earthworms tunnel and fertilize soil, I guess. The moths make tiny tubes—air holes, you might call them—and help us breathe. We probably couldn't survive without them. They tunnel up and back, every day. And when they come back down, they bring back pictures of what they see."

"How is that even possible?" Ollie's head was spinning.

"Honestly? I have no idea. But it makes for a hell of a show, as you can see." She pointed again at the burrowed holes in the ceiling. "That spot there leads right up to the Boston Common. The moths emerge near Frog Pond. They fly around for a bit, eat, linger, whatever, before making their way back down here. That's why their wings have so many pictures of pigeons, and paths, and people walking. They're all scenes from the park. Look, right there: That's the Tadpole Playground. You see it?"

He did see it. The arch. The slides. The fishing frog statues.

The Common. *His* Common.

The momentary pang of loss was strong enough to stop his breath. Then he collected himself. "Is this what's been making you upset?" he finally asked. "All of this? Are you missing home?"

She turned to give him a gentle smile. "No," she said. "I mean, yes, I do miss it, all of it, but this is my home now. And I'm good with that. I brought you here because of something else. Something we've seen. On the moths."

"Ohhkay," he said slowly, drawing out the syllables.

Tera licked her lips. She seemed to be looking for a place to start. "Sometimes, people up on the Brickside use the moths to communicate. With us. To send messages."

"What people?" he asked, puzzled.

"Well, people in the know, obviously. And there aren't many of those."

"Like, the WRC people?"

"Yes," she nodded. "Exactly."

The WRC, or Women's Resource Center, was a Brickside organization with a mission that went well beyond its bland, slightly misleading name. Yes, the staff did provide "resources" to Boston-area women in need. But mostly, the WRC existed to help victims of domestic violence escape their situations safely. The organization had a long history, and a long menu of options to choose from. Some clients sought therapy, or legal help. Others wanted to go into hiding somewhere up on the Brickside. For this, the WRC worked with other, similar centers to create an "underground" network that ferried clients secretly from one city to another.

Of course, relocation offered no guarantees. Perpetrators often had plenty of resources of their own, and sometimes managed to track down their victims no matter how well they were hidden. It was an abusive song-and-dance as old as time: *If I can't have you, then no one else will, either.* And it too often ended in tragedy.

As Ollie understood it, the Neath had been created to provide abuse victims with something a little more airtight—a literal underground, instead of just a metaphorical one. A sanctuary safe from all of the grift, and loopholes, and risk. This was the option that Tera had chosen, when she had wanted to escape her dangerous childhood. "Option Three," as she called it. That was six years ago, when Tera was just 13. She had left her old life, and her old name, and her old, oxygen-breathing lungs behind. For good. And then she had found a new—and better—family in the depths.

According to legend, it was George Herrick who had helped the witches create this strange and magical underworld—his idea of paying penance for the wrongs he had committed as Deputy-Sheriff of Salem Village during the infamous witch trials. And at first, that was all it was: a safe haven, hidden far below the surface. But sometime later—Ollie was still a little fuzzy on the details—something had changed in the Neath.

Up above, the system wasn't working. Victims stayed victims, and perpetrators rarely suffered consequences. Corrupt judges, priests, and government officials ruled with iron fists. And so, naturally, some escapees began to ask a new kind of question. Not: *Where should I go?* But instead: *Why should I go?* They wondered: *Why must I be the one to run and hide? I've done nothing wrong.* They began to demand justice. After that, it didn't take long for the desire for justice to give way to a lust for revenge.

That, it seems, was when Herrick's End had been created: a dank, disgusting, degenerative hellhole designed with vengeance in mind. From that point on, victims who approached the WRC had one more, radical option to choose from: Instead of sending themselves to a new home, the injured parties could choose to send the wrongdoers instead. "Runners" like Laszlo would help with the transport, and witch "Readers" would confirm the prisoners' guilt before condemning them to a crumbling cell. Forever. Then, the WRC clients would return to the Brickside with nothing but a conscience to bother them.

That was the world Ollie had found when he landed in the Neath. Before he had met Ajanta, and Meatball, and the others. Before Tera had been taken. Before they had shaken up Herrick's End and morphed it into something different. Something better.

But what did any of that have to do with the Mirrormoths?

"I don't understand," Ollie said. "Did the WRC people send you a message?"

"No," Tera answered. Her mouth had gone tight. "We got a message...about them."

"What sort of a message?"

She sighed. "First, it was just rumors. And then, finally, we got confirmation."

When she paused, he pressed: "About what?"

"They're gone, Ollie. All of them."

"What do you mean, gone?"

"I mean, gone, gone. Someone took them, as far as we can tell." Tera wrung her hands and stared up into the kaleidoscope of flapping wings. "Someone broke down the door and...just...took them." Her voice broke a little on the last word.

Ollie gulped.

The WRC had been Ollie's first stop on his journey to the Neath, back when all this began. He could still picture the door at the bottom of a dark staircase on Henchman Street. The small sign on the brick, no bigger than a folded sheet of stationery: "Women's Resource Center," it had announced quietly, in tiny letters. "Open 24 Hours." Not the sort of place you'd notice. Which, he now realized, was exactly the point.

He remembered the security cameras whirring on either side of the stairwell, and the tiny but tenacious woman who had answered his questions but had not invited him inside. At the time, he had wondered about the cameras. They had seemed liked overkill. That was before he knew what kind of work the staff and volunteers were really doing behind that door. The kind of danger they faced down each day.

"Do you know who did it?" he asked, knowing full well it was a ridiculous question. It could have been any one of the angry abusers who had lost track of their favorite punching bag. Those kinds of folks didn't take too kindly to interference. "One of the husbands? Or a parent?"

Tera shrugged. "Maybe. But I don't think so."

"Why not? What other explanation could there be?"

"Because...there's more. After we learned about the kidnapping, we got another message. A very weird message. On a moth." She pointed up at the circling flock.

He nodded. "Okay. A message about what?"

"Well, about...you."

Ollie's body stiffened. *"Me?* What about me?"

Tera sat up, looking resigned. "C'mon. I'll show you." Taking his hand, she pulled him off the stone recliner and led him across the room. The other ticket-holders took little interest as Ollie and Tera walked and ducked through the path of the darting, gigantic insects. When they reached the far wall, Ollie saw a table holding a clear glass dome. It looked like the top of a cake stand. Inside, something flopped and bounced against the glass. Trapped.

"What's that?" he asked warily.

"It's a Mirrormoth," Tera paused a moment before continuing. "They're holding it in there for us. For, uh, safekeeping."

Ollie took a step backward, repulsed.

She watched him with sympathetic eyes. "You might want to take a sec, Oll, before you look. It might be a little...upsetting."

A little upsetting? In a place where understatement ruled, that could only mean that he should brace for the worst. Ollie balled his hands into fists, inhaled, and nodded.

"You ready?" she asked, gently.

He nodded again. He wasn't sure what he was waiting for—an actual push? *Move, dammit.* Finally, he inched forward, then forward again. The colorful wings flapped helplessly inside the dome.

At first, Ollie saw nothing but colors. Brown, pale yellow, pink, peach. Then, he realized the peach was a face, and the brown was hair. A girl's face, with long chestnut locks. The pink was a shirt.

And in the center...something white. Rectangular. A piece of paper?

Yes.

Ollie leaned closer. It was young woman, holding up a piece of paper. Holding it up in front of her chest, like a sign.

The Mirrormoth's wings flapped, then fell still—just long enough for Ollie to get his first clear glimpse. His limbs went cold.

Not just any girl.

It was Nell.

Ollie spun, looking at Tera with wide eyes. "It's—" he began, but couldn't seem to finish.

Tera nodded sadly. "Yeah, I know."

Nell was his friend—his only friend—from his life back on the Brickside. They had attended Lighter Tomorrows weight-loss support-group meetings together, twice a week. They had commiserated about the lousier aspects of their lives. She had been a life preserver when he had needed it the most, after his mother died and he had been left stranded in a blizzard of wintery grief.

"I... I don't understand," he stammered. "What is she doing? Why is she just standing there?" All the other people depicted on the Mirrormoths had been caught in mid-motion: walking, running, biking, talking. But Nell was just...standing there. Staring straight ahead, as if she was looking into a camera.

As if she had known the moth was there, and she had wanted it to see her.

"Is she all right?" Ollie asked. The panic was rising. *Not again,* he thought. Was it happening again? Nell had already gone missing once. That was how he had ended up down here to begin with. Had she gone missing again?

"You have to read it," Tera answered in a quiet voice.

"Read what?"

"She's holding a note."

He bent forward, haltingly. The moth crashed itself against the glass a few times, then paused. Ollie took the opportunity to focus in on the piece of paper in Nell's hands. He could see now that it was covered in thick, black letters. All capitals. They blurred together and then, finally, cleared enough to form a coherent, terrible sentence.

SEND OLLIE UP OR THEY ALL DIE

The creature's wings fluttered again, stealing the words from his sight.

Ollie reached out for the edge of the table to steady himself. A buzzing had started in his ears. A strange, persistent heat began to burn beneath his skin.

"What the hell is this?" he whispered.

Behind him, Tera answered: "We don't know."

"What does that even mean? 'Send Ollie up?'"

"Just what it sounds like, I guess."

"But...why me?"

When she didn't reply, Ollie turned to face her. He could feel the blood draining from his face, which had probably left him looking even paler than normal. One blonde curl fell into his eye; he pushed it away. "Tera, what's going on?"

She looked grim. "That's what we're trying to find out."

"Is Nell okay? Did they... Is she...?"

Tera touched his arm. "As far as we know, she's fine. They're all fine. For now. They seem to be...hostages."

"Hostages? What the hell for?"

"As leverage, Ollie. For you. Someone wants you up there, back on the Brickside."

"Why?"

"I told you, Babe. We don't know."

He spluttered and threw up his hands. "This has to be some mistake. Some joke. I'm a nobody, Tera! Less than a nobody! What does anybody care whether I'm here or there? I doubt anyone even noticed I was missing, other than maybe Mr. B." Mr. Bonfiglio had been Ollie's employer and landlord; one of the only people Ollie had regretted leaving behind. He shook his head. "This doesn't make any sense. Are we sure that was even my name on that sign? Maybe it said Olivia. Or...Collin, or something. I only got a quick look."

"Maybe," Tera answered, slowly enough to betray that she didn't believe it. She, apparently, had gotten a better look. Probably more than once.

"But...why them? Why the WRC people? I don't have anything to do with them! Hell, they never even let me through the door when I visited. I only talked to the one lady, that one time."

"Well, you also went to the Visitor Center," she pointed out.

Oh, right. The little gingerbread house Visitor Center on the Boston Common. That was where he and Laszlo had secured the key they'd needed to transport Ollie to the Neath through a hole in the Freedom Trail. Two women had helped them, behind the counter. "Are they...?"

"Yep," Tera nodded glumly. "They're gone, too."

He felt nauseous as he digested her words. "Is this...my fault? Because I came here?" Laszlo had bent the rules to get Ollie to the Neath. He had never been an "official" visitor. Had his presence upset some sort of unseen balance between the two worlds?

"No! Of course not!" she answered quickly. Too quickly. "It just seems like we might have started, like, a chain reaction. When we did what we did at the prison."

He held up his palms, confused.

"Look, we made reforms, right?" Tera continued. "That's a good thing. We got rid of the torture, and now Leonard is the new warden—" She stopped, held up a hand, and corrected herself. "Sorry, the new *Superintendent of Operations*. And he's doing a great job. And you rescued me, right? So that's all good stuff. Lots and lots of good things." She smiled weakly.

"But?"

Tera cleared her throat. "Well, we also prevented new arrivals at Herrick's End. No more prisoners."

"Right. And isn't that a good thing, too?" Ollie was confused. They had all agreed: No more revenge. The front gate had been closed to new inmates, and that was how it was going to stay—at least until they got a better handle on things.

"Yes, of course. Of course it is. But now..." She threw a pointed look at the glass dome on the table. "It seems like not everyone is a fan."

"What do you mean? Someone is pissed off about the changes, and they're blaming me? That makes no sense. It was all of us. I'm literally the least important person here."

"Well, I wouldn't say *that*," Tera protested. She ducked as a particularly large Mirrormoth flew past her purple-swirled hair.

"I would! Jesus, I'm lucky to get my shoes tied around this place. If somebody thinks I'm, like, the Mayor of Neathtown, they've been watching the wrong channel. If anything, they should want you. Or Derrin, or—" He stopped when he saw her face. "Not that I want *you* to..." He backtracked. "This is just ridiculous, that's all I mean. Just...senseless."

"Well, senseless or not, it's happening. The WRC staffers are gone."

"And Nell?"

"And maybe Nell, too. Yes. But it's even worse than that, Oll."

With dismay, he glanced back at the flailing, incarcerated moth. "How could it possibly be worse?"

She took a deep breath and folded her arms. "If the WRC *staff* is gone, that means the WRC is gone. Nonfunctioning. And that means that no one else can get down here, either. No offenders *or* clients. The Neath is officially closed for business."

"So the victims..." he started, then stopped.

Tera nodded. "So the victims up there are stuck with what they've got. No options, no escape, no help."

They stared at each other for a long moment. Both of them knew what that meant: Life on the Brickside had just become a whole lot more dangerous for a whole lot more people.

Ollie rubbed his eyes, felt himself swaying again, and walked to the nearest empty reclining stone seat. He collapsed onto it and stared up at the swirling flurry of colored wings.

A moth landed on Ollie's knee, its images hidden from sight as the wings folded together. Ollie didn't shoo it away. *No feeding, no touching.*

"So, what now?"

"I don't know, Oll. But this is bad. It's really bad."

He let that settle for a moment in his gut. It felt heavy, like an extra-large slice of ricotta pie. "What about Laszlo? Can he help?"

As a Runner, Laszlo was one of the few with the permission, and the knowledge, to travel freely between the upper and lower worlds. As long as he didn't stay too long in the Neath when he visited, his lungs maintained the ability to function on the Brickside. For years, he had worked closely with the WRC to secretly ferry survivors to the Neath sanctuary—and, in some cases, to ferry their abusers to Herrick's End.

"I already sent him up to look into it."

"And? What did he say?"

"He was supposed to be back this morning, to give me a full report. But he never showed up."

"Laszlo stood you up?" That didn't sound plausible.

"He did. And now...no one knows where he is."

Ollie swallowed thickly. "So, you're telling me these women were taken, and now Laszlo is missing?"

She sat down next to him, her body dropping hard in defeat. "That's what I'm telling you."

Possibilities spun in Ollie's mind, none of them good.

SEND OLLIE UP OR THEY ALL DIE

The all-caps, the lack of punctuation... It was like a note from a churlish child. Which somehow made it seem all the worse. "All right," he said, pushing out a gust of air and rubbing his palms on his pant legs. "All right. So, what do we do?"

She gave a small, sad smile. "That's the problem. There's not a lot we *can* do."

"Tera, if I don't go up there, those people are all going to die."

"We don't know that."

"It literally says exactly that."

She opened her mouth, said nothing, then closed it again.

They eyed each other as the truth of the matter dangled like visible strings.

Whatever Nell was doing in the park, with that sign, she wasn't doing it voluntarily. Something sinister was going on here—he could almost smell its foul tang. And now, looking at Tera, he could tell she knew it, too.

Ollie felt a heavy cloud of dread descending. And then, suddenly...anger. Lots and lots of anger. Nell... Laszlo... The others... Where were they? Who had taken them? Who had the goddamn nerve to take them, and then write *his* name down? To implicate *him* in something so unspeakable? And now...what? He was just supposed to do what they said? To blindly follow orders?

He had felt a strange heat under his skin when he first read the note on the Mirrormoth's wings. Now, the burn grew stronger. Hotter. Hot enough to make him pause, pull up his jumpsuit sleeve, and stare down at his arm. Was his skin getting red? Was he having some sort of allergic reaction to the insects? Or to this entire infested grotto?

Ollie looked up, eyes narrowed. The flying moths looked less miraculous, now. More malignant. Their shadows passed over him like shifting demons—blackened, mercurial stains in the torchlight.

His face fell into temporary darkness as he whispered: "I caused this."

Tera shook her head. "C'mon, that's not—"

"It's true," he interrupted, his voice low. "I didn't mean to, but I did. Just by being here. Just by doing what I did. What do they call it... Chaos Theory? Ripple effects?" Ollie glanced up at the swarm over his head: an iridescent blur of scattered flight. "A Mirrormoth flaps its wings in a cave, and a storm rages half a world away," he murmured.

"Ollie, what the hell are you talking about?"

"I think..." He looked up at the ceiling, and, by inference, at the world beyond. His anger was ebbing into dull resignation. "I think I have to go."

"That's exactly the problem, Oll. Even if you wanted to go, you can't. It's impossible."

She was right, of course. He couldn't leave the Neath. No one could, once their lungs had acclimated. One step above the surface would lead to instant respiratory failure and death.

But...whoever wrote that note would have known that, too. If they had known enough to send a message via Mirrormoth, then they must also have known all about this place and its limitations— which made the demand to "send Ollie up" all the more puzzling.

So maybe they, whoever "they" were, wanted him dead. Was the transaction as simple as that? One dead Ollie in exchange for multiple live hostages? Revenge for what he had done to the Warden, perhaps?

Or maybe the note-writer wasn't from the Neath, at all. Maybe they didn't understand how things worked down here. An interloper who had coerced information from the WRC hostages? A Bricksider? An outside interest? But why?

He sighed forcibly, flubbering his lips. At this point, the details and motives hardly mattered. Ollie couldn't leave. Period. And yet, if he didn't leave, horrible things would happen. Things that were definitely, unmistakably, all his fault.

Impossible. How many times had he spoken that word? Not too often, before he came down here. But ever since? A lot. If he remembered right, he had uttered it, or at least thought it, when he had first contemplated the odds of escaping the confines of Herrick's End. And then again, when Tera had been taken. And again, when he'd had to figure out a way to win a bizarre drinking game against a professional lush, and rig a fighting contest, and drag his father's heavy, unconscious body out of the tower, and, finally, trick the Warden into falling into a trap of his own making.

Every last bit of it, impossible. And yet, here they were.

The Mirrormoth on his knee fluttered, rose into the air, and hovered between their faces for a long, luminous moment. Ollie stared at the picture on its wings—dappled sunlight on the branches of a tall maple at dusk, so colorless it was almost black-and-white—and the image made something catch in his throat.

He thought, suddenly, of another achromatic object: A magnet his mother had hung on the fridge, long ago. The magnet had featured a black background with white letters that read, "Hang on, let me overthink this." As a kid, Ollie didn't get it, and once asked his mom to explain why the saying made her laugh. "Oh, *Bambino,*" she had said, rumpling the top of his head. "Sometimes, you just have to stop thinking and *do*. You know what I mean?"

He didn't, at the time. But he did now.

"You should have told me sooner," he said to Tera sternly.

"Yeah, okay. Fine."

"And next time...?" he asked.

"Next time, I will tell you sooner." She leaned in to kiss him lightly, as if sealing the pact.

"All right, then," Ollie said. He watched the maple-tree moth vanish into the multitudes above his head. "I guess we'd better get moving."

"Get moving, where?" Tera asked. Her forehead scrunched in confusion.

"We need something to eat."

"Now? Why?"

Ollie squeezed her hand. "Because you should never attempt the impossible on an empty stomach, that's why," he said. Then he stood, walked over to the table, and lifted the glass dome. The Mirrormoth didn't hesitate: With one mighty flap, it was gone.

Three

After swinging by the market for sustenance, Ollie and Tera's next stop, naturally, was Ajanta's house—though "house" might have been a generous term for the one-room, cobbled-together dwelling. Constructed from a hodge-podge of fabric, wood planks, and metal sheeting, it was wobbly, uneven, and definitely not watertight. Despite all that, the structure had already served as a safe haven and stronghold for Ollie more than once during his brief tenure in the Neath. As his mother used to say, "People look for strength on the outside. But that's not usually where it is." Ollie had found that to be true not only for this house, but also for the people living under its patchwork-quilt of a roof.

He had barely stepped through the curtained front door when he was accosted by a wiggling ball of brown fur. The trog had waddled across the floor, climbed up Ollie's pant leg, scuttled around his torso, and landed on his shoulder in a matter of seconds.

"Hey, buddy!" Ollie said, reaching out to scratch Meatball's head. Or what he assumed was his head. Trogs' eyes were mostly hidden, so Ollie usually just aimed for the spot a few inches above the animal's protruding, platypus-like beak. Meatball snorted eagerly, knowing that Ollie most likely had a treat or two tucked away for their reunion. He wasn't disappointed; with a smile, Ollie reached into a pocket, pulled out a strip of pickled wormwalker, and dangled it. The long blue morsel vanished with a noisy slurp.

His view still partially blocked by tufts of fur, Ollie peered through the fuzz to see Ajanta wiping her hands on her apron. In the center of the room, Derrin and Kuyu sat on a log near the crackling fire.

And to his right, he heard a voice. It was thickly accented, and deep. "This hurts me deeply," the voice said. "I think you must like that creature more than you like me, no?"

Ollie spun.

"Laszlo!"

The strapping, limber man was leaning against a stack of shelves with his arms folded across his chest. Dark hair hung to his shoulders, looking a bit tangled. His hooked nose pointed down at a wide, mischievous grin.

"Laz!" Tera pushed past Ollie to run to their friend. She hugged him tightly, then stepped back to hold him at arm's length. "I thought you were gone!"

"Gone? Ach." The Ukrainian man waved an arm. "Not gone. Just late. I am sorry, my little *sonechko*. I did not mean to make you worry."

"What happened?" she asked. "Did you find them? Did you learn anything? Who took them? What's going on?"

Laszlo's mouth stayed partially open as he fielded the barrage of questions.

"Krite, Tera, give the man a minute," Derrin said.

"Yes," Ajanta agreed. "Come in, both of you. Sit down. We have much to discuss."

Ollie didn't like the sound of that. He and Tera looked at each other and begrudgingly made their way over to the fire, where Kuyu was stirring a steaming pot with one hand and holding Derrin's knee with the other. Ollie had come to think of them as the Neath's premiere power couple. He sometimes contemplated giving them a tabloid-worthy nickname—Deriku? Kuyuin?—but doubted the gesture would be appreciated. The two women were like the human version of a yin and yang: Kuyu was short, round, and of Asian descent, with a head full of tight, dark curls. Derrin towered over her with abnormally long limbs, thin blonde hair, and the gossamer skin and strange facial features seen in the Neath residents who had been underground for many generations. One was mighty; the other was scrappy. Neither one, Ollie had learned, was someone he wanted to cross.

"Fungi tea?" Kuyu asked him, holding out a small brown cup.

Ollie's stomach did a little jump of disgust. "Uh, sure," he replied. "Thanks." Cautiously, he took a tiny sip. It tasted like an oversalted egg-drop soup. And old, wet leaves. He did his best to smile and let out a "mmm."

Kuyu ladled out the remaining cups and passed them around. Laszlo chugged his drink down in one gulp and landed beside Ollie on the log.

"You had us worried, there," Ollie told him.

"Yes. I am sorry for that," Laszlo responded, holding out his cup for seconds and giving Kuyu a nod of appreciation when she complied. "Things went little, how do you say, sidewinding."

"Sideways?" Ollie supplied.

"Yes, this is it. Sideways." He rubbed the back of his sinewy neck. "Not straight line, what is happening here."

Ajanta stepped closer and put a hand on the big man's back. "Laszlo ran into some trouble," she explained, her voice gentle. "I'm afraid he didn't quite get the answers we were hoping for."

Tera looked from one to the other. "What the hell does that mean?"

"Our friends, at center, they are still not found," Laszlo said, his face darkening. "Police people have the yellow tape all around. I sneak inside, of course, but I find nothing. Just chairs and pencils and other office things, all over the floor. These women..." He paused. "I know these women. They would not have made it easy. They would have fought like Carpathian Mountain badgers. It must have been many men, many people, who came. Not just one. Unless..."

Unless.

He didn't have to finish the sentence. They all knew what he meant. *Unless there was magic involved.* And that, somehow, seemed much worse.

A moment of silence descended. Ollie looked around the little circle of faces, all sipping moldy tea and watching Laszlo with concentrated focus.

Finally, he continued: "Then I am thinking. Maybe there is clue at Ollie's apartment, yes? Above the caffe? Something to help? And so I go there. But—"

He stopped abruptly.

"What?" Ollie asked, feeling goosebumps rise on his skin.

Laszlo, who also happened to be an accomplished, astonishingly flexible, and most likely double-jointed acrobat, bent his wrists backwards. Then he said, "When I get to caffe, I see yellow tape there, too. Police tape."

Ollie jumped to his feet. "What do you mean? Why? Did you see Mr. B? Is he okay?"

"He's okay," Ajanta said quickly. "He'll...be okay."

"What do you mean, *be* okay?"

She ran her fingers along her braid before answering. "It seems Mr. Bonfiglio got a little...roughed up."

"Oh my God!" Ollie started pacing. "Oh my God. What the hell happened? Who would go after Mr. B?" The small, portly man was one of the most beloved residents of the North End. Kind. Gentle. Cheerful. Never a harsh word for anyone, or anything. The idea of someone hurting him was...unthinkable. Unbearable. Ollie squeezed his eyes shut.

"It seems I was not only one wanting to see your apartment," Laszlo said with a frown. "People came, at night, but your Mr. B tried to stop them. That did not end very well for him, I am afraid." He shook his head.

Ollie's face fell into his hands. His apartment was located above the caffe, requiring any potential intruder to first enter the bakery and walk to the back stairs. This was his fault, again. He had put Mr. B in harm's way. The nicest man he had ever met. The man who had given him a job, and a place to live, and a chance— however slim—at happiness.

"Your apartment, I am sad to say, is mess. Like WRC office. Many things tossed around. Many things broken."

Ollie cringed. Someone, clearly, was trying to send him a message, though he had absolutely no idea what that message might be. None of this made any sense at all. "Where is Mr. B?" he whispered.

"He is in hospital. Is recovering. He will be fine, but..."

Again, Laszlo's unfinished sentence was clear enough: *But* it might happen again. And the next time, it might be more dire. Until they figured out what was going on here, Mr. B and the others would remain in grave danger.

"I will learn more." Laszlo gave a firm nod. "I will do breaking in, at police station. I will find out what they know."

"Break into a *police station?*" Ollie asked.

The wiry man shrugged. "Yes. Of course."

"But...how?"

"Ollie Delgato," Laszlo said, his voice full of disappointment. "After all we have done, you must ask me this question? You know who I am."

Ollie did know. His friend was Laszlo Kravchenko, nephew of the Famous Flying Kravchenko Brothers of Ukraine. Ollie maintained secret doubts about the closeness of that familial relation and the actual famousness of the supposedly famous brothers, but he had seen enough with his own eyes to know that Laszlo was, like his uncles, a lithe and powerful acrobat of unparalleled skill. If he wanted to break into just about anywhere, he could do it easily. Without being detected, without breaking a sweat.

"Don't bother. The cops won't know anything," Kuyu said glumly.

"We don't know that," Tera insisted, folding her arms. "Why not let him try?"

"Kuyu is right," said Derrin. "This has the Warden written all over it. The Brickside police won't have the first clue."

"The Warden is frozen in a chair!" Ollie protested.

"Maybe so. But he didn't operate in a bubble. He had allies. Friends. Thugs. And all of them were living high on the hog in the old system. The new one? Not so much."

"Yes, but they're all down here, not up there."

"We don't know that," Ajanta interjected with a small shake of her head. "We have no idea how wide this thing goes. He might have friends everywhere."

That thought set them all brooding.

Moments later, Ollie spoke over the crackling of the fire. "I have to go up there," he said quietly. "It's what they want. It's the only way."

"What *who* wants?" Tera argued. "We don't even know what we're dealing with, yet. And I hate to keep repeating the obvious, but you *can't* go. You'll die."

Kuyu poked the flames with a stick, sending up sparks. "Well, to be fair, the note didn't specify that he had to be alive," she said with a shrug. "It just said to send him up."

Tera looked at her incredulously. "What are you saying? That we should send Ollie as some sort of human sacrifice? Is that what you're proposing?"

"I'm not proposing anything," the curly-haired girl replied. "I'm simply pointing out that the note didn't specify either way."

"Oh, you'd like that, wouldn't you," Ollie muttered. Kuyu had made no secret of her distrust of Ollie from the moment he'd arrived in their house as a fugitive prisoner, all those months ago. Even after all they'd been through, she still seemed to have it in for him.

"What I'd *like* is for things to go back to the way they were," the pint-size girl retorted. "It might surprise you to know that before you came here, we weren't always running for our lives. We were fine. Happy. People weren't getting kidnapped every ten seconds. That's the plain truth of it. Read into that what you want."

"All right, now," Derrin said, dropping a calming hand on her girlfriend's knee. "Let's settle down."

"I won't settle down!" Kuyu snapped. "I'm not the one who's causing all the problems around here!"

Tera jumped to her feet. "You're a psycho, you know that?"

"Better a psycho than a love-sick idiot!"

Tera's mouth hung agape. "Are you kidding me right now? Like you're not curled around Derrin every minute of every day?"

"Well at least I have sense enough not to let her get captured by Reds!"

Tera's face darkened. She lunged forward

"THAT IS ENOUGH." Ajanta's voice boomed throughout the room, stopping Tera mid-motion and silencing them all. "Who are we helping with this arguing? Hmm? Who?"

No one answered. Ollie hung his head.

"Sit back down, all of you. This is not why we're here."

Dutifully, they returned to the logs. Tera and Kuyu glared at each other across the flames. Ollie inhaled a whiff of smoke and coughed.

"Well?" Derrin asked. "What are we going to do? We can't just leave them up there like that, right?"

Around the circle, heads shook.

Laszlo took a deep, decisive breath and slapped his Lycra-wrapped thighs. "I will go again," he said. "I will do looking. If there is something to see, I will see it."

"No," Ollie said. He stood up again. "*I* will go. This is my fault."

"It's not your—"

"It is. And anyway, it's me they want. I don't think we have a choice."

Another hush fell over the room. On Ollie's shoulder, Meatball curled himself into a tighter ball.

"But, Babe," Tera began. "You know that's just not—"

"Don't say it's not possible!" he insisted, looking from face to face. "There has to be some way! Look where we are, for Krite sake! We have Blackheart Powders. And magic friggin' moths. Hell, we had a whole bunch of kids turned into slave zombies by some stupid, sparkling liquid! All I'm talking about is breathing up there, just for a short time, and then coming right back down. There *has* to be a way."

No one immediately responded.

The quiet went on for so long that Derrin's voice, when it finally came, startled him.

"There might be one thing," she said.

Five heads snapped in her direction.

"What?" Tera asked.

"I've heard...rumors." Derrin's nearly translucent skin shimmered in the firelight, highlighting the thin blue veins in her jawline.

"What kinds of rumors?" Ajanta sounded skeptical.

"Just...rumors. Of a mechanical type of thing. A device. Supposedly, it makes it possible for people like us to breathe. Up there."

Tera leaned forward. "Is it real?"

"I don't know," Derrin admitted. "Probably not. It's just one of those passed-down tales that you hear. You know, my great-grandmother told my grandmother, that sort of thing."

"Who made the device?"

"No one knows for sure. I mean it's not, like, written down or anything. But..."

"But what?"

"They say there was some kind of place. Like, a lab, or whatever. The place where they built it. Or tried to build it, anyway. No one knows if they ever succeeded."

"Who? Who was doing this?" Tera was leaning so far forward she seemed about to lose her balance.

"That's the crazy part."

"What is?"

"Well, if you believe the rumors, which I'm not saying I do..." Derrin looked around the room hesitantly. "But if you believe it, then the person who made the lab, and built the device, was...George Herrick."

Ollie and Tera looked at each other.

"George Herrick," Ollie repeated.

"Yep."

"The dead guy. In the park."

"One and the same."

"The guy who came down here with the witches, three hundred and fifty years ago, to help them build this place? To make up for all the awful things he had done?"

Derrin sighed. "Unless there was another George Herrick running around down here, then yes."

"Why would Herrick have wanted to make a device to help him breathe on the Brickside?" Kuyu interjected. "Was he planning to go back there?"

"How should I know?" Derrin said, frustrated. "Maybe he was some kind of mad scientist. Maybe he regretted creating this place. Maybe he wanted to unite the two worlds in peace and harmony forever. I have no idea. I'm just telling you what I've heard. Which means nothing, because I doubt a single word of it is true."

"But if it is true..." Laszlo began, letting his voice trail off.

"If it is true, then it's possible!" Tera finished. She steepled her fingers and pressed them against her lips.

Ollie sat motionless on his log as he tried to absorb this strange new knowledge. Or supposition. Or flat-out fiction.

Ollie had been there, two feet away, when George Herrick died. So close that most people assumed that Ollie himself had killed the man. Herrick had somehow foreseen Ollie's arrival here in the Neath, and had left cryptic breadcrumb clues to help all of them navigate the dangerous fate that had awaited them in his namesake prison. According to the scuttlebutt, he had been granted long life—361 years long, as it turned out—in exchange for helping the persecuted witches build this safe underground haven. But somewhere along the way, he had been tricked into drinking a potion that had rendered him all but frozen for more than a century. That all came to an end a few months ago, when Herrick finally took his last breath inside a crumbling, ancient body while Ollie looked on in horror.

Why would a man like that have tried to build a laboratory? Or a device that would enable Neath residents to breathe on the Brickside? By all accounts, Herrick had been a simple man: a deputy, or a sheriff, or something along those lines. Something to do with law enforcement. As far as Ollie knew, he had possessed no scientific knowledge beyond what the typical 17th-century Massachusetts Bay Colony resident might know about tides and agriculture and blacksmithing. And even if he had wanted to achieve such a feat, when would he have had the time?

Ollie looked down into his half-empty cup. It wasn't until he swirled the liquid into a tiny whirlpool that the thought occurred to him: He was asking the wrong questions. This was not a place of science, after all. This was a place of...something else entirely. A slow smile began to spread across his face.

"What are you grinning about?" Derrin asked him.

All eyes turned in his direction.

Ollie handed the cup back to Kuyu and stood up. "I have to go."

"What, now? Why?" Tera's eyes went wide with surprised annoyance. "We're in the middle of something, here!"

"We want to know, right? If the rumors are true?"

"Well, yeah. Of course."

Ollie's smile widened. "I know someone who might be able to tell us."

Three someones, actually. And as luck would have it, they all owed him a favor.

Four

With Meatball settled firmly on his shoulder, Ollie followed the directions exactly as they'd been written: Two bridges, three islands, one sharp left. Check. Straight down into the Dribbling Acid Ditch ("move fast and don't touch the sides"). Check. Then all the way around the Sacred Guano Mound ("not over—never over") and through the Dry Sponge Thicket ("ignore the name… it's more of a marsh than a thicket, and the sponges are definitely not dry"). Check and check. Ollie was wiping acid and bat poop from his shoes and dripping with smelly sponge juice by the time he emerged into the clearing, looking for the witches' house.

He wasn't sure what he was expecting. A crooked Victorian, maybe, covered in moss. Or a storybook gingerbread cottage topped with peppermint-candy shingles. Or even a dilapidated houseboat half-submerged in a swamp. Not a one of those setups would have surprised him. But instead, he saw…nothing.

The clearing was fairly small, as clearings go, bordered by the Dry Sponge Thicket on one side and a stalagmite forest on the other. The stalagmites were different than others he had seen, though. Rather than looking like squat, solid Christmas trees, these were as narrow and tall as pines. Exceptionally pointy. And one of them, he now saw, was capped with something circular. It looked almost like the brim of a massive stalagmite hat, though that, of course, would be preposterous. Wouldn't it?

Ollie stepped closer. The ringed platform was made from hundreds of twigs and reeds, all stuck together with bits of lichen and chunks of what seemed to be dried mud.

A nest?

It was certainly big enough to host a family of giant crows. He could see Mrs. Paget settling in there quite nicely with one or two of her feathered friends. But this particular nest did not echo with caws or tweets. Instead, Ollie heard something that sounded like out-of-tune music. And was that...laughter? Yes. Cackles, actually. Lots and lots of cackles. The sound reminded Ollie of his mother's occasional late nights with the Bingo ladies, after too many rounds of Scarlett Flozzie martinis.

A crick started to ache in his neck as the realization dawned. This was not a birds' nest—at least, not anymore. Now, it was a witches' nest. His destination. And it was mounted some thirty feet off the ground, with no obvious way to reach it.

On his shoulder, Meatball was grunting in displeasure and trying to shake the thicket's residual dampness from his fur. Ollie gingerly set him on the ground, where the trog undulated hard and fast enough to send drops of sponge-tree sap flying in every direction.

Ollie hopped out of the way of the deluge and walked closer to the towering stalagmite nest. "Hello?" he called out. He didn't know their names, he suddenly realized. He had only ever thought of them collectively as "the witches." They certainly knew his name, though: They had somehow known it the minute he had unlocked the door to their dank and terrible cell at Herrick's End, where the Warden had imprisoned them hundreds of years before. *Hello, Ollie,* they had said, calm as fish in a bowl. *We've been waiting for you.*

Now, he craned his neck and shouted up at the matted wad of sticks and mud: "Hello? It's me!" After a pause, he added, "It's Ollie!" He wanted to add, *You know, the guy who saved your life?* but didn't.

No one had been looking for them after they disappeared. As the decades and centuries had passed, the other Neath residents assumed that the witches had died, perhaps, or returned to the

Brickside. Only George Herrick—long mute and paralyzed by a dose of Dark Heart Powder—had known the truth. He had also known, inexplicably, that Ollie would appear in the Neath and eventually give the evil Warden a taste of his own medicine—or, in this case, a taste of his own poison.

Herrick's prophetic, handwritten messages had guided Ollie on his journey and made all of that possible. But how? And why? Had the witches endowed George Herrick with the gift of foresight? Or did he already have it on his own? And if the old man really had been all but petrified in his chair, how, then, did he manage to write notes? Ollie still had no idea. But he supposed it didn't matter much now, anyway. George Herrick was dead, along with his secrets. Ollie, on the other hand, was very much alive. And happy. He had Tera, and his friends, and his little buddy Meatball, and a new, better life in the Neath. All that unpleasantness was behind him.

Or, at least, it had been. Until a Mirrormoth had arrived from the surface with an open threat etched all over its wings.

He curled his spine backwards, hands on hips, and looked up at the massive nest. "It's Ollie *Delgato*!" he clarified. In case there was more than one.

Still, he got no response.

"Hey!" he yelled. "I know you're all up there! I can hear you! I have to talk to you. *Now*. It's important. And I swear to God, if you don't answer me in the next two minutes, I swear, I'll... I'll..."

Ollie was saved from having to come up with a plausible ultimatum when a small object tumbled, suddenly, from the nest above. He dodged it as it fell, just narrowly missing his head. Meatball crawled up his leg and torso, and they examined the new arrival together.

It was a swinging basket. Woven, with a handle, not unlike something Little Red Riding Hood would have toted through the woods for a picnic with Grandma. It hung from the nest above by a long stretch of twine. Inside the basket, Ollie saw three small glass bottles, each filled with colored flakes and affixed with a label. The first label read, "TO FLY," in neat, block writing. The second read, "TO DIG." And the last read, "TO BURN."

Puzzled, Ollie glanced at Meatball. The trog was sniffing the basket and the bottles, no doubt hoping for something tasty. Above their heads, the discordant music continued to play, accompanied by something that sounded like the steady thump of a bongo. And more cackling.

Meatball tried to get closer but only managed to push the hanging basket with one webbed foot, making it sway. Ollie watched the swinging motion, feeling oddly hypnotized. That was when he noticed another item tucked away with the bottles: a rolled-up parchment, wrapped in a string. Ollie reached for it, tugged open the knot, and read the message inside.

Hello and welcome
To our humble home!
No stairs here to climb,
No wings here to roam.

You see, we are shy,
And not used to guests.
Those who will join us
Must first pass our test.

For someone to climb,
A ladder must drop.
Lose the connection
To reach to the top.

We'll give just one chance
And one simple clue:
It's meant to destroy,
And not meant for you.

P.S. No refills.

Ollie's brow furrowed. Not meant for him? What, the basket? Or the clue? Who was it meant for, then?

"Seriously?" he yelled, looking up again at the underside of the nest.

No one answered.

"Goddammit, let me up!"

Nothing.

Reaching out to steady the swaying basket, Ollie sighed and looked again at the bottles. It didn't matter, he supposed, who the clue was meant for. He was the one who was here.

He read the labels again: TO FLY; TO DIG; and TO BURN.

It seemed simple enough: Each bottle contained a substance that would endow him, if only temporarily, with the ability listed on its label. And of those, TO FLY seemed like the most obvious choice. He was down here, and the witches were up above. How else to get there but to fly?

Tentatively, Ollie reached for the first bottle and opened the tiny cork. He lifted it to his nose. On first sniff, he detected a faint odor of...bacon grease? Christmas ham? Definitely something piglike. He sprinkled a few of the flakes onto the palm of his hand. They were multicolored in earth tones: greens, tans, browns. Taking a deep breath, he popped a few of them into his mouth. And waited.

Nothing happened. Despite their bacony smell, the flakes had no taste at all. He ate a few more, then jumped, half-expecting to find himself launched into the air. But gravity seemed to work as well as it ever did, holding him tight to the ground. Finally, he tipped the bottle upside down and poured a pile of flakes onto his tongue. They dissolved. Seconds passed, then minutes. Foolishly, Ollie flapped his arms. But he did not fly.

Not meant for you.

Ollie held out the bottle. "Maybe they're meant for trogs?"

Meatball's long tongue darted into the bottle, cleaning out whatever remained. He didn't fly, either.

Ollie heaved a deep breath. Fine. Flying was too easy. This was a puzzle, after all. What had they called it? A "test." He eyed the second label: TO DIG. It was counterintuitive, but maybe that was the point. You didn't expect to rise by digging. He peered at the rough gravel around his feet. Perhaps there was something he had to find under the ground, like a set of wings. Or a firefighter-style extension ladder. Or a passageway leading to a set of stairs that climbed right up through the center—like a Keebler's Elf stalagmite house with a hidden, delicious world tucked away inside. That made him think about chocolate-drizzled cookies, which made his stomach rumble.

Focus, he told himself. He popped the cork from the second bottle, shared some of the flakes with Meatball, and poured the rest into his own mouth. Ollie chewed and swallowed thoughtfully, tasting a hint of banana. After a moment's pause, he crouched onto the ground and started scratching. All he succeeded in doing was building up a crust of muck under his fingernails. He stomped, jumped, and pounded his fists on the dirty gravel, but seemed to have no greater digging abilities than he'd had a moment before. Then he tried pawing at the stalagmite crust, which was as hard as...well, as calcium carbonate. Probably because that's exactly what it was.

Meatball imitated him, scratching his tiny claws in futility.

"This is stupid," Ollie said. He tilted his head back and shouted it: "This is stupid! Just let me up!"

No one answered.

Warily, he let his eyes fall on the last bottle. TO BURN.

Ollie did not want to burn. He did not even want to pick up a bottle that had the words TO BURN written on its side. And he certainly didn't want to solve a puzzle that required him to sizzle himself into a barbecued crisp.

Meatball was staring at him.

"What?" Ollie asked.

The trog gave three quick snuffs through the air holes on his beak.

Ollie covered his face with his hands and spoke into his palms. "Fine. Fine! I cannot believe I'm doing this." Stepping forward, he reached for the last bottle, popped open the top, and cautiously removed a few of the flakes. They smelled overwhelmingly like French onion soup. "You're not trying this one," he told Meatball. Then he took a deep, shaking breath and stuck out his tongue. *Just do it. Just do it, dammit.*

He had watched a TV show once about strange, unsolved phenomena. It had included a segment about something called "spontaneous human combustion:" recorded instances in which people die in sudden, inexplicable, and contained fires. Some theorized that the flames had somehow originated within the victim's body. One image in particular stood out in Ollie's memory: a photograph of a burnt-up easy chair. Supposedly, the guy had been sitting there, relaxing with a Bud Light and a high-def playoff game, when—bam. Fireball. "Happens more than you think," the FBI agent had drawled in the narration. Now, standing below a witches' nest with a handful of potentially flammable magic flakes, Ollie thought back to that crispy recliner and the husk of a burned body on top. Maybe this explained it all.

P.S. No refills.

Last bottle, last chance. As he stood there, motionless, willing himself to potentially, voluntarily, join the illustrious ranks of "spontaneous human combustion" victims, he thought about the witches. They wouldn't actually hurt him, would they? Or make him hurt himself? He just couldn't believe it. No. This had to be part of the riddle, that's all. Just part of the game.

The test.

Ollie paused. Instead of lowering the fateful flakes onto his tongue, he dropped them back into the bottle. Then he reached again for the rolled-up parchment and reread the last few lines: *We'll give just one chance, and one simple clue: It's meant to destroy, and not meant for you.*

Not meant for him.

His eyebrows lifted as recognition dawned. They weren't talking about the riddle; they were talking about the *solution.* The bottles, the flakes: They weren't meant for Ollie, at all.

Meant to destroy.

Destroy what?

Ollie's eyes traveled back to the basket, and to the length of twine that held it suspended. The rope was frayed, flimsy. And it was the only thing that reached all the way to the nest above.

He skimmed the rhyme again: *For someone to climb, a ladder must drop. Lose the connection to reach to the top.*

Absently, Ollie ran his fingers over Meatball's thick fur coat. He read the label on the last bottle: TO BURN. Then he shook a pile of flakes onto his palm, twisted his face into an expression of hopeful trepidation, and threw the purple, onion-scented fragments directly at the dangling rope.

The "poof" came fast and colorful, like a magician's trick on a Vegas stage. Violet clouds temporarily blocked his view, then cleared to reveal a small but steady flame on the twine. The fire grew and traveled, eating the string inch by inch on an upward trajectory. The basket, suddenly untethered, fell to the ground. And when the flames reached the nest at the top, Ollie heard a plink, a pop, and a short moment of silence before a coil of thick rope and rungs unfurled and fell almost all the way to the dirt at Ollie's feet.

A ladder.

Ollie wanted to feel annoyed at all the trouble. Instead, he felt elation—and, he had to admit, a weird puff of pride. He lowered Meatball onto the ground. "You'd better stay here," he said. "I'll just be a minute." And then, for the second time that day, he eyed a flimsy set of rungs, prayed that they would hold his six-foot-six, extra-round frame, and started to climb.

Five

Any hope of a graceful entrance vanished when Ollie reached the top of the ladder. The nest had no ingress or threshold. No convenient swinging door. It soon became apparent that he'd have to hoist himself up and over the edge, drag his body across the surface of countless sharp sticks and mud clumps, and then somehow touch down on the other side. He managed to do this, barely, but did not manage to land upright. Instead, he found himself lying in a heap at the witches' feet—moss stuck in his hair and scratches splayed across his skin.

They did not seem at all surprised to see him.

"Let me guess," Ollie said, struggling to stand. "You've been waiting for me?"

A loud laugh erupted from the closest one. "We wait for all, we wait for none!" she said gaily, swinging her long hair from side to side in a blissful, swaying dance. The other two, another woman and a man, seemed amused at this. Or maybe just amused in general. Either way, Ollie definitely had the feeling that he'd interrupted a party.

All of them wore ratty, flowing robes.

The man was banging a wide drum in a steady rhythm. His long beard partially covered the drum's surface, which looked like it was made from a thick animal hide. He had a cherubic, kindly face, with fewer wrinkles than one might expect, given his age.

The non-dancing woman was reclined and drowsy, sucking on something that looked like an oversized straw and blowing out teal-tinted smoke. Her hair, frizzy and thick, wrapped her entire head and torso. Her features were pointier than the man's. More pinched and stern.

The swaying witch, meanwhile, interrupted her dance to pour steaming white broth from a narrow pitcher into a glass. She gave off a gentle, patient air, like a long-suffering battlefield nurse that everyone looked to for comfort. She offered the drink to Ollie; he politely declined.

"What's with the riddles?" he asked.

The witches ignored his question. Each was seemingly enthralled with the effects of the white drink and whatever else was swirling in the thick, hazy air. They looked much the same as he remembered them, though he had to admit that he hadn't gotten a great look that day, due mainly to the sudden and debilitating case of lung catastrophe and unconsciousness. Moments after his collapse, the witches had breathed air—or possibly something else—into his tissues and given him the gift of time. He had used those precious moments to make the toughest choice of his life: stay in the Neath, or return to the Brickside? In the end, he had decided to stay, and his lungs had become irrevocably adjusted to life underground.

The closer woman set down the pitcher and resumed her dance. Music enveloped the entire nest: Not just the drum, but other chaotic, stringed symphonies coming from...somewhere. A radio? An invisible chamber orchestra?

Then Ollie saw them: a row of absurdly oversized insects, lined up along the rim of the nest like sailors waving from a departing ship. They resembled grasshoppers, but bigger. And yellower. Each bug seemed to be playing itself like an instrument: sliding legs, shimmying wings, and contracting abdomens, all combining to emit melodic sounds into the ether. Their protruding eyes were half-closed by massive, hooded lids, as if they'd been hypnotized by their own song.

Ollie stared, dumbfounded, momentarily forgetting why he had come.

"Welcome, welcome, Ollie, Ollie," the man said. He spoke the words in a chant. "Welcome, welcome, welcome. You are always welcome here."

The two women smiled and repeated it in harmonious synchronicity: "You are always welcome here!" Their faces were dreamy; blissed.

Good God, Ollie thought. These witches were hammered.

"Hi," he said, feeling as awkward as a seventh grader at the eighth-grade dance. "Hello. Great to see you, again."

The man lifted his hand in a happy, distracted wave. The two women said nothing.

Ollie gave another sideways glance at the insect symphony, then raised his voice. "Look, I don't want to...uh, take up too much of your time. I just have a quick question, and then I'll be on my way." He paused, in case someone wanted to say, *Wonderful, ask away!* When no one did, he pushed forward: "It's about the WRC. The Resource Center. You guys know the place?"

If any of the witches recognized the name, they gave no sign.

"Anyway, I was hoping... I know it sounds crazy, but I was hoping you might be able to help me get access to the Brickside. Me and Tera. Just for a little while. Not permanently or anything. Just for, like, a few days."

The music continued to play.

"The women, at the WRC... It seems like they might be in a bit of danger. And there was this note, with my name on it, and...I have to go up. Well, I want to. I mean, it's important. That I go up."

The witches swayed and hummed and smiled.

Had they even heard him? He cleared his throat. "So, uh, like I said, I was hoping you might be able to...help. With that."

"No going back up there, little shaver," the seated witch said. She held up her palms as if to say, *too bad, so sad.* A fresh puff of teal smoke escaped her tube.

"Right. Yeah, I know, it's tough. The lung thing, and all that." He looked from one to the other. "But you guys, being magic and all... Maybe you can do it? Or do...something?"

The tall woman refilled her glass. "A noble thought for a noble gent," she said. "Alas, dear Ollie, we are nested."

Ollie blinked. "What does that mean?"

"It means, we are incubating," said the man. "Physicking. We cannot fly."

"Welllll…" The seated witch raised a finger in disagreement.

"We *will* not fly," he corrected himself. Then he pounded the drum with extra emphasis. *Whomp.* "We will be but vessels for the pestles." *Whomp.* "A stewed pottage, simmering on the flame of prestidigitation." *Whomp.* "Aye, mere pots hung from trammels, building in flavor, darkening with the might of ever-bigger rigor!"

The dancing woman shimmied and raised her glass, as if to toast his verbal gymnastics.

The seated witch, likewise, lifted her smoking tube slightly before returning it to her lips. She leaned back in her seat; her eyes began to close. Nearby, the jumbo grasshoppery creatures continued to buzz and vibrate and whir, creating a resonant thrumming that echoed unpleasantly in his ears.

Ollie looked from side to side, bewildered. "So, that's a no?"

"Aye, a beautiful no, spoken with the resonance of a thousand sanguine seraphs," the man said.

Plucking moss from his hair, Ollie waited for one of them to say something that made sense. When that didn't happen, he asked, "But…why not?"

The seated witch reopened her eyes. The amusement was starting to drain from her expression. "We have reasons aplenty, young man. Reasons that need not stating."

"But didn't you hear me? They're in trouble. Missing. A whole bunch of people. Maybe in danger."

"That may be. But their troubles are not my troubles, nor do I wish to make them so."

"How can you say that?" he sputtered. "Don't you want to help? What's the matter with you?"

The tall witch's dancing stilled. The man's drumming slowed. The bugs continued to play their symphony, though even they seemed to understand that the mood had shifted. And in her reclining seat, the frizzy-haired witch was stiffening.

"Okay, fine," Ollie said, holding up his hands with innocent detachment. "I get it. Fine. You won't help, or un-nest, or whatever. But there's this other thing. A machine, or a spell, or some kind of potion. I don't know, exactly. Rumor is, this thing exists, somewhere down here, and it helps you breathe. Up there."

The three witches shared a long glance.

"What?" he asked, looking from one to another.

"Rumors do not travel well, my son," the man said. "Whatever their original shape might have been, they tend to arrive at their destination quite disheveled. Crinkled and wrinkled and puffity-pinkled."

"Sure. I know. That's why I'm here. I figured if anyone might know more about it, the truth of it, it would be all of you."

This time, they made a concerted effort not to look at each other. Which piqued his interest even more.

"What?" he asked again. "Does it exist, or not?"

"We do not know anything about such supposition," said the seated woman casually. Too casually.

"Don't know? Or won't say?" he challenged.

"Your questions have been asked and answered, young sir," she said in a clipped tone. "It has been the greatest of pleasures to cast eyes upon you this day. Be sure to take a pocketful of whortleberries for your trog friend below. Now, if it please you, leave us our peace."

"Your *peace?*" Ollie repeated, his eyes agog. "Whortleberries?"

The witch nodded. The yellow bugs continued their serenade.

His hands landed on his hips. "Is this what you do all day?" he finally spluttered. Then, the words started to spill faster than his teeth could trap them. "You just sit around and...drink? And dance? And smoke? It's like goddamn Woodstock up in here. People are suffering, you know. Not just these WRC people. Lots and lots of people! They're getting abused, like, everywhere. Little kids. Women. Old people. Helpless people. You have magic, for Chrissake! *Magic!* You could be...I don't know...doing something. Anything. You could be helping them. Helping *me,* right now. And instead, you do *this?*" His eyes flitted around the strange roost, landing on the drums, the smoke, the warbling insects, the clear glass pitchers. "You do nothing?"

At this, the seated woman narrowed her eyes.

The man, likewise, stopped his drumming. "Your tongue wags beyond its boundaries, young fellow," he said, a note of warning in his voice. "We will forgive this trespass. But best be on your way, now."

"No!" Ollie said, his voice almost a shout. "I won't be *on my way!* I need your help, dammit. And...and..." He took a deep breath before finishing his sentence. "And you owe me!"

The frizzy-haired witch jutted her head forward. "We owe *you?*"

"Yes," he answered stubbornly. "I got you out of that cell, didn't I? And now all I'm asking for is a little help. Not even for me! People are missing, somewhere up there, and they need us. And you won't even get off your asses and answer a simp—"

Her body rose like a thunderclap, stopping him mid-sentence with a blur of rapid motion that landed her face only inches away from his. Not enough time had passed for her to travel the distance, and yet, there she was.

"You know not of which you speak," she hissed, her lips grazing his ear.

Ollie jumped back, startled.

"Go on now, Ollie," the other woman said, tugging his sleeve. Like the man, she, too, sounded like she was issuing him a warning. "Go on home."

"Oh, I don't think so," the now-standing witch sneered, pushing her cohort aside. "Our young friend here seems to think we are in need of education, does he not? And that he is to be our schoolmaster? How very lucky for us. Fortune has smiled upon us this day."

"Elisha," the taller woman said, an urgent note in her voice.

"Aye, it is fine. It is right, this way." The witch they called Elisha had moved her face even closer to his. Ollie could smell something fermented on her breath. "You think we do not understand defilement, young sir? You think we do not understand what it means to endure?"

"Elisha, stop!" said the man. Even the insects had gone quiet.

Ollie began to shake. Too late, he could see his error. "I'm sorry," he said. "Look, I'm sorry. I shouldn't have—"

"No, you should not have," Elisha agreed, her voice cold and calm. "But like all those of your time, you fail to grasp the sacrifices and sufferings of those who came before."

"You're right," he said, holding up his hands. "Of course, you're right. I'm sorry."

"You think we do nothing? You think we know nothing?"

"Elisha, this is not—"

"Now, now, Lizbeth. Our young Ollie is but a whelping pup, is he not? His eyes are not yet open. So, let us open them. We shall let him see what we have seen. We shall let him feel what we have felt." Her last words dropped to a harsh whisper. "Every sharp and bitter thing."

Six

Before the others could intercede, and before Ollie could react or protest, Elisha grabbed him by the shoulders and spun him. Fast. Unnaturally fast, as though his feet had been perched on top of a lazy Susan. Ollie's vision swam with the sudden smear of his surroundings: the faces, the browns and greens, the pointy tips of the stalagmite forest. His perceptions, his reality, swerved into a skid.

He heard Elisha's voice: "Where shall we start? Perhaps at Valais!"

And then, with the force of a shove, Ollie found himself somewhere else. Some*when* else. He could sense it in the air, in the stench, in the unfamiliar clothes that draped his body. He was wearing a tunic of some kind, thick, like a rucksack, with something else wrapped tightly around his neck. A rope, if he wasn't mistaken. Sharp and scratchy and tight enough to make breathing a struggle. More ropes bound his wrists together.

The shock of it blasted like a furnace. Ollie struggled to straighten his thoughts, his posture, but found he could do neither. He was shuffling down a street, pressed along by a crowd—men and women, all with roughly shaved, bleeding scalps and downturned faces. They limped and stumbled beside him, in front of him, and behind him. Some cried out loud, some prayed. Most were deadly silent, their eyes awash in terror.

Ollie felt a tremor shake his limbs. He could hear a deafening chorus of jeers and angry shouts echoing from all sides; when he dared a peek above the heads around him, he saw the gathered horde of spectators. Taunting. Spitting. Yelling threats and insults in a language he didn't understand.

"Sorcieres!"

"Concubines du diable!"

The hatred was as thick as the smoke in the air.

So much smoke. It snaked down Ollie's throat, choking him. And something else, too: the stench of cooking fat and flesh. Wails of agony cut through the other sounds to send a shiver of horror up his spine. As he approached the open square, the grisly source of the fetor and shrieks became all too clear. Dozens of rounded pyres filled the space, each stacked high with straw bales and planks. They were also stacked with people. Screaming, burning people, tied to poles. The flames shot skyward, thundering, spurting sparks and ashes. Floating flakes of charred skin swirled in the air, falling down around him like dirty snow.

Ollie froze. Tried to backtrack. Tried to turn, to free his tethered arms, to run. But it was no use. Meaty hands grabbed him, pulled him toward the square. The angry crowd threw rocks at his face, his chest, his back.

"Bruler avec le diable!"

"Bruler, sorciere!"

The thick smoke stung his eyes. Tears washed his cheeks. The plaza, the flaming pyres, grew ever closer. Then another voice, a closer voice, broke through the panic and pain.

"Elisha! Enough!"

Ollie heard the witch's voice, again, in his ear. "Aye, let us move, then, to Aberdeen. To Ross! To East Lothian and Fife!"

With a blast of soot, the fires vanished. The smell of cooking human skin and filthy tunics evaporated. In their place, Ollie found himself suddenly inhaling the scents of simmering food, chopped wood, body odor, and stale, indoor air. Once again, he realized that his hands and feet were bound—this time, while sitting on a chair inside a low-ceilinged cottage.

Ollie blinked, trying to clear the residual smoke from his vision. His eyes fell first on a book. It sat on a table directly in front of him, open to the title page. At first, the letters swam. Finally, he was able to focus and read the unfamiliar words: *Malleus Maleficarum,* written in ornate calligraphy on yellowed, thick paper.

Next, he saw the woman. Not standing or sitting, but bent over on the table next to the book. A man stood next to her, wearing a hat, a short woolen jacket with a pleated shirt, and a stern, cruel expression. The woman wore a peasant's house dress and apron. She was young, and possibly beautiful. It was hard for Ollie to say, exactly, because her face was contorted in agony.

"Confessen!" the man growled.

When the young woman said nothing in response, the man reached for a device sitting next to the book on the table. It looked like a wrought-iron press of some kind, with the woman's thumb trapped between two of the iron rods. The man spun a lever on the top, causing the prisoner to scream as the rods crushed her finger.

"Confessen, wicche!" he shouted.

She only sobbed.

This went on for minutes, or possibly hours, as Ollie watched in despair. He struggled against the ropes that bound him, and the gag in his mouth, to no avail. Finally, the man gave up on the finger-crushing vise and ushered in some helpers from outside the cottage. They bound the woman's head with thick ropes, wrapping her face and hair, then pulled so hard that Ollie was sure her skull would buckle from the pressure. She screamed and begged until the pain became too great for even that; then, she slumped, slipping in and out of consciousness.

Stop! Ollie yelled in frantic desperation, if only in his head. *Leave her alone!*

Elisha's voice interrupted the scene, snapping into his mind like a whip: "Witches' Tower, Lancaster!" she said.

And just like that, he was gone from the cottage and lying on the floor of a dank cell.

Bodies pressed around him on every side. Old women, and teenagers, and every undefinable age in between. Each person was tethered by an ankle cuff and chain to a single metal ring in the center of the room. One of the prisoners seemed to be already dead;

her body lay untouched by the seeping stone wall. The stench of decomposition and filth and excrement burned his nose. The cold left him shivering uncontrollably in his wet clothes, soaked clean through by the puddles on the ground and the constant, maddening drips from above. Hunger clawed ceaselessly at his stomach.

Time jerked; Ollie found himself dragged out of the cell and into the sudden, harsh sunlight. The gallows awaited him, and yet another jeering crowd.

"It's the short drop for ye!" one woman yelled triumphantly, pelting him with mud as he passed.

"Devil's whore!" shouted another. Up ahead, he watched the nooses tightening around the necks of the unlucky souls who had reached the platform before him. Saw the leather boots kicking out the stools, saw the feet twitching in the open air as strangulation landed its slow, final blow.

And then, he heard the voice again: "Reign of the Witchfinder General!" Elisha said, this time in a harsh whisper.

Ollie stood on a bridge over a moat. Woozy, and sick. He looked down to see an old man bobbing in and out of icy water, gasping for breath. Another man, this one younger with a wide-brimmed hat, told the crowd to gather and observe. "Now we swim the witch!" he called out.

The elderly man in the water coughed and struggled as the assembled townspeople watched from the bridge. His arms seemed to be tied behind his back.

"He floats!" one of the gathered yelled.

"Aye, he be a sorcerer!" another agreed.

The third voice was Elisha's. "And Torsaker," she rasped into his ear.

Ollie groaned in misery as the vision of the moat and the drowning man faded into one with more flames, more pyres. With retching revulsion, he realized that the victims in these fires had also been beheaded. He saw hundreds of scorched bodies and mounds of severed heads, stretching into the horizon. Children gathered nearby in a weeping, wailing crowd. Ollie felt his own sobs rise in his throat as the grotesque scene blinked in and out like a TV channel with faulty reception.

"And let us not forget Salem Village," he heard the witch say.

With that, the smoke-filled vista was gone. Now, Ollie found himself traveling along a rutted, hilly road. He tried to catch his breath, to identify his new surroundings. He seemed to be in a cart, pulled by horses and driven by a hunched-over man. Ollie was near the back, trapped with three other filthy prisoners in a crude cell constructed of latched-together poles. One of his fellow captives was praying feverishly; another was crying. The third rose to her knees, reached an arm through the bars, and grabbed the sleeve of the driver.

As Ollie watched, the driver turned, clearly startled by the woman's grip. He slowed the cart and pulled her fingers from his arm. The two had words, muttering at each other in low tones that Ollie couldn't hear. Then the driver pushed his hand against the prisoner's face, forcing her backward. "You are mad, old woman," he spat. "Mad, and cursed."

The prisoner gripped the bars with both hands. "Can you not see it?" she cried out. "I am no more a witch than I am a cloud in the sky. You have imprisoned innocents! It is not too late for you to save us, and to save yourself. I beseech you now, open this cage! Stop this injustice! By your own hands, you bring us to death, George Herrick! You bring us to hell!"

Ollie straightened from his slump in the corner of the makeshift cage. Did she say...Herrick? He strained to catch sight of this driver, who was snapping the reins with angry precision. At first, Ollie could only see the back of the man's head. Then, a slight profile. The jostling made a clear view difficult, and the driver did not seem inclined to turn and peer at his prisoners again. If anything, he seemed determined to ignore them altogether, as though he and his horses were alone on this desolate stretch of rutted road.

The cart picked up speed. Ollie reached for the bars, trying to steady himself. That was when he saw them: a row of silent, mostly hidden figures in the tree line. Four people. Five?

Witches. *His* witches. Elisha, Lizbeth, the man. Others. They looked much the same then as they did now; long-haired and hollow-eyed. They watched the rickety vehicle pass by, lingering in the echo of the old woman's screeching accusation: "You bring us to hell!" They looked at George Herrick and at his passengers. Then, they looked directly at Ollie.

Heart pounding, he jumped forward to grab the bars. "Enough!" he shouted. "Please, I understand! Please, let me out! Make it stop!"

"Elisha, bring him back," a man's voice said sternly.

"Fine," Ollie heard her say. "He wants to return to the present? Let us bring him there. Ollie Delgato, welcome to India in the twenty-first century. And Tanzania, and Congo, and Ghana, and Papua New Guinea!"

With another bone-rattling shove, Ollie landed in a village. In front of him, a young, dark-skinned woman wearing modern clothes was being chased by a crowd. When they caught her, they shouted the word *"Dakan!"* with harsh repetition and beat her mercilessly with rusted, metal bars. That scene melted away to reveal another: two old women, forced to strip naked and parade past jeering crowds, filmed all the while by onlookers with cell phones. Then, a mother and her four children, all drowned in a well. Bodies bloated. Then, shaved heads and mob lynchings. Men, women, and children accused, examined, and burned alive, this time with fires lit not by ancient torches but by plastic lighters. On and on it went, each scene grislier and more unthinkable than the one before.

Ollie whimpered, crumpled.

"Elisha! Enough!"

With a convulsive shudder, the visions grew muddled, then dim. And finally, they disappeared. Ollie found himself back in the witches' nest in the Neath, curled into a ball with tears running in fast streams down his cheeks. He touched his arms, face, legs...checking for damage, amazed to find none. No scorched skin. No rope burns. No biting fleas or trails of blood. He whimpered piteously, aghast at the sounds pouring from his lips. Aghast at the things he had seen. Wishing he could wash out his brain and forget it all.

"Why?" he heard himself say, though he wasn't sure who he was asking. God? The witches? The world? So much suffering. So much death. And for what? *Why? Why, why, why?* The exhaustion and revulsion and pure, utter helplessness left him stuttering.

The three witches hovered over his curled-up body, their faces grim.

The one called Lizbeth crouched down beside him. She placed a hand on his arm and smiled gently. "It is hard to see the truth of things," she said, her voice low and quiet. "But we cannot change what we cannot see."

His head whipped up. "Change?" he whispered. He thought about the horrific things he had been shown in Africa, in India. Endless scenes of death and mutilation. "That was now! Today!"

"Aye," she acknowledged. "Hatred and ignorance persist, it is true. But the world is changing. We are changing it. *You* are changing it. One soul at a time."

Ollie sat up, resting on his hands. His muscles were shaken and spent. "No," he said, the word catching in his throat. "Nothing ever really changes." And it was true, wasn't it? Some scars were inflicted by strangers; some, by those who were supposed to love you. Was one worse than the other? He thought about his own mother's suffering at the hands of his father. Thought of his bullies back on the Brickside. Of the relentless mistreatment that had forced Tera to escape to the Neath. Of the endless, endless, endless cycle of abuse from parents to children and back around again.

"Anyone can change," the man said, pressing his hands together. His voice was gentle. "Even those with the most to atone for. Just look at George."

"George...Herrick?" Ollie asked.

Lizbeth nodded. "Back in his own time, Elisha decided to teach him a lesson, of sorts. She showed him all that she just showed you."

"And then some," the man added.

Elisha shrugged, unapologetic, and wandered back to her seat.

"Yes, and then some," Lizbeth agreed, giving Elisha a stern look. "As you know, George did some...terrible things, back in Salem Village. He believed terrible things. He followed orders without question, even when those orders were wrong. But then he saw the truth of the past, and of his own misdeeds, and he understood. He grieved his part, and he wanted to atone for his sins."

"It was George who suggested we create the Neath," the man added. Ollie still hadn't caught his name. "He wanted a sanctuary for all the oppressed. A place where the victimized could go to find peace and safety."

Ollie nodded, and nodded, and nodded. Yes. He knew all that already. What he didn't know was why they wouldn't help him now. With this. He couldn't go back to his friends with nothing. There had to be a way. His hands, he realized, were still shaking from his ordeal. He shoved them into his jumpsuit's pockets.

"And I want to do something, too," Ollie said, looking from face to face. "Let me go up there. Help me find them."

Elisha had reached again for her strange smoking straw. Her face was still clouded. "So that you may play the hero?" she asked.

"What? No, that's—"

"Ah, dear Ollie. Even now, you do not heed your lessons."

"What are you talking about?"

"You may tell yourself any story you want, young man. But do not expect us to believe that you do this thing for others. Helping those women is but a pleasant side effect to helping yourself."

"That's not—"

"Stop," she snapped, her back rising from the reclined seat. "I will not tolerate lies."

His lips pressed shut.

"Tell us the truth of the matter, and only the truth," Elisha said. Her blue eyes sparked. "If you cannot find the truth of it inside of yourself, then you cannot hope to find whatever else it is you seek."

The other two witches nodded, not unkindly.

A slow, gentle song began, and Ollie realized that the insects had cautiously restarted their music. The resonance seemed to vibrate the entire nest, amplifying his already stark sense of vertigo.

With effort, Ollie rose to his feet. He looked at each witch. They stared back, alert and expectant. The hazy-dazy atmosphere he had stumbled into earlier was long gone. Now, the nest felt less like a drug-addled music festival and more like a courtroom. He imagined a sketch artist nearby, expertly drawing the befuddled expression on his face.

He swallowed.

"Okay," he said, holding up his palms. He could feel the shame creeping into his face with a hot flush. "Okay, fine. It's my fault they got taken. Is that what you want to hear?"

No one answered.

"I wasn't supposed to come down to Neath. I kind of...snuck down here. Or whatever. So I must have thrown off the balance of something. Or maybe I just pissed off the wrong people. I don't know. So yeah, maybe I'm asking partially for myself. Out of guilt. Is that so wrong? What difference does it make, in the end? As long as they get helped?"

Again, his question was met with silence.

Then, the man spoke. "He does not yet know," he said, his voice laced with surprise.

"Bert," Elisha said warningly.

"Do you not yet know?"

"Know what?" Ollie asked.

"Bert!"

But the round-faced man ignored the admonition, stepping closer to peer into Ollie's eyes. "It is no accident you are here, our dear, young giant. It is your kismet."

"My...what?"

"Your kismet. Kizzee, kizzee, kaleidoscopee! Your divine providence!" The man wore a suddenly urgent expression. He began to advance.

Startled, Ollie tried to step out of the way, but stopped short when his back pressed against the nest's scratchy rim. He watched in dismay as the witch moved ever closer. The man's eyeballs had started to jitter in their sockets, jerking left and right as though watching a far-off tennis match. He held out his hand.

Ollie pulled backwards. "What are you—"

But it was too late. The witch named Bert had pushed up both of Ollie's sleeves, grasped his forearms, and flipped them over. "Have you felt it, yet?"

"Felt...what?" Ollie's eyes darted around the nest.

"It. *It*," Bert said. "It! The change. The burn of metamorphosis-o-sis. Transmutification. Inflammereria." The man peered down at Ollie's now-exposed skin, squinting. Impatient.

"I don't... I'm not—"

Before Ollie could complete the half-formed thought, Bert reached up and pressed a palm, hard, against Ollie's forehead. And started humming. At first, the abstract sound mingled with the insects' music. Then, it morphed into words.

"Water, earth, air," he said, his voice buzzing like a chainsaw.

Ollie winced and wiggled, trying to pull away.

"Bert!" Lizbeth called out. "For heaven's sake! Stop that!"

Bert ignored her. His eyes were closed. "Water, earth, air," he intoned again. "Water, earth, air. Water, earth, air. Three pieces, one key. Ollie's key. Kizzee, kizzee, kismet. Water, earth, and air."

Ollie stared in bafflement at the blissed-out, ranting man.

Bert's eyes flew open. Then he smiled kindly. "A message for you," Bert said. "Just for you. Water, earth, and air."

Ollie's throat had gone dry. "A message from who?" he finally asked.

"From the one who wishes you to have it."

"What does it mean?"

At that, the witch grasped Ollie's cheeks and squeezed. The gesture reminded Ollie of the Italian *nonnas* back in the North End, forever pinching and squishing whatever faces they happened to come across. "You will need it. That is all I know."

"Need...what?"

"The message, of course! Water, earth, air. Water, earth, air. First place, second place, third place." He began to dance, and then, as though overcome with sudden glee, he ran to his drum. "WATER!" *Whomp.* "EARTH!" *Whomp.* "AIR!" *Whomp.* "He will need it, way up there!" *Whomp.*

The insects, now seemingly caught up in the mania, sped up their shimmying; the strident symphony grew louder.

Bert jumped and pounded: "WATER, water! EARTH, earth! AIR, air! He will need it, way up there!"

What the...? Ollie ran a hand through his thick curls, bewildered. Then, Lizbeth stepped in front of him, blocking his line of sight to the drumming man. "Don't mind our Bert, dear," she said, waving a hand. "He's a bit touched."

"Touched," Ollie repeated.

"Yes, touched. You know, woo-woo. Confused."

"His head is emptier than his drum," Elisha interjected wryly.

Ollie doubted that very much. Touched like a fox, maybe. He peered around Lizbeth to look, again, at the quirky, thrumming man. "What's he talking about, 'way up there?' Is he talking about the Brickside? Can I go? Is there a way?"

Elisha, clearly annoyed, took another drag on her hollow stick and didn't answer. Teal smoke rose into the air between them.

Ollie folded his arms. "Okay, then. I guess Bert is the only one interested in talking. Or singing. Maybe I should ask him to expand a bit more on his theories about... What was it? Kizzee, kizzee, kismet? He could create a ballad, maybe. Or a long limerick? I have plenty of time. And I'm sure we'd all like to hear more about—"

"All right, all right. Fine," Elisha interrupted, holding up a hand in irritation. She looked Ollie up and down, as though he were an item available for purchase. Finally, she gave a resigned sigh. "There was something, once. I am not sure if it still exists."

At this, he perked, but left his arms folded. "What is it?"

"I am told it was a device," Elisha said. "Only half completed, or perhaps not even that." She reclined to look up at the massive swirl of wormwalkers crawling across the cavern's ceiling high above. "At some point, apparently, some of the Neath residents thought it would be a good idea to create a way to...visit. To move back and forth. To find a way to see their loved ones back on the Brickside."

She shrugged, as if the notion was a silly one. Ollie found himself leaning forward.

"Alas, too late, they realized the error of their plan," she continued. This seemed to amuse her; she gave a short laugh. "If they made it possible for themselves to leave the Neath, then, theoretically, it would also be possible for anyone to leave the Neath. Including the prisoners at Herricks' End."

At this, Ollie swallowed.

"For years, for decades, they had been dragging the worst sorts of humans down to our depths, as a way to protect those on the Brickside. What would happen, do you suppose, if those same, vile inmates suddenly had access to an escape from our realm? A way to revisit their old world, and their old victims?" She tented her fingers. "Revenge works both ways, as we know. Can you imagine what those prisoners would do if they could get their hands on the people who had condemned them to hell on earth?"

Ollie didn't answer.

Elisha paused, sucked on her stick, and blew out a plume. "And so, it was decided. Work on the device would cease. The tunnels leading to the lab would be blocked. Collapsed, I believe?"

She looked for clarification at Lizbeth, who nodded.

"But the lab is still there?" Ollie asked.

"I suppose so, yes."

"And the device might be there, too?"

"Again, I can only suppose. As you might recall, we have been locked in a stone cell for several hundred years." Elisha gave Ollie a wan smile that was not a smile at all. "George Herrick might have known the answer to your questions, but alas..."

Sad looks traveled around the nest. *Alas, he is dead.*

That he was. But...

Ollie shifted his weight. For a fleeting second, he considered telling them about the note.

Though he didn't like to think about it much, that damn frayed piece of parchment had nonetheless spooked him every day since he'd found it tucked into Meatball's bedding on the floor. George Herrick's cryptic prophecies, ripe with prescient riddles and hints, had guided Ollie through his trials of imprisonment and escape. There was no getting around the truth: Herrick had somehow known what was going to happen before it happened. Every gory detail. And he had decided to share that knowledge, albeit in a roundabout way, with Ollie.

So far, all this note-writing weirdness had worked to Ollie's advantage.

So far.

He wanted to be thankful. And sometimes, he was. But more often, he was just disconcerted. What was the saying... Knowledge is power? Even now, Ollie had no knowledge—not really. Just snippets and impressions and ambiguous warnings, all doled out like a slow, dark drip into an espresso cup. And until that changed, he knew, he would have no power. No control at all over his own life.

He had stumbled across the most recent note by accident. That's what he told himself, anyway. He hadn't wanted to find it. And once he did, he had tried his best to forget it. But the words, it seemed, had other ideas.

They had arrived, this time, in the form of a rhyming poem. A taunting poem, really. A big letter O had been scrawled at the top of the page, leaving little doubt about who the message was intended for. And none of it, of course, made any sense:

Hows and Abouts
Souls and mates
Find him his,
Seal your fate.

Water green,
Three on high.
Air and breath,
Truth and lie.

Good is bad,
Beast will bite.
Steer the course,
Bend the light.

Mud to brick,
Dark to sun.
Soon, you choose:
All
   or
     one?

He hadn't told anyone about the poem—not even Tera. Talking about it would have made it real. Instead, Ollie had chosen the path of complete and utter denial. He told himself that his Herculean trials were over. His tough decisions had all been made. And that he and Tera were now settling into a bump-free, happily-ever-after ride of sympatico bliss.

But now, the words marched out again. They twirled batons and shook tambourines and blew trumpets of reminders in his head. Unavoidable.

Water green, three on high.

Three on high?

Ollie stared at the three witches lounging in their nest. Their *high* nest.

A prickle began to lift the hairs on his arms. It was already in motion, wasn't it? The prophecies were coming true. Again. George Herrick had known Ollie would come to this very place, today, in this very minute. He had known all of this would happen.

Ollie rubbed his forehead, frustrated. So what, anyway? What good did that do him? What possible difference could it make? Even if Ollie did have some sort of weird, dead, poetry-writing guardian angel, it didn't seem to be getting him any closer to his goal. *Three on high. Big deal,* he thought. *Give me something I can use.* Then he said, out loud, "Where is the lab?"

"It does not matter, my young friend," Bert said, tapping the wide drum in time with his words. "The tunnels"—*tap*—"are"—*tap*—"gone."

"Okay, then, where *was* it?"

The three witches looked at each other.

"Somewhere that a human like you cannot go," Lizbeth said. "Not without the tunnels."

Resentment mounted in Ollie's throat; he did his best to swallow it. To stay calm. The bug music was growing ever-louder now; Lizbeth had begun to sway again. Elisha's eyelids were starting to droop. He was losing them, he could tell. Their attention was waning fast, dissipating into the cavern air like the steam from their alabaster drinks. Apparently, it had been tiring to drag him along on an involuntary tour of horrors past.

"Please," Ollie begged. Then, again, louder: "Please!"

Elisha's eyes had all but closed. She opened them for a brief flash, seemed to consider him again, and said, "If anyone can get you there, it would be the Novas."

"Who's that?" Ollie asked, looking from face to face. "Where do I find them?"

Lizbeth smiled and held up her glass. "Ask your friends," she said. "They will know where the Novas dwell. But please, dear one, do not get your hopes lifted. You must understand, this is...how do you humans say it? A target that is hard to hit?"

"A long shot?" Ollie supplied.

"Yes. This one, I'm afraid, is a long shot." Lizbeth's expression looked almost apologetic.

He sighed. Of course, it was. He was starting to wonder if there was any other kind around here.

Ollie's hands had finally stopped shaking, though the visions of fires and nooses and screaming, agonized faces lingered in his peripheral vision. It was the victims' surprise, he now realized, that haunted him the most: the pure, plain expression of shock that had registered on each face as their final moments had arrived. As if they had never truly believed the worst could happen. As if they had thought, right up until the very end, that someone would intervene to stop the atrocity.

But no one did.

He supposed it was just human nature, to hope for a good outcome despite all evidence to the contrary. And Ollie was, if nothing else, human.

Too human, perhaps, for this place. And for the challenge that lay ahead.

"Don't forget the whortleberries," Lizbeth said, pointing to a small sack on the table.

"Whortle, hortle, thine immortal!" Bert added gleefully. "Farewell, dear Ollieberry! We shall see you again!"

Ollie lifted his hand in a feeble wave, hoping that was more of a promise than a goodbye.

Seven

The Nova Scotian Water Nymphs, or "Novas" for short, lived in and around the rocky ledges of the lake. You wouldn't find them unless you were looking for them—and looking for them was usually not a great idea. They were extraordinarily beautiful, extraordinarily clever, and extraordinarily cruel. The "mean girls" of the Neath.

According to Derrin, anyway.

Derrin had also informed Ollie that the Novas were able to remain underwater or on land, interchangeably and amphibiously, for as long as they pleased in either place. Which also made them the salamanders of the Neath, he supposed.

The scuttlebutt was, they liked their water cold and their men transitory. But above all, Nova Scotian Water Nymphs were known for being insular, secretive, and highly territorial.

"They won't talk to us," Kuyu said, hanging the pot over the fire.

"They won't talk to *you*," Derrin corrected. "They'll talk to me." She sounded confident, though annoyed. Something about this subject had raised her hackles.

"Why?" Ollie asked.

Derrin flashed him a look that said the question was too irritating to answer. Then, she answered it anyway. "Our families have existed here, together, for centuries," she said. "My father once—" She stopped, cleared her throat. "My father...knew them. One of them. Not too long ago." Her gaze traveled to her feet.

Ah. Ollie nodded. Even in the Neath, every family had its dirty little secrets.

"And you know how to find them?" Tera asked. She was rocking back and forth, heel to toe. Her purple swirl was tilted slightly, like a piece of ribbon candy in mid-melt.

"I do."

"Awesome! When should we go? Today? Tonight?"

Derrin filled her bowl with broth, bits of blindfish, and something that looked like chopped-up roots. She lifted a spoonful and sipped, seemingly in no hurry to answer the question. Finally, she wiped her mouth with a sleeve. "We can leave whenever you want," she said. "But only a few of us. They won't like a crowd."

Tera nodded. "Like, how many?"

Derrin took another slurp and looked at the assembled group. "Me, Tera, Ollie, and...Laszlo."

Ollie winced. He knew what was coming even before it came.

"*What?*" Kuyu burst out. Her black curls bounced. "Why not me?"

"There's no need for you to be there," Derrin answered, firm. "Or Ajanta. Four is already more than enough. Tera and Ollie have to go because...well, because it's their deal. I have to go because I'm the contact. And Laszlo should come in case we need muscle."

At this, Laszlo grinned with pleasure.

"Muscle?" Ollie asked. "Why would we need muscle?"

Derrin shrugged. "You never know."

"Is true," Laszlo agreed solemnly, straightening and puffing out his chest.

"Good," Tera said. "Then we'll leave after dinner."

Ollie's eyes swept the room; each person, it seemed, was stewing in a different emotion. Kuyu was sullen, Laszlo was preening, Derrin was irked, Tera was impatient, and he was just feeling his customary confusion.

Only Ajanta remained neutral: a stoic mama bear in a den of complaining cubs. She carried an armful of wood to the fire pit in the center of the room and dumped it with a clatter. Her shining braid wrapped over her shoulder and reached almost all the way down to her stomach. "I will make preparations," she said.

Derrin and Tera nodded.

Ollie watched Ajanta walk away, toward the overflowing shelves of potions and packages and fabrics. "Preparations for what?" he asked.

"For anything," Tera answered. She was staring straight into the fire, her mouth set into a line. Whatever she was feeling, she kept it to herself. The unspoken thoughts stacked around her like bricks on an impenetrable wall.

What did she mean, "anything?" What did she know that he didn't? Weren't they just going to talk to the Novas? He waited for someone else to elaborate, or explain. Instead, a peculiar quiet descended around the room. No one met his eyes.

He thought suddenly of Nell, holding up the sign with white knuckles and frightened, wide eyes. Where was she now? Where were the others? Ollie didn't want to envision it, but he could. Oh, he could. Too easily. Thanks to his time at Herrick's End, he had already seen enough hellish cages, claustrophobic cells, and blood-splattered, scream-filled tunnels to fill in all the imaginary blanks. Maybe they were all waiting for him, despairing, somewhere in the dark. Waiting for him to find them.

Or maybe he was already too late.

He wrapped his arms around Meatball's furry torso, squeezing tight. The trog grunted in response. And for the first time since seeing his name etched in a delicate threat on a Mirrormoth's wings, Ollie felt afraid.

⸻ ∽ ⸻

They walked in a line: Derrin at the front, followed by Ollie, Tera, and finally Laszlo, who belted out a steady stream of what he called "Ukrainian traveling songs" until Ollie thought he might lose his mind.

"Stay behind me," Derrin told him, more than once.

"All right, all right," he muttered in response. Why would she think he had any interest in walking out front?

Back when Tera had been captured by the Herrick's End guards and Ollie had found himself alone in her studio, he had stumbled across her hand-drawn map of The Neath. Most of the sections had been neatly labeled with the names of the various islands, bridges, caves, parks, and even crow-boat routes. But one section had been notably blank: no names, no markings, no topographic indications at all. "Here be dragons," it might as well have said, so immense was its emptiness. It was that section, he believed, that they traveled in now.

Up hills, down hills. Past clusters of dilapidated dwellings. Into and out of narrow cave passageways, each one dripping with stalactite formations so huge and sharp they threatened to scrape clean through the top of Ollie's scalp. Marshes turned inexplicably into dirt paths, which turned into patches of rhizer farmland, and then back again into marshes. On and on they walked. Every once in a while, a wormwalker would fall from the cavernous ceiling above and land nearby with a gruesome splat; the sound would wake Meatball from his slumber on Ollie's shoulder and send the trog scuttling to the ground to slurp up whatever was left.

Ollie was soon exhausted. The combination of uneven ground, humid air, unrelenting exercise, and Laszlo's off-key warbling had left him panting and bleary. He wanted to ask where they were going, or at least whine *Are we there yet?* like a kid in a station wagon. He could only imagine what Derrin's reaction would have been to that.

When she paused unexpectedly, Ollie darted to the right to avoid walking into her back. She was looking for something in her bag. He continued moving forward, one step, two steps, and then stopped short—so short that Meatball lost his balance, let out a squawk of protest, and fell onto the path below.

"What's the matter?" Tera asked Ollie.

"I...don't know," he answered. He really didn't. He had walked past Derrin, only a few steps, and then saw everything in his peripheral vision go fuzzy. "I think there's something wrong with my eyes."

"There's nothing wrong with your eyes," Derrin said. "I told you to stay behind me."

"I did! I mean, I was, and then—"

"I told you to stay behind me because it's dangerous," she interrupted.

"What is dangerous?" Laszlo said, coming up to stand beside them. "I see only path."

Derrin looked weary. "Yes, that's exactly what they want you to see. But it's just an illusion."

Laszlo scrunched up his face. "Like, in desert?"

"Right. Like a mirage in the desert. You think you see it, but it's not there."

Ollie, Tera, and Laszlo followed her pointed finger to gaze at the scene ahead: a narrow road that led through a dense, stalagmite forest. Then, cautiously, all three approached with hands outstretched. Their fingers made the image wave and wobble, like tendrils of disturbed smoke.

"What...is it?" Ollie asked.

"The Novas build them," Derrin explained, rolling her eyes. "They like their privacy."

"So how do we get by?" said Tera.

"They like you to leave a token," said Derrin. "Then the mirage disappears, and you can pass."

Tera looked dubious. "What kind of a token?"

"All sorts of things. But these are their favorites." Derrin held out an open palm.

Ollie took a step closer. The object in Derrin's hand looked much like a sea star from back home, except smaller. And more...bejeweled. It had been painted in some kind of gloss and covered with an assortment of shiny tokens: scraps of metal, maybe, and polished coppery shards. The result was a bauble that looked like it might appeal to a scavenging magpie.

"Dried lakestars?" Tera asked, sounding puzzled.

Derrin approached a large rock at the edge of the path. Its center was hollowed out and smooth. Without speaking, she placed the lakestar onto the curve of the stone and held up her hands. "Ta da."

Almost instantly, the air around them began to shimmer. The scene ahead blurred, then cleared. Ollie stepped forward cautiously, his hand outstretched.

The path—the real path—veered off to the left. And straight ahead, where the illusionary road had been, he saw a deep pit. It was lined with something thick and black, like tar. If he had been alone, and had fallen in, there would have been virtually no chance of escape. This wasn't just a mirage. It was a trap.

"What the hell?" he said, spinning around to face them.

Derrin nodded grimly. Tera and Laszlo looked at each other with eyebrows raised.

"Are they actually trying to *kill* us?"

"Like I said, they like their privacy," Derrin said. "The men who visit them know to leave the tokens. But as for everyone else..." Her sentence trailed off.

Laszlo whistled.

"That's friggin' diabolical," Tera said, folding her arms.

"Yes," Laszlo agreed. "Is that."

Derrin hoisted her bag. "So. You going to stay behind me now?"

Ollie's head bobbed.

"Good. Then let's keep going."

The foursome continued the journey, now stopping intermittently to leave bedazzled lakestars in hollowed-out rocks along the way. The path turned and twisted, but never in the same direction that it appeared to at first glance. And each time, a tar-lined pit awaited those who might make the wrong choice. Ollie made sure to stay several steps behind Derrin. At one point, a lakestar went missing moments after they placed it in the rock; panic ensued until Tera spotted one of the five points hanging out of Meatball's bill.

"Control your animal," Derrin snapped.

"Bad trog," Ollie said, not really meaning it.

Meatball crunched happily, not really caring either way.

Finally, after they had averted five death-pit traps, Derrin rounded a bend and stopped. Ollie peered over her shoulder, expecting to see yet another carved-out stone on the ground. Instead, he saw a steep incline leading down to the lake. The cliff's edge was stepped with rock outcroppings, so evenly spaced they might have been seats at an outdoor stadium. And on those ledges he saw ten or so women, lounging. Murmuring. Leaning back on their elbows. Turning their faces to the ceiling as though they were soaking up ultraviolet rays from the glowing blue wormwalkers above. Sunbathers without a sun.

The first thing he noticed was the hair. So, so much hair, and all of it was red. The shade and intensity varied slightly from head to head: crimson, maroon, cherry, light rose, candy-apple, raspberry, vermillion, deep wine. They were like paint chips come to life with textured, thick abandon. Some had afros; others had straight locks, braids, waves, or a style that his mother used to call a "pixie cut." But every last strand of it was red.

Do not adjust your screen, he thought. Their heads seemed too big for their bodies. Their fingers seemed too long, as did their toes, which were gripping the rocky ledges with unnatural dexterity. They reminded Ollie of caricature drawings he might see at the Topsfield Fair: exaggerated features, oversized eyes, bulbously swollen lips.

Despite all this, the rumors were true. The Novas were beautiful. Stunning, really. He couldn't stop staring.

"Stop staring," Derrin muttered. "And whatever you do, don't call them mermaids. They hate that." She hoisted her jumpsuit and strode forward with resigned purpose.

Ollie watched her departing back with rising dismay. He wasn't *planning* to call them mermaids, and yet now it was all he could think about. They didn't look like mermaids—at least, not like the mermaids of his childhood fairy tales. No swishing tails. No naked torsos. These creatures had spindly legs, clothing made from something that might have been wrapped kelp, and a radiance that defied the murky gloom that surrounded them. He pressed his lips together as though the word might pop out of its own free will. *Mermaid, mermaid, mermaid.* He looked at Tera, who shooed him forward with her hands. Then he scrambled to catch up.

The Novas did not seem surprised to see them approach. A minute later, Ollie realized why: Several of them were holding and examining the glittering lakestars that Derrin had left along the way. One was pinning a star into her auburn hair; another was waving the five points in the air like a Fourth of July sparkler. How was that possible? How had the lakestars traveled from the scooped-out stones all the way to this cliffside before Ollie and his friends had even arrived?

No matter. They were, unmistakably, the same tokens. So, the Novas had been expecting visitors. They were not, however, expecting *these* visitors.

"Oh," the closest one said, eying Derrin disdainfully as the group approached. "It's you."

"Hello, Eelia," Derrin said. The name poured like sludge through her lips.

This Eelia had silver eyes, brown, sparkly skin, and russet hair exploding in tight curls that reached nearly a foot above her head. She gazed at Derrin for a long moment, smiled sweetly, and asked, "How is your father?"

The question elicited its intended response; Derrin seethed and glared. Then she recovered her composure. "He's fine, thank you," she said. Clipped. Neutral.

"Yes, he certainly is," the Nova agreed. A grin curled at the edges of her magnolia-pink lips.

The tension between them would have chilled a lava flow. Ollie darted his gaze back and forth, afraid to move. Tera and Laszlo stood beside him, also silent. The other Novas, meanwhile, continued their whisperings, listening while pretending not to listen.

Eelia was leaning back on one hand and cradling a dried lakestar with the other. The attached metallic bits glinted as she held it up. The stars reminded Ollie of the cobbled-together crafts his mother had once made with the neighborhood ladies. Ollie wondered, suddenly, how Derrin had come across them. Did she buy them at the Tea Party market? Had she somehow stumbled across a glue gun at Nikki and Floyd's Brickside Curiosities shop and spent hours making them herself? Somehow it didn't seem likely.

"You bring what we like," Eelia said, waving the star.

"I do," Derrin nodded.

"Everything that we like," the silver-eyed Nova added. Her gaze slid over Derrin's head and landed squarely on Laszlo. She looked the acrobat up and down like a jeweler appraising a precious stone.

By now, the entire group of nymphs had paused their preening to scrutinize their visitors, though their eyes skipped right over Tera and Derrin. Ollie's skin prickled with self-consciousness as he felt the heat of their attention.

Leaning close to Derrin, he tried to speak without moving his lips: "Why are they looking at me like that?"

"Just ignore it," she muttered, still wearing a forced smile. "It's mating season."

Mating season? Panic mounting, Ollie moved as slowly and unobtrusively as possible as he stepped backward to try to hide his giant frame behind Tera's tiny, five-foot-two body. She looked up at him with mild amusement, shook her head, and turned back to face the gathered creatures on the rocks.

"My name is Tera," she said. "This is Ollie, that's Laszlo, and I guess you know Derrin. Thank you for letting us visit your realm." Her voice sounded formal and pinched.

Derrin turned around to face her, eyebrows raised. *Your realm?* she mouthed.

Tera ignored her friend and continued. "We come today to humbly ask for your assistance. We seek something, and the nesting witches told us that you might have the knowledge to help us find it."

Laszlo leaned toward Ollie and whispered, "Why does she talk like game show host?"

Ollie shrugged.

Tera glared at them both before pressing on: "We were told you might know of the location of an old laboratory. Closed, now. But once open. There is something inside it that we need."

Giggles erupted from the gathered nymphs.

Tera bristled. "Something funny?"

Ollie put a hand on her shoulder. This was going south, fast. Eelia, clearly the elder of the bunch, wasn't buying what they were selling. The younger Novas, similarly, were regarding the newcomers with somewhat disappointed merriment, as though the circus had come to town and it wasn't all that impressive. He tried to think of something to say or do. Something helpful. But in the end, it was Laszlo who intervened.

"Ladies," he said, striding forward. "Please. Is honor to meet you all. My name is Laszlo Kravchenko. You are wondering, like famous Flying Kravchenko Brothers of Ukraine? Yes. Is true. They are my uncles."

His grin was a beacon; almost instantly, dozens of bright eyes fixed on his cheekbones. His shoulders. His bulbous muscles, stretching the limits of his tight, elastic shirt. Laszlo turned to give

Derrin, Ollie, and Tera an almost imperceptible wink. Then he spun back around to face his hostesses.

"Please, tell me, are your names as beautiful as your faces?" he asked, spreading his arms wide. "Come, please! Tell me all!"

They advanced like bees to a marigold, scrambling up the rocks with inhuman speed. Now that they were closer, Ollie could see that the Novas' hands and feet were webbed, and that their skin was covered with tiny, phosphorescent scales.

"I am Nerida!" said the one with straight, auburn hair.

"I am Crinni!" said another.

A third pushed past them. This one had fire-engine-red curls and almond-tinted skin. "I am Potemedes!"

A pale-faced Nova behind them practically shouted, "I am Limnia!"

Ollie, Tera, and Derrin shrank away from the onslaught. But Laszlo merely put his hands on his hips and pushed out his chest.

"Wonderful!" he bellowed, his voice tinged with pride as though he had named them all himself. They called more names from the rocks, and he nodded at each one approvingly.

"Are you from the Brickside?" the one called Crinni asked. She crept closer. The tip of her webbed finger stroked his arm.

"Yes," Laszlo said solemnly, the word landing like a pronouncement.

"Do they speak of us there?" another wanted to know.

Laszlo paused only a moment before answering. "Of course! Legend of Mighty Nova! Even in Ukraine, we speak of it!"

From all directions, their eyes sparkled; their bodies pressed against him. Only Eelia held back, seeming annoyed by the throng.

"What do they say of us?" Nerida asked breathlessly.

Laszlo paused, cleared his throat. Then he turned to Ollie. "Where to start? They say so many things, don't they, my friend?"

Ollie froze. His mind raced. Finally, he said, "Right. So, so many things." He chewed his lip. "Well, obviously they talk about your good looks, of course."

"Of course," Laszlo agreed.

"And your...amazing abilities," Ollie continued. "The swimming, and the, uh, diving. And the breathing underwater."

Tera took a small step forward. "And your great speed and strength," she added. "No one on the Brickside can do anything like that."

"Right," Ollie nodded. "Yes, that, too."

The one named Potemedes leaned forward. "Do they speak of the Nova victory in the legendary Battle of the Whirlpool? Or of the defeat of the Great Horned Serpent in Kejimkujik?"

Ollie blinked, then bobbed his head. "Definitely. Like, all the time."

"Yes, that is big one," Laszlo said. He turned back to the gathered group, who were now nearly motionless as they drank in his words. "When men gather on Brickside, tales of great Nova Scotian Water Nymphs flow like vodka! The serpent battle, yes. The Keja... Kejik..."

"Kejimkujik!" someone shouted.

"Yes! That! So many songs they sing. But is things they say about your brains..." He stopped, ran a hand through his hair. "Those, I am sorry to say, seem too much to be true."

"What?" Crinni asked, straining her eyes up at him. "What do they say?"

"Weeeellll..." Laszlo stretched the word like taffy. "They *say* Novas are not only most beautiful, but also most smart. Most smart of any creature in whole ocean or lake!" He puffed his cheeks and blew out a breath. "But I said, no. No, that cannot be truth. How can one creature be so many things?"

At this, Eelia finally stepped forward. Her arms were folded, her eyes narrow. "You doubt our wisdom?" she asked.

"No!" Laszlo insisted, holding up his hands. "It is just that, the things they say... They are too much to be truth!"

"What do they say? Tell us!" pleaded the smallest nymph. Limnia.

This time, it was Tera who answered. Her voice rang high and strong. "Aboveground, they say you know everything about these waters, and this place. That you remember everything that ever happened here, and everyone who has ever been here. You know all, and you see all. And that you never, ever forget."

Eelia lifted a single eyebrow, smug. "But all of that is true."

An expression of delighted surprise crossed Laszlo's face. "No! It cannot be!"

"It is!" squealed Nerida.

"Remarkable!" he said, spreading his arms. "Is truth? I should have known. I should not have doubted! You are most wonderful creatures, my Novas of the Neath!"

They beamed up at him, the gossamer scales on their faces glinting in the cavern's blue glow.

"Perhaps, then, you might be smart enough to even remember this place? This lab?" He paused, held up a hand. "No. I ask too much. I am sorry. That was too long ago for even you to remember, I am sure."

Limnia clung to his leg. "I remember!" she said.

"No, *I* remember!" shouted another.

"The lab is in the lake! I can show you where!" shouted Potemedes.

And then, the battle ensued: a frenzied swirl of red hair and long limbs, all of them clawing and climbing and scratching in an effort to curry Laszlo's favor.

"One at a time, beautiful ladies!" he shouted over the din, his deep laugh like a bass note to their treble. "No fighting over Laszlo! Is enough Laszlo for all!"

Behind him, Derrin rolled her eyes. Tera and Ollie exchanged a glance. Only then did Ollie understand: Derrin hadn't brought Laszlo along "for muscle." She had brought him for bait. Nova mating-season bait. And it had worked like a charm.

"Enough!" came a sharp voice. It was Eelia, now standing above them all. She swatted the other Novas away with a simple flick of her wrist.

In the silence that ensued, Ollie saw an opening and grabbed it. "The lab is in the lake?" he asked.

Eelia folded her arms. Begrudgingly, she answered: "It was. Many years ago. The humans built tunnels to reach it."

"But...why?" he asked. It made no sense. Why build a laboratory that was so hard to access?

"I long ago stopped trying to figure out why the humans do what they do," Eelia said, her face hard. "In any case, it makes no difference now. The tunnels are gone. Collapsed."

"Have you seen the lab?" Tera asked her.

"If it is still there, none of us have seen it in quite some time," Eelia answered. The others stayed silent behind her, blinking their extra-wide eyes.

Ollie pointed at Potemedes. "But she just said—"

"Never mind what she said," Eelia snarled. "This is our lake. Our home. And the secrets contained within it are ours, too."

Ollie raised a hand, foolishly, as if he were an elementary schooler in math class. Meatball shifted on his shoulder with a grunt. "Could you just...swim around a bit and look for it?" he asked. "Or, like, take us to it somehow? We'd really, really appreciate it."

But the suggestion only seemed to anger her further. "Why would I do that?"

Ollie had no answer. *Because I unknowingly made some kind of terrible mistake and now lots of innocent people are in danger?* Somehow, he doubted the Novas would believe it. Or care, if they did.

In the silence that followed, Laszlo swaggered past them all, moving toward Eelia. Wordlessly, he climbed one step and then another, until the two of them were face to face. Ollie watched, agog, as Laszlo reached out to run his callused knuckle along the Nova's smooth cheek. Even from a distance, her shudder of pleasure was visible.

The lake's small waves lapped against the shoreline below. The scent of something burning traveled through the hazy air. And Ollie realized, suddenly, that they were all holding their collective breath.

"Is true, we ask too much," Laszlo said, staring into Eelia's silver eyes. "But perhaps, you could do this thing...for me?"

She didn't answer.

"And then, when all is done, I could return," Laszlo crooned. "And I could tell you all of the things. All of the, how do you say, discoverings?"

"Discoveries," Eelia said, her voice the barest whisper.

"Yes," he smiled. "Discoveries. Wonderful, wonderful discoveries. And we could celebrate, together, yes? Just you and me?"

Ollie watched the scene unfold with stunned admiration. He had seen Laszlo work a crowd, back at Faneuil Hall, coaxing dollar bills out of pockets and into his black hat with just a few words and tricks. Hell, he had even taken a few of Ollie's dollars. But then, he had had been an acrobat. A street performer. This was something else entirely. Was Laszlo really that handsome? Ollie hadn't thought so. The Ukrainian's crooked nose, long face, and scraggly hair would never be featured on the cover of a magazine back home. No, it wasn't his looks that attracted people—and apparently water nymphs—to Laszlo. It was his magnetism. Pure, animal magnetism. Ollie didn't understand it, and he knew that he would never possess it. But he had to admit, it was a marvel to see it in action.

To Ollie's left, Tera and Derrin were also watching in wide-eyed silence. And all around the rocky, stepped cliff, the younger Novas swooned with rapt attention. Each wishing they were standing in Eelia's webbed feet, no doubt.

Something like a sigh escaped from the elder Nova's throat. When she spoke, her voice was loud enough to carry to Ollie's ears.

"The structure you seek is in the deep," Eelia said. "You may go, if you wish. But we will not take you. If time has taught us anything, it is to stay clear of human folly."

"But...how can we do that?" Tera asked. She looked from face to face in confusion. "Is there some kind of a boat or something?"

Eelia smiled, but not kindly. Derision flashed behind her eyes. "There is no boat."

Ollie shoved his hands into his jumpsuit pockets. *In the deep.* What did the Novas expect them to do? Build a submarine? Pull some scuba-diving gear out of their packs?

"We can help you breathe!" Crinni said. "Under the water!" She was speaking, of course, to Laszlo.

The acrobat's face betrayed his confusion. "I do not understand, little one," he said, reaching out to touch the top of her strawberry-colored head. "How is such thing possible?"

"Oh, it's easy," she said with a wave of her hand.

"We do it all the time!" Nerida added.

The others nodded in agreement, all looking quite pleased.

"For how long?" Tera asked. Doubt weighed down her voice. "I mean, how long could we stay under the water?"

"For as long as we like," Eelia said dismissively, as though the query were a silly one. Ollie couldn't help but notice the pronoun:

Not, "as long *you* like," but, "as long as *we* like." Something about it made his pulse quicken. *Is this really a good idea?* he thought, and then realized that he seemed to ask himself that question a lot these days.

A familiar kind of terrible feeling settled suddenly into Ollie's stomach. A flashback swam into his head from his childhood days: the other kids luring him around the corner of the playground, promising something wonderful, and delivering anything but. These Novas sounded exactly like that, as though they would enjoy watching him writhe.

"Who will go, then?" Eelia asked, pointing to the shore below. Her patience with this strange little show seemed to be reaching its end.

"What, right *now?*" Ollie asked. Panic roiled his gut.

"Yes, now," the elder Nova barked. "Now, or never. Who will go?"

Ollie, Tera, Laszlo, and Derrin looked at each other. For a moment, no one spoke. This was what they had wanted, right? To find the lab. And here it was, the way forward, opening like a smooth, sliding door. So why did Ollie feel like they were about to fall headfirst into one of the Novas' tar-pit traps?

Tera slid her hand into Ollie's. "I'll go," she said.

"Me, too," Laszlo nodded.

"I'll stay here," Derrin said. "Report back to the others."

With that, all eyes turned to Ollie.

"Wait... What's down there?" he asked feebly. He thought again of all that vast, blank space on Tera's map. *Here be dragons.*

The Novas exploded in giddy laughter.

"Water, silly!" said Potemedes.

"You'll be fine," Crinni added, wrapping her long fingers around Laszlo's thigh. "Big, strong man like you." Then, like an afterthought, she added, "Just stay away from the Hermit."

"The Hermit?" Ollie injected, his voice sounding too loud. "Who's that?"

Eelia waved a hand; the subject bored her. "Avoid the lights. That is all."

"Wait, what lights? Who's the Hermit?" Ollie's eyes flitted over the Novas' faces, then Derrin's, then Tera's. Sweat began to soak his armpits.

"If you see the lights, just swim away!" Potemedes said. She spun in a circle, her merlot-colored hair flying out in all directions.

The others echoed her with a daffy, impromptu song: "Swim away! Swim away! Swim away! Close your eyes, close your ears, don't delay!" They danced and laughed, delighted in their camaraderie.

Ollie shivered. The scene, oddly enough, was conjuring up a long-forgotten memory of his mother—a summer memory. She had taken his hand in hers and led him to the shoreline at Revere Beach. "It's a beautiful day for a swim!" Francie had said when he protested. The water was too cold, he had insisted. The sun was too hot. The clumps of seaweed were too thick. In truth, of course, he just hadn't wanted anyone to see his overly round body on display in his bathing suit. *A beautiful day for a swim.*

But his mother had never seen this kind of day. And she'd never seen this kind of water, murky and greenish and somehow thicker than water should be. And she'd certainly never imagined the kinds of ghastly creatures that were probably watching from below the surface at that very moment, lips smacking, just waiting for his meaty, helpless, pathetically human body to submerge.

"But...we don't even know where we're going," he said.

"Ah, my Ollie," said Laszlo, jumping down from his rock perch. "Does anyone ever really know where they are going?"

"Yes," Ollie insisted. "People know where they're going all the time. Most of the time. That's usually how this kind of thing is done." Directions and GPS and helpful advice from friends. Not tossed into the waves with vague instructions to avoid lights and loners.

"We will not worry!" Laszlo said, clapping him on the back. "We will see what we can see, yes? If we see this place, this lab," he paused, curling his fingers into air quotes, "then we will. If we do not, we do not, and we will come right back up here to these lovely ladies. Am I right, lovely ladies?"

The Novas twittered with fawning delight.

Ollie groaned inwardly. He turned to Tera. "Look, maybe this isn't a great idea. Maybe there's something else—"

"There's not," Tera interrupted.

"But maybe we can—"

"We can't."

Then he noticed her hand, still squeezing his so tight he could feel his fingertips starting to tingle from lack of circulation. Tera's face was staunch, but her hand gave away the game: She was scared.

Courage doesn't mean you're not afraid, his mother had told him that day on the beach. *Courage is being afraid, and doing it anyway.*

Ollie looked up at the group with as real a smile as he could manage. "What are we waiting for?" he asked. "It's a beautiful day for a swim."

Eight

If he'd had the choice, Ollie would have inched into the lake like a toddler at a cold community pool, step by step by ridiculously cautious step. Sadly, that wasn't an option. There was only the steep cliffside and the water below, with nothing in between but air.

Solid, liquid. Brave, cowardly. Simple states of matter.

At the very least, he wanted to be the first to jump. And so, he was—arms wrapping his torso, eyes squeezed shut, feet first, heart pounding. He plunged into the water and sank. And sank, and sank. The pressure pushed in from all sides. Finally, Ollie opened his eyes. Bubbles. Weightlessness. It took a moment for the panic to set in.

He snapped his head up, searching for the surface. Too far. Frantically, he began to paddle and claw. *Air. Must have air.*

But he had plummeted too deep. He'd never reach the surface in time. How had he sunk so far, so quickly? Ollie stretched his arms as far as they would reach and pulled them downward. Again, again, again. His knees bent and straightened in desperate frog kicks. He was moving up. Definitely up. But not nearly fast enough.

His body flailed in one last, furious attempt. His vision spun; the bubbles seemed to buoy him and smother him all at the same time. It was no use. His lungs were bursting, burning. Ollie stared up at the surface, tantalizingly close and yet impossibly far. All logic fled; he opened his mouth, and he inhaled.

The Novas had told him he would be able to breathe underwater. It would be "easy," they had said. It was their gift to grant as they wished. But he had not truly believed them. Not then, back on beautiful, oxygen-rich dry land, and certainly not now, in what was surely about to become his watery grave. People—regular, human people—do not, *cannot,* breathe underwater. Not even in the Neath.

And yet...

He was.

He was? Ollie dropped his chin, looking down. His chest seemed to be...rising. And falling. The scorching sensation in his lungs had disappeared. All around him, the water wrapped less like a strangle and more like a hug, embracing him as one of its own. He stared down at his hands in wonderment. They looked the same as they always had; just hands. But down here, suddenly, they felt like something more. Something better.

Meatball had followed him. Now, the trog was darting and spinning in happy circles, paddling his webbed feet through the water in an effortless dance. His thick, brown fur burst out around him like rays from a sun. No lung adjustment necessary: Meatball was built for the submersion, at home in the depths.

To Ollie's right, he saw a disturbance in the water. Tera. He watched her plunge, then panic, then claw, just as he had. He wanted to reach out to her, to reassure her, but knew now that there was no way around it—only through. Tera gasped, inhaled. Her purple hair billowed above her head as she paused, finally, in an astonished stillness that mirrored his own.

Laszlo came last, landing somewhere to Ollie's left. Ollie and Tera stayed in place, undulating their arms and legs. The acrobat sank, struggled, and then, with difficulty, accepted the transition.

At last, all three of them faced each other. And smiled.

They did not talk, of course. That would have been impossible. Then again, they didn't have to. This place had its own language, and Ollie was surprised to find himself instantly fluent. Tera, he somehow knew, felt content and eager. Laszlo felt excited and curious. Neither of them felt frightened. And oddly, neither did he.

From the surface, the lake water had seemed thick and murky. But down here, it looked nearly clear. Full of brightness and possibility. Ollie scanned his surroundings and saw everything in sharp detail. Tiny specks of plankton. A pair of albino squid. A school of polka-dotted balloonfish, each as round as Meatball. Ollie didn't know how he knew their names: only that he did. Below his feet, a buck-toothed lakeshark glided past. He had the vague feeling that the shark would have concerned him, maybe even terrified him, not too long ago. Now, he merely watched it curiously.

Tera told them, without actually saying anything, that it was time to get going. She had a direction in mind. She turned to begin the journey, and they followed.

The swimming was easy. Easier than walking. His body knew the way, felt the streams and currents, navigated the ebbs and flows. He inhaled deep, cleansing breaths. Felt his lungs fill with something he could only describe as an elixir of purified liquid energy.

They moved together, as a unit. When Tera swayed, he swayed. When Laszlo lunged up or down, he followed. Meatball darted playfully between their bodies. If there was a bottom to the lake, it was far below—too far for Ollie to see, though he did spy soaring formations of fluorescent coral and the creatures that lived in and around it. Their names popped into his head, somehow, the moment he spotted them: zebra lakeslugs. Hammerface eels. Thorny-shelled turtles. Cerulean blennies. Poisonous tangerine lakegrass. Up above, all the blindfish had looked identical to him. Down here, they were as unique and recognizable as human faces. As familiar as friends.

Hello, friend. Hello!

Time passed. How much, he could not say. It might have been hours or days. What was more, he didn't care. Where were they going? Why was he here? There had been a reason, he was sure of it. They were...looking. For something. The thought nagged at him, but only for a moment before dissipating into the eddies. Blissfully gone. Now, he wanted nothing but this. The warm wrap of water pressure. Tera ahead, Laszlo behind. The silent circus of swimming creatures. The endless expanse of liquid, vast and wondrous, somehow carrying his future and his past in every drop.

Then, up ahead, Ollie saw something else.

A light.

No, two lights. More?

They were so...beautiful. The rays shone like tiny beacons. Full of color. Like Tera's paintings, vibrant and electric and otherworldly.

Come, see.

Laszlo and Tera followed. They were close to him, now, one on each side.

See the lights!

White. And yellow. And emerald. Blinking. Swirling.

The spectacle jogged a memory he couldn't quite place. Something the Novas had said. Something about...light?

Mesmerized, he swam closer still. The luminescence brightened and swelled until it engulfed his entire field of vision. *Yes, I see the lights. I feel them!* They were wonderful, magical. Ollie surrendered to myopia. In that moment, he could not imagine ever regretting it. He could not imagine anything at all other than this rapturous, perfect peace.

———⸎———

His throat was sore.

Sore and scratchy, as though he'd been screaming. How very odd.

Ollie saw nothing, then realized his eyes were closed. Stuck. With effort, he pulled his lids apart. They were coated in some kind of crusty ooze. He blinked and squeezed, trying to clear the haze.

He was in a darkened space. A cave, he guessed, though deep shadows and the goo on his eyes prevented him from confirming his suspicions. His legs felt tight, cramped. He tried to stretch them and found that he couldn't. Ollie wiggled his fingers, relieved to feel the movement. He tried his arms; those, too, felt free. He tipped his neck from side to side in an effort to ease the dull muscle pain that radiated in all directions. He smelled dampness, and smoke. And the slow rot of wet, decaying things.

What the hell was going on?

Slowly, the recollections began to flash. He had been swimming. Breathing under the water! It had been wondrous.

Even now, the euphoria pierced: the fishes; the cool water; the extraordinary creatures that had circled around him. Welcomed him.

And then...what? Lights. Blinking, dazzling lights.

Avoid the lights, that is all, the Novas had told him. *If you see the lights, just swim away.*

But he hadn't moved away, had he? He'd moved directly toward them. He'd been unable to resist. And now...

With a hard jerk, Ollie tried to move his legs again. And again, he found that they were stuck.

His arms were weak, but at least they seemed to be under his control. He lifted one and wiped the smear of ooze from his face. That helped. His vision somewhat cleared, he looked at his hands, his arms. Then, moving his gaze downward, he saw the top of his jumpsuit—but not the bottom. Instead of seeing pant legs, Ollie found that he was looking at something white. And smooth. No, not quite smooth. It had ridges. Curved ridges, repeated in a pattern that went around and around and around...

What the—?

It was a shell. A giant, hard, swirling shell. Bigger than a suitcase. Bigger, even, than a pile of suitcases on a luggage cart. Unnaturally, mind-bogglingly big. And it was completely encasing his body from the waist down.

Now in a full-on panic, Ollie jerked and twisted, yanking at his legs. They wouldn't budge. No matter what he tried, his lower body remained tight and sheathed inside the shell. Trapped. He heard himself whimper as a tingle of terror traveled up his spine.

Ollie looked to his right and saw two more shells, each as large as a tractor tire. Tera's upper body protruded from one; Laszlo's from the other.

Both of them looked unconscious, their heads lolling at grotesque angles. Ollie's stomach clenched. *No. No, no, no, no...* What if they were—

"Wake up!" He spoke as loud as he dared, wanting to rouse his friends while at the same time *not* wanting to rouse whatever else might be lurking in this dim, shadowy cave. "Hey! Guys! Wake up!"

Nothing. Neither of them moved.

As the hysteria rose, so did his voice. "WAKE THE HELL UP!"

He went weak with relief as he saw Laszlo stir, then Tera. *Alive.*

Laszlo made an unidentifiable sound, something between a grunt and groan.

Tera lifted her head, slowly, and fought to open her eyes. "Ollie?"

"Yes! It's me. I'm here."

"Where are we?" she croaked.

"I don't know," he answered.

Laszlo was noticing the shell for the first time, struggling to free his legs. "What is...this thing?"

"I don't know," Ollie said again.

Then it was Tera's turn to panic, grapple, and pull. All in vain. "Why am I in a shell?" she shrieked.

"Shhh!" Ollie warned.

Her voice had echoed in the cavern, bouncing off walls that looked to be made of polished stone. The space was about as large as his studio apartment back home. Off to the sides, crevices and narrow passageways led off into parts unknown.

"What happened?" Laszlo asked.

Ollie sighed. "The lights."

"What?"

"We were supposed to swim away from the lights," he said. "We didn't."

"Ah."

The three friends sat in silence for a moment, remembering. Then, Tera pointed a shaking hand. "What the hell is all that?" she asked.

Ollie followed her finger to the floor of the cavern. It was made of the same glossy stone as the walls, with intermittent patches of sand. As his eyes became more accustomed to the darkness, he began to make out shapes along the ground. Piles. Leaning up against walls, lumped into disparate heaps.

The three of them stared. Only Laszlo was brave enough to voice what they all were thinking: "Is bones," he whispered.

Yes, Ollie thought, his stomach clenching. *Is bones.*

Lots and lots of bones. Rib cages. Femurs. Skulls. Tiny, pencil-length cartilages, and ones that were astronomically bigger. Some fanned out like fins, or tails. Others looked disturbingly...human.

A chill whipped up his back.

Tera was close enough to reach him; her hand shot out and he grabbed it. They squeezed. A blur of motion caught his eye near the ground; Ollie looked down and felt a momentary respite: "Meatball!"

The trog was waddling around near the base of Ollie's shell, a long green leaf hanging from his beak. When Ollie called his name, Meatball lifted the air and sniffed. Then he ambled up the side of the shell and settled on a flat section, munching amicably. Ollie reached out to pat his head, feeling alternate waves of comfort and frustration. At least Meatball was free. But why hadn't Ollie trained him to do things? Fetch things? Free his best buddy from confinement in a ludicrously large nautilus?

Laszlo's voice broke through his musings. "Friends, this is bad situation, I think."

"You think?" Tera snapped. Then she shook her head. "Sorry. Sorry. This is... I feel...so fuzzy. What's the matter with my head?"

"I think we were drugged," Ollie said. It came out more chipper than he had intended, as though he were sharing good news.

"We have to do something," Tera said, pushing against her shell. "There must be a way out of these things."

Ollie nodded, more out of reassurance than agreement. He had already wriggled harder than a politician caught in a lie, with no progress whatsoever. There was no way his big legs were getting out of that narrow shell slot. Whoever, or whatever, had put them in these things knew what they were doing. They had a plan. And based on the myriad piles of bones around them, Ollie had a sinking feeling he knew what that plan was.

"We just have to think," Tera said. "Okay? Everybody think."

Laszlo and Ollie nodded. A long period of uneasy quiet followed.

Ollie could still feel the effects of the drug, or venom, or spell, or whatever it was that had lured and subdued them. His head felt heavy; his senses, dull. He hoped like hell the others were formulating brilliant plans, because all he could think about was how fast his legs and feet were falling asleep. Dozens of tiny needles, pricking everywhere. Shooting and stabbing. He bit his lip to keep from letting out a whine. No matter what he did or how he shifted, he couldn't move them an inch.

Without warning, a memory intruded, snapping his consciousness back to a long-ago visit to a wax museum. Ollie had been only a kid, maybe eight or nine. After the usual parade of jaundiced historical figures and pop stars, the museum had offered up an exhibit of something more gruesome—a recreation of a torture chamber in some old-world dungeon. Hooded henchmen and scrawny victims had toiled in frozen agony beneath a bevy of helpful, descriptive signs. *This, dear visitors, was "the rack." Diabolical, wasn't it? And here, the "rat head cage." And "the hook." And, perhaps worst of all, "the confinement." Feast your eyes, visitors, on the tiny, carved-out hole in the wall, in which the victim would be confined. Too small to accommodate the body, it prevented the prisoner from stretching out his back or legs in any way, contorting him into a permanent crouch that he could never hope to uncurl...*

Ollie shuddered and frantically convulsed his thigh muscles, to no avail.

Think of something else, he told himself. *Think of something else!* Which led, of course, to thoughts of food. This proved to be almost worse than the leg pain as the images swam and beckoned: Heaping plates of French fries, dipped into pools of shiny red ketchup. Natural-casing hot dogs in crispy, grilled buns. Clam chowder from Quincy Market, sprinkled with pepper. Buttery corn on the cob. A sack of miniature chocolate-chip cookies, still warm in the bag.

And then: Home. The North End. Specifically, Luciano's on Prince Street. Ollie heard himself groan as he visualized the gold-and-white menu and let his mind's eye skim the options. Chicken Milanese. Puttanesca. Butternut-squash ravioli. Vanilla-bean gelato with caramel sauce. Braised short rib and sausage lathered over al dente fettuccine, topped with whipped ricotta and thick shavings of aged parmesan...

Ollie's stomach let out a pitiful growl. He glanced over at Tera; she was still holding his hand, but looked drowsy. Laszlo's eyes, similarly, were mostly shut. The shadows seemed to be lengthening. Meatball was already snoring. So much for thinking their way out of this.

"Hey," he said. Then again, "Hey!"

Their heads snapped to attention.

"We have to stay awake!" Ollie told them. "We have to keep talking."

"Right. Yes," Laszlo said, clearing his throat. His face was mostly covered by strings of dark hair.

"Yes," Tera parroted blearily. "You're right. What should we talk about?"

"I don't know..." Ollie's mind skittered over possible topics, preferably unrelated to dungeon torture chambers or melted cheese. "Tell me about the women," he finally said. "From the WRC. I don't really know anything about them."

Laszlo thought a moment before responding. "They are tough cookies." Even in his bleary state, the tone of admiration was clear. "They will be all right, until we find them."

Tera nodded, or seemed like she was trying to nod. She was having trouble righting her head once it had been tipped.

"I don't even know their names," Ollie heard himself say, his voice quiet. Not that it really mattered. Not to them. But it seemed important, suddenly, that he at least hear the names of the people he had apparently, unintentionally, condemned to a terrible fate.

Laszlo hesitated. "I am not so good with the names. Maybe was...Jennifer? Yes, was one Jennifer. And a Tracey, and a Claudia...no. How do you say...Claudette?" He stopped, shook his head. "More, too, I think. I am sorry. Is drug. Our brains are sleepy, yes?"

"Mmm," Tera agreed. Her eyes had closed again.

"How many were taken?" Ollie whispered.

"That, I do not know, my friend," Laszlo answered. "Maybe... five? Or more? Or maybe not so many, we can hope. But like I say, they were—"

"Are," Ollie interrupted.

"What?"

"You said 'they were.' Like they're dead." Ollie felt his pulse quickening.

"Right, yes. *Are.* They are tough cookie ladies."

"Do you think they're dead?" Ollie asked, his voice going high.

"No! Not dead. I am just slee—"

"Do you know something? Laz, if you know something, you have to tell us!"

"I know nothing! I am sure you worry for nothing. Our WRC friends are just fine. If anyone can be fine, is them. They are—"

"Yeah, yeah, I get it," Ollie groaned. "Tough cookies." Even as he said it, images of pizzelles, shortbreads, and black-and-whites danced in his head. Those were *not* tough cookies. Those were delicate, and sugary, and crumbly, and coated with the barest sprinkle of powdered sugar...

Stop, he told himself.

Like a punishment, he forced himself to repeatedly recite the names in his head: *Jennifer. Tracey. Claudette. Jennifer. Tracey. Claudette.* And probably more. Just regular people. Regular, brave, innocent, hard working people. People worth saving. And now, maybe, no one ever would. Krite. How had he already screwed this up so completely?

Stop!

He had to stay positive—and he had to stay alert. Ollie tried to think of another topic for discussion. Everyone's favorite color, maybe. Or favorite song? But before he could formulate the words, a sound caught his attention.

The others had heard it, too. In unison, they swiveled their heads. Even Meatball woke and snuffled.

It was coming from the direction of the far wall, where a wide opening broke through the stone. Beyond it, Ollie saw only murk.

The sound came again:

Clack.

Clack, clack, clack.

Ollie's heart began to pound. Tera clenched his hand; none of them spoke.

Clack, clack.

As his brain scrambled to translate what he couldn't see, Ollie realized it was the sound of something sharp and hard against something equally solid. A tapping on the polished ground.

Clack. Clack, clack.

The noise was getting closer. Louder.

Ollie looked at Laszlo, then Tera. The whites of their eyes shone.

Clack.

Clack, clack, clack, CLACK, CLACK, CLACK.

It emerged at once from the shadows, scattering loose bones as it moved. For one long, hideous moment, Ollie couldn't look away. He couldn't run, or fight, or even feel his legs. He couldn't do anything at all but stare at the advancing horror and pray that he was actually still asleep, caught in the throes of a grisly, inconceivable nightmare.

Wake up wake up wake up

But Ollie didn't wake up. The nightmare was real.

And it was closing in fast.

Nine

The creature stood nine or ten feet high.

On first glance, Ollie would have called it a gargantuan crab: six coral-colored, multi-sectioned legs moving in awkward, lumbering locomotion, carrying the weight of a massive brown-and-white shell on its back. But in the front, where the tentacles and eyes should have been, something else sprouted, instead. A torso.

A human torso.

The thing advancing toward them seemed to be a grotesque fusion of man and crab. No arms. Just the six, spider-like legs and claws, tapping in irregular staccato against the hard ground. Its eyes were thinned into slits, and focused solely on its captors.

One of the claws seemed to be dragging a large, burlap sack.

What fresh hell...? Ollie thought, his body going limp with terror. It was revolting. Unspeakable. How could such a thing in exist in nature? Or in...whatever this place was?

To his right, he could hear Tera and Laszlo gasping. Tera had dropped his hand; Ollie flailed around for it but found only empty air.

Clack, clack, clack, clack. Then, the dragging bag: *Shhhew. Shhhew.*

The vile creature was creeping closer.

Clack.

Clack.

Shhhew.

The sounds radiated through Ollie like infrared waves of fright, making him shudder. This was it, then. It was over. After all he'd been through, all the challenges he'd faced in this strange and desperate place, he'd finally reached the end. And what an end! Stabbed in the gut by a gigantic crab claw, sliced into pieces, and then shoveled into that humanoid mouth. Not only him, but Tera and Laszlo, too. All of them—reduced in a few bloody seconds to nothing more than captured prey. And then their bones would rest in piles with all the others, waiting to greet the next bunch of unsuspecting morons who were stupid enough to end up here.

Ollie struggled and pulled uselessly, hysterically, at the binding shell. Out of the corner of his eye, he saw Laszlo and Tera doing the same.

The monster continued moving toward them—*clack, clack, clack*—until it was close enough to cast a shadow on their trembling, trapped bodies. It watched them. And finally, it opened its mouth, dripping thick rivulets of drool all over the shiny ground.

Ollie pushed Meatball, hard, trying to rouse the trog into making a break for it. *Run, run, run!* With no remaining hope of escape for himself, he could only hunch and squeeze his eyes shut. Tears of fear and despair welled. He heard his mother's voice in his head: *Saint Francis, pray for this small soul.*

He braced himself.

And then he heard another voice. An actual voice, not in his head. It was squeaky and high:

"Oh, you're up! Sorry I took so long. I thought you all might want something to eat. You're humans, right? Humans like fish. I've got plenty of those. See? Plenty of fish. I guess that won't surprise you, though, considering where we are!"

The sack flew through the air and landed with a wallop. Dozens of slimy blindfish slid out.

Ollie had been cowering, his hands over his face. Now, he gingerly opened one eye and peered through his fingers.

"I know you need them cooked, so don't worry about that. I have a fire. Well, I don't have one right this minute, but I will. I can do lots of things that might surprise you. Because of the claws, I mean. They work just as well as hands, sometimes, for most things. You'd be surprised! You really, really would."

The creature was talking. The top half, anyway. The person half. His mouth looked much like any other man's mouth Ollie had ever seen, though the teeth were longer and sharper. Their points dug into his lips a little while he spoke, like fat white needles poking into a pincushion.

Slowly, Ollie lowered his hands.

"Let's see... There are three of you, so I should cook...fifty fish, or so? Will that be enough? I confess, I don't remember how much humans eat. I usually don't remember much at all, really. Oh well. Can't have it all, I suppose!" He smiled, baring his oversized teeth.

Meatball, who had fallen to the ground with Ollie's shove, waddled back into view.

"Oh! Four of you. This one is not human, though, is it? I wonder if it will still eat fish?"

Ollie dared a look at Tera and Laszlo. They were both motionless, staring at the monster with eyebrows raised.

He seemed to be waiting for them to speak. When they didn't, he hung his head. "Of course. Fifty is not enough. But that's okay! I can get more. You just wait here, and I'll—"

"It's enough," Tera interrupted, her voice cautious. "Thank you. It's more than enough."

Relief washed the creature's face. "Oh, good. Good! Wonderful."

Ollie finally dared to speak. "You're not going to...eat us?" he asked.

The man-crab looked aghast. "*Eat* you? Goodness, no! Why would I do that?"

"I...I don't know."

"I eat greenie-greens," the creature said, smacking his lips with a thick, purple tongue. "And wigglers, and sometimes fish. But humans? Ugh. No. Never, never, never." He grimaced, then leaned closer, as if sharing a secret. "I'm part human myself, you know. Can you guess which part?" He smiled again.

Ollie looked at the others, not sure if they were actually expected to answer.

"Then why do you lock us in shells?" Laszlo asked suspiciously.

The creature seemed surprised at the question. "Well, to protect you, of course," he said. "You were all soft and squishy, with no shell whatsoever! Just those...legs." He waved a hand dismissively. "You won't survive very long down here with nothing but those, I can tell you that! Take it from me. Down here, it's all big fangs and big bellies. You need to protect yourself. That's what I always say. Protect yourself, protect yourself, protect yourself." He looked proud.

Ollie straightened suddenly and pointed. "The Hermit!"

Laszlo and Tera looked at him in surprise.

"He's the Hermit!" Ollie said excitedly. "The Novas told us to watch out for the Hermit, remember? I thought they meant, like, a loner. But they meant a hermit *crab!*"

Ollie remembered the tiny hermit crabs of his youth at Revere Beach. Crawling and brawling in yellow plastic buckets. Burying themselves in the sand. Scurrying across barnacle-covered rocks. They had no shells of their own; instead, they would "adopt" abandoned shells as they came across them. When they outgrew one, they would simply ditch it and move into bigger digs. Nature's original squatters.

"That's very kind of you to think of us," Tera said, her tone still tentative. "They are beautiful shells. But I wonder... Is there a way for us to get out of them? Just to eat our dinner, perhaps? Human legs need to move, you see. For circulation."

The Hermit nodded solemnly. "I lose legs, sometimes. Then they just grow back. Yours might not grow back. Anyway, you can get out any time you like. But I wouldn't recommend it. Like I said, it's really not too safe."

"How to get out?" Laszlo pressed.

"You only have to wish it to be so," the creature answered with a shrug.

Tera rested her arms on the outer rim of her shell and smiled. Ollie recognized it as her patient smile, the one she used with kids. Or with him, when he was being dense. "But you see, Mr. Hermit, we've already—"

"That's not my name," he interrupted.

"Sorry," she said, and held up her hands. "Sorry. I just meant to say that we've already wished and tried to get out, many times, and it doesn't seem to be working."

"No," the hermit said.

"I'm...sorry?"

"No. You haven't been wishing to get out, or you'd already be out."

"But we have," Ollie insisted.

"No! You've been *wanting* to get out. But wanting and wishing are not the same."

"They are not?" Laszlo asked, sounding puzzled.

"Well, of course not. You are humans, aren't you? I would think humans would know that." He lifted one of the front claws to scratch his face absently. "Go ahead, then. Try it. Go ahead and wish."

"All right," Tera said, flashing Ollie a look that said, *what the hell?* She glanced up at the ceiling of the cave and said, "I wish to leave this shell."

Tera pressed her hands against the rim, hoisted her body, and then, incredibly, she was out. Her legs were covered in some kind of pink goo; it dripped down the side of the shell and oozed onto the floor. A look of ecstatic relief flashed across her face.

A minute later, Ollie heard Laszlo's voice: "I wish to leave this shell." The acrobat's legs made a sucking sound as he lifted himself free.

Everyone stared at Ollie. Feeling like a six-year-old in front of a candlelit cake, he closed his eyes and said, "I wish to leave this shell."

His legs resisted the motion at first, stuck as they were in the suction of goop. Moments later, they were out. Ollie groaned as he leaned down to rub his thighs, both completely numb and coated in the slimy, thick mucus. He banged his feet against the side of the shell and winced at the sharp stabs of tingling pain.

"I shall cook the fish now, I think. Would that be all right?" the creature asked. He didn't wait for an answer before continuing. "I shall leave the heads on. The heads have wonderful nutritional value. I do remember that. I don't remember much, but I do remember that. And we shall eat, and talk, become friends. Or perhaps we are already friends?" He looked at each of them in turn, confusion and optimism flashing across his features.

"Yes, of course," Tera told him. "Of course, we are friends."

He lifted his two front legs in celebration. "Wonderful! Friends already! How lucky for us. You can never have too many friends, can you? Not in a place like this. We will be friends forever, I think! Forever and ever!"

They nodded in unison: Yes. Friends forever.

The crab-man wasn't kidding about his claws: They were every bit as useful as promised. With rapid-fire motion, he gathered clumps of something that looked like dried seaweed from around the edges of the cave, made a hefty pile, and scraped his left front claw against the floor until it made a spark big enough to light a roaring fire.

Ollie, Tera, and Laszlo shot each other wary glances as the mutant busied himself with meal prep. Soon, dozens of fishes were hanging head-down over the flames; Ollie found himself staring at them longingly and swallowing the build-up of saliva in his mouth as they cooked.

He leaned to his left and whispered, "Should we eat them?"

"No," Laszlo muttered, crossing his arms. "I do not trust this crabby man."

Tera shrugged and whispered: "If he wanted to kill us, he could have done it already."

In the end, Laszlo did eat the fish. Three of them, in fact. Tera ate two, Meatball ate one, and Ollie ate a whopping five—but not the heads, despite the hermit's repeated exclamations about the nutritional superiority of brains and eyeballs.

They ate, and the creature talked. And talked, and talked, and talked.

He talked about the cave: "I sleep in the sand, over there. I like it all the way over my head. You'd think I couldn't breathe, but I do! I breathe just fine. You'll see. You can sleep in the sand, too, if you want. I won't mind. It's warm and soft. I know humans need lots of sleep. I don't remember much, but I do remember that."

He talked about the polished stone: "I keep it nice and shiny. Do you like it? I like it shiny. I polish with these cloths, see? Left behind by other humans like you." At that, he used one of his long claws to lift a beige jumpsuit from a pile on the ground. "See? I shine it up nice, all day long. You have to keep on top of it, you know. Things can get very dirty very fast if you don't keep on top of it. That's just the way it goes down here."

He talked about his light-tipped tentacles, which emerged from the space between his human torso and shell as he rambled on. "See? I have beautiful lights." To Ollie, they looked like fishing lures, tender and thin, blinking in a kaleidoscope of different colors. "They help me catch friends," he explained cheerily. "Friends like you."

And of course, he talked about food: "I do like the greenies the best. Little bits and smidges. Yummy, yummy, yum. They're easy to find, too. Floating everywhere. I go out, and I find the greenies and the wigglies, and I scoop them right up. I know where to find them. I'm really good at it. If you want some, I can bring some back for you, too! Do you think you'll want some?"

Ollie, Laszlo, and Tera nodded. Sure. Greenies.

"Excellent! We can eat them together. All together, all the time. I'll take good care of you, I promise. I'm really good at it."

"Sounds great," Tera said. "Doesn't it guys?"

Ollie and Laszlo nodded again. Laszlo had finished eating; Ollie was still gnawing on a charred fish carcass.

"We sure do appreciate your helping us," she continued. "And giving us the shells, and this wonderful meal, and...everything."

The hermit beamed.

"But the thing is, we're actually trying to help some people, too. People who need us to find them. Just like you found us." Tera smiled. "So, I was wondering, since you're so, uh, helpful, if you might be able to help us with that, too."

"I am helpful," the hermit agreed. "I am very, very good at helping. I don't remember many things, but I do remember that."

"Right!" Tera said. "And all you have to do to help us now is just to show us the way out. That's it! So easy! And I bet you'd be really good at it!"

The creature looked puzzled. "The way out of the cave, you mean?"

"Yes! That's right," she said.

"Oh." His forehead wrinkled. "Well, that's the way out, over there." He pointed to a crevice in the far wall.

"We will fit?" Laszlo asked, looking doubtfully at the opening.

"Yes, I don't see why not. If I fit, then you will certainly fit, don't you think? Sometimes I am surprised at the places I fit. In the coral, and the rocks, and all the other places. You just never know, I suppose! Things are like that, sometimes. Surprising. Don't you think?"

"Yes, they sure are!" Tera answered, her voice ringing with false cheer. "Thank you again, so much, for everything!" She stood up and shot Ollie and Laszlo looks; quickly, they followed her lead. Ollie tossed the rest of his fish onto the ground as he scrambled to his feet, scooping up Meatball on the way.

"Is nice to be meeting you," Laszlo said with a wave.

They were backing away, now. Slowly. Away from the fire, and the vacant shells, and the giant crab-man. Tera kept a smile plastered on her face; Ollie tried to do the same as the trog squirmed in his arms.

"It's no problem at all," the hermit assured them. "I love to help my friends. We're friends now, right? Forever and ever? Because I don't like to be alone. I really don't. I like lots of things. Lots and lots of things. But I don't like to be alone."

He was following them as they moved. *Clack, clack, clack, clack.*

"Yes! Good friends!" Laszlo boomed heartily.

"Such good friends," Tera parroted.

Ollie said nothing. Instead, he just kept walking. All three of them moved backwards, stepping carefully toward the crevice.

The crab-man followed. He was starting to look confused. "Are you done already with your meal?" he asked them.

"Yes, I think so," Tera said. Her pitch was rising. "Thank you again. So, so delicious. But I think we have to go now." *Step, step, step.*

The creature didn't answer. He only watched with a tilted head.

The crack in the wall was closer, now. Just a few feet away. Ollie sped up his steps, half expecting one of the giant claws to lunge suddenly. To skewer him like a kabob. What was one less friend, after all, when you had so many to choose from?

Tera reached the wall first. From the corner of his eye, Ollie saw her slip one leg, then an arm, then her whole body through the crevice. And suddenly, she was gone. Laszlo gave a hearty wave and followed her. And then Ollie found himself standing alone in the cave with a half-crab, half-man abomination as flames flickered shadows all around them. He reached out an arm, felt the edge of the opening, and tried to steady his shaking hand.

"Thanks, buddy!" he said, avoiding the hermit's eyes. "Thanks for everything! Goodbye!"

The creature opened his mouth to say something, but Ollie didn't wait to find out what it was. Instead, he took a deep breath, leapt backwards, and slammed directly into Laszlo's back.

They were standing in a dark, tight hallway. The ceiling was low and riddled with wide fissures.

"That was close one," Laszlo said.

"Let's get out of here before he changes his mind!" Tera hissed. She turned and started to run.

Ollie felt weak with relief. He didn't know where this narrow tunnel would lead, but it had to be better than being trapped inside a goddamn shell. In a claustrophobic cave. With an overly chatty monster that looked like it might have been cobbled together from the leftover broken parts in a child's toy chest.

They ran without talking. The hallway was short; Ollie could already see a glimmer of flickering light at the end. As before, Tera was the first to pass through, then Laszlo, then Ollie. He burst through the opening behind them, short of breath. Excited. Then he looked up to see—

The hermit.

Smiling. Tapping his two front claws together.

Ollie turned around, confused. Tera and Laszlo were doing the same.

"What...happened?" Ollie asked.

Was this another hermit? In another cave? Turning back around, he saw the three empty shells surrounded by puddles of pink goo. The chewed fish carcasses. The roaring fire.

Same hermit. Same cave. But how was that possible?

"Would you like more fish?" the creature asked. His gray eyes blinked expectantly. "I have plenty. But I can get more if you want. I'm very good at finding fish. I will take good care of you."

"Uh, thank you," Tera said. Her eyes were darting left and right. "But I thought you said that was the way out." She jerked a thumb behind her, obviously perplexed.

"It is."

Laszlo was pressing a hand against his forehead, as though massaging a headache. "Did we take wrong turn?" he asked.

"I don't think so. It is the way out. And also, the way back in." The Hermit tap-tap-tapped in a giddy little dance and continued: "It's a loop. I think that's the right word. I don't remember much, but I do remember that. A loop! Around and around and around. Like a circle. No beginning, no end."

"What are you saying?" Ollie asked, trying to control the hysteria that had started to burrow under his skin. "There's no way out?"

"Of course, there is! Don't be silly. I get out all the time! How do you think I caught all these fish? I like to catch fish. And swim. And find greenies, of course. Lots of greenies. I have to get out for that, don't I?"

Tera was standing with her hands clenched into fists at her sides. When she spoke, her voice was hard and even. "Yes, but how do *we* get out?"

"I have to let you out," the crab-man said. "I have to wish for it. Remember? The wishing?"

They nodded numbly. They did remember the wishing.

"All right," Tera said. "All right. Then... I wish for us to leave this cave." She spoke the words loudly and solemnly.

"Not *you,* silly," the creature said. Her mistake seemed to delight him. "This is *my* cave, remember? I have to do the wishing."

"So, all you have to do is...wish us out?" Ollie asked. "And then we can leave?"

"Yes."

"Great!" Tera said, her eager smile returning. "So...maybe you can do that? Like, now?"

"No, I'm sorry," the hermit answered. He looked genuinely contrite. "I can't do that."

"Why not?" Laszlo demanded.

"Because I don't wish it! Wishes only work when they're true."

Tera clenched her jaw. When she spoke, her voice was dangerously low. "*Why* don't you wish it?"

"We're friends now, remember?" the creature said, lifting two claws. "I will love you, and I will take care of you. Forever and ever. If you leave, how can we be friends?"

Herrick's Lie

Ollie's eyes fell on the piles of bones and clothes scattered around the cave, remnants of all those who came before. And for the first time, he saw the scene clearly.

The hermit had not hurt anyone. He had simply loved them all to death.

Ten

The fire burned down to almost nothing. Meatball lay on his back near the glowing embers and crunched fish bones with gleeful abandon, entirely unaware of the dire situation in which he'd found himself.

Ollie, on the other hand, was all too aware. He stared glumly into the low flames, knowing they would soon vanish. Knowing the cold would set in soon after. Knowing the hermit-man would probably say goodnight, submerge himself into the sandy corner, and leave Ollie and his friends to shiver and wander and run their hands along the perfectly shiny, perfectly polished walls. Forever and ever and ever.

Several hours had passed since they had traveled around the loop and ended up right back where they had started. They attempted it one more time, for good measure, with the same depressing results. Then Tera had tried reasoning with the crab-man. Laszlo had tried charming him. Ollie had shared the story of the missing women and stressed the urgency of their mission. They begged. They embellished. They even drummed up a few tears.

Nothing worked. The creature either didn't understand, or didn't care. Either way, his answer was always the same: He loved them. And he wished for them to stay.

At some point, Laszlo had returned to the charm offensive. Now, he was asking the hermit about his past, his interests, and his daily habits, feigning interest in it all. Ollie was barely listening. Exhaustion—along with its cousin, resignation—had seeped in, leaving him all but useless in the effort.

"Do you know others?" Laszlo was asking. "Others...like you?"

"No," the Hermit said, sounding proud. "I am the only one."

"Ah, is good," the acrobat said with a nod. "You are, how do you say, one of kind!"

"Yes, I suppose I am. Someone made me, you know. I don't remember much, but I do remember that. I wasn't always here, like this. I used to be someone else. And then I went to the place where they made me. But after a while, I got out. Escaped. All by myself. I'm very clever, you see. Cleverer than you might think! I got out, and I found this place, and I learned how to polish and how to find greenie-greens and how to catch friends. And now I am here, with you, and we are so happy!" He grinned, the long teeth flashing like silvery hooks.

At the mention of "the place where they made me," Ollie shot Tera a surprised and apprehensive look. What the hell did that mean? Tera shrugged in answer, looking equally bewildered.

Laszlo had picked up on it, too. "Where is place where they made you?" he asked.

"I don't remember. I don't remember much."

"Do you remember *who* made you?" Tera interjected.

The subject seemed to agitate the creature; instead of answering, he started to tap his claws against the stone in rapid-fire, irregular rhythm. *Clack. Clack, clack, clack. Clackety-clack.* The movement reminded Ollie of a person bouncing their knee.

Laszlo glanced over at his friends and changed the subject. "And your name, is not Hermit?"

"No." A frown emerged. *Clack, clack, clack.* "That's not my name. I don't have a name."

"Don't have name?" Laszlo said. "How is possible? Who does not have name?"

The crab-man tilted his head. "Me. Well, I suppose they might have given me a name and I don't remember. Anything's possible. And I don't remember much. But no, I don't have a name."

"We must change this!" Laszlo boomed, rising to his feet. He gestured to Tera and Ollie. "We must change this, yes? Right now!"

The creature's dour expression brightened. "Now?"

"Yes! No time like the now! That is what they say, no?" Laszlo pivoted, folding his arms. "What kind of name does crabby man want?"

"I...I don't know. What are my choices?"

"Any choices!" Laszlo said, casting a glance at Tera. "Right?"

"Right," she nodded.

Ollie said nothing. He wasn't interested in playing these games. Not anymore. He was tired. Beyond tired. What did Laszlo think, that naming this monster was somehow going to get them out of lake-cave jail? It wouldn't work. Nothing would work. Ollie reached out to scratch Meatball's exposed belly and stared stubbornly into the smoldering mounds of seaweed in the pit.

He tried to think positively. Things could be worse, he told himself. If you had to be imprisoned, it was better to be stuck in a cave with friends than languishing in a cell at Herrick's End. And he would know. He clung to that thought, remembering the agony he had suffered in the decrepit tower, hoping it would make him feel better about his current, relatively less hideous incarceration.

It didn't.

Laszlo pointed a finger in the air. "Herman! Like Hermit, yes? But different!"

The creature's nose wrinkled in distaste.

"What?" Laszlo protested. "Is good name!"

"Maybe...Fred?" Tera piped in.

"No," said the hermit decisively. "Too short."

"Too short," Laszlo nodded. "Ah, I see. Is long name you want. Long name like...Oleksandr! Oleksandr is fine Ukrainian name."

"But I'm not Ukrainian," the creature said.

"That, you do not know for sure," Laszlo pointed out. "You say all the time, you do not remember. Maybe you are Ukrainian." He turned to Tera. "Yes? Is possible."

"Sure," she shrugged. "Maybe."

The crab-man was about as Ukrainian as a leprechaun standing in a County Cork field of clover, and they all knew it. But Ollie could see that Tera, too, was tiring from the conversational effort. She was giving up. The firelight was dwindling, and so were their chances of winning the creature to their side.

"Okay, okay, no Oleksandr," Laszlo acquiesced. "How about—"

"Yes!" the hermit shouted suddenly. He pointed a claw. "Yes! That one."

"What one?"

"That name. The one you just said."

"Oleksandr?"

"No, the other one."

Laszlo's brow furrowed. "I said no other one."

"You did," the creature insisted. "Howerbout."

"Hower—?" Laszlo stopped, tipped back his head. "Ohhh. You are confused. I said, *'how about.'*"

"Yes," the Hermit said. "That's the one I like. That's my new name!"

"That's not a name," Ollie piped in crossly, still staring at the fire.

"What difference does it make?" Tera snapped. "If that's what he wants for a name, let him have it." The exhaustion was making them all irritable. "Crabby," his mother would have called it. The irony of that should have made him smile. It didn't.

Ollie tossed a chunk of blindfish carcass into the flames and watched it burn. *Stupid fish,* he thought. Stupid fire. Stupid, stupid crab. Too stupid to know that "how" and "about" do not make a stupid name.

He reached for another hunk of leftover filet, started to throw it, and then stopped. His hand froze in midair.

How and about.

"What?" Tera was watching him. "What's wrong?"

"Nothing," he answered, shaking his head. But that wasn't true. A phrase had started ringing in his consciousness.

Hows and abouts.

"What?" she asked again.

Ollie set down the fish. He felt a tingling in his extremities. A sudden clarity in his thoughts. The dwindling flames seemed brighter, somehow. The crackling seemed sharper.

He turned to look at her. He flashed what he hoped was an apologetic smile. "Okay, don't get mad."

Tera's eyes narrowed. "Not a good lead-in," she said.

"Yeah, I know."

"Why would I get mad?"

"It's just that..." He let out a sigh of resignation. "Okay, here's the thing. There was another note."

For a moment, no one spoke. Then Laszlo asked, "Another Herrick note?"

"Yes."

"For you?"

"I think so, yes," Ollie answered. In reality, he didn't just think so, he knew so. But that would be a little harder to explain.

"What's a Herrick note?" asked the hermit. Now, apparently, called Howerbout. They ignored him.

"When?" Tera asked.

"Um, a while back. You know, after it all...happened."

When she spoke again, Ollie could tell she was trying to keep her voice even. "Why didn't you say anything?"

"I didn't want to worry you!" he said, starting to talk fast. "Everything was nice, for a change. Easy. And we were happy, and it was all so good, and I guess I just figured, why? Why say anything? It would just ruin everything, and make everyone worry, and it was probably nothing anyway, so I just...didn't. Say anything," he finished lamely, realizing that he was sounding like their long-winded captor.

"Probably nothing?" Laszlo said. "Herrick notes are never nothing, my friend!" The acrobat had received his own Herrick note, not too long ago, which had said simply, *"When you find the lost boy looking for the lost girl, send him to me."* Days later, Laszlo had spotted Ollie trying—and failing—to locate his missing friend, Nell, and put the pieces together. And so, he did what he was told. He sent Ollie on a journey along the Freedom Trail that he knew would lead to the Neath. Even if he didn't know why.

As Tera had once explained: *That's what you do around here when the 350-year-old creepy founder guy gives you a job to do. You do it. End of story.*

She had been wrong about that last part. Those notes never seemed to be the end of the story. Not even goddamn close.

"What's a Herrick note?" Howerbout asked again.

Still ignoring him, Tera folded her hands in her lap. "What did it say?"

"Well, there was one part that—" Ollie stopped. "It's weird. You won't believe me."

She raised her eyebrows in an expression of annoyance and disbelief. Then she gestured at their improbable surroundings. "Seriously?"

"All right, all right. It said, uh..." Ollie searched his memory. He wanted to get it right. "It said: Hows and abouts, souls and mates, find him his, seal your fate."

Meatball continued to crunch. The others stared at Ollie blankly.

"Hows and abouts," Ollie repeated. "Isn't that weird?"

"Say it again," Tera said. "The whole thing."

Ollie did.

Laszlo looked from one to the other. "I am not understanding the English. What does that mean?"

Tera had a sudden, faraway look in her eye. She repeated it out loud, though she seemed to be talking mainly to herself: "Hows and abouts, souls and mates, find him his, seal your fate." She paused, then looked at Ollie. "Find him his."

"What's a Herrick note?" interjected the creature. Again.

For the first time in several hours, Tera turned, looked up, and gave Howerbout her full attention. "They're messages, left for us sometimes," she explained.

"Left by who?"

"By a man who's dead."

For once, their captor didn't seem to know what to say.

"He left them before he died," she added. "His name was George Herrick. He seemed to know what was coming, I guess you could say. Like, the future. For all of us. But for Ollie in particular."

Ollie shifted uncomfortably.

"The notes are like clues," Tera continued. "Puzzles, sort of, that only become clear when...well, when they become clear." A smile was spreading across her face.

"What?" Ollie asked.

"Don't you see?" Tera looked from face to face. "Hows and abouts. That's him." She pointed at the creature. "Souls and mates. Obviously, he's lonely, right? I think we've established that."

Howerbout scrunched his face. "I'm not lonely!" he protested. "I have you, don't I? Aren't we friends? Forever and ever?"

"Yes!" Tera assured him. "Yes, of course. But you need something more than that. You, sir, need a soul mate!"

Silence settled around them, weaving through the flickering shadows.

Laszlo rubbed a bulging bicep and said, "I am not understanding. What is this...soul mate?"

"A soul mate is, like, your number-one person," Ollie said. "The person you were meant to be with. Your other half." His eyes flickered automatically back to Tera, and his heart jumped several beats when he saw that she was looking at him, too. Something passed between them, then: something charged and ethereal. It made his breath catch.

Tera blinked, then broke away to look again at their captor. "That's why we're here," she told him. "I see it now. We were meant to be here. It was our destiny to help you find *your* destiny. Your soul mate."

Herrick's words lingered in the back of Ollie's mind... *Find him his, seal your fate.* A nugget of uncertainty began to tingle. "Seal your fate" could mean any number of things, after all. Not all of them good.

But it was something. It was more than they had five minutes ago.

And Tera looked so certain. Unreasonably certain, he realized. As if she knew something that he didn't.

"How are we supposed to do that?" Ollie asked her. "Find his soul mate?"

Tera waggled her eyebrows. "That part is easy," she said. "You only need to ask."

"Ask...who?"

Instead of answering, she tapped a finger against her lip and gazed up at Howerbout again. "Would you like to find your soul mate? Someone you were meant to be with, forever and ever?"

The crab-man looked confused, but solemn. "You're not my soul mates?"

"I'm afraid not," Tera told him gently. "I think that's what Herrick is trying to tell us. You do have a soul mate you're meant to be with, and we're the ones who are meant to find that person. Or, uh, crab. Creature."

"It would be nice to have a soul mate," Howerbout said, his claws clacking in thoughtful rhythm.

"Yes, it would!" Tera said. "Do you want us to do that for you?"

He seemed to think for a moment, then nodded. A bit of drool dribbled from his thick lips. "Yes," he said. "I think I would."

"Excellent," she replied, pressing her hands together as if in prayer. "I think I can make that happen. But first, you have to do two things."

"Two?"

Tera nodded. "The first thing is, you have to give me some of your sweat."

Three heads swiveled to stare at her.

"Did you say...sweat?" Ollie asked. "Like, *sweat,* sweat?"

"*Sweat,* sweat, yes." She looked around thoughtfully, then pointed at the pile of leftover clothes-turned-polishing rags. "I think I can use one of those to soak it up."

Ollie looked at the creature's human torso, slick with perspiration, and grimaced.

"Would that be okay?" Tera asked Howerbout.

"I...guess so," he answered, looking doubtful.

"Great! Awesome. And the second thing is, you have to let us go. You have to wish for it."

The crab-man looked stricken. "Oh, no," he said. "I couldn't possibly do that."

"Why not?" Ollie asked, frustration mounting in his chest.

"Because I don't wish it! I've already told you! I wish for you to stay!"

"Yes," Tera interjected. "But you also said you wish for us to find your soul mate. Right? So, we'll do that, and then we'll come right back. With another friend!"

"You won't," Howerbout said dolefully. His head hung.

"What?"

"You won't come back. That's what happens. Friends say they'll come back, and then they don't. They say they love me, and then they don't. And then I'm all alone, with no one to talk to, forever and ever." All six legs buckled at the top joint, causing his massive, speckled shell to drop to the floor with a thud. He went silent, and morose. A still-life portrait of crustacean grief.

Ollie considered the point. Howerbout was right, wasn't he? If they did get out of there, were they really going to come back?

"I will stay," Laszlo said.

They all swung around to look at him.

"What are you talking about" Ollie asked.

"I will stay, and you will go," the acrobat said. "And me and my new friend here will have fun time until you come back. Fun, fun time."

Howerbout seemed to brighten at the suggestion.

"No," Tera said. "No way. That's not happening."

"Crabby man needs some company," Laszlo said, patting the big brown-and-white shell affectionately. "We are good friends. Yes?"

Howerbout smiled, exposing his fangs.

"This is only way," Laszlo insisted. "He will have me here, and he will wish for you to leave. And you will go, and do this...thing, and then you will come back for me. Bam, boom. Like that. Quick as bunny rabbits, we will be doing hellos and the huggings and all together again."

Ollie stared at him, this wiry, muscle-bound, acrobatic oddball, standing with arms outstretched. Laszlo made it sound like the plan for a grand, wondrous time. Like the itinerary of the Titanic voyage must have sounded right before it met the iceberg. "Dude, you're crazy," Ollie said. "We're not leaving you here. There's no way."

"I am *genius,*" Laszlo corrected, waggling a finger. "You know is true."

"Laz, you have to get aboveground!" Ollie told him. "Soon! What if we take too long?" As a Runner, Laszlo could only stay in the Neath for a limited amount of time before suffering irreversible consequences to his lungs. It was an unacceptable risk.

Laszlo waved a hand. "I have weeks yet. You will not take weeks, no? Neath is not so big."

"We don't know how long it will take," Tera said firmly. "And it doesn't matter, anyway. You're not staying."

"*I'll* stay," Ollie told them.

"You're not staying either!" Tera yelped. Her voice was getting higher pitched by the second. "We'll think of something else! Krite!"

"There is no something else," Laszlo said, now leaning up against Howerbout's shell as if the two were long-lost comrades. "We need to keep moving, no? Is my fault, all this...trouble. And I will do this now so we can find lab, find device, find people. All of missing people."

"What? Laz, it's not your fau—"

"*Is* my fault," Laszlo interrupted, his face darkening. "It was my job, to do the protecting. *My* job."

Ollie was shocked to hear a catch in his friend's voice.

"I make promise, swear my oath, to protect them," Laszlo continued, now staring at the polished ground. "They trust me. This was my job."

"Laz, there's no way you could have known—"

"Does not matter what I know, what I did not know!" the acrobat said. "I *should* have known. They did the counting on me. They did not worry, because they had me. But when they needed me, where was I? I was not there! And now..." He paused, collected himself. When he started again, his voice was hoarse with anguish. "Where are they? We do not know! They are gone! And if we do not find them again, if we never find them...Is my fault. *My* fault!"

Ollie was stunned, and speechless. All this time, he had been blaming himself for the WRC kidnappings. It had never occurred to him that Laszlo had been doing the same. Finally, he said, "We'll find them."

At that, something came over Laszlo. He lifted his head and straightened. When he spoke, his voice was stronger. Louder. "We will, Ollie Delgato of the North End Delgatos," he agreed. "We will. But only like this. There is no other something." With a determined expression, he looked up at their captor. "I call you Howerbout?"

"Yes," the creature said happily.

"Good. Is good name. Me and Howerbout, we will stay. We will be good team. Yes?"

"Yes," Howerbout agreed.

"And you will let these two leave, and the rodent?" He jerked his head toward Meatball, still laying on his back by the fire. "You will wish for it?"

A pause. And then: "Yes."

"Wonderful!" Laszlo tossed an arm over the curve of the giant shell. "Tell me, crabby man. Do you know any Ukrainian traveling songs?"

Howerbout looked confused. "I don't think so."

"Ah. Better get to wishing, then, my new friend. We have much to do."

Eleven

There was, of course, one slight snag in Laszlo's generous and unorthodox plan: Water. Lots and lots of it.

Howerbout's cave, they had to assume, was an air-pocket respite located far below the surface of an unfathomably deep lake. Unswimmable for mere mortals. And they had no way of knowing if the underwater-breathing trick on loan from the Novas might have already run its course. The nymphs had not specified how long it would last, and Ollie wouldn't have put it past that preening bunch of narcissistic beauties to yank it away haphazardly for fun. If the breathing allowance was done, then Ollie and Tera were done. There was no way to make it topside without it.

Either way, they had no choice but to try. And so, they left—really left, this time—through Howerbout's cracked cave wall, with Meatball in tow on Ollie's shoulder. From there, it was a short jaunt through a narrow passageway until they reached a ledge lapped by water. This was it. No turning back now.

There were worse ways to die than drowning, he told himself. He had heard somewhere that it was actually kind of pleasant: first, fear, then, a kind of euphoria, and then...nothing. Or so a few back-from-the-dead survivors had claimed. He hoped they were right.

Standing side-by-side on the ledge, Ollie and Tera looked at each other. He felt like he should say something, but what? *See you on the flip side? If we don't make it, it was great knowing you? You are, and will always be, the love of my life?* The more he reached for the right sentiment, the more the words piled up like an I-95 multi-car crash on his tongue.

Tera stopped his musings by standing on her tiptoes to give him a long, gentle kiss. It worked like a sedative: The jitters floated up and away to the jagged ceiling, leaving him feeling calm. Resolute.

She winked. He smiled.

Then they squeezed their hands together, took two synchronized deep breaths, and jumped.

Ollie plunged, struggled, and felt a surge of bliss as something like high-octane air filled his lungs. It was absolute perfection, like salve on a burn, or lemon slush from a Boston Common pushcart on summer's hottest afternoon. He made a mental note to never underestimate the Novas again—and to bring them a whole damn bouquet of sparkly lakestars as soon as he got the chance. Meatball seemed equally overjoyed; the trog was already darting and gliding with practiced skill through his native aquatic habitat.

As the murk began to clear, Ollie saw that they had to swim down, not up, in order to travel the passageway that connected Howerbout's cavern to the big, open water. They descended further, toward a beckoning light. He could see vague flashes and colors in the distance.

Finally, an opening yawned ahead. The tunnel ended. And when an unexpected current pushed from behind, the force expelled two humans and one trog into a wonderland of almost unimaginable scale.

It came back to him in a sudden swoosh of pleasure: the ecstasy of it, the beauty. The water, *his* water, had become as clear as crystal, speckled with a floating confetti of animals, plants, and multi-hued flecks of sediment. He felt like nothing more or less than one of them, drifting and melding, at home in the flotsam. Upside down, right side up. Then, there, tomorrow, yesterday. None of it mattered. All that mattered was here. Now. This delirious pressure, nudging from all sides. Suspending his weightless body in its gentle grasp.

The aquatic creatures, he sensed, were mildly amused by his presence. As before, their names came to him, simply entered his brain, as he glimpsed each one: fat pufferpines with long, sharp quills. Orange-striped Mandarin eels. Lakehorses—not like the seahorses of the Brickside, but instead shaped like actual, land-based equines with four legs and flowing manes, galloping through the water in slow motion as though a starting gun had set them off in disparate directions.

They all circled his body, curious. Unhurried. What, he wondered, would they call the likes of him? Did they have a name for visiting humans? Fishes-out-of-water, in reverse? Humans-out-of-land, perhaps. Or people-out-of-air. The notion made him want to laugh, but the idea of opening his mouth and expelling a sound seemed impossibly foreign, somehow. A vestige from another time.

Ollie wiggled his toes inside his sneakers. His clothing felt almost obscene: so heavy and unnecessary. More vestiges. He considered stripping it all off. Watching the jumpsuit and shoes and crunchy, old underwear float away into the deep. The water, he knew, would feel extraordinary against his skin. Therapeutic. Yet something about this notion made him hesitate, as though he might regret it later. He wasn't sure why. What could be wrong about stripping down to the bare essentials, especially in a place such as this?

He watched as a one-eyed scuppergill nibbled at his finger, then swam away.

Tera was there, too. Smiling. Next to him—so close. Her presence surprised him in the most wonderful way. *Tera Martinez. Underworld angel.* He floated in place and marveled at her, there in the currents. The water had made her more vibrant, somehow. More alive. The violet of her hair seemed brighter. Her big brown eyes reflected all of the lake's swirling, unnatural colors in a startling prism. A school of phosphorescent dewdrop carpies had surrounded her like a living net, swimming in concentric circles. They were drawn to her. Of course, they were. She was magnetic. Magical. So magical she made even the actual magic around her seem bland by comparison.

Their eyes met. Ollie's pulse scampered. Something was pulling them toward each other with inexorable force. The water was like air—like nothing. No barrier at all. When they found each other, a cocoon of carbonation formed around them, protective and warm. Was it real? Or did he just imagine it? He kissed her and felt the tiny bubbles fizz and pop against his skin. Their lips formed a seal against the water. He felt her heartbeat through her lips, through the liquid, through the hundreds of bubbles that frothed all around them. And he knew: This was why he was here. Why he was alive. He needed nothing else, and he never would.

Tera.

And then, something jarring. An unwelcome interruption. Brown and fuzzed, brushing up against his face. With reluctance, Ollie broke the seal between them and pulled away.

He stared at the creature for a long moment before awareness surfaced. *Trog.*

Meatball was swimming laps around their heads. When they ignored him, he spun faster, darting between their faces. Separating them.

Ollie felt himself frown. Meatball's webbed feet grazed his arm. Ollie felt the claws, sharp and insistent. Once, and then twice.

The trog was poking them. Reminding them of...something.

Tera moved backwards. Ollie saw something dawn in her expression.

As before, they were able to talk without talking. It was time to go, she was telling him. *Why?* he wanted to ask. He knew that he didn't want to go. But he also knew that he didn't want to be here without her. Even in his current addled state, he realized that was the most important thing. *Tera.* Always, Tera. She started swimming and he followed, reluctantly. Though the world around them seemed directionless, he somehow knew in which direction they were heading: up.

And up, and up, and up.

It might have taken minutes, or hours. Ollie genuinely couldn't say. He was working hard, using the full force of his muscles to move through the liquid, but he didn't feel tired. He had vague memories of that feeling, "tired"—of straining and struggling and crying and hurting—but those sensations seemed almost ludicrous to him, now. Exceedingly far away. He could feel each water molecule lifting him, pushing him, and becoming a part of him, in every possible, impossible way.

When the surface light appeared above, harsh and refractive, Ollie felt a crushing disappointment. If not for Tera, and the niggling sense of something important to be done, he would not have left. He would have gladly stayed there forever, wrapped up in curly lakeweed. Frolicking among his new, unblinking friends. Hiding inside the fast-moving schools of fishes. Sinking like a mighty stone to the bottom of the lake—if a bottom even existed. Somehow, he doubted that it did.

The thought did not dissuade him. If anything, the possibility of boundless expanse beckoned with a crooked, curling finger. *Come. Stay. All that you have known is but the beginning.*

Tera burst through the surface first. He followed, grudgingly, gasping the unpleasant air. So...rough. Like oxygen coated with spikes. It hurt to inhale. But after a minute or two, Ollie acclimated. He pushed a lock of wet hair from his face, treading water. The hangover hit almost immediately: harsh and deadening, with a wave of nausea—something like the opposite of seasickness, he supposed—that came out of nowhere.

Meatball's lithe body encircled them in laps.

They were close to land, at least. Ollie saw a stalagmite forest, indistinguishable and yet comforting in its familiarity. Perhaps they were not too far from their goal.

The thought made his head clear. *Their goal.* Of course. They were here for a reason. They had things to do—very important things.

Laszlo.

He pictured the garrulous acrobat, trapped in a cave and spinning nonsensical conversations with his captor to buy them time.

The missing women.

How many were gone? Had still more been taken since he'd seen the picture of Nell and her note? Had anyone on the Brickside noticed their absence? Were they suffering? Or...worse?

Mr. Bonfiglio. Was he still in the hospital? Was he still in danger?

Nell. Who had forced her to hold that sign? Where was she now?

The questions heightened his nausea. When did things get so complicated? He and Tera had started out with one simple goal:

Find the lab. But they hadn't found it—not yet, and maybe not ever. If anything, they seemed to be getting further away. No lab, no device, no clear information. And now, no Laszlo. One rescue mission had somehow, alarmingly, turned into two. Instead of making things better, they were actively making them worse.

With a jolt, a row of block letters flashed like neon in his brain: SEND OLLIE UP OR THEY ALL DIE

Ollie balled his fists, began to sink below the surface, and then spread his fingers again. *Shit. Shit, shit, shit.*

Tera was splashing, scanning the scenery. She looked woozy, too.

Ollie ignored his queasy stomach and caught her eye, mustering an optimistic smile. *Enough.* Whatever he hoped to do, it wouldn't happen while he was flailing around like a startled cat in a bathtub. Like it or not, it was time to kick this dubious expedition into gear. "C'mon," he called out, pointing to the narrow beach.

Together, they swam to shore and climbed, dripping, from the lake. Ollie's wet jumpsuit clung and hung; he tried to wring it out without much success. Face flushing, he remembered his earlier, water-borne desire to tear off all of his clothes. Now, he threw up a silent prayer of thanks to whatever impulse or deity had prevented him from washing up stark naked, all of his bits and bobbles and fat rolls on full display in the glowing cavern light.

Tera was glancing right and left. Her usual gravity-defying swoop of hair had been flattened to her head. She ran a finger through the wet strands, looking concerned.

After a moment, Ollie cleared his throat. "You do know where we're going, right?"

"Yes! I know where we're going," Tera answered, though she wore a troubled look. "I just don't know...exactly...where we are. Yet."

As Ollie watched her, his uneasiness grew. She was staring down at her feet like she'd never seen sand before. Tera, lost? He didn't think such a thing could be possible.

"How about that way?" he finally asked, gesturing toward a slender opening in the stalagmite thicket. He didn't want to point out the obvious: that the only alternative seemed to be diving back into the water.

She nodded, but still seemed a bit muddled. "Yeah. Sure. Let's give it a try."

They plodded along slowly in their soaked clothes. At first, side-by-side, then, with Ollie in the front and Tera following behind. He felt as if he were waking from anesthesia, groggy and incapable of conversation. Tera, he guessed, must be feeling the same—which was why she seemed so preoccupied. So...off-track.

It's fine, he told himself. *Just keep moving.* It was the same refrain he had repeated to himself countless times during his endless, arduous days at Herrick's End. Ignore the obvious calamities all around you and just keep moving. Like a shark. Or a contagious virus. Or a kid sticking his fingers in his ears at the sound of bad news.

For a long while, nothing changed. The stalagmites surrounded them in infinite shades of russet, fatter on the bottom and pointy at the top. They endured a short urinestorm from the wormwalkers above. That was nothing new. Normally, Ollie and Tera would have simply reached for their tool belts and pulled out umbrellas; on this jaunt, however, their tool belts—along with pretty much everything else—had been lost somewhere along the way. In truth, Ollie was already so wet that he hardly noticed.

Meatball, as always, kept an eye out for falling wormwalkers. Each time one of them dropped from the ceiling and splattered nearby, he tensed his body, lifted his head, and scurried to the ground to inhale the flattened snack.

The wormwalkers had moved into a dark phase, which would last about a week. With their usual bright cerulean glow dimmed, Ollie was finding it hard to spot the ruts in the ground. The wet sneakers didn't help. He stumbled awkwardly, repeatedly.

Tera was having similar trouble. Finally she tripped and fell outright, tumbling into a pointy stalagmite protrusion. "Ow! Shit!" she yelled.

He hurried to her side. "Are you okay?"

"Yes, yes, fine," she said, struggling to stand up. She smoothed back her wet hair, took a deep breath, and blew it out in a lip-rattling rush. The anxious expression had not left her features; if anything, it looked more pronounced. Then, she gave up on the standing and crashed back down to the ground. "No, dammit," she said, draping her arms over her knees. "I am not fine. This is not fine."

Startled, he looked down at her. "What do you mean?"

"Ollie, what the hell are we doing? The Novas, the crab, this friggin'..." She gestured wildly. "This friggin' endless path to nowhere? And now, Laz is stuck down there? What are we doing? I think we're just making things worse!"

It was as if Tera had read his thoughts from just a few moments before. Hearing the words from her, though, made them seem twice as bad. "What? Where is this coming from?" he said quickly, waving away her concerns with a hand. "That's not true."

Her eyes searched his. "I don't think we're ever going to find them! What were we thinking? I don't think we can do this!"

"Of course, we will!" he said, sitting down beside her. "You know where you're going, right? You said it yourself. The soul mate...thing? You said you knew the right place to go to fix all of this. One step at a time, that's all. Easy does it, and one thing leads to another, and...all that. Of course, we'll find them!" He strung the cliches together with a certainty that he didn't feel.

"I don't know, Oll..." Tera's voice wavered. Her gaze focused on something behind him; something far away. "Something is off. I can feel it."

He knew exactly what she meant. He had been thinking the same thing since the moment he had first read his name in block letters on the wings of a moth. What was really going on here? Ollie recalled Laszlo's long-ago advice about surviving the Neath: *Forget your eyes,* Laz had said. Then he'd tapped a finger against Ollie's head and heart. *Your eyes do not know as much as those.*

What was he missing? What was illusion, and what was real?

Tera continued to stare into the distance. "Sometimes I think... I think I made the wrong decision," she said hesitantly. "Coming down here."

"What? No way."

"I'm serious," she said, shaking her head. "Maybe I should have stayed on the Brickside. Helped them fight the good fight. Helped to change things, up there. Instead, I took the easy way out. I could have been one of those women, working at the WRC. Maybe if I had been there, I could have stopped—"

Ollie interrupted her mid-sentence. "Of course you did the right thing! You did the only thing you *could* do! You were thirteen, for God's sake. An abused, neglected kid. Give yourself a break."

"And now I've dragged you into all this." Tera continued as though she hadn't heard him. "I made you stay down here."

"Tera, you did not make me stay."

"Well, maybe not, but I think you stayed because..." She hesitated. "I think you stayed because of me. Even though I told you not to do that, and—"

"I stayed because I wanted to stay," Ollie said. "Because my life is here. With you."

When Tera spoke again, her voice was nearly inaudible. "It's my fault they were taken, you know."

"What the...what?"

"You broke into that damn prison to rescue me, and look how that turned out!"

"It turned out...great," Ollie answered, perplexed. "Here we are, right? Safe and sound?"

"Yeah, but now someone wants payback, and they're targeting you, and they're targeting those women, and your friend, and your old boss...and none of it would have happened if I wasn't down here. Or if I hadn't gotten caught that day, by those Reds. Don't you see? It all leads back to me." Her expression was pained; her gaze dropped to the ground.

Ollie's mouth had fallen open. He was blaming himself, and Laszlo was blaming himself, and now—Tera was blaming herself, too? This was ridiculous.

"Tera, none of this is your fault. Do you hear me? The only people to blame are the people who did these awful things."

She didn't reply.

"I wouldn't change any of it," he added. "We did the right thing, making those reforms at the prison, no matter who it pissed off. I did the right thing, staying here. And you did the right thing, coming down here when you did. Thank God the WRC helped you. Thank God you came down here, or..." His voice trailed off. He didn't even want to think about the alternate possibilities for Tera's younger, more vulnerable self.

No response.

"Not to mention, the reason you got caught by the guards in the first place was because you were helping me. Remember? The idiot who got himself trapped in Herrick's End? I'd still be there now if it wasn't for you. So if there's anyone to blame around here, it's me."

Again, she stayed quiet.

Ollie struggled to think of one of his mom's useful sayings. Something to help drive his meandering point home. Oddly, though, it was his father's voice he heard in his ear—sudden and clear. *Regrets are like a backpack full of cannonballs,* the old man had once told him, long ago. *Not useful, just heavy.*

The recollection was so startling that it made him stiffen. Why had he never remembered that before now?

Ollie blinked. Then he said, "Tera, listen to me. Look at me."

Slowly, she turned her eyes up.

"You are the toughest, smartest, strongest person I know. Even though you've been through so much. Maybe *because* you've been through so much." Ollie shook his head, frustrated again, searching for the right words. "You're like... a paper cut, you know? So small, but so powerful. You never expect a paper cut to do what it does. To affect you so much. But then, there it is, and damn. It's always more than what it should be—more than you ever expect it to be. And nothing can touch it, you know? It's invincible. Nothing can heal it but time."

At that, she straightened. The beginnings of a smile began to curl her lips. "Just what every girl wants," she said wryly. "To be compared to a paper cut."

"You know what I mean," Ollie said, squirming.

"Is this what passes for romance on the Brickside these days? 'Be My Paper Cut' written on little candy hearts?"

"Well, yeah, until things get serious. Then it's more like, 'Be My Gushing Wound.'"

"Ah, of course."

"Band-Aid sales go through the roof on Valentine's Day," he added.

"Wow. Things really have changed up there."

"You have no idea."

As they grinned at each other, Ollie felt the familiar rush of jittery infatuation and contentment. He wanted, in that moment, to stop time. To forget about everything other than the glow of her bronze skin, the allure of her collarbone peeking through the drooping jumpsuit, the ever-present twinkle in her deep, brown eyes. Maybe he could start a Valentine's Day tradition in Neath. Why not? Tera deserved at least that, didn't she? Ollie would give her a whole bouquet of sparkly lakestars. Or a bucket of paints for her studio. Or both. Or more. Of course, he'd have to figure out when February 14 was. Come to think of it... Did they even have calendars down here?

Meatball interrupted his thoughts with a sudden, rapid waddle up Ollie's arm. The trog nibbled at his sleeve, insistently, then hopped down to the ground and started poking at Tera's feet with his bill.

She watched the trog with amusement. "Looks like somebody wants us to keep moving."

Weirdly, it did look exactly that way. Ollie regarded his furry friend with confused fascination. What was really going on inside that little brain?

"He's not wrong," Ollie said, reluctantly. He slapped his palms against his thighs, as though that might kickstart his moxie. "C'mon. We should get back to it. 'No time like the now,' as Laz would say."

"Yes, he would," she agreed.

Her voice was chipper, but Ollie saw through the bravado. His Tera—his brave, unflappable, self-confident Tera—was freaking out. Doubting herself, and indulging regret. And he didn't like it one bit.

Ollie kissed her forehead. "You can do this," he insisted. "*We* can do this. And hell, even if we screw it up, I'm sure Meatball can just take over and wrap the whole thing up. Trogs to the rescue. I already made him a little red cape."

She looked like she was trying to smile, but didn't.

That was when he reached for her, enveloping Tera's small body in his. He stopped talking and squeezed. She was crying, he realized. And much to his surprise, he didn't panic. She clung to him, and he stayed firm. Solid. He did not loosen his grip.

"Shhhh," Ollie murmured. "It's okay. It'll all be okay."

Maybe it would, maybe it wouldn't. But he would stay there as long it took to make her believe it.

Eventually, Tera's tears subsided. Ollie wished he could say the same about his own growing disquiet. But, like any good Catholic, he stuffed his feelings under a blanket of guilt and obligation and "put on a good face." A *faccia buona,* as his Nonna would have said. Then, with Meatball's continued prodding, they rose to their feet and started off again.

As the stroll stretched into a walk, which stretched into a hike, Ollie tried to quell the mounting suspicion that this entire leg of the journey might be a trick. Yet another mirage created by the Novas for God-knew-what reason. Or by Howerbout himself, in an effort to keep them from returning to rescue Laszlo. Or even by some other bizarre, scheming creature he had yet to meet. None of those scenarios would have surprised him in the least.

What did surprise him was a sudden parting in the stalagmites. An opening.

A road.

Ollie stopped short.

"What is it?" Tera asked from behind his back. When he didn't answer, she stepped around him.

Despite the dim wormwalker light and a thin film of fog, Ollie could see footprints—lots of footprints—in the wide dirt street. This was a thoroughfare, for sure. He could also see residential shacks in the distance, smoke rising from chimneys, and a cluster of brown, black, and white trogs chasing each other around a wheelbarrow filled with fabric sacks. Meatball did not move to join them.

Tera's face betrayed surprise, then delight. She pointed to a clump of buildings nearby. "I know where we are!" she exclaimed. "We're not far!"

"Far from what?" Ollie asked. He still didn't know what Tera had in mind. In truth, he had been kind of afraid to ask. As his old Herrick's End cellmate, Dozer, used to tell him, *Less questions you ask down here, the better.* Ollie had quickly learned he was right— and that even when you did ask, you rarely liked the answers.

But Tera's inner turmoil seemed to have dissipated at the sight of the small village ahead. She looked up at him with a victorious and relieved expression. "We're going to see the Salt Collector," she said.

"The what, now?"

"The *who,*" Tera corrected, pulling him along as she started to walk along the road. "You'll see. She has certain…skills."

"What kinds of skills?" he asked, letting himself be pulled. Yet another question he probably didn't want an answer to. Still, it was good to see some pep return to Tera's step.

"All kinds."

"Like finding soul mates?"

"Among other things."

Other things. Anywhere else, the phrase would have made him mildly curious. In the Neath, it made him want to turn and run. "And why is she called the Salt Collector?"

Tera looked up at him with raised eyebrows. After a beat, she said, "Because she collects salt."

"Oh. Right. But…why?"

"Hell if I know." Tera turned left and started to march.

This was more like it, he thought: Tera in charge, leading the way. A clear goal. And him just along for the ride.

"And you think she'll help us?" Ollie asked.

"For a price, yes."

Ah, he thought. *Of course. For a price.* Everything in this place had its price. Some steeper than others. "Yeah, but… How do you know? That she'll help?"

Tera gave him another sideways glance. "I live here, remember? I ferry people around all day. I hear things. I know things. It's kind of my job."

"Okay, okay," he said, holding up his hands. "I trust you. Salt Collector, here we come."

After just a few more turns, the road forked: The dirt path continued to the left, while a geometrically elaborate, stone-paved walkway appeared on the right. No signs were posted. Tera veered right.

The irregular stone pavers led them over a rise and then down into a similarly paved, circular area. It looked, to Ollie, like a suburban, backyard patio that had been dropped into the middle of nowhere. This particular patio, however, had no barbecue grill, or outdoor dining set, or raised flower beds. It had only a podium in the dead center, where a man waited, hands folded, wearing a regulation blue jumpsuit. He had a five o'clock shadow and an enormous beer belly, as though he had a standing nightly appointment at Moseby's tavern. He watched Ollie and Tera approach with the focus of a hunting hawk.

"How many for entry?" the man asked.

Ollie sighed inwardly. These podiums. Living in the Neath sometimes felt like an endless attempt to get a table when you're not on the list.

"Two," Tera said.

"And you've brought an offering?" he asked.

"We did." She reached inside her shirt—inside her bra, Ollie realized with surprise—and pulled out a packet of tightly wrapped lakeweed leaves. A waterproof package, Howerbout had assured them. At its appearance, Meatball stirred on Ollie's shoulder. He leaned over to sniff the leaves in Tera's hand, then lost interest and returned to his slumber.

The man at the podium also seemed unimpressed by the package. "Just one?"

"Well, yes," Tera said. "But it's a good one."

The attendant scrunched his face with displeasure. "Fine," he said. Then, in a more authoritative voice, he added, "Two for entry." He swept his hand toward a nearby clump of ferns that formed a sort of archway.

"Thank you," Tera said. She gave a curt smile to the man and tugged on Ollie's sleeve. "C'mon."

Ollie followed her through the opening in the greenery, quickly forgetting about the patio and the strange podium attendant as soon as he pushed the last of the leaves from his face.

They had stepped out into a clearing that contained the base of something...big. It was as high as a city apartment building, though that's where the similarities to a conventional structure ended. The mound, or temple, or whatever the hell it was, jutted and bent at cockeyed, random intervals, zig-zagging its way up toward the cavern's high ceiling. Bounteous, gravity-defying terraces hung from its sides. It reminded Ollie of something he might have seen in one of his childhood picture books: cartoonish and illogical. Stranger still, it seemed to get wider as it went up, with all of the weight somehow balanced on the pointier base.

The structure had an overall whitish tint: some sections seemed to be translucent, while others were more opaque. Ollie squinted: The terraces, he now saw, were connected by a series of rope bridges. And those were connected to the ground by a meandering, rough-hewn staircase, carved directly into the mound itself.

Stairs.

Ollie groaned.

"More climbing?" he whined. The complaint came out before he could stop it. He was so *tired*. So, so tired. And hungry. What had he eaten last? The fish, in Howerbout's cave. That seemed like a lifetime ago.

"Just up to there," Tera said, pointing to a scraggly, distant hut. It perched at the peak like a wedding-cake topper.

Was that supposed to reassure him? There had to be hundreds of steps. Thousands, maybe. Ollie's legs ached at the sight of them. This was an underground world, wasn't it? *Under*ground. So why the hell did he always seem to be going up?

Heartbreak Hill. That's what they called the big incline on the Boston Marathon route back home. The term had always made him shudder.

"Can't we just take a break, first?" he pleaded. "Two minutes. Five, tops. Right here, on the ground." Never had a patch of dirt looked so appealing. "Or maybe a snack? There must be something around here. Just something small?"

Tera gave him a sympathetic look. "No time, Oll."

And of course, she was right. She was always right. They had no time for hunger or cowardice or exhausted, feeble legs. Not now, when so much was apparently dependent on Ollie and Tera's ability to carry a bunch of soggy lakeleaves to the top of one very tall, very weird, and very goddamn heartbreaking hill.

Twelve

It was probably no coincidence that "hell" and "hill" differed by only one letter.

This thought occurred to him first when they began the climb, and then repeatedly afterward as they continued it. The steps were cruelly steep; at some points, he had to lift his foot almost to waist-level just to reach the next one. They were also lumpy, and crooked, and varying in size from normal to gigantic to teenier than a box of Good & Plenty. But the staircase, he soon realized, was going to be the least of their structural problems.

The first rope bridge appeared within five minutes or so. On first glance, it made Ollie think of the so-called "Wiggly Bridge" he and his mother had once visited in York, Maine: That crossing had been fun and adventurous, scenic and safe. These bridges? Not so much.

Constructed of frayed and too-thin ropes, the spans stretched across open air and led from platform to platform. "Wiggly" would have been much too generous a term for the motion Ollie felt as he crossed them. "Quivery" might have been more accurate, or "terrifyingly jerky," or "nauseating to the point of actual, rising vomit." They came one after another, after another, as Ollie and Tera continued to trek up and around the strange, white structure.

With each jump in height came an equally high jump in his blood pressure. The ground was getting further away, but the catwalks were not getting any more stable.

It didn't help that Meatball seemed to consider the entire behemoth his personal jungle gym; the trog raced across bridges, skittered up and down stairs, and darted under Ollie's feet with abandon. At each crossing, Ollie insisted that Tera wait until he reached the other side before stepping her own feet onto the scaffold. If anything was going to make these precarious suspensions tear free and crash to the ground, it would be his enormous, heavy body. And he'd be damned if he was going to let Tera go down with him.

After six or seven crossings, they seemed to be about halfway up. Ollie paused for a rest on one of the terraces, panting and leaning against the wooden railing. Tera, also breathing heavy, came to stand beside him.

"Check this out," she said. Then she slid her finger against one of the structure's jagged outcroppings, brought her finger to her mouth, and licked it.

Ollie grimaced. "What the hell are you doing?"

"Go ahead, try," she smiled.

"No! That's disgusting!"

"Aw, go ahead," Tera said, giving his arm a playful shove.

Hesitantly, Ollie reached out and copied her motions. The surface was firm and white, with a granular, somewhat loose coating. He touched his finger to his tongue.

"Salty!" he said with surprise.

Tera nodded, looking pleased.

He looked around, suddenly seeing the topsy-turvy tower with fresh eyes. "Is this... Is it all...salt? Like, *made* of salt?"

"I think so, yeah."

"But...how?"

"Who knows?" she answered.

Who knows. Those two words could have been the official motto of the Neath, Ollie thought. Somebody should embroider it onto a flag. He took another taste of the salt wall, instantly regretting it as thirst pinged his mouth. "Let's keep going," he said, hoping against hope that this Salt Collector, whoever she was, happened to have a refrigerated soda-vending machine in that hut of hers. And plenty of quarters, too.

They didn't talk much—couldn't talk much—as they completed the last of the climb. Around and around they went, from stair to bridge to terrace ad nauseum, until finally reaching the peak. Ollie bent over, hands on knees, heaving. He was amazed to have made it. After several minutes of coughs and gasps, he glanced up. The hut was there, just a few feet ahead. And it did not, amazingly enough, look like it was made of salt.

Like the other houses in the Neath, this one seemed to be constructed from a hodge-podge of collected materials. Sheet metal, wood planks, and fabric made up the walls, while the roof looked like dried fern leaves that had been stacked and flattened into shingle-like clumps.

Meatball was already digging curiously through a nearby pile of brush and discarded trash.

"See? Not too far," Tera said.

Ollie looked at her from his bent-over position. His lungs felt like they had just passed through the surface of the sun. "Are you kidding me right now?" he wheezed.

She smiled sweetly.

Ollie waited until he could inhale without pain. Then he straightened.

"Ready?" Tera asked.

He nodded.

"Alrightee, then. Let's do this." She marched ahead with determined strides; Ollie and Meatball scrambled to catch up. When they reached the hut, there was no door to knock or bell to ring. There was only a sign:

Please wipe face and neck thoroughly before entering.

Ollie tilted his head. He couldn't help but think of another sign—the very first thing he had seen after falling through the Freedom Trail and landing, butt-first, in the Neath. *Please take only one.*

That sign had been posted near an assortment of torches. This one hung next to a basket that held two folded, colored cloths: one orange, one brown. Ollie and Tera looked at each other in momentary confusion, then complied. He chose the orange and handed her the brown; he had to admit, it felt good to dry his face.

Refreshing. When they were done, they returned the used cloths to the basket and lingered in hesitation, until they heard a voice emerge from deep inside.

"I don't suppose you came all this way just to stand on the stoop."

Ollie and Tera looked at each other again. Meatball climbed Ollie's torso and settled onto his usual spot. Then all three of them stepped through the doorway.

The space was well-lit, with dozens of flickering wall sconces casting a warm glow in every direction. A few throw rugs and sparse furnishings added to the overall sense of hominess: one table, one chair, and one small bed pushed to the outer edges, surrounding a central firepit with a cooking grate. And on every wall, every shelf, every surface, he saw jars. Clear glass jars, all filled with crystals of varying shades and opacities. Most were white; some were pink, or gray, or yellowed.

Salt, Ollie realized. The array was seemingly endless: jars stacked on top of jars, piled everywhere, teetering and toppling—some even hanging from the ceiling by thick coils of string, like the macrame hangars his mom used to bring home from flea markets.

Ollie had not realized that so many varieties of salt existed in the world. He wondered, briefly, how they had all come to be here. And why anyone would possibly want them.

"You bring an offering?" the raspy voice said.

It was coming from behind them. Ollie and Tera spun around to see a rotund, short woman, swaddled from head to toe in thick fabric. Her head was wrapped in a scarf; her body, in something that looked like a woolen, knitted afghan. Everything about her was swollen. Her face made Ollie think of a split baked potato, fresh from the oven, topped with melting lumps of butter. A pair of sunken, dark eyes peered out from the potato suspiciously.

Ollie was too startled to speak. Luckily, Tera piped up: "Yes."

"What offering do you bring Weelichka?" the woman asked.

"We bring a rare specimen," Tera answered.

"Bring it forward, then," the woman croaked, her voice scratching like an insult against the open air.

So much for pleasantries, Ollie thought. He trailed behind Tera as she joined the woman—was her name Weelichka?—at the fire pit. Tera pulled the leaf-wrapped package from her bra and held it out.

The puffy-faced woman frowned. "I hope you have brought Weelichka more than rotten lakeweed," she said crossly.

"Yes," Tera said. "Of course. That's just the, uh, wrapping. To protect it. We were underwater."

Weelichka's stern expression didn't change.

Hurriedly, Tera tore the leaves and pulled out the prize inside: a sodden, stinking rag, soaked clean through with Howerbout's pungent sweat. Ollie took a step back, his face twisting in revulsion.

Weelichka, in the other hand, broke out into a wide smile. She reached out to clutch the rag with both hands. "Ah!" she breathed. "This is rare, indeed! From where does it come?"

"It's, uh..." Tera paused, looking at Ollie.

"It's from a crab-man," he said.

"Crab-man, you say?" Weelichka repeated, looking doubtful.

He nodded. "Like, half crustacean, half man."

"Hmm." The Salt Collector seemed to consider this, running her fingers along the fabric. "Very well."

At that, she went to work. Ollie and Tera moved out of the way as Weelichka began to whirl around the hut like a spinning spider, tossing logs onto the fire pit, banging pots against each other, and murmuring indecipherable incantations. Finally, she selected one medium-sized frying pan, dropped it onto the cooking grate, poured in a spoonful of greenish liquid, and held the soggy rag over the pan ceremoniously.

For a moment, Ollie held his breath. He watched the rag. Would it burst into flame? Change colors? Explode into sparkling fireworks?

But the rag did none of those things. Instead, it just... stayed a rag. And Weelichka the Salt Collector began to squeeze it. Twist it. Talk to it.

Ollie looked at Tera, then back at the strange old woman. She was wringing it out, he realized. Squeezing Howerbout's sweat from the fabric's pores and watching it dribble into the pan. *Drip, drip, drip.* He covered his mouth, disgusted. Meatball lifted his head and snuffled the air, as if noticing something amiss.

After several minutes, Weelichka had apparently wrung all of the stinky moisture she could out of the rag. There didn't seem to be much; maybe a tablespoon or two. She tossed the cloth to the ground and reached for a big wooden spoon. Then, she began to stir.

The woman twirled the spoon into rapturous circles, humming and singing and even dancing around the fire as she worked. And as Ollie and Tera watched, the liquid—the sweat—began to evaporate. It bubbled away into puffs of short-lived smoke, leaving behind a small but distinct clump of yellowy-brown crystals at the bottom of the pan.

Salt.

Ollie's gag reflex kicked in; he pressed his arm against his mouth. Tera rubbed his back, though she, too, looked like some of the color had drained from her face.

And just when he thought the worst was over, Weelichka the Salt Collector pinched a few crystals between her thumb and forefinger, brought them to her mouth, and...tasted them.

Ollie slammed his eyes shut in revulsion. But he couldn't escape the sounds—the delirious, slurping smacks—of the old woman savoring her latest creation.

When he finally, reluctantly, reopened his eyes, he saw Tera take a thick swallow, fold her arms, and ask, "It's good?"

"Oh, yes," the woman smiled. "Weelichka likes this. Very, very good."

"Great," Tera said. She cleared her throat again. "So, you'll help us?"

"That is the deal," the old woman said, shrugging with disinterest. "One offering, one answer."

Tera glanced at Ollie with the barest nod and continued: "This creature, this crab-man. We need to find his soul mate."

"Ah, soul mates," the woman said, as though the word brought back fond memories. "The strings that connect us. The structures of our being." Her dark-pit eyes took on a faraway look.

"Right." Ollie resisted the urge to wave a hand in front of her face. "So you can find him? Or her? Or, uh, it? The soul mate?"

"Of course I can," Weelichka said, sounding mildly insulted. "It is what I do."

Among other things, he thought, but didn't say it out loud.

"I need only a piece of that person, or that creature. This, you have already brought," she added, pointing to the crystals in the pan. "You understand what it is, a soul mate? You understand what question you are asking?"

"Well, yeah," Ollie said. "It's like, your person. The love of your life."

Weelichka shook her head. "This is a common misconception," she rasped, sounding almost sad. "A soul mate is not, necessarily, a romantic partner. It can be, of course, but it need not be. A soul mate is simply that. A mate for your soul. Someone you have met, or will meet. Someone who will touch your life in profound ways. Ways you might not even recognize at the time."

The old woman looked from Ollie to Tera and back again. "This person might be still living, or already passed. You might have known the person for decades, or mere moments. Sometimes, you will recognize your mate's importance to your story right away. Sometimes, much later. And in rare cases, you never do. It makes little difference. All of us were destined to meet our mate, at one point or another. And when we do, our lives are altered profoundly."

The speech was so long it threatened to outlast her voice; by the time she was done, the croak had been reduced to a barely audible sibilation.

Ollie was wondering how to get her back on track when the potato-like woman scooped all the remaining salt in her hand and brought it up to her face. She inhaled so deeply that Ollie thought some of the crystals might have been swept up into her nose.

Weelichka smacked her lips. She hummed some more. And then she opened her eyes.

"This creature's soul mate is still living," she said, staring up at the ceiling in a kind of trance. "The location is nearby. You will find the mate in the dark place where cages rest, where all things are like he is. Half of one, half of another altogether. An unclean place. Crowds gather. Nefarious and foul crowds, with nefarious and foul intentions. You will need entry, but entry is not free. The sign above holds a name: Carmichael. I see the name clearly. But that name does not belong to the mate."

Weelichka paused, or maybe stopped altogether. Ollie couldn't tell. In the silence that followed, he looked at Tera, whose entire body had stiffened.

"What is it?" he asked. "What's wrong?"

"I know who that is," she said.

"Who, Carmichael?"

Tera nodded and rubbed her forehead with three fingers. Back and forth, back and forth.

"Great! So let's go see him!" Ollie said.

"I can't."

"Why not?"

She didn't immediately answer; instead, she reached for Meatball. Lifting the trog off of Ollie's shoulder, she held him tightly in her arms. Ollie could see that her jaw was clenched. She began patting Meatball with an intensity and speed that seemed to unnerve the rotund little creature. But when he wiggled, she gripped him even tighter.

"Tera!"

"What?"

"Easy, there," Ollie said, pointing to the struggling trog.

"Oh, sorry."

"What is it?" he asked. "Why can't we go see this guy?"

"Because if I see him, I might kill him," she muttered, still raking her fingers like an angry gardener through Meatball's fur. "And the asshole can't talk if he's dead."

Her mouth clamped shut, her expression hardened, and Ollie knew better than to press. Whoever this Carmichael was, and however he might have wronged her, Tera was done talking about it. When she was ready—if she was ready—she'd share.

Meatball managed to escape Tera's overzealous affection and hopped to the ground, sniffing his way around the cottage.

Alrightee. Since that subject seemed to be prematurely closed, Ollie used the awkward moment as an opportunity to ask their host for a drink. He braced himself for what that might mean to Weelichka: a briny slush, maybe, or a warm, dirty, metal-tinged solvent. Instead, much to his surprise, she brought them two glasses of ice-cold, clean water. Just...water. It was more than he could have hoped for. Perfectly perfect perfection. Both Ollie and Tera gulped the glasses to empty and then asked for seconds. Weelichka seemed happy to comply.

Ollie decided to push his luck. "I don't suppose... Do you have something to eat?"

"Eat? Yes, of course." The question seemed to confuse her.

When she didn't move, he added: "For us, I mean."

Weelichka wiped her hands on her crocheted wrap, considering the request. "I will bring you poonchkee," she finally said. "You wait here."

The waddling woman disappeared for a moment behind a drawn curtain, then emerged with a tray heaped high with something that looked like puffy, doughy balls. She set the tray down in front of them. Ollie's eyes went wide as recognition dawned: They looked like...doughnuts! Browned with beautiful precision. Dusted with powdered sugar. Could it possibly be? Did he even dare to hope?

Poonchkee, she had called them. Ollie lifted one to his nose and inhaled. The smell brought him back in a startling instant to his former life aboveground: Bonfiglio's Caffe, bakery boxes, biscotti lined up in tidy little rows. Cappuccino. Tiramisu. Sfogliatelle. An insanely thick, layered concoction that Mr. B had called "Chocolate Lasagna." Every crumb and creamy dollop slammed into his memory bank like a freight train of forgotten delectability. Ollie licked the powdery coating on his finger. His eyes widened.

"Sugar!" he said to Tera.

They beamed at each other with surprised delight.

Ollie's stomach roared, echoing in the air around them. He took an enormous bite without even realizing he was doing it: just opened his mouth, chomped down, and prepared to savor. A fraction of a second later, he froze mid-chew. His tongue rejected it before his brain could catch up—the next thing he knew, he was spitting out the mouthful all over the floor.

"What's wrong?" Tera asked, jumping back.

"Thalt!" Ollie sputtered. He was scraping his tongue clean with his fingertips. The entire cavity of the pastry was filled with tiny, white, sparkling crystals. Enough to fill a shot glass. Or two.

Weelichka folded her arms. She gave a disapproving look at the spit-out wad on the floor. "Of course, it's salt," she said, her voice scraping with the gravel of a pack-a-day smoker. "What else?"

It was a fair question, he supposed.

Tera put a hand on his arm and stepped forward with a smile. "Forgive us, Weelichka," she said. "We don't yet have your refined palette. Do you have anything that's just...plain?"

"Plain? No. There are no *plain* poonchkee." The idea seemed to disgust her. Then, she sighed. "But I do have others. Others with—" She paused, as though the words were difficult to say, then valiantly finished: "With no salt."

"That would be great, thanks," Tera said. "We'd really appreciate it."

Ollie reached for his glass and slurped what was left of the water, wiping his mouth with the back of his hand.

When Weelichka returned, she had a much smaller plate with a much smaller pile. Just four poonchkee, this time, though they looked much the same as the one Ollie had already tried. He eyed the quartet suspiciously.

"Let me," Tera muttered. She reached for a dough lump, held it up to Weelichka in a gesture of thanks, then took the tiniest of tiny bites. Then another, and another. Her tongue darted out to lick her lips. The skin around her eyes crinkled with rapture. "What…is this?" she asked.

"Ach," Weelichka said with a dismissive wave. "Custard. My grandmother's recipe. Horrible woman."

Custard? Ollie's arm shot out to grab the nearest poonchkee. He hesitated only a moment before taking a cautious nibble. He tasted fried dough, and powdered sugar, and…something remarkably sweet and tart. Something stupendous. His eyes actually watered with the joy of it. "Raspberry jam!" he said.

"Yes, yes," Weelichka said, decidedly unimpressed. "And that one is plum, and that one is apple."

Ollie and Tera stared at each other wordlessly, chewing with glee. Perfectly perfect perfection, again. After taking another bite, Ollie held out his raspberry poonchkee to her. She nodded eagerly, and they switched. Ollie went more slowly with the custard, marveling at the sensation of smooth, sweet cream mingling with the rich, heavy dough. He tore off a piece and shared it with Meatball, who snapped it expertly into his bill.

Tera stared down at the last bite of pastry in her hand. "It's…it's…"

"It's heaven!" Ollie finished for her and meant it. He looked up at the Salt Collector in wonder. "Weelichka, you're a genius! You should make these for everyone! You could open a stall at the Tea Party!" He resisted the urge to drop to his knees.

"No," the old woman rasped, shaking her head firmly. "Poonchkee are only for those who make offerings."

Ollie was already reaching for another. The sugar and fat swept through his veins like an IV infusion of blood to a dying man. Weelichka was still talking, but he had stopped listening. And by the time he felt the runny plum filling dribbling down his chin, Ollie had forgotten all about soul mates, and ransom notes, and underwater labs, and anything other than the heavy, sweet deliciousness in his hands.

Thirteen

"Ollie."

He licked his fingers.

"Ollie!"

"Hmm?" He looked up, dazed. All at once, Ollie envisaged what he must look like: hunched and grunting and covered with smears of powdered sugar. A Poonchkee Troll.

He straightened. "Sorry. Did you want some of th—" He realized with sudden shame that he had eaten the entire plum-filled doughnut and already started in on the apple. "God, I'm sorry. Here." He held out what was left.

"You keep it," Tera said, letting out a small groan and clutching her stomach. "Those things are like lead weights."

He probably should have insisted, or at least argued. Instead, he closed his eyes and continued to gobble the apple pastry, drowning happily in cinnamon and nutmeg and thick, gelatinous goo.

When he opened them again, he saw Tera helping their hostess straighten up, carrying the frying pan to a basin sink. Ollie watched the two women chit-chat as they worked. He luxuriated in the feeling of a full belly. He pondered his situation. And then, slowly, he began to formulate an idea.

Tera was his partner, his love—his destiny. She had to be. His life had been transformed when he met her. He thought about her all the time. He'd probably kill for her. Or even die for her. Hell, he'd already given up his whole life aboveground just to be with her, and he would happily do it again.

Granted, Tera hadn't had a whole lot of other options when she met him—it's not like the Neath was crawling with eligible bachelors. But still, he had to believe that they had been destined to find each other. How else to explain his feelings? And their connection? If ever two people were soul mates, it had to be Ollie and Tera. There was no doubt in his mind. But here, now, in this place, he could do more than just believe it.

He could prove it.

And once it was official, Tera would understand, *really* understand, that they were meant to be together, forever. And then Ollie could stop worrying about losing her.

Because he did worry about it. Constantly. All the time he used to spend obsessing about his weight had been replaced by time obsessing about Tera spotting some handsome Neath hunk— maybe a vendor at the Tea Party, or some fare in her boat, or another clueless Brickside expat needing rescue—and realizing that she had options. Better options than the likes of him.

But if Weelichka could confirm what he already knew, that would change the game entirely.

Unfortunately, he also knew that the old woman wouldn't do that. Not a chance. She had made it clear when they arrived: One offering, one answer. Period. And they had already used up their quota.

Ollie slumped. He gazed fondly at the last bit of poonchkee before tearing it, giving half to Meatball, and popping the rest into his mouth. He chewed thoughtfully. He examined his surroundings, contemplating everything he had seen in his short time on this wonky, salty mountain. Then he looked up. His mouth still half full, he said, "This is a nice hut."

"Thank you," Weelichka answered. Her voice had a note of pride.

"Why'd you decide to build it way up here?"

She paused her pan scrubbing to look at him curiously. "What do you mean?"

"It must have been hard, lugging all the materials up here. Seems like it would have been easier to build it on the ground."

"Maybe so," Weelichka said. "I like the view."

Ollie looked around. "There are no windows."

She turned toward him, hands resting on her hips. "What's your point?"

"My point is, there's no logical reason for you to live all the way up here. So I was just wondering why you do."

Weelichka didn't answer. Tera was giving him a warning look.

"I have a guess," Ollie said, rising to his feet. He wiped his sugary hands on his jumpsuit. "I think you want people to have to work really hard to get here. You want them nice and sweaty when they arrive, don't you?"

The old woman's mouth set into a hard line, and Ollie knew he was right.

"You make us climb and kill ourselves, and then you leave those cloths in your fancy basket at the door, and then, as soon as we leave... Jackpot. You're stealing our sweat."

Tera's eyebrows shot up.

"That's how you fill all these pretty little jars, isn't it?" he pressed.

"Weelichka is doing no such thing," she answered defiantly, folding her arms.

"Then you won't mind if we take them with us," Ollie said, keeping his tone casual. "The towels, I mean. Hey Tera, would you mind grabbing the—"

"Those are my cloths!" the old woman interrupted.

"And that's our sweat," Ollie retorted, pulling himself to his full height and looking down at her sternly. "Which means we didn't bring one offering, we brought three. By my count, that means you owe us two more answers."

Weelichka's potato face glowered beneath her scarf. After a hesitation, she tightened her wrap on her shoulders. "Fine. Two more answers, and then you will leave."

"Great," Ollie smiled. He glanced at Tera, who looked bewildered. "We'd like to know *our* soul mates."

Did the woman roll her eyes? He could have sworn that she did. "Always the same with your kind, isn't it?" she grumbled. Then she pointed to Tera. "You. Girl. Give me your arm."

"What do you mean?" Tera asked, recoiling.

"Your arm! Your arm!" Weelichka waved her own limbs through the air with impatience. "You want the reading, or not?"

"I...guess so," Tera said. She looked at Ollie in continued confusion. When he gave a quick nod of encouragement, she lifted her left arm into the air.

"Closer," muttered the Salt Collector. "Closer. *Closer*. Hello? Closer, girl!" Finally, when Tera was only inches away, the woman grasped her arm, leaned in, and...licked it.

Tera scrunched her face in disgust. It looked like it was taking all of her willpower to keep her arm extended as Weelichka probed the skin with her tongue. "Is this really necessary?" she asked, holding her body stiff.

The Salt Collector ignored the question. She tasted. She paused. She seemed to be considering something. Then she made her pronouncement.

"I'm afraid, my dear, that your mate has passed."

For a moment, no one moved. Then Tera asked, "Passed what?"

"Passed *on,*" Weelichka said. "Died. Your mate is deceased."

Tera seemed dumbstruck.

"That's impossible," Ollie said.

"Alas, it is very possible," the old woman said. "You remember, as I told you: Your mate might have already left this life."

"I don't understand," Tera said. "Who is—who was it?"

Weelichka closed her beady eyes. "I am seeing only...a word. I do not understand this word. It sounds like...Aboo...Aboo, whale...a."

Tera's hand clasped over her mouth. *"Abuela!* My grand-mother!"

"Yes," agreed the Salt Witch. She puffed her already puffy cheeks and looked up at the ceiling, as though watching a projection. "I am seeing... I am seeing that your *abuela* protected you for as long as she could."

Tears sprang to Tera's eyes. She nodded rapidly. When she spoke, her voice was unsteady. "She did. She really did."

"She wishes she could have done more," Weelichka said, her tone matter-of-fact.

Ollie looked from one to the other. What the hell was going on here? That couldn't be right. "That's ridiculous," he said, the words popping out before he could stop them.

Tera looked at him, aghast. "Ollie!"

"No! Wait a sec! I don't mean your grandmother was ridiculous. I mean..." He was making it worse. Now flustered, he turned to look at Weelichka. "You're wrong! *This* is wrong. Her grandmother can't be her soul mate."

"Why not?" the old woman asked.

"Because *I* am!"

But Tera was clutching her chest, almost reverently. Thinking about her *abuela,* he could tell.

"Here, do me!" he shouted, shoving an arm under Weelichka's nose. "Then you'll see! Go ahead."

Annoyance flashed across the Salt Collector's features. "Fine." She gave a long look at her guests, then leaned forward and sniffed Ollie's arm. He flinched as her tongue darted out and grazed his skin. It felt like a cat's: sandpapery and furtive. Again, the proclamation came in a sudden rush:

"Your mate is here, in the Neath," she said.

"See?" Ollie blurted, looking at Tera with an eager smile.

"Wait," Weelichka said. She licked his arm a second time then paused, giving Ollie a look of suspicion. "What are you trying to pull, young man?"

"Huh?" Ollie took a small step back. "Nothing."

"What is this about?" The woman's eyebrows furrowed; her tongue dabbed at her lips as though tasting something foul.

"What is what about?" Ollie said. "You're the one who's supposed to be all...soul-searchy. So tell her! Go ahead! Tera's my soul mate. Tell her!"

"Your mate is male," Weelichka growled. Her eyes darted left to right. "But this doesn't make sense."

"Damn right, it doesn't!" Ollie yelped. "You're wrong." A leaden weight was beginning to settle on his chest. This was a mistake, he suddenly realized. This whole thing was a mistake. They shouldn't have come here.

"Weelichka is not *wrong,*" the witch said. "Weelichka is never wrong. Not about this."

Tera nodded in reluctant confirmation. "It's true," she told Ollie.

The old woman rubbed her lumpy head. "But you... I don't understand. Your mate is here. Well, was here. Then, mostly here. But not entirely?" The shawl had slipped from her shoulders; she righted it. "You have a very close connection. Yes. My goodness, yes. It's...a..." She closed her eyes, opened them again. "He communicates with you directly. Writing? Words? Yes. He gives you words without speaking them directly. He is gone, and he speaks to you still!"

No.

No, no, no.

Ollie looked at Tera, who let out a long, low whistle. "Damn," she whispered. "Your soul mate is George Herrick!"

"What? No! Jesus! Of course not! This is ridiculous," Ollie sputtered.

Weelichka puffed out her cheeks again, looking confused. She started to speak, then stopped. With a sudden gasp, she dropped Ollie's arm and backed away. The color seemed to have drained from her face.

"What?" Ollie said.

The Salt Collector lifted a shaking finger. "You!"

Her expression was unnerving. She was looking at Ollie like he was radioactive. Contagious. Covered in swarming maggots. Reflexively, he reached for Meatball. But the trog was several feet away, using his flippered feet to scrape dribbles of poonchkee filling off the floor.

"You should have told me about the rest!" she screeched.

"The rest of...what?" Ollie asked, genuinely bewildered.

"Of that!" Weelichka pointed to Ollie's arm, at the spot she had just licked.

He looked down and saw the skin reddening, like before. This time, small bumps had started to form. When did that happen? Was his Brickside skin reacting badly to Weelichka's tongue? Wait—were the little bumps...glowing? They looked almost like freckles. But brighter. Ollie furrowed his brow, perplexed. But he had no time to ponder it before her voice accosted him again.

"Why do you come here?" the old woman demanded. Her already pasty skin was growing pastier by the second.

Ollie and Tera threw each other glances. "We told you," Tera said. "We need to know—"

"Why do you bring *him* here?" Weelichka amended, not taking her gaze from Ollie's face. There was no doubt about it—her curiosity had turned to fear. She was afraid. Of him? The possibility was laughable.

Ollie lifted his palms. "Listen, ma'am. I think you're confusing us with—"

"You need to leave," the witch interrupted again. Her rasp had deepened. "Now. Both of you."

"Oh, c'mon!" he protested. "This is...I mean, this is just..."

His voice trailed off as the old woman began to tremble. It wasn't a normal kind of a shaking—more like the menacing quake of a rattlesnake tail. Ollie took a step back, alarmed, as a series of frantic thoughts began to dart through his head. First, he wondered if she was having some kind of a seizure. Then, he wondered if he remembered his CPR lessons, taken at the Engine 8/Ladder 1 firehouse five—six?—years ago. Then, he wondered if CPR even worked in the Neath. Or on witches. And finally, he wondered why she had suddenly stopped shaking and grabbed his arm.

Ollie tried to pull away, but found his efforts useless. She was dug in, nails and all.

Weelichka's eyes had gone pink and glazed over like two tiny candy apples. Then, a voice escaped from the cavern of her mouth. A voice that sounded unlike her own. "I deliver a message," the voice said. "For you."

"For...me?"

"I deliver a message," she said again. "For you. Three points. One key. Water, earth, air."

Ollie startled. *Water, earth, air.* Those were the same words Bert the Witch had spoken to him, back at the nest.

Weelichka started to moan, then chant. Her eyes closed. "Water, earth, air. Water, earth, air. Three points make one key. Not here, but there. Not down, but up. Up and up and up."

Ollie's breath caught. Something about the woman's strange words felt like pinpricks.

"Water!" she groaned. "Water first. The water of your youth. From Myrtle to Coral, and then further still." She dipped her head, continuing as if in a trance. "Earth! Earth second. Herrick's home.

The place of his sin. The remnants of the victims will guide you." Weelichka stopped, hummed, twisted her neck.

Tera was gripping his back; Ollie's feet felt like they had grown roots into the floor.

The old woman continued: "Air! Air third. Two-twenty-one, two-ninety-four. Climb to fly. Walk the sky."

Her head dropped—then, just as suddenly, snapped back up. She stared through shiny-red, unseeing eyes. "Your rage will show you."

Tera and Ollie looked at each other in bewilderment, then back to the woman.

"Show me...what?" Ollie asked.

"Your rage will show you who you are."

The assertion made him feel oddly defensive. What the hell was that supposed to mean? "I...I know who I am."

She gave a harsh, mean laugh. "You know nothing. But your rage will show you. Soon, your rage will show us all."

Weelichka wobbled. The candy-apple coating on her eyes began to fade, leaving two black, angry dots. "Enough," she coughed. Her voice sounded more like her own. "It is done. I have delivered your message. You have received your answers in fair barter. Now you will leave this place and not return." She swept her hands forward, as if shooing flies.

Ollie opened his mouth to protest. This witch was batty. And obviously confused. If anyone had a rage problem around here, it was her—not him. But before he could speak, Tera grabbed his arm.

"Let's go," she muttered.

"But—"

"Let's *go*." Tera had already scooped up Meatball and was hugging the trog tight.

The room started tilting as they moved toward the door.

But, but, but...

This didn't make any sense. None of it.

Water, earth, air? *What about them?* he wanted to scream.

When Ollie was a kid, he had taken a school field trip to an amusement park in New Hampshire, where he had waited in line for a ride called the "Turkish Twist." The experience was a lot like being trapped inside a clothes dryer, spinning faster and faster until your body was squashed up against the wall of the drum by the simple force of gravity. That's what Ollie felt like now. Flattened. Dizzy. Moments away from upchucking the ten pounds of poonchkee he had scarfed down only minutes before.

Weelichka's vague "messages" had left him reeling with dozens of unanswered questions. But in that moment, he only cared about two:

What did it mean, if George Herrick was his soul mate?

Worse, what did it mean if Tera wasn't?

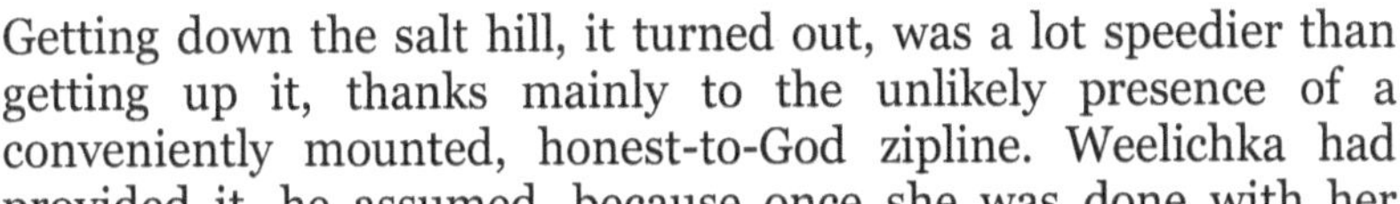

Getting down the salt hill, it turned out, was a lot speedier than getting up it, thanks mainly to the unlikely presence of a conveniently mounted, honest-to-God zipline. Weelichka had provided it, he assumed, because once she was done with her visitors, she wanted them gone as fast as possible. And she didn't care how sweaty they got on the way out.

Ollie had never used a zipline. He had never even *thought* about using a zipline. And if he had, he was fairly certain he would have started thinking about something else as soon as possible.

Tera hooked the harness around his crotch, which made him redden. She yanked on the wire and reassured him that the line was sturdy and safe. Then she flew down first to prove it. He watched her go, his fearless love—her purple hair lifted in the rush of air, her graceful arms wrapping the harness rope—and felt a similar rush of admiration and desire. Would he ever tire of watching her, of wanting her? Would he ever stop counting every lucky star for her existence in this strange, dark, and spectral place? A minute later, she landed safely at the bottom and unhooked herself from the contraption. She waved, and he was ready to fall back to her.

"Hold on tight, buddy," Ollie said to Meatball, his voice wavering.

He needn't have worried about that: The trog's claws nearly tore holes through his shoulder as they jumped from the ledge and sailed through the air. The line dipped, then straightened, sending them flying downward at ever-increasing speeds. A high whine emitted from Meatball's nostrils.

"It's okay," Ollie heard himself say, not sure if he was talking to the trog or himself. He clung to the harness rope with shaking arms as the wind whipped his face. "It's okay, it's okay, it's okay..."

Tera was getting bigger by the second. He kept his eyes fixed on her body. As the line leveled out, he slowed. Finally, the ground appeared within miraculous, wonderful reach, and he stepped onto it.

"See?" she said. "Nothing to it."

"Right," Ollie said with a shrug he didn't feel. "It was...fun."

He unclipped his carabiner and removed the harness. Tera's equipment was already lying in a heap on the ground. Together, they left the zipline and the Salt Collector behind and started to walk. Since Tera, as usual, seemed to know exactly where she was going, he simply followed along. Ollie didn't want to talk about what had just happened.

In fact, he decided, maybe it would be best just to forget all about that crazy potato-faced woman and her crazy ramblings. Yes. That's exactly what he would do. Weelichka had been right about Howerbout's soul mate, and wrong about his. And that was all there was to it.

They crossed a small bridge, walked through a rhizer agricultural field, and approached a pond choked with vibrating hummingtail reeds. A path of flat stones in the water provided an easy crossing. The hummingtails grew louder as they approached. Like the cattails back home, these made Ollie think of corndogs skewered on green sticks. Unlike Brickside reeds, though, the hummingtails contracted and expanded like tiny accordions, letting out a harmonious, buzzing song that radiated across the pond. Thundered, really. Ollie pressed his hands against his ears as he stepped on the first of the crossing stones.

"So, we're, uh, going to see Carmichael?" he shouted over the din.

"Looks that way," Tera answered, jumping from one stone to the next.

"And you know where that is?"

"Yep."

He waited for her to elaborate. She didn't.

Who is Carmichael? he wanted to ask. Instead, he pressed his lips together. *Patience, you idiot. Patience.*

Three more stones. Hop, hop, hop. Then five more. Finally, they had crossed the entire pond and left the hummingtail cacophony behind. The question still weighed on his tongue: *Who is Carmichael?* Ollie told himself that she would share when she was ready. If she was ever ready. And if she wasn't, that was fine, too. Totally fine. Her past was her past. He should just be glad that he got to share in her present. After all, it was none of his busin—

"So, who's Carmichael?" he blurted. Then sighed.

The wet pond had given way to a thicket of giant ferns; Tera pushed her way past a snowshoe-sized leaf before parroting Ollie's question. "Who is Carmichael?" she said, as though contemplating the query for the first time. "Hmm. Well, you know that guy up on the Brickside, the one who drives the biggest, most threatening-looking pickup truck he can find?" she asked. "With stupid giant tires and smoky exhaust? And then he covers it with stickers that say stuff like, 'My kid banged your honor student's math teacher?'"

"Uh huh," Ollie said. He certainly did.

"And then he takes it onto the highway, and he weaves in and out of traffic, and tailgates, and flashes his high beams at everybody to scare them into moving the hell out of his way?"

Ollie nodded.

"And when he sees his exit, he cuts off two lanes of traffic without even glancing into his mirrors, and nearly causes six different pileups, and doesn't give a shit?"

"Yep," Ollie said.

"And then he gets off the highway, and he rolls through every stop sign, because he thinks the rules don't apply to him, and nobody in the world matters *but* him? And when he finally gets where he's going, he parks in the handicapped spot? Even though he's not handicapped? And nobody dares to confront him, because everybody knows he's probably got a shotgun stashed somewhere in the cab of that truck, and who wants to risk that? And so he just gets away with it? Every single goddamn day?"

"Uh huh."

"Yeah, well, that's him," Tera said, a scowl pulling at her face. "Except that he probably wouldn't be caught dead in a pickup truck. More like a... I don't know. I don't know cars. Something flashy. Because God forbid everyone isn't looking at him every minute of every day." She rolled her eyes. "But you know what I mean."

"So, your basic douchebag," Ollie said.

"You got it," she answered grimly. "That's Michael."

Ollie tilted his head. "Wait a sec. I thought his name was Carmichael."

"That's his last name."

"So, his name is...Michael Carmichael?"

"Yep."

"Huh," Ollie muttered. "Well, that probably explains a lot."

Tera shrugged, then kept moving. The subject of Michael Carmichael, Douchebag Extraordinaire, seemed to be closed once again.

Once they pushed through the ferns, they walked for only a few hundred feet or so before coming across a road. They had reached civilization again—or at least what passed for civilization in this part of the world. Huts, and wheelbarrows, and smoke rising from holes in ceilings. There were a few larger buildings, too, off in the distance.

Ollie let his gaze sweep the vista, then stopped short.

"What?" Tera asked, turning. "What's wrong?"

"Nothing. It's—" He cleared his throat and jutted his chin toward a big structure at the bottom of the hill. Too big for a single house. "I think that's the care place, over there. The clinic. The place where...my dad is."

"Ohhh," Tera said, nodding knowingly. "Yes, that's it."

Ollie took a step back, as though the building might somehow come rushing up the road and start making demands.

"Have you, uh, been in there, yet?" she asked.

"No."

Ollie had rescued his father, Matteo, from Herrick's End a few months prior. Not that the old man had deserved any such kindness. Matteo had been physically abusive to Ollie's mother, Francie, and verbally abusive to both of them throughout Ollie's childhood. No doubt, Matteo would have soon turned his fists onto his son if Francie hadn't taken matters into her own hands.

Working with the WRC and Runners like Laszlo, Francie had sedated and transported her husband to the Neath. She had then checked him in for a lifelong, less-than-luxurious stay at Herrick's

End prison before returning to Ollie on the Brickside. This had all happened, apparently, when Ollie was just a boy. It was the only solution she could find to keep herself, and her son, safe. Still, the guilt of it had eaten Francie alive. When the breast cancer hit a few years later, she believed the illness was her penance. A bill that had come due.

Ollie had been shocked to learn that his scumbag father—whom he had always assumed was either dead or shotgunning cans of Michelob somewhere in the Florida sun—had instead been languishing, all that time, in a torturous, underground tower. At first, Ollie had resisted the idea of rescuing dear old dad. Then, finally, he had relented. He still wasn't sure why. Maybe it was just pity. Or a secret fear of inheriting some of his mother's malignant guilt.

During the prison break, Ollie had banged his head and fallen unconscious. And then, somewhere in the mists of dreamy oblivion, he had heard his mother's voice.

Forgive him, Francie had said.

Never, he had answered.

Now, Matteo was living in the health facility, still lingering in a mysterious coma-like condition that no one could seem to identify or cure. Ollie paid for his dad's care with money he earned at Ollanta's. Every time he handed over the cash, he asked himself if it was worth it. He asked himself why he continued to support the subsistence of a man who had abused him and his mother. He never did come up with a good answer.

Ollie stared at the flat roof of the facility in the distance, imagining his father inside. Sitting upright. Staring out a window, maybe. Drooling. Eating mashed-up gruel from a wooden spoon.

"I'll go with you, you know," Tera said quietly. "I mean, if you ever want to go."

"I won't," Ollie said. "I hate him."

She didn't press. Probably because she saw the layers of emotions behind his simple words. Tera, of all people, understood the complexities of survival, of escaping damaged parents and family secrets. She knew that sometimes, there were no great solutions—only temporary, shoddy fixes.

Ollie's hands moved to his midsection. Thinking about his father always seemed to make his stomach roil. Either he got nauseous enough to want to puke, or he got hungry enough to glom-glom-glom his way through every food vendor in the market. Right now, neither was an option. So he changed the subject.

"We should keep moving," he said, turning around to put the big building at his back. The path ahead was in rough shape: pitted and narrow. Rarely traveled, from the looks of it. Stalagmites bulged inward from both sides, occasionally forcing Ollie and Tera to step around them as they made their way. It was slow going.

"So, what are we walking into, here?" he asked.

Tera sighed. "I'm not exactly sure. Last I heard, Carmichael ran some kind of a zoo."

That got Ollie's attention. "A zoo?"

"Well, sort of. Word is, it's a sleazy kind of place. I don't know what kinds of animals he's got in there. To be honest, I've never wanted to know." She gave a shudder. "It's down near Moseby's."

"Ah," Ollie nodded. "The wrong side of the tracks." Not long ago, he had visited Moseby's with Derrin to extract a favor from the pint-sized, foul-tempered owner. Derrin had used her influence to get them inside, where he had found a raucous tavern crawling with depraved patrons. Moseby had made Ollie play a drinking game with fizzing, fetid grog, which had almost leveled him. It had been worth it, though: In the end, his efforts had started a chain of events that had led to Tera's release. Sometimes Ollie could swear he could still taste the sting of that foul drink in his mouth.

"To be honest, I don't know how we're going to get in," she said.

"What do you mean?"

"He's got bouncers. Of course. And he knows me."

"Isn't that good?"

"Uh, no," Tera said. "Let's just say we're not exactly friends."

"Okay, so I'll go in."

"No way," Tera said, stepping around a wide pit in the dirt road. "We don't even know what we're looking for. *Who* we're looking for. And even if we do manage to figure it out, we don't know if they'll come willingly. Either way, Carmichael isn't going to let you just take them. Not without a fight."

Ollie's stomach began to ache again. "This is starting to sound complicated."

"It is," she agreed. "And it's definitely not a one-person job."

"So, let's go back to the house," Ollie suggested. "We can get Derrin." When it came to Neath bodyguards, Derrin was always his first choice.

"No can do. He knows her, too. And Ajanta, and Kuyu."

"And...let me guess. He's not exactly friends with them, either?"

She gave him a sardonic smile. "No. Carmichael doesn't like people who don't put up with his shit." Her expression turned thoughtful. "We need someone who's never met him. Someone who can get past the bouncers. Someone who's tough enough, and smart enough, to get in there with you and figure something out on the fly."

The next pothole in the road was bigger; Ollie had to back up and take a running start before leaping across it. When he landed, he straightened Meatball on his shoulder before flashing her a grin.

"What's that look for?" Tera asked suspiciously.

"This look?" he answered, pointing at his face and adopting his best southern drawl. "Well, I reckon it's the look of a guy who's happier than a clam at high tide."

She lifted one eyebrow. "Oh yeah? Why's that?"

"Because I know exactly where we have to go."

Fourteen

"Well, lookie what the cat drug in."

The wiry black man stood silhouetted in his doorway, staring down at Ollie and Tera with one good eye, a stubbled face, and a surprised smile.

"Hey, Dozer," Ollie said. Just the sight of his friend sent a shot of endorphins through his system. He looked cleaner than Ollie remembered, and calmer. Like an after-work guy rocking on a front porch, watching the world go by, satisfied with his lot. Freedom, it seemed, had been good to him.

Dozer scratched his arm through the off-white jumpsuit sleeve as he looked them up and down. "If you don't mind my saying, you two look like you been rode hard and put up wet."

"Uh, yeah. Something like that," Ollie said. "You have a second?"

"Sure do. Got lots of 'em, last I checked." He turned to Tera. "Nice to see you again, pretty lady." His southern accent melted the words into a lazy river.

"Hey, Dozer."

"And who's this little fella?" he asked, pointing to the trog on Ollie's shoulder.

"This is Meatball."

"He bite?"

"Only if you deserve it."

"Mmm," Dozer nodded. "Sometimes I do, sometimes I don't." Tentatively, he reached out to scratch Meatball's fur. The trog snuffled, pushed his head further into Ollie's neck, and continued to snore. "Guess I'm good today." He adjusted his eyepatch—a new one, Ollie noticed—and regarded them thoughtfully. "I'm guessing you ain't here for a social call?"

Ollie and Tera looked at each other.

Before they could respond, he stepped back and swept his arm through the doorway. "Better get on in, then."

Dozer had been Ollie's cellmate in Herrick's End. And, eventually, his friend. From the moment they had shared their first stick of loosemeat, Dozer had tutored Ollie in the ways of the prison and saved him from despair. Well, maybe not from *all* despair—a hefty chunk of the stuff was inevitable, considering the circumstances. But he had at least kept Ollie alive and functioning long enough for Tera to come along and rescue him. Ollie owed Dozer, big time, and he always would.

Yet here he was, asking for another favor.

As he stepped through the doorway, Ollie's eyes widened. The shack's interior was startlingly spartan. One small window on the back wall. One bed with a brown blanket. Empty walls. One sink, one shelf. It looked like... *Krite almighty*. It looked like their old cell! A swift, spiky rush of flashbacks made his skin prickle. He reached out for the wall to steady himself.

"Nice place," Tera said, though the look on her face said the opposite.

"Aw, not really." Dozer waved a hand. "I ain't gotten around to much, yet."

"Dude, what the hell?" Ollie burst out. He couldn't help it.

"What?"

"*What?* Seriously, man? Look at this place! It looks like you never left the goddamn tower!" The lone window on the back wall disturbed him the most. It was uncannily reminiscent of a similar, round window with bars, leading to a courtyard, leading to... He shuddered.

Dozer gazed around his small home as though seeing it for the first time. Then he chuckled. "Well, I'll be. I guess a man gets used to a thing."

Ollie didn't see the humor. "I hope you're not still pissing in a bucket, too."

"Nope," Dozer replied, a note of pride in his voice. "Got me an outhouse around back."

"Good," Ollie said, folding his arms. At least there was that. He didn't know why this place bothered him so much. It wasn't actually a prison cell, after all. Dozer was free to come and go as he pleased. Maybe Ollie just wanted better for his friend. Or maybe he was feeling a sudden, crushing guilt to realize that he'd been so busy luxuriating in his new life with Tera that he hadn't even bothered to see the inside of Dozer's house before now.

"Sweet tea?" Dozer asked them.

Their eyebrows shot up in surprise.

"Well, it ain't *exactly* sweet tea," he acknowledged. "But probably the closest we're gonna get, in these parts."

They accepted two cups of brown, room-temperature liquid. Ollie took a sip and coughed. It looked and tasted like murky New England pond water—the kind you choke on in early autumn, when it's still warm enough for swimming but the leaves have already started to fall and decompose.

"Only got the one chair," Dozer said, pointing unnecessarily. "You two take the bed, there, and start talking. I got a feeling this might take a while."

He was right. They told him the story from the beginning, meandering through the details of their visits with the Novas, the crab-man, and the Salt Collector, until finally reaching the part where they ended up on Dozer's doorstep.

"So, lemme get this straight," he said when they finished. "You don't know who, or what, this soul mate is."

"Right."

"And you don't know how to figure out who it is."

"Right."

"And even if you do figure that out, you got no plan for grabbing her from this Carmichael guy's zoo or whatever the hell it is."

"Right."

Dozer looked from Tera to Ollie and back again. "Sounds like neither of you could find your ass with both hands in your back pockets. What's any of this got to do with me?"

They smiled.

In the end, Dozer agreed to help, with one condition—he insisted that Ollie and Tera nap and clean themselves up first. "No offense, but you two smell like deviled eggs three days after the picnic."

They had half-heartedly protested. Then, because they had to admit they were pretty tired and smelly (though perhaps not as smelly as all that), they took turns in Dozer's backyard tub before collapsing together onto his bed. Meatball slept at their feet. After a few hours of dreams and drool, Dozer shook all three of his guests awake.

"Time to go," he said. And out they went into the darkened Neath, latching the door behind them.

Dozer passed out snacks as they walked: white crunchy things; yellow chewy things; and hard, round pinkish things—one of which almost broke Ollie's tooth. He was too hungry to ask what any of them were. The journey took about twenty minutes across two islands. The wormwalkers' luminescence seemed even darker than it had been the day before, casting an air of added gloom over the entire affair.

The surroundings grew progressively dingy as they traveled. Their head lamps' beams illuminated only slivers of the packed-earth road ahead, leaving Ollie's imagination to wonder about the scratching, panting, and skittering sounds he heard in the shadows all around them. When he turned his head, his lamp caught the glint of hooded eyes leering at them from tattered tents along the sides of the road. Indecipherable red graffiti marred the surface of nearby stalagmites—written in what kind of "paint," he didn't want to know.

Then, the path brightened with the sudden appearance of torches planted in the ground. They were beacons, he realized, lighting the way to Moseby's, just ahead. As they neared the entrance to the tavern, a scattering of empty buckets, bottles, and bags littered the path so completely that Ollie found himself stepping as carefully as a cat to avoid twisting an ankle.

The place looked much the same as he remembered it, with a rowdy, impatient crowd out front, a roped-off entryway, multi-colored flames, and strange music thumping from somewhere deep inside the cave. The rhythmic beats shook the ground as they passed. Inviting. Titillating. Hot with the promise of liberation.

That was the entrance. Further down, the exit was another story altogether: People who left Moseby's, it seemed, did not get very far. Not right away, anyway. Most were staggering, slurring, or slumped, or some combination of the three. Ollie cringed at the sight, remembering his one-and-only taste of Moseby's hospitality, and the horrible concoctions he'd had to consume in order to extract the "favor" he'd needed from the tiny, braided bar owner. When he'd left that night, he must have looked just as foolish and incoherent as all of these vagabond souls, with one big difference—he'd had Derrin to watch his back. These people were not so lucky.

Some of the drunken patrons wandered like zombies. Others had given up even that, propping themselves against the wall of a nearby longhouse for blackout naps. Ollie, Tera, and Dozer stepped over the assorted pairs of splayed legs as they continued along the narrow road.

"There," Tera said, pointing.

Ollie followed her finger to see another roped-off entrance, this time leading to an asymmetrical wooden door in a wooden wall. It was flanked by two large, red-and-white striped poles that made him think of Fabrizio's Barber Shop back home. A sign above the door read, *Carmichael's House of Unnatural Wonders*. Each letter had been painted a different hue of blue, white, red, or yellow and embellished with carnival-like stripes and spots. Nearby mounted torches made the words seem to flicker and jump.

Whatever "unnatural wonders" lay beyond the doorway, plenty of people seemed eager to get a glimpse. The two muttering women at the front of the line were sharing a bottle of something fizzy as they waited their turn. The man behind them was openly scratching his crotch. And behind him, a group of greasy-haired Neathians passed around a smoking stick, creating a thick, orange haze over everyone's heads. Ollie grimaced. This place was seedier than twelve-grain bread. And he wasn't even through the door yet.

Ollie was not at all surprised to see that the two gigantic men guarding Carmichael's entrance were dressed like clowns. Not happy children's clowns, either: more like demented, Halloween-costume clowns with patchwork suits, dripping makeup, and blood-red, bulging noses. He was guessing that the noses wouldn't squeak if squeezed, though he planned to leave that particular theory untested.

"They look fun," Ollie muttered, eying the harlequin guards.

Tera looked around. "Give Meatball to me," she said, reaching out to lift the trog off of Ollie's shoulder. "You guys go get in line. I'll wait over there, behind those crates. If you need anything, just..." Her voice trailed off.

"Just what?" Ollie asked.

She shrugged. "I don't know. Just...yell, I guess."

"Yell from where? Inside the circus from hell? How would you hear me?"

"Oh, c'mon," she smiled. "You'll do fine."

"How am I supposed to do fine when I don't even know what I'm supposed to do?" His words came out more high-pitched than he intended.

"You do know," Tera said, holding his face in her hands. "Find Howerbout's soul mate. That's all. In, and out."

Ollie inhaled sharply. "Right. And I'm sure it'll have a sign just hanging there above its head. The Bearded Lady, the Sword Swallower, and the Soul Mate. Step right up."

Tera grinned. "You'll know it when you see it. I believe that." At his skeptical look, she insisted, "I do! Herrick gave you that message for a reason. We met that crazy crab-man for a reason. We're here because we're supposed to be here. We have to just...trust the process, I guess."

"What process?" he asked, wiping his sweaty palms on his pant legs. "This isn't a process. It's a shitstorm. It's like we're jinxed or something." One of his North End neighbors had once had a black cat they called Jinx. Between the color and the name, the poor thing had been a pariah among the superstitious Italians on Fleet Street.

"We're not jinxed."

He folded his arms stubbornly.

"We're *not* jinxed," she said again. "Look at me. Do you trust me?

"Of course I trust you." *Always,* he thought.

"Great. Now, trust yourself." She pinched his face gently. "Everything's going to be fine."

Ollie rubbed his cheek where her fingers had fallen. Even if he and Dozer got in, even if they figured out what they were looking for, they still had to somehow get it out. He had been wrong when he called this a shitstorm. It was more like a category-5 shit hurricane. And he was about to walk right through the eye.

"All right, now," Dozer interjected, holding up a hand. "No need to get your boxers in a bunch. We won't need nothing, and we won't do no yelling. We got this. Right, buddy? We've handled worse."

Technically, Dozer had handled worse. Ollie had mostly just watched. But he nodded anyway.

"Let me just do one thing before we go in," Dozer said. "You wait here."

A moment later, they were both gone—Tera behind the wall of wooden crates, and Dozer back to the row of sleeping drunks. He seemed to be talking to each one in turn: leaning in close, patting their arms. Ollie looked left and right on the dark street, tamping down his panic.

Finally, Dozer returned to his side.

"What were you doing over there?" Ollie whispered loudly.

"Just giving a little visit to my brothers and sisters," Dozer answered, clapping Ollie on the shoulder. "Like my mama used to say, some folks are so poor they can't afford to pay attention."

"What does that even mean?"

"Watch and learn, my little grasshopper. Watch and learn."

As they approached the line for Carmichael's, Ollie tried to affect a casual, curious saunter: something that said, *I was just wandering by…Well, what have we here? This looks interesting!* They took their place at the end of the line, waiting impatiently as the clown-suited bouncers let in small groups of two and three at a time. After a half-hour or so, it was their turn. Dozer shoved a few bills into the closest guard's oversized glove and beckoned Ollie to follow him through the off-kilter doorway.

Once inside, Ollie lifted his head and yelped in surprise to see a wavy, ginormous man staring down at him. A yelping, wavy, ginormous man. It took a moment for Ollie to realize that he was looking at himself: a distorted version of himself, reflected in a series of funhouse mirrors. They were mounted on the wall of what appeared to be a man-made, carved-out bunker.

He heard a groan from Dozer. Then a colorful stew of expletives.

Ollie turned away from the zig-zagging reflection to follow his friend's gaze. He saw, inexplicably, an oversized grog barrel mounted sideways in the passageway. It was spinning. Beyond that, he saw a stairwell. To get to the stairs, it seemed, they'd first have to pass through the barrel.

"You've got to be kidding me," Ollie said.

Dozer threw up his hands. Then he approached the barrel, jumped in, and landed on his feet defiantly, as though daring it to mess with him. The revolving cylinder complied almost instantly, tossing the big man onto his side, back, and belly with all the elegance of a garbage disposal eating a spoon. Dozer sputtered and swore, making little sense and even less progress. Ollie tried to suppress a smile, then an outright laugh, as he watched his friend flop and flounder and, eventually, make it through to the other side.

Ollie cupped his hands around his mouth. "Hey, Dozer! You look like you've been rode hard and put up wet!" he said with glee.

Rubbing his arm, Dozer fixed Ollie with a one-eyed stare. "Keep laughing, big fella. Ain't so funny when it's your turn."

He was right, of course. Ollie's path through the rolling barrel was even more awkward and bruise-inducing than Dozer's had been. His face hit the slats, hard. His feet twisted out from under him more than once. By the time he crawled out the other end, he was dizzy and winded. But still somehow grinning.

Dozer gave him a playful punch in the arm and started down the steps.

The stairwell was cold, damp, and eerily quiet, as if trying to quell the silliness of all that came before. It was lit only by occasional torches on the walls. Ollie couldn't help but think of all the times he had followed Dozer in other, similar stairwells, back in Herrick's End. This one, at least, had to be an improvement on all those. It had to lead to something better. Something less...dungeony. Less torturous. Surely even this place could rise above such a low bar.

At first, Ollie struggled to identify the permeating smell. It reminded him of Mrs. Paget's old barn, crowded with giant crows and equally giant piles of bird poop. The odor grew stronger as they went. Once at the bottom, they rounded a corner, then another corner, finally reaching a dim opening with a sign. Like the one out front, it read, *Carmichael's House of Unnatural Wonders*. Unlike the one out of front, this one had an exclamation point—*Unnatural Wonders!*—and no color at all.

The stench of manure and concentrated urine wafted through the doorway and hit Ollie's nose with a wallop. "Ugh," he muttered into Dozer's back, holding a hand to his face. "What the hell is that?"

Dozer remained uncharacteristically quiet. No "hold your horses." No "I reckon." No quips about britches or rising creeks or turnip trucks. That silence, more than the smell or the darkness, set Ollie's nerves on edge.

"What?" he asked his friend, afraid to look. "What do you see?"

"I..." Dozer seemed unable to finish his sentence.

"*What?*" Ollie asked again.

Dozer shuffled forward, moving through the doorway. Ollie followed with tiny, cautious steps, instantly forgetting about the stink as he took in his new surroundings.

The House of Unnatural Wonders did not look like a circus. Or a carnival, or a zoo.

It looked, to Ollie, like an animal shelter. Like the world's most depressing animal shelter, to be more specific. Granted, he had never seen an animal shelter that looked particularly appealing, but this one took bleak dreariness to another level entirely.

A wide, center aisle stretched out in front of them, lined with gravel. On either side, cages loomed. Each was slightly higher than the top of Ollie's head. The bars appeared to be made of bamboo stalks, or perhaps swamp reeds, wound together into tightly knit mesh. Probably stronger than they looked. The stench was oppressive. The gloom was oppressive. The ceiling was low enough for him to reach with his fingertips, if he wanted to. He didn't.

Up and down the aisle, visitors sauntered. Murmured. Pointed.

Dozer, still silent, had approached the nearest cage, on their right. Ollie walked closer to stand beside him. Then, together, they stared at the unfathomable sight within.

Ollie's mind raced to make sense of what he was seeing. In many ways, the creature inside the cage resembled a walrus. A baby walrus, maybe, considering its smaller-than-the-average-walrus size. Gray skin. Bounteous rolls of blubber. A pair of white tusks protruding from a thick, brushy mustache above its lips. Chunky, flippered legs. On a checklist of walrus characteristics, everything fit.

Everything but the wings.

Those were long, dark, and leathery, with visible boning. Bat wings, to be sure. But they were not on a bat. They were, improbably, on a walrus.

They were also enormous, though Ollie had to wonder how enormous a pair of wings would have to be to lift a walrus—even a baby-sized walrus—into the air.

"What in the Sam Hill am I looking at?" Dozer whispered.

Ollie tried to answer, then tried to shrug, and ended up doing neither.

The freakish creature stared back at them, stretching its wings and blinking its black, walrus eyes. A sign hanging on the bars helpfully provided its name to visitors: "Specimen 625: Blumbat."

As if in a trance, Ollie moved down to the next cage. This one contained three animals. All identical. They had feathered seabird bodies and turquoise, webbed feet; blue-footed boobies, if he'd had to guess. But their heads...were not heads at all. Not really. To Ollie's horror, each head looked like nothing more than a bulging brain coral, all twists and turns with a glistening sheen. The beasts waddled together in aimless, unseeing circles, bumping repeatedly into each other and into the walls of the cage. According to the sign, they were "Specimens 271-273: Ceecilfeet."

It went on like that all the way down both sides of the aisle, cages and names and critters, each as perverse and horrible—or *more* perverse and horrible—as the last.

The Gerstysnake, a.k.a. Specimen 172, had scaly skin, sidewinding locomotion, and a flicking tongue. It also had hundreds of quills poking ominously out of his out of its back: a slithering, menacing pincushion. Ollie backed away slowly.

A pair of bird-like monstrosities, identified as Screechwhits on their sign, resembled tiny screech owls. Each feathered head was somehow spinning in a continuous, sickening circle, like wind-up toys—or owl exorcisms—gone wrong. Specimen 197, the Janedoe, appeared to be nothing more than an ordinary, spotted fawn. Then, Ollie realized that its spots were actually gaping holes—some of which went clear through the animal from one side to the other.

Cage after cage, the names and atrocities kept coming:

Kimmerswimmers. Salamandovers. Garabarnacle. Champer-chomper. Hilligator.

Ollie reeled. He felt sick. He also felt indescribably sad. What was this place? And why would someone create such hideous, helpless things?

Now, at least, he knew where Howerbout had come from. The crab-man had alluded to "the place where they made me." Where else but here? And if Howerbout had originated from this carnival of depravity, then it was likely that his soul mate did, too. And that the creature, probably, was still here.

But which one?

He kept walking, half-hoping to see a blinking arrow. A smoking gun. Something. *You'll know it when you see it,* Tera had said. But Tera couldn't have imagined this place. The variety of specimen numbers and names seemed inexhaustible, like deformed bits of a nightmare come to life: *Cassavacat. Hoopdeedoop. Llarsonllama. Stumeleon. Lonepayone.* Shrimp, turtles, groundhogs, rabbits, clam shells, beetles, sea gulls, felines, coral, toads, lobsters, and even plants, all stitched and gummed together in a grotesque parody of life as he knew it.

It was too much. It was impossible. Ollie froze in place, stupefied, barely noticing as other gawking visitors pushed past him in the aisle.

"Hey, Roomie?"

At the sound of Dozer's voice, he looked up in a daze. "Mmm?"

"I think you're gonna wanna give a look-see over here."

Dozer jutted his head toward a cage on his left. Wordlessly, Ollie approached. The first thing he saw was the inhabitant's name and number on the sign: "Specimen 222: Jinx."

He stiffened. What had he just said to Tera, out in the road? *It's like we're jinxed.*

Taking a step closer, Ollie caught sight of the creature inside. It had a man's torso and face, merged seamlessly into an oversized hermit crab shell. No arms. Just six fat, orange crab legs, clawing into the dirt below.

Dozer propped his hands onto his hips. "Ain't that just like the other fella you told me about?" he asked. "The crab-looking fella?"

Ollie walked forward. He grabbed the bars with both hands. The crab-man caught sight of him and waved happily, enthusiastically. He even gave a little hop. The creature seemed relaxed. Content. He didn't seem the least bit concerned that he had been confined to a cage and forced to sit on display in a dreary, underground sideshow of sleaze.

He didn't even seem concerned that his mouth had been taped shut.

Ollie waved back. His hand felt heavy, like it was moving through a bucket of syrup. When he found his voice, he answered simply: "No."

"No, what?" Dozer asked. "It ain't like the other fella?"

Ollie shook his head. His field of vision narrowed; the cacophony around him echoed like distant shouts in a canyon. "It isn't *like* Howerbout," he said. "It *is* Howerbout. Dozer, that's the exact same guy."

Fifteen

Ollie stuck his face through the narrow gap in the bars. His skin stretched; his eyes bulged.

"Howerbout!" he said in a loud whisper. "It's me! It's Ollie!"

The crab-man seemed delighted at the prospect of interaction. He jumped with excitement and toddled closer.

"What's going on? How the hell did you get here?" Ollie asked him.

The creature lifted one of his claws and pointed, insomuch as a crab can point, at the tape sealing his mouth. The human torso shrugged apologetically.

Ollie sighed. "Dude, your legs are free. You can rip off the tape."

A look of surprise, then elation, registered in the crab-man's eyes. Lifting a claw, he pinched the edge of the adhesive and began to peel it from his face.

"Not the sharpest cheese on the tray, is he?" Dozer muttered.

Ollie sighed again. Then he braced himself for the deluge to come.

It started the moment the rosy lips and pointy teeth were free. "Hello, friends!" the crab-man exclaimed. "My goodness, hello! Thank you for visiting me. I don't get many visitors. Well, I mean,

I do. We all do, of course. But not many want to stop to talk to me. Or tell me such smart things! Thank you! I didn't like that tape on my mouth. I didn't like it at all."

Dozer took a step back.

"I don't understand... How did you get here?" Ollie asked, still gripping the bars. "Where's Laszlo?"

Now it was the crab-man's turn to look confused. "I don't remember how I got here. Then again, I don't remember much. This is where I live. Me and all my friends. And the people who visit us, like you. I know I've been here a very long time. A very, very long time. So long I can't remember anything before it! Then again, I don't—"

"Yeah, yeah," Ollie interrupted. "We know. You don't remember much. You have to *think,* Howerbout. Think hard. *Where is Laszlo?*" He spoke the final three words slowly, stretching them out. His heart was starting to pound. None of this made sense. Why, and when, had Howerbout left his cave? More importantly, what the hell had happened to Laz?

"Think. Yes." The creature nodded. "I will think." He paused and stared up at the ceiling. Two seconds later, he looked back at Dozer and Ollie. "I still do not remember," he said with a wide smile, as though sharing good news.

Ollie's knuckles turned white on the bars. "Why did you leave the cave?"

"What cave?"

"*Your* cave. In the lake."

The human brow furrowed. "I do not have a cave. Well, I have *this* cave. Is this a cave? I'm not sure. I've always wondered. I mean, it's sort of like a cave. Dark and wet. And deep, too. At least, it seems deep. I guess I've never really known for sure. The Fancy Man doesn't tell us much." He looked over at Dozer. "Is this a cave?"

"I, uh..." Dozer's eyes widened. "I guess so. Sure."

"There you go," the crab-man said. He looked back at Ollie with a satisfied smile. "This is my cave."

"No, it's—" Ollie took a deep breath, trying to calm himself. "This is *a* cave, Howerbout. This is not *your* cave."

"Why do you call me that?" the creature asked, looking puzzled again. "That's not my name." He pointed to the sign on his cage. "That is my name. Jinx. Do you like it? I like it well enough. It's fun to say. Jinx. Jinx. Jinx. Jinx. Jinx..."

He continued on like that for several seconds. Ollie and Dozer flashed each other dismayed looks.

"...Jinx. Jinx, Jinx, Jinx, Jinx..."

Finally, Ollie interrupted with a shout. "Stop! We get it! Listen to me: I need to know where Laszlo is. Do you understand? *Laszlo.* Remember him? Bulging biceps. Flexible. Big nose. Lots of Ukrainian traveling songs. You have to think. You have to tell me where he is."

"I am sorry," the crab-man said. And he did, in fact, look sorry. "I do not know anyone named Laszlo. I wish I did. You seem to want to find him, and I wish that I could help you. I really do. But I don't know anyone, really! Just the people who pass through here. And none of them tell me their names." An expression of deep sadness passed over his face. "Would you tell me your names? I would like that very much. Then we could be friends. Real friends, forever and ever."

As Ollie watched him talk, a slow realization began to dawn. He took a step back and let his gaze land, one at a time, on the other exhibited creatures up and down the aisle. Some, like the Gerstysnake and the Blumbat, slithered, flapped or flopped alone in their cages. But some lived in groups: Ceecilfeet. Salamandovers. Screechwhits. Multiples of the same species, housed together. Each one looking much like the next.

No, not similar—identical.

The architects of this place weren't just messing with mutations: They were also making clones. But who would do such a thing? And why?

Ollie turned back to look at the crab-man inside the cage, who, he now realized, was not Howerbout at all.

"Your name is Jinx," he said. It was a statement, not a question.

"Yes," the mutant nodded. "Jinxy Jinx Jinx. That is my name."

My lucky Jinx, Ollie thought. He was looking for a soul mate, and he had found a clone. If that wasn't a blinking-arrow, smoking-gun, unmistakable sign, then what the hell was?

"Nice to meet you, Jinx. I'm Ollie. And this is Dozer."

The crab-man waved a claw. "What wonderful names you have! So wonderful. You must be wonderful people, too. I just know it. We're going to be such good friends. Such good, good friends. This makes me feel so happy I could just bury my whole head in the sand and blow bubbles! Are you feeling happy, too?"

Ollie let go of the bars. "Well, to be honest, buddy, we're not doing so great right now. But I think you might be able to help. How would you feel about going on an adventure? With us?"

"How would I *feel?*" Jinx gasped, his eyes widening. "How would I *feel?* He clacked two of his claws together and hopped up and down on the remaining four.

"I think I can guess how he feels," Dozer said dryly.

Ollie folded his arms in satisfaction. He had done it. He had found Howerbout's better half. Or worse half. Or...exactly the same half. It didn't matter. One crab, two crab, red crab, blue crab. All that mattered now was figuring out how to get this yammermouth out of that cage and into the lake. And then he'd never have to see *either* half again.

———⌇∞⌇———

"Gentlemen! Welcome!"

The voice came from behind, smooth as tomato skin.

Ollie turned slowly.

"I see you've met our talkative friend. My apologies. I usually try to keep his mouth covered." The voice belonged to a man, who was flashing his teeth. Holding out a hand. "Pleased to meet you. My name is Carmichael. I'm the proprietor of this fine establishment. And you are?"

This man, this *proprietor,* was standing abnormally close. Ollie could smell his breath: a sweet mix of licorice and vanilla, with a chaser of rum. His hair was a wondrous, shining sheen of black satin. Carmichael was as tall as Ollie, but not nearly as round. Instead, his body formed that perfect inverted triangle that women seemed to love so much, with broad shoulders hovering above a trim waist. Ollie could see his waist clearly, because he was wearing a thick leather belt atop pressed pants, along with a bedazzled suit jacket and expensive shoes. Proprietors, it seemed, did not wear beige jumpsuits. The man had Asian features and a complexion

185

that somehow glowed, despite the dim surroundings. And his teeth... They looked to Ollie like square, polished pearls, all lined up for display in a jewelry-store case.

A top hat balanced on his head. It was about half the size of a standard top hat, and tipped at a jaunty angle.

Dozer stepped forward to shake the man's hand. "I'm Dozer," he said. When Ollie didn't speak, he added, "This here's Ollie."

Ollie nodded dumbly.

"Pleasure to meet you both," Carmichael said, though his cold eyes, car-salesman demeanor, and abnormally wide smile said otherwise. He had two earrings in each lobe; all four were sparkling gems. "What's this I hear about an adventure?"

"Oh, Fancy Man!" Jinx exclaimed. "Isn't it wonderful? These are my new friends! They said they need my help! I've never helped anyone before. Never, never. But I think I'd be good at adventuring. And helping. They want to take me with them!"

"Is that so?" Carmichael gave a hearty, forced chuckle. "I'm afraid we don't usually issue day passes around here."

"Oh, we ain't looking for no day pass," Dozer drawled. "We're looking to adopt."

Carmichael gave them a pseudo-sympathetic smile. "It seems you've got the wrong idea, gentlemen. This is Carmichael's House of Unnatural Wonders." He spread his hands in the air as though asking them to imagine the Broadway marquee above their heads. "We're not a store. We're an *experience*. A unique, one-of-a-kind experience that combines the very best of—"

"That's the same thing," Ollie interrupted.

"Excuse me?"

"Unique and one-of-a-kind. They mean the same thing." Ollie had no idea why he was being so unnecessarily petulant. Or why he was fighting the urge to punch this pompous idiot square in his chiseled, perfectly moisturized face.

Dozer gave him a hard look, then turned back to their host. "Sure is an amazing place, I'll give you that. I ain't never seen nothing like it. Where do all these critters come from? You make 'em yourself?"

Carmichael seemed glad to turn his attention away from Ollie. "Oh, no. Nothing like that. I'm more of a host. An entertainer. The face of the place, you could say." He chuckled again. "We have…generous benefactors. They take care of all the nuts and bolts at the lab, and we take care of the glamour." He rubbed a finger along the jeweled edge of his lapel, looking pleased.

Lab.

The word made goosebumps rise on Ollie's skin.

"What lab?" he asked. Was it the same one he and Tera were looking for? How many labs could there be in the Neath? His brow furrowed.

"Oh, it's nothing you need to concern yourself with," Carmichael answered with a dismissive flick of his fingers. "As you can see, it's the end result that matters."

"Where is it?"

"The lab?" Their host seemed surprised at the question. "I don't know. Nor do I care, frankly. They create things and keep what they want. And whatever they don't want, they bring to me. So in a way, you could call this a sanctuary. A warm and welcoming home for all the discarded, magnificent freaks." He spread his arms magnanimously. Again. "And I am their caretaker."

Ollie snorted. Caretaker, his ass. This place was about as "warm and welcoming" as the wire monkey in those cruel psychological experiments. Carmichael didn't care about these creatures or their comfort. Ollie had just met the man, and already he knew: There was only one thing Michael Carmichael cared about in this world, and it rhymed with Schmichael Carschmichael.

The top-hatted proprietor continued blathering, this time with a sales pitch: By any chance, would they be interested in paying a little extra to enjoy an enhanced experience? Perhaps they would like to feed one of the animals? Some of them, like the Hilligator, could even be petted. For a small added fee, of course. Though they'd need to wear protective gloves.

Ollie ignored the spiel. His mind was racing.

Now what? How were they going to get an enormous half-hermit crab, half-human monstrosity out of here without anyone noticing? There was no way they could head back up the stairs. Even if they somehow managed to get Jinx past that asinine rolling barrel, they'd still have to deal with the clown-faced guards. There might be a back door, he supposed. But a back door to what? Probably not a convenient alley with a waiting, helpful cab driver. And now that Carmichael had taken an interest in them, things looked even worse. The guy was already watching them like a hawk. Half-hawk, half-man.

Maybe they'd have to knock this "Fancy Man" out. Just...smash his head with something. Then they'd have to unlock Jinx's cage, somehow, and—

Dozer interrupted his spiraling machinations.

"Well, like I said, we sure have taken a shine to this here crab," his friend was saying. "What's it gonna take for you to let him go?"

"And like *I* said, it doesn't work like that," Carmichael countered. "And even if it did, I don't do business with folks I just met. But you gentlemen are welcome to come back anytime for a visit."

"Actually, you do know a friend of ours," Dozer said.

"Oh, yeah?" Carmichael's charming grin turned skeptical. "Who's that?"

"Name's Tera."

Ollie's head snapped up.

"Tera...Martinez?" Carmichael asked, a spark of interest alighting in his eyes.

"One and the same. We're real tight with her. Matter of fact, she's the one that sent us. Says she's a fan of yours. Loves this whole place."

Ollie tried to glare a hole through Dozer's skull. It didn't work.

"Well, what do you know. Tera Martinez." Carmichael spoke the name slowly, as though tasting it in his mouth. He waggled his manicured eyebrows. "Damn. A real spitfire, that one. Funny, I always got the impression she didn't like me."

"Well, I don't know about all that," Dozer said. "She tells us you're one of the smartest fellas she's ever met. And that you clean up real nice, too." He winked.

Ollie stared at him with a loose jaw.

Carmichael, meanwhile, ran a finger through his glossy locks. "Did she, now?" He leered. "Tera, Tera, Tera. Now there's one I'd like to—"

"You'd like to what?" Ollie interrupted, his voice cold. He stepped closer. Their eyes were at the same level. Ollie narrowed his lids and held the stare.

"Hey, there," Dozer said lightly, placing a hand on Ollie's arm and giving him a pointed look. "We're all friends, here. Right? Friends who do business."

"No, Dozer, I want to hear this. What exactly would this fine proprietor like to do to Tera?" Suddenly, all he could think about was reaching out and ripping that stupid tiny top hat off the guy's head and stuffing it down his throat.

"Ollie," Dozer snapped. "Hush your mouth. Let the grownups talk."

The spell broke. Ollie took a step back. What was wrong with him? Dozer was just working this guy. Buttering him up. Obviously. Tera had no interest in Carmichael: She had said so herself: *If I see him, I might kill him,* were the exact words, if he remembered right.

Still, the doubt sucked at him like a trog on a wormwalker. As the old saying went, there's a thin line between love and hate. Maybe Tera didn't want to get near Carmichael because she didn't trust herself to be near him. Because she felt a magnetic pull toward his charm, his abs, his expensive clothes, his peppermint-Chiclet smile. What girl wouldn't be attracted to this guy? Michael Carmichael was better looking than the male underwear model on the billboard near Ollie's old apartment—the billboard they'd had to take down, reportedly because women *and* men kept crashing their cars into the guardrail when they spotted the stud in his skivvies hovering forty feet above the intersection.

"Come on now, friend," Dozer continued. "You said so yourself... These are just the rejects, right? Nothing special. We'll give him a good home."

Carmichael folded his arms, looking suddenly suspicious. "What's your interest in this crab, anyway?"

"It's like I said," Dozer shrugged. "I just took a shine to him. Nice to have someone to talk to, around the house."

Carmichael chortled. "Oh, he'd be plenty good at that."

In his cage, Jinx jumped and nodded.

"Right. And that's exactly what I'm looking for. It's tough living alone. He seems like good company, that's all."

Carmichael went quiet, considering. Then he shook his head. "Can't do it. Sorry."

"Not even for this?" Dozer pulled a wad of colored bills from his jumpsuit pocket.

For a moment, the slick carnival barker lost his cool. "Wow, that's... I..." He collected himself, then shook his head. "No. It wouldn't be right. Jinx is part of the family."

"I understand," Dozer said solemnly. "That's mighty admirable of you."

Carmichael nodded.

Dozer smiled and shrugged. It looked to Ollie like he might be giving up. Then he adjusted his eye patch, reached into his other pocket, and pulled out another stack of bills. He dropped it on top of the first, creating a barely balanced tower of cash on the palm of his left hand. "Final offer," he said.

Ollie had once seen a pharmaceutical commercial that advertised a drug to treat bulging eyes. The patients, apparently, suffered from a thyroid condition that caused their eyeballs to literally protrude from their faces. In the commercial, the poor sufferer stared into the camera with orbs as big as apricots. That's exactly what Michael Carmichael looked like, in that moment, ogling the tantalizingly close pile of bills.

Ollie wondered how long, exactly, it would take for the dapper dan to change his mind. He began to count: *One Mississippi, two Mississippi*. He didn't even get to three.

"Deal," Carmichael said. He snatched the cash and gave a withering look at Jinx, all pretense of affection abandoned. "Maybe now we'll get a little peace and quiet around here. But if anyone asks—"

"We were never here," Dozer finished.

Carmichael gave them a curt nod.

Ollie and Dozer shot each other looks of pleasant surprise as their host pulled a set of jangling keys from his jacket pocket.

"Do we, uh, take him back up them stairs?" Dozer asked.

"No need," Carmichael said. "We've got a loading dock, out back."

As Ollie watched him approach Jinx's cage and fumble with the keys, he leaned over to whisper to Dozer: "Where the hell did you get all that money?"

Dozer gave a noncommittal, slightly guilty shrug.

Ollie's brows lifted as he put the pieces together. "The drunks, outside! You weren't 'supporting' them. You were stealing from them!"

Another shrug. "If I did—and I ain't saying I did—but if I did, it would've been for the greater good, don't you think?"

Before Ollie could answer, Carmichael inserted a big brass key and turned it with a snap. The cage door swung open to reveal an ecstatic Jinx.

"Are we going adventuring now?" he asked, all six claws bouncing in spasmodic jitters.

"Like June bugs on a Jet Ski," Dozer answered. "Pack up, big fella. We're taking you home."

Sixteen

They traveled by crow boat, in the darkest of the dark.

Mrs. Paget propelled them from the stern, flapping her broad, black wings as Tera steered atop the giant bird's back. Ringlets of fog swirled all around. The row of bench seats created a challenge for Jinx, who didn't fit comfortably anywhere. In the end, the crab-man climbed over all three benches and rested his shell along their tops, like a cookie on a cooling rack. Ollie, Meatball, and Dozer, meanwhile, squashed themselves into the edges of the hull and tried not to fall into the churning, green water.

Somewhere out in the middle of the lake, Tera dropped the reins. She instructed Mrs. Paget to take Dozer and Meatball back to the islands. The crow squawked in agreement.

At this, Ollie felt himself frowning. They had all agreed that it would probably be best for the trog to stay behind for this leg of the mission, for the sake of simplicity and speed. Quick trip, in and out. The fewer distractions they had, the better. And Dozer had agreed to take good care of him. Still, as he watched Meatball climb amiably up Dozer's leg, Ollie felt a twinge of regret. He didn't like to be separated from the little guy. He didn't even like the *idea* of being separated from him. Not that he would have admitted it to anyone.

Dozer encircled the trog with his arm and nodded reassuringly. Ollie gave them both a short, somewhat pathetic wave.

Then, Tera told Ollie and Jinx to jump.

Before his face hit the water, Ollie had been worried about many things. Would the Novas' breathing assistance still work? How many more plunges could his sneakers and jumpsuit survive before dissolving into waterlogged tatters? Would Meatball be okay while he was gone? How would they find Howerbout's cave? And even if they did, would they be able to enter?

Once he submerged, however, the now-familiar bliss enveloped him. Ollie inhaled it all: breath, sight, and knowledge, in one satisfying gulp. It made him think of a verse from Herrick's note:

Air and breath, truth and lie.

He inhaled the words, too. And once he did, all of his questions floated away with the bubbles.

They led Jinx over forests of lakeweed, through schools of fishes, and around the multitudes of other fantastical, aquatic beings. When the air pocket appeared above, Ollie recognized it immediately. How a person could recognize an air pocket, he didn't know, but he recognized it nonetheless. He smiled at Tera and pointed, and she smiled in return. Not long after, they found themselves standing on their feet, breathing regular old oxygen again, in a cave. In *the* cave. A crack in the wall ahead beckoned.

Jinx started to talk; Tera shushed him with a stern finger to her lips. She told him to wait there, *quietly,* just for a minute, and reassured him they'd be back soon.

Ollie walked through the opening first.

He immediately spotted Laszlo lying on his back, spinning a set of fish bones like batons in his fingers. Ollie's legs all but buckled at the sight. Only then did he realize how afraid, really afraid, he had been for his friend.

"Laz!"

The acrobat's head snapped around. A wide grin appeared on his narrow lips as he jumped up. "Ollie! You come!"

Tera followed close behind, joining them in a laughing group hug.

Ollie succumbed to equal parts elation and surprise as he squeezed his friends' shoulders. Had they actually made it? They had promised to return to Laszlo, to bring the soul mate, and they had done exactly that. Hot diggity. An unfamiliar surge of pride welled in his chest. If ever there was a time for a slo-mo, pan-out scene, this was it. Here they were, together again. Hugging. Laughing. Victorious.

Now, there was nothing left but the introductions—*Howerbout, meet Jinx. Jinx, meet Howerbout*—and then they'd be on their way. With any luck, one or both of the crab-men would know something about the lab's location, and they'd even get a shortcut. Bing, bam, boom. It had taken a little doing, and more than a few detours, but here they were. Almost to the finish line. He caught Tera's eye and saw the joy reflected there: genuine, relieved joy. It made him feel like he could float.

Clack, clack, clack.

"Welcome back, my friends!"

Ollie turned to see Howerbout dancing on his claws. *Clackety, clack, clack.*

"I'm so happy to see you! My new friend Laszlo and I have been having so much fun! Haven't we, Laszlo?"

"Yes, we—"

"So, so much fun. The most! Did you have a nice journey? Did you see lots of things? I'll bet you did. Lots of greenies, maybe? And other things, too? Did you find what you were looking for? You were looking for something, I think. Something big. I don't remember what. Then again, I don't remember much." His human shoulders shrugged.

"We were looking for your soul mate, Howerbout," Tera reminded him gently. "Someone you could be friends with forever and ever. Remember?"

"That sounds nice!"

"Yes," Tera nodded. "And we found him! Well, Ollie found him." She looked at Ollie proudly and patted his arm, then turned back to the crab-man. "Are you ready to meet him?"

"Yes, yes, yes!" Howerbout exclaimed, dancing again. *Clack, clack, clackety clack.*

"Great! I'll go get him." Tera gave Ollie and Laszlo a conspiratorial wink. Then she walked to the crack in the wall, vanished, and reappeared moments later with Jinx trailing behind her.

Ollie glanced at Laszlo, who was agog at the sight.

"I know, right?" Ollie muttered.

"There is *two* of them?" Laszlo whispered.

"It would seem so."

The creatures approached each other and circled cautiously. It was like watching one animal observe itself in a mirror. Claws lifted and fell. Heads tilted. Clacks echoed against the shiny rock walls all around.

Neither spoke. Ollie suspected it was quite possibly the longest moment of silence in crab-man history.

Then, Howerbout said, "You look like me!"

"You look like me!"

"I just said that."

"And I said it, too."

"Why would you say something I already said?"

"I like to say things. I said things a lot, back at my other place. Unless the Fancy Man puts the tape on my mouth. Then I didn't say anything."

"Who's the Fancy Man?"

A pause. "I don't remember, exactly. I don't remember much."

"I don't remember much, either."

"Why not?"

"I don't know. Why?"

"Why, what?"

"I...don't know."

"You don't know what?"

"I told you. I don't remember much."

"No, I told *you* I don't remember much. Don't you remember?"

Ollie, Tera and Laszlo shared a series of nervous glances. Tera's smile, which had been wide and eager, started to shrink.

Laszlo leaned closer. "He is...twin?"

"A clone, I think," Ollie murmured. "Someone's making them in a lab. We're not sure who."

"Lab? But you are looking for lab, yes? Is same one?"

"We're not sure about that, either."

Laszlo dropped the spinning bones onto the ground and clapped his hands together. "This is it. You have done it! We will find all of the missing people!"

"Oh, Laz. I hope so," Tera said.

"I can say now, I have never been so happy to see any two people in my big, whole life. This crabby man never shuts mouth. Never. All day long, with the talking, talking, talking. It is enough to make—"

Laszlo stopped short, interrupted by a staccato burst of raised voices behind him.

"I told you! Don't you listen? I told you what they are called. I said, they are ca—"

"But I told *you,* I don't know what—"

"Why don't you listen more?"

"It is you who will not listen! I was just trying to tell y—"

"If you would just let me finish, I could—"

The nonsensical bickering continued. And continued, and continued. Thirty minutes later, to Ollie's horror, they were still at it.

"I don't have enough greenies to share."

"I don't want your greenies."

"You will! You will, when you get hungry."

"I won't! And you can't make me!"

"You won't ever want to eat, ever, ever again? That doesn't even make any sense! How can you never want to—"

"I won't eat them, and you can't make me!"

It was like a rap battle with no rhymes. Or logic. Laszlo, Tera, and Ollie each took turns refereeing, which mainly involved trying to force one to listen while the other talked, and vice versa.

After nearly two hours with no progress, Ollie was exhausted and dismayed. Tera had gone nearly hoarse from her efforts at reconciliation. And Laszlo slumped in the corner, covering his ears with his hands. "No more!" he moaned. "Dear God, no more!"

The identical mutants ignored them all.

"You are not like me at all! If you were, you would know that it's—"

"I am like *me.* You are *not* like me. Now that I think about it, you don't even look like—"

"What do you even do here? Do you get visitors? I used to get visitors every day. Lots and lots of visitors! I don't want to stay here with—"

"I don't want you to stay here either!"

"Good! Because I don't want to, anyway!"

Tera grabbed Ollie's arm and dragged him into a corner of the cave. It was the closest they were going to get to privacy.

"I don't understand!" she whispered. "What's wrong with them?"

"I think..." Ollie paused wearily, looking over his shoulder at the quarreling crustaceans. "I think maybe they're too much alike."

"They're clones," Tera said. She left the "duh" unspoken, but it hung in the air between them anyway.

"Maybe it's an opposites-attract kind of thing. Like, opposites attract, and clones...don't."

"But they're soul mates!"

Ollie shrugged helplessly.

Tera's expression turned suspicious. "They are, right? Soul mates?"

"Yes! Of course."

"Are you sure?"

The nervous feeling that had been nibbling at his stomach lining began to chomp. Hard. "Sure, I'm sure."

"But how do you know?"

He threw up his hands defensively. "What do I look like, a freakin' Salt Collector? I made a guess."

"Yeah, well, it looks like maybe you guessed wrong." She folded her arms.

Ollie mirrored her movements, folding his own arms in a panicked huff. "Maybe I did! But what the hell was I supposed to do? Just grab some random half-snake thing and make a run for it? I saw what I saw. Maybe if you had gone in there like I wanted you to, you could have done it better."

He felt, suddenly, like he was floating above his own body, watching the scene from afar. In the other corner of the cave, Laszlo had lifted his head and was staring at them. Even Jinx and Howerbout had quieted.

He and Tera were fighting. Really fighting. She was pissed. At him. The knowledge left him feeling hollow and, somehow, even more angry.

"You knew why I couldn't go in there," Tera said.

"Oh, right," Ollie countered, a sarcastic edge to his voice. "I forgot. The hot guy in the suit. You didn't trust yourself to be near him, isn't that right?"

"Ollie, what in the actual hell are you talking about?"

"You know what I'm talking about!"

"Please, enlighten me."

Her calmness infuriated him even further. Of course she wanted Carmichael. What girl wouldn't? He was the perfect package. Unlike Ollie, who had...nothing. Nothing! No answers. No optimism. No suggestions of any kind. All he had was this anger, splashing and bubbling in the cauldron of his gut. He felt impotent, and cornered, and pissed.

And...hot.

Really, crazy hot.

Ollie looked down, tugged up a sleeve. There it was again: the reddish glow on his skin. The bumpy, crimson freckles—small at first, then bigger. And bigger again. Growing before his eyes, like poison ivy on a deadline. Somehow, the sight only made him madder.

"I screwed up, okay?" he heard himself shout. The words, and the vehemence, surprised even him. "I screwed it all up. Just like I screw everything up. I did it up on the Brickside, and now I'm doing it here. You were wrong to trust me. Newsflash. Now you know."

"Krite, Ollie. Pull it together, will you? We have to fix this."

"There is no fixing this! We just keep making it worse!"

"What are you saying? That we're not going to find the women?"

"Yes! That's exactly what I'm saying! We're not going to find the lab, we're not going to make it to the Brickside, and we're sure as hell not going to find any missing people. Wake up, Tera! We're not even going to get out of this goddamn cave!"

She jerked back as though she'd been slapped.

He had gone too far. He knew it the minute he said it. The rash on his arm seemed to know it, too. Ollie felt the freckled protrusions expanding, pushing against the confines of his jumpsuit. Felt the heatwave spreading down his torso and limbs.

But...wasn't he right? And didn't some part of her already know it?

Anyone could see: They had no shot of making this happen. They never had, despite what they had told themselves. If they had taken off their rose-colored glasses for even a minute, they would have realized it was impossible—mainly due to the inconvenient fact that they were trapped in this ridiculous, underground world with lungs that didn't work anywhere else, and all they'd had for "help" was a bunch of stoned witches hiding in a bird's nest, a sweat-licking old lady, a riddle from a dead guy, and a couple of supposed soul mates who, apparently, hated each other's guts. Not exactly a recipe for success.

Howerbout would never let them out—not like this. They'd never find the lab, or the device, if it even existed. Ollie had had his chance to fix this, and he'd failed. No: It was worse than that. He had taken a concerning situation and made it absolutely wretched. Who does that? It was like a gift. His one true skill. When God was handing out talents, he'd looked down at Ollie and said, *I grant thee the eternal ability to Make Matters Worse. Go, now. Share your gift with the world.*

Instinctively, he reached for the ball of fuzz on his shoulder...and found it empty. *Meatball.* Why the hell had he agreed to leave the trog behind? What had he been thinking? Now, he was separated from his furry friend by an endless expanse of water and time. Would Ollie ever see him again? The horrid void on his shoulder felt abnormal, and wrong. Almost catastrophic. *Trogastrophic,* he thought. *Calamity caused by the sudden, unexpected absence of snorting sounds in one's ear.* He would have laughed if it didn't make him want to cry.

His chest tightened. His teeth began to chatter. The mushrooming heat under his skin made him sway as rivulets of sweat dripped from his forehead.

It was too much. All of it. He'd never be enough: not for Tera, not for this place, and certainly not for this mission. He had let her down. Let them all down. And hadn't he known he would, all along? Hadn't the Widow Hibbins told him that from the very start?

You did nothing, she had said. *You were nothing. And so, that is how you shall remain, within these walls, until the end of your days. As nothing.*

What did he think, that he would actually get away with it? That he could have friends, and a home, and a trog, *and* a beautiful, brilliant girlfriend? It was good while it lasted, he supposed. Like a mid-afternoon daydream interrupted by a honking horn out the window.

Tera would leave him now, as she should.

Well, not *leave* him, leave him, because she couldn't actually go anywhere. More in the metaphorical sense. In the actual sense, she was going to be stuck down here with him for an eternity, condemned to life in a claustrophobic, echoey cavern with two squabbling nincompoops. She would spend the rest of her days glaring at Ollie through the fire-pit smoke, probably wishing she'd never met him. Probably wishing him dead. He wouldn't blame her if she did. And since wishes seemed to count for something down here, that might just be the end of it. *I wish for Ollie to be dead*, she would think, offhandedly, and over he would keel: one more pile of bones for the collection.

He'd never asked to be a mastermind. Or a leader. Hell, he'd never even asked for a soul mate. All he had ever wanted was to be a little less alone. But even that, it seemed, was too much to ask.

As the despair washed over him, Ollie's thoughts turned to his mother. The papery, warm grip of her hands—still strong, even after the cancer came. Her legs crossed on the gold, upholstered couch, one fuzzy slipper swinging back and forth, back and forth, as she gossiped with the ladies. The smell of her Chanel No. 5 perfume. Lemony dish soap in the sink. Ciabatta bread baking in the oven on a Sunday afternoon.

The loss of her still punctured like an ice pick, every day, all the time. But especially in times like this. *Mama*, he wailed silently. *I need you. What do I do?*

Ollie tilted his head back, staring hard at the rocky ceiling. Straining to hear her voice. Her spirit. Anything.

But all he heard was the distant whistle of trapped, restless wind.

That is how you shall remain, within these walls, until the end of your days, the wind said. *As nothing.*

Ollie's head dropped. His veins ran cold; his limbs went limp. The wind was wrong. He wasn't nothing: He was less than nothing. Less than a speck of algae in the churning lake, less than a grain of salt in Weelichka's vast collection, less than a single, slimy pore on the Blumbat's walrus-gray skin.

He was less, even, than the underground wind itself, whistling its unheard song of pain throughout the centuries. Crawling relentlessly through the deep and the dark, where no wind should be. Never landing, never slowing, never belonging.

I wish to be the wind, Ollie thought.

But even as he wished it, he knew it was no use. Down here, wishes only worked when they were true.

Seventeen

Tera took another step back. Her face had blanched. "Ollie, stop it. I'm serious."

"No, *I'm* serious," he countered. "You're better off without me, okay?" It felt freeing to say it out loud, finally. It felt noble. "You were going to figure that out eventually, so it might as well be now. I'm just slowing you down."

"You are not slowing me down."

"I am!"

"You're not," she said, more gently.

"I don't belong here, Tera! Don't you see that? I shouldn't have stayed. I'm not like you guys! I'm not tough, or smart, or, or"—he thought of Carmichael—"or handsome. You can do better. You *need* to do better. So you go. Please. Make this right. Take Derrin, and Kuyu, and Ajanta, and whoever else. And I'll just...stay out of the way." He lifted his chin a little. He might be losing Tera, but he would not lose his dignity, too.

"Oh, yeah? How exactly does that happen?"

"I'll stay here, with Howerbout. He'll let you go if I stay."

"What, forever?"

Ollie straightened. "If I have to, yes." He would stay, and Howerbout would wish for the rest of them to leave. And then he would just wait for the yammering crab-man to push him over the edge into insanity. With any luck, he'd inherit his father's propensity for lapsing into unconscious limbo. At this point, it was probably the best he could hope for.

Tera massaged her forehead with her fingers. "Jesus, I thought those two idiots were the ones who couldn't remember anything."

Ollie pursed his lips. Still looking chivalrous, he hoped.

Tera sighed. "Listen to me, you big dope. Let's take a little walk down memory lane, okay? When I was locked in that fighting pit, who came to my rescue?"

He lifted one shoulder. "Well, I mean, there were a few of—"

"Who?" she interrupted sternly.

Ollie shoved his hands in his pockets. "Me," he muttered.

"Sorry? I didn't hear that."

"Me," he said again, louder.

"That's right. And when I asked for help on this ridiculous impossible mission, or anything else for that matter, what did you say?"

He hesitated.

"You said yes," she finished for him. "You always say yes when I need you. And when things get complicated, you always figure out a way through. I'd say that qualifies as both tough *and* clever. And as for handsome..." After a pause, she reached out and slowly started walking two fingers up his arm. "Well, I think we've established my opinion on that particular subject."

He blushed.

Laszlo, Jinx, and Howerbout were dead silent now, hanging on every word.

"Oll, you told me that I was like a paper cut. Remember that?"

He nodded.

"You said paper cuts were small but mighty, and that nothing could heal them except time."

He looked down and scuffed the toe of his sneaker into the sandy cave floor.

"You were wrong about one thing," Tera continued. She bent forward and titled her head, trying to catch his eye. "*You* heal me. If I'm a paper cut, then you're a Band-Aid. You heal me, Ollie. I need you. Don't bail on me now."

He swallowed down the lump in his throat. Something hard in his chest was softening. Still firm, but softening. The heat under his skin was receding. The bumpy rash, if it was still there, had stopped itching.

When he finally trusted himself to speak, he said, "I never thought I would want to be compared to a Band-Aid."

"Yeah, well, it's better than being compared to a paper cut," Tera countered.

A smile dared to tug at his lips. Clearly, they had a long way to go in the romantic metaphor department. But he didn't care. Ollie pressed his hands together into a steeple. "You know, Band-Aids have actually improved a lot since you've been down here," he said. "Some of them have waterproof coatings now. And twisty fabric, and cartoon characters. Different colors, too."

Tera looked impressed, then shook her head. "Sorry. You're just the regular kind. Plastic. Little holes."

"No Bugs Bunny?"

"Nope."

"Yeah, you're probably right."

They grinned at each other. Laszlo and the two crab-men stayed quiet.

"So," Tera said, clapping her hands together. "Now that we've settled all the first-aid questions, can we move on? Because I don't know about you, but I don't plan to spend the rest of my life down here. We have work to do."

"Like what?" Her clap had snapped him back into the present. What work was there to do? They were out of options. Short of hypnotizing Howerbout into making a wish against his will, they weren't getting out of that cave anytime soon.

The crabs had started arguing again.

"For starters, I think it's safe to say we got the wrong soul mate," she said. "*We* got the wrong one, not just you."

Ollie looked at Howerbout. Or at least, at the one he thought was Howerbout. "Maybe he'll agree to let us go, anyway."

"He won't."

She was right, of course. He let out a puff of frustration. "So now what?"

Tera twisted her lips to the side, deep in thought. Then she said, "Now...we go back and get the right one."

Ollie assumed she was joking. "As if. Carmichael won't sell us another one of his creatures, trust me. And even if he did, we still don't know which one to take! What are we supposed to do, just keep going back and forth until we finally get it right?"

"No. That would take too long." Tera propped her hands on her hips and spread her legs wide. The full power stance. "We're going once more. That's it. And we're going to get them all."

"Get them...all?" Ollie stared at her. He was starting to worry that she had finally, seriously, lost her mind.

"Yes." Her voice was louder now. Firmer. "We're going to get every last one of those poor creatures out of that hellhole and bring them back here. One of them is the soul mate. I know it. And maybe one of them knows where the lab is, too. We're going to make Howerbout happy, free Laszlo, and find that damn mad scientist and his damn mad laboratory. And then we're going to go to the Brickside, figure out where they're keeping those women, and set them free."

She sounded so confident, Ollie almost believed it.

In the corner, an eavesdropping Laszlo jumped to his feet. "Nooo!" he wailed, desperation straining at his features. "Please, say is not truth! You are not leaving me here again! Not with them!"

"I'll stay!" Ollie interjected. "Take Laszlo. Leave me here."

At this, Howerbout spun and stamped a claw. "No! No, no, no, no! I want my friend Laz! Not that one!" Another claw lifted into the air and pointed at Ollie. "I want my friend Laz! I won't wish for anything else." His lower lip jutted out, punctured by two sharp teeth.

Tera turned to Laszlo, lifting her palms apologetically.

The acrobat's head fell. "Fine," he moaned, scraggly black hair covering his long face. Then he looked up at her plaintively. "Is fine. Just hurry, yes? Fast as bunnies."

"Faster," Tera assured him. "Fast as bunnies making baby bunnies. I know you've got to get back up to the Brickside soon. But you've still got time, right? Can you be patient a little while longer?"

"Ahhhgh." Laszlo dropped his forehead into his hands again. Without looking up, he waved a woebegone arm. "Go, now. Just go. Go, go, go, go." The word lost volume with each repetition.

Beside him, the crab-men resumed their marathon altercation.

Ollie stared at the scene in bewilderment. If Dozer were here, he would tell Tera she was crazier than a soup sandwich. But Dozer wasn't here. And who was Ollie to argue? He was the one who had picked the wrong soul mate and screwed everything up. Clearly, he had ceded any rights to group decision-making from here on out.

"But...how?" he asked timidly. "Dozer and I can't go back in there. There's no way. Carmichael will know something's up as soon as he sees us."

"Yeah, I know." Tera sighed again. "You're not going in. I am."

"I thought you said you couldn't go in there because he'll remember you."

"Oh, he'll remember me," Tera said, her face grim. "I'm counting on it."

———⌘———

"Remind me again why I'm doing this?"

"Because you're a very, very good friend," Ollie answered. "And I'm giving you free Ollanta's rhizers for a month."

Dozer gave him a dubious sideways glance.

"For a year," Ollie amended.

Dozer grunted in agreement.

They were crammed together in a space that was much too small to accommodate both of them. It was an oppressive, stuffy wooden box, with little light and even less breathable air. They tried to keep their voices low, their breaths shallow, and their bodies as still as humanly possible, though they were doing none of those things particularly well.

It didn't help that they were also sharing the cramped space with a pair of spindly, flailing crow legs. Every few seconds, one or both of the crow's feet would kick one of them in the side, producing a muffled "oof" of pain.

Howerbout had agreed to wish for Tera and Ollie to leave his cave—again—on two conditions: one, Laszlo had to remain behind—again—and two, Jinx had to leave along with them. That had been fine with Jinx, and not so fine with Laszlo. But, as the acrobat himself grudgingly admitted, "You cannot get always what you want." And so, it seemed only fitting that none of them got what they wanted, in the end. Well, none except Jinx, who left their side the minute they hit the water to find an empty lake cave of his own—presumably as far from Howerbout's as he could get.

Now, after a brief, confused reunion and a flurry of preparations, Ollie and Dozer had found themselves at the shadowy loading dock at Carmichael's House of Unnatural Wonders. Trapped inside a box. Underneath the body of a massive—and massively unhappy—bird.

A pair of brown eyes peered in through the box's air holes. "You guys doing okay in there?" Tera whispered.

They grunted in reluctant agreement.

Behind her, a noisy chain began to turn a wheel. A door began to rise. And Michael Carmichael stepped out onto his dock, staring suspiciously at the loitering boat that bobbed in the water behind his fine establishment.

"Who's there?" Carmichael asked, shielding his eyes for a better view.

"Look away, boys," Tera muttered into the air holes. "This won't be pretty." She pinched her cheeks, pressed her lips together twice, and ran her fingers through the purple, messy mohawk. Then she turned and raised a hand in greeting. "Hey, Mikey!"

As recognition dawned, pleased amazement splayed across his features. "Martinez? Is that you?"

"Sure is," Tera answered, striding forward. "How's the handsomest man in the Neath?"

Ollie stiffened; Dozer gave him a warning look and a head shake. Or tried to give a head shake, anyway—an actual head shake would have been impossible, given that Dozer's head was wedged into the corner of the box. Either way, Ollie got the message: *Chill.*

Right, Ollie told himself. *Chill. It's all an act. You know that. She hates this guy. Or at least, she said she hates this guy.* He dug a fingernail into the fat folds in the palm of his hand. *Get a grip, you idiot. Do your job.*

"How am I? I'm better now, baby." Carmichael said, lifting one eyebrow and one side of his mouth. It was like an asymmetrical ode to lechery.

Then Tera did something that shook Ollie to his core: She tucked a piece of hair behind her ear, and she giggled. She actually giggled. She also seemed to be twisting herself into the shape of the letter S and sidling up much closer to Carmichael than was necessary for normal conversation.

Their voices dropped. Ollie strained to hear the conversation but caught only snippets—exclamations, mostly, on her part, and deep, seductive murmurs on his. Tera seemed amazed, absolutely amazed, by every stupid sentence that left his mouth. Her smiles flashed fast and hard, accompanied by an array of gratuitous gestures: slow, wide-eyed nods. Fingernails running along the nape of her neck. A gentle stretching of her back, as though she was trying to work out the kinks of a long day.

Carmichael looked more objectively attractive than he had the last time Ollie had seen him, if that was even possible. The guy was like a walking actor's headshot. He was wearing the colorful coat, again, and the tight belt. And of course the expensive shoes, which seemed as out of place in the Neath as a bottle of sunscreen. The tiny, tilted top hat was back, too, though this one was cobalt blue instead of black.

The flames from the dock's torches gave a carnal gleam to the Fancy Man's eyes and a warm glow to his already flawless skin. Casually, and yet not so casually, he tossed an arm over Tera's shoulder.

She seemed to be explaining something, now, and pointing to the boat. They walked closer. Ollie pulled his face away from the air holes.

"Since when do you do jobs for the Doc?" Carmichael was asking.

Tera shrugged. And giggled, again. "Oh, you know how it is. Another day, another dollar." Then she gave him a playful punch in his six-pack abs. "But look who I'm talking to. You don't have to worry about that kind of stuff. You must be the most successful guy down here! Everybody says so. This thing you've created…" She shook her head as through overcome with admiration. "It's really something, isn't it? Really something. I don't think anyone else could have done anything quite like it." Tera smiled sweetly.

Carmichael shrugged with faux modesty. He gave her a wink— an actual wink!—and pointed to the boat. "What is that thing, anyway?"

"That," Tera said proudly, "is a guppy-crow. Direct from the lab."

Caw! said Mrs. Paget. Whether she was confirming or objecting, Ollie couldn't say.

Just a few hours before, Tera had recruited Ajanta, Derrin, and Kuyu to help her brush every last one of the big crow's feathers with streaks of pink, silver, yellow, aquamarine, teal, and white. They had emptied nearly every tube of paint in her studio. But in the end, they had all agreed: It had been worth it. It was, Tera said, her best creation yet.

Mrs. Paget's once-dark feathers now looked like a rainbow of scales. Guppy scales, specifically, colored from the memory of Tera's childhood fish tank. Thanks in part to the blue glow from the wormwalkers above, the "scales" glimmered with an iridescence that would have looked right at home in the lake's deepest depths. Her beak and eyes remained stark, solid black.

Caw! she said again.

Half crow, half fish.

One hundred percent bullshit.

And Carmichael was eating it up like an elf at a peppermint factory. "Damn! That's a cool one," he said. "They're really cooking up some crazy shit over there."

"Yeah," Tera nodded. "They did run into a few problems, though. No legs." She gestured toward the spot where Mrs. Paget's lower body rested on the box. "That thing has wheels. That's how you get her around."

"Oh," Carmichael said in surprise. "So we're just supposed to...keep her on there? Like, all the time?"

"I guess so," Tera gave a convincing shrug, as though this was the first time she had considered it. "Like a wheelchair, I suppose."

In reality, Mrs. Paget's legs and feet were not only intact but also, at that very moment, kicking the eye patch off of Dozer's face. The big man grimaced, shoved the black foot away, and reaffixed the patch over his missing eye. A few hours before, they had cut two small holes in the box and slid Mrs. Paget's legs inside, leaving her to rest her body weight along the top. Throughout it all, the crow had sat stoically. Barely a squawk.

Ollie had to admit: The whole thing had made him reassess his opinion of the big black bird. So she did occasionally want to peck his eyeballs out. So what? He couldn't think of too many others of her kind who would willingly submit to feather painting and leg subjugation in a wooden box. Ollie's mother used to have a saying for some of their more hardened North End neighbors: *"She's a tough old bird."* Now, finally, he knew what she had meant. Mrs. Paget was, truly, a tough old bird. And a loyal one, too.

He gave her spindly leg an affectionate pat. In response, the limb kicked out and clocked him in the cheekbone. Ollie groaned.

Dozer pressed a finger to his lips.

Out on the dock, Carmichael was asking a question: "Does it have a name?"

Ollie peered through the tiny hole at Tera, who was suddenly looking like a kid who hadn't raised her hand but got called on anyway. She blinked rapidly. "Uh... Huh. If they told me, I don't remember it." She lifted her palms helplessly. "Hey, why don't you name it? You're so good at that!"

"Yeah, okay," Carmichael agreed. He studied Mrs. Paget, who, Ollie assumed, was returning the Fancy Man's stare with one of her own. "We'll call it the... Crowerfish. No, the Gupperscupper."

Tera nodded encouragement at each suggestion.

"Or how about...Rainbowcrow?" Carmichael continued. He snapped his fingers. "Wait, no! I've got it. Fisherswisher! Like, fishing and flying. At the same time."

Tera didn't immediately answer, probably because she was waiting for more pronouncements. When none came, she nodded agreeably. "Sure! Sounds great."

He flashed two rows of pearly, straight teeth. "Fisherswisher it is."

In the box, Ollie rolled his eyes and snorted.

Dozer kneed him in the side.

"I don't know, though, Tera," Carmichael said, rubbing his chin. "No one told me about any new shipments. I'm not really ready for new merchandise. And damn... This one's *really* big. It's going to eat a *lot."* He looked at Mrs. Paget dubiously.

"I've got you covered," Tera answered, walking to the boat and lifting a bucket full of seeds and squirming insects. "They told me to give you this."

He nodded, then paused. "Yeah, that should help for a couple of days. But it's just weird, though. A shipment out of the blue, like this. The Doc has never done that before."

Tera rubbed his shoulder. "It's probably just because he has so much faith in you, Mikey. He doesn't even have to think about it, right? He knows you can handle anything, so he just, boom, sends it off. Sounds like a pretty big compliment, to me." She was practically purring. Leaning in close.

Michael Carmichael straightened. "I guess so. Yeah." He looked thoughtful again. "I did have one cage open up recently... And this one would look good on the posters. Colorful and all."

"Definitely," Tera agreed.

"Hey, Martinez, maybe you can make a few new posters for me. Like in the old days." His hand ran down her back, then traveled lower.

Tera deftly darted just out of reach. "Sure, why not. I can do that."

He smiled down at her. "All right, then. I'll get the cage ready tonight. We can bring in our Fisherswisher tomorrow."

"Tomorrow?" A look of mild panic crossed Tera's face. She covered it quickly with a more benign expression. "You're just going to leave her—uh, it, out here? All night?"

He shrugged. "Yeah. What difference?"

Tera cleared her throat. "No difference to me. But why do you have to clean the cage? It's just a stupid mutant. Don't tell me you're going soft on me, Mikey."

"What? No." He shifted uncomfortably.

"Then let's get the thing inside and get it over with so we can concentrate on more...important things tonight." She waggled her eyebrows.

Carmichael looked pleased, then uncertain. "Not that I'm complaining, but... Where's all this coming from, Martinez?"

"What do you mean?"

"The last time we saw each other, I got the impression that I was maybe not your favorite person."

"What?" Tera allowed a look of shock to cross her face. "Nah. C'mon. It's a small world down here, isn't it? We're all in this together. And when I got this assignment, I just figured, you know..." She pointed to Mrs. Paget. "Two birds with one stone."

He grinned.

"Did I mention I also brought a little gift?" she added.

"Oh, yeah? What's that?"

She pointed to a barrel on the side of the boat with fizzing grog bubbling over its edges.

His eyes widened. "Is that...?"

"Moseby's finest," Tera confirmed. "She owed me a favor. But it's too much for one person, obviously, so I thought maybe you could help me make a dent in it." This time, it was her turn to wink.

Carmichael laughed out loud. "Hell, yes. Now you're talking." He stepped back to appraise her. "I don't know what's gotten into you, Martinez. But I like it. I like it a lot."

"Oh yeah? If you like this, you're going to love the rest."

"I'm sure I will, baby. I'm sure I will."

Inside the box, Ollie scowled. Dozer gave him a placating thumbs up. And somewhere above their heads, Mrs. Paget let loose with a loud caw as she and her two hidden companions found themselves suddenly rolling up the dock and though the doorway. Behind them, a gear began to crank. A chain began to spin. Seconds later, the heavy door hit the floor behind them with a bone-rattling thud.

Tera had done it. They were in.

Come one, come all, to the magnificent, the mystical, the freakish and peculiar House of Unnatural Wonders, Ollie thought with a grimace. He could already smell the stink.

Eighteen

Ollie and Dozer tumbled out together onto the hay-scattered cage floor, which was still soaked with the remnants of Jinx's crabby urine.

"Damn, son!" Dozer said, coughing and pressing an arm against his face. "What've you got me into, here?"

"Sorry, sorry," Ollie muttered. He got to his feet and wiped his knees clean. Well, as clean as he could get them, given the circumstances.

Caw! Mrs. Paget said.

"I know!" Ollie told both of them, holding up his hands. "This will be quick, I promise!" It had to be, if they had any hope of finding Laszlo coherent and functioning upon their return to Howerbout's cave.

"How quick?" Dozer asked. He peered around the dim cage unhappily. "You know I ain't looking to be locked in no dungeon again."

"We're not locked in," Ollie said.

"That so?" Dozer pointed at the closed latch on the door. "'Cause that sure looks locked to me."

"Well, *technically,* yes," Ollie allowed. "But don't worry, man. Tera's got this." If he'd had a watch, he would have glanced at it. Instead, he tapped his fingers against his thigh.

The racket echoed all around them: screeching; clacking; splashing; bleating; roaring; barking; peeping; growling. And a few other, scarier noises that Ollie couldn't identify.

Dozer rubbed the stubble on his chin and moved toward the bars. Poking his face through, he let out a whistle. Ollie knew what Dozer was seeing: Headless Ceecilfeet. Slimy Salamandovers. Groaning Garabarnacle. Hissing Cassavacat. A sad blur of feathers, fur, saliva, and stench. He never thought he would see any of these creatures, or this place, again. And now here he was, locked in right beside them.

"What'd that gussied-up guy say? All these things were made in a lab somewhere?"

Ollie nodded glumly. "He said these are just the rejects. Whatever they don't want, they send here."

"So there's *more* of these things, somewhere?"

"Seems so, yeah."

"Damn." Dozer gave a slow shake of his head as he gripped the bars. "That ain't good. That ain't good at all."

"What do you mean?"

"If these are the rejects, then what in blue blazes do you think is back at that lab?"

"I...don't know."

"Who runs this here lab?" Dozer asked, folding his arms.

"Uh..." Ollie didn't want to say *I don't know* again, so instead he said, "Carmichael just mentioned a guy he called 'the Doc.' Maybe him?"

Dozer scratched the skin under his eye patch. "Hmm. Don't ring no bells. Either way, we're going to have to find out right quick."

"Find out what?"

"Find out what's really going on here. With these animal...things."

"What? No. Uh, uh." Ollie shook his head. "We're not here for that. We've got to get them all out of here, and that's it. Laszlo's running out of time down there, and those women are still missing."

"As far as you know."

"Well, yeah. As far as I know. And my Brickside friends might still be in danger. Nell, and Mr. B. So whatever else is going on, it's got nothing to do with us."

"As far as you know."

Ollie held up his palms in frustration. "Yes. *As far as I know, it's got nothing to do with us.*"

Dozer tilted his head to the side. "Boy, you still don't know where you are, do you? I thought I taught you better than that. Everything down here has to do with everything else. Everything. There ain't nowhere to hide in the Neath. So if something bad is happening, we'd damn well better know what it is."

Ollie could feel a fresh wave of exhaustion kicking in. Suddenly, he desperately wished for a recliner and a ginger ale. No—a latte. A mocha latte. And a soft fleece blanket. Lights down low. Some kind of cooking show on the TV.

Just the thought of it made him tingle with longing.

Then, with a sigh, Ollie returned to rude, latte-free reality. And the barnyard fumes. And the bone-rattling, ceaseless discord of his fellow bunker prisoners. "C'mon," he asked. "How bad could it be? I mean, what could be worse than Herrick's End?"

They sat quietly together for a minute, sharing the grim memory. Did Dozer try to forget, like he did? It was an impossible task, of course. Every grisly detail lived just under the surface of his skin, always, like a tattoo: the filth, the torture, the confinement, the hard labor, the starvation—and of course, the brutal Knockdown tournaments.

"I can't think of nothing worse," Dozer finally said, his voice hard. "But I reckon the Warden and his Reds can. And did."

"Yeah, well, the Warden's frozen now," Ollie said. "So there's nothing to worry about. Not anymore."

Dozer snorted. "If you believe that, I got a bridge to sell you."

"What's that supposed to mean?"

"It means, the Warden's got friends. What do you think, he's the only one with designs on this place? C'mon, boy. You can't be that wet behind the ears. Just because you got that man sitting still in a chair, that don't mean trouble's sitting still with him."

Ollie opened his mouth to interrupt, then closed it again.

"Think, kid. Who's gonna go through all this ruckus and bother just for a carnie sideshow?" Dozer gestured to the long rows of cages. "Nobody. Whoever's doing this, they got something else in mind. And I'm telling you right now, it ain't nothing good."

Ollie was silent for a moment. Then he said, "Aren't you the one who told me that it's better not to ask too many questions down here?"

"That's rule number one," Dozer nodded. "And rule number two is, sometimes you got to forget rule number one."

Caw! Caw!

Ollie looked up at Mrs. Paget. She was attempting, and failing, to flap her thickly painted wings.

At the end of the aisle, the sound of laughter—Tera's laughter—and intermittent thumping erupted from somewhere inside Carmichael's office.

"Sounds like a party," Dozer said wryly.

Caw!

"Something like that," Ollie answered, eyeing the closed "Proprietor's Office" door. "Won't be long, now."

He hoped he was right.

With that, they settled reluctantly into the damp, sticky hay. And they waited.

———⁂———

Ollie didn't know how long they had been napping—Ollie and Dozer on the ground and Mrs. Paget on her wheeled perch—when a clinking sound awakened them.

"You guys look awfully comfy," a voice said. "Maybe I should let you sleep."

Ollie lifted his chin from the hay to see Tera standing outside the cage, dangling a set of keys from her hand. He scrambled to his feet, still groggy.

Mrs. Paget shook her head with a corkscrew twist.

Dozer wiped his one good eye, blinked, and asked, "What happened?"

"What do you think happened?" Tera answered, looking mildly insulted. "I kicked ass and took names. And addresses." She smiled. "Are you guys ready to help, or do I need to do the rest myself, too?"

Ollie ran to the bars. "Get us out of here."

"I don't know..." she said, looking doubtful. "I hate to interrupt nap time."

He flashed her an unamused look.

"All right, all right...geez." Still grinning, Tera lifted the key ring. "Get my girl out of that thing, would you?"

Dozer and Ollie struggled to free the crow's legs from the box while Tera tried various keys in the lock. Finally, it snapped open.

"Voila," she said. "Free at last. By my count, that makes twice, now, that I've sprung you from captivity. And you've only rescued me once."

"Guess I'll have to owe you one," Ollie answered.

"Luckily for you, that won't be necessary. None of us will be needing any more rescue from here on out."

"Well, besides Laszlo," Dozer interjected.

"True," Tera said. "And our new friends, here." She looked down the aisle with her hands on her hips as Ollie, Dozer, and Mrs. Paget pushed through the cage door. "I suppose we'd better get started."

"Where's the pretty boy?" Dozer asked.

"He's, uh, sleeping. For a while," Tera said, her face blank. "He won't be bothering us."

"What about the guards?" asked Ollie.

She waved a hand. "The place is closed for the night. They probably went home hours ago."

Caw!

Ollie and Dozer glanced at each other. Neither commented.

"Everybody ready?" she asked.

Nods all around.

Together, they approached the nearest cage to the right and peered at its inhabitants: seven tiny, deranged-looking Kimmerswimmers, dribbling foam from their fangs. From the back, you would have thought they were ducklings. Yellow. Fluffy. Adorable. From the front, you would have thought... Well, you probably wouldn't have thought anything, because you'd be too busy running away. They made odd gurgling sounds as they waddled closer, clearly curious about the hubbub near the door of their cage.

Tera handed Ollie and Dozer each a knife. "Here, just in case," she said. "I found them in the office."

Dozer looked at his knife, and at the Kimmerswimmers, with obvious concern. "They gonna bite?" he asked.

Tera lifted her hands and eyebrows in a *who knows?* kind of gesture that Ollie did not find reassuring.

Above their heads, Mrs. Paget gave a loud, guttural squawk. Clearly, she wasn't planning to allow any Unnatural Wonders—fuzzy or otherwise—to harm her Tera.

Neither was Ollie. "They'll be fine," he said. They had to know, didn't they? Somewhere deep down, all these creatures had to understand that this place was bad, and that leaving it was good. Even still, he found himself clutching the handle of his own knife tighter than was strictly necessary. And feeling glad that Meatball was safe back at home with Derrin, Kuyu, and Ajanta. "Open it," he said.

After a brief pause, Tera complied. Ollie could feel Mrs. Paget tensing beside him, probably readying her deadly beak to stab.

The Kimmerswimmers craned their necks, looking up. The drooling and gurgling sounds continued. Then, the small creatures waddled out of the cage and into the aisle, snuffling curiously at the ground and at their visitors. One of them climbed onto Ollie's big foot, sniffed his ankle, and sat on his laces. The others loitered nearby. They reminded him of commuters on the Green Line, waiting for the next train to arrive.

"Hey, little guys," Tera said. "You want to come with us?"

The Kimmerswimmers, unsurprisingly, didn't reply.

"Herd them down there, will you?" she asked Ollie, gesturing toward the opening that led to the loading dock door. "Then we'll start on the rest."

Ollie bent and used his hands to lead the mutant ducklings in the right direction. When they reached the opening, he told them, "Wait here." They burbled in reply. Did they understand him? He had no idea. But they didn't move, so he returned to his friends to help keep the process moving.

They worked with assembly-line efficiency for the next five minutes or so: Tera unlocked the cages and spoke soothingly to the inhabitants; Ollie and Mrs. Paget herded the newly freed creatures down the hallway; and Dozer served as a guard of sorts for the growing crowd near the exit door.

Some of the mutants came easy. Others, however, created what his mother would have charitably called a *piccolo problema.* The fishy, suction-mouthed Champerchomper had to be carefully carried in its glass bowl. A huge, turtle-like creature meandered at a speed that made tectonic plate movement look like a bullet train. The Blumbat's wings opened and closed sporadically, knocking over anything, or anyone, nearby. And the furry alligator kept snagging its claws on its own long hair as it walked. In each case, Mrs. Paget provided incentive with a series of gentle beak prods.

Progress was steady, but slow. Too slow.

Ollie fought the urge to scream *"Hurry up!"* as he watched the creatures inch along—some in the right direction, some in the wrong direction, and some in no particular direction at all. *Hurry up, hurry up!* What would the Fancy Man do if he woke from his drunken stupor to find them stealing his prized specimens?

Crouching and sweating, Ollie kept his voice low, his pulse quick, and his eyes on Carmichael's office door. *Hurry, hurry, hurry.* Locks, opening. Feet, shuffling. Growls, growling. It wasn't until they reached the end of the aisle, with just a few cages left to open, that he realized his mistake.

He had been watching the wrong door.

The squeal was long, and ear-splitting: the unmistakable sound of complaining hinges.

Ollie froze. Then, slowly, he turned.

The main entrance doorway near the stairwell had been closed and dark just a moment before. Now, it was open. And entirely filled with the hulking bodies of two enormous, angry clowns.

They were about equal in size, wearing ruffle-neck collars, puffy harlequin shirts, and tight, red-and-white striped pants. Their faces were smeared with thick makeup, applied messily. One had a bright green wig; the other sported a bald head. They were ridiculous and menacing at the same time.

Oh, shit.

Ollie heard the motion behind him slow as the others noticed the guards, too. For a moment, all the humans stared at each other. No one moved.

Then, the bald one advanced. His face was a blur of white paint, red nose, and oversized, sneering lips. A blue star had been drawn around one of his eyes, but had melted into more of a sweaty smear.

Ollie started walking backwards. Reaching out an arm, he found Tera and pushed her further behind him.

"Uh, guys? I think we'd better skedaddle," Dozer said.

Skedaddle? They couldn't skedaddle! Not now! They weren't done! Ollie's mind raced, looking for a solution. But all he found was blankness. At his feet, confused creatures skittered and flopped and scratched at the dirt.

The guard was bearing down, holding a weapon. Ollie recognized it instantly: the cruel prod used by the Reds back at Herrick's End. Sparks flew from its tip haphazardly, landing on the scattered clumps of hay below. He knew from experience that one zap from that thing would send him flying—and leave him writhing on the ground in pain. Useless. Helpless.

Defeated.

All that he had suffered... All the progress they'd made... For what? For nothing?

The bald clown was so close now that Ollie could see the clumped, black eyeshadow on his lids. Ollie stared into those blue, hollow eyes and felt...heat.

So much heat.

The furnace started in his belly, spreading and crackling. He didn't have to look at his skin to know that it was changing from white to crimson. The blistered freckles were appearing, and rising. Pushing against the fabric of his clothes.

Goddamn Reds, he thought, teeth clenched. *Goddamn clowns. Goddamn cattle prods and cages and powerful idiots running roughshod over everyone else.* He'd had enough. Enough of feeling small. Enough of seething quietly while injustice reigned. Enough of standing by and watching selfish, sanctimonious, hypocritical assholes hold the rest of humanity under their tyrannical thumbs.

Ollie gripped his small knife. Steadied it. With new, sudden clarity, he could feel the energy pulsating around him—the energy of the creatures. He could see their colors radiating. Colors he had not seen before. He tasted their gifts, their improbable powers, their four-dimensional shapes.

And in that brief, crystalized moment, Ollie understood: He had underestimated them. The creatures were mutants, yes. But they were *his* mutants. Where he led, they would follow. What he asked of them, they would do.

Ollie stared at the advancing clowns as the fury rose within him like a full-moon tide. His shout, when it came, surprised even him:

"Get them!"

The words echoed against the bunker walls. For a moment, only silence followed. No grunts, no whines, no protests or questions.

Ollie inhaled and held his breath. He felt the red-hot glow coursing through his capillaries. Then he raised the knife, lunged forward—and instantly felt himself topple. The next thing he knew, he was face-down, staring at the gravel.

What the…?

A blur of long, low hair passed through his vision, and it took him a minute to realize what he was seeing: the wooly Hilligator. Its mouth was open, baring rows of sharp, mildewed teeth. The creature had pushed past Ollie, knocked him to the ground, and was now steadily advancing toward the guard.

The bald clown stopped, sneered, and held out the prod. If he was intimated by the sight of a mutant on the loose, he didn't show it.

The face-off between the human and hairy alligator was interrupted by a sudden, yellow blur. Ollie watched with morbid fascination as the gaggle of Kimmerswimmers padded past his face, climbed over the Hilligator's back, and swarmed the guard: a mob of deformed, maddened ducklings, all teeth and feathers and drool. In response, the clown started waving his weapon frantically, but couldn't seem to find a target.

The Hilligator took advantage of the distraction to chomp its mouth around the guard's foot. The man's red-painted lips formed an oval as he screamed.

The others followed in a frenzied throng: Screechwhits, heads spinning and wings flapping. Salamandovers, waving tentacles and spreading slime. The Gerstysnake, hissing and sidewinding its way down the aisle, wrapping an exposed clown ankle with a back full of spikes. And, of course, Mrs. Paget, slowed by her painted feathers but deadly accurate with her beak.

There were others, too—too many to count. Ollie found himself scooting backwards on his hands and butt in an effort to escape the pandemonium. He waited for the second clown, the one still in the doorway, to come to his comrade's aid. Instead, the horrified man tore off his green wig, tossed it like a useless shield, and ran away.

The bald guard, meanwhile, was still screaming and swatting at the onslaught. Finally, he managed to peel enough attacking mutants off his limbs to make a break for it. Brandishing his weapon, the hulking clown spun around and limped his way through the doorway, up the stairs, and out of sight.

Ollie gaped as the menagerie—some with teeth still bared— watched the guard retreat. They landed on top of each other, creating a sort of multi-hued, multi-textured lump on the gravel. Their chirps and snorts and snarls quieted; then, calmly, each creature in the clump disentangled itself and began the slow saunter back down the aisle. Toward the loading-dock exit.

Ollie stood, finally, and looked at Tera and Dozer. His friends stared back with astonished shrugs.

"Guess Carmichael's guys ain't too loyal," Dozer said, glancing at the empty doorway and the sad, green wig lying on the ground. "Maybe he should've given them that raise."

The joke landed flat; no one laughed.

Ollie swallowed and dropped his knife onto the ground. He peeked at his skin under the sleeve: The red was gone, as were the bumps. The odd, eerie clarity was gone, too. What *was* that? Some kind of hallucination? Or sickness? Why did it keep happening? Much as he hated to admit it, he knew it was possible—more than possible—that his body wasn't acclimating to the Neath as seamlessly as he had hoped it would. Maybe the adjustment came with side effects.

And then, an unwelcome thought: Was this what had happened to his father? Had Ollie started some kind of slow, neurological slide?

"Let's keep moving," Tera said. "Those two might have friends."

Ollie cleared his throat. "Right," he said. Whatever was happening to his head and body, now was not the time to ponder it. For all they knew, the guards were merely regrouping.

Several frenzied minutes later, all the cage doors were finally open. All the mutants were free and gathered near the exit. And all remained quiet, for the moment, behind Michael Carmichael's office door.

"That everybody?" Dozer asked.

Tera looked at the assembled, chattering group. "I think so."

"Good. Then let's blow this pop stand."

Ollie craned his neck to look up at the overhead door. It was bigger than a typical garage door, but not quite as big as the ones he had seen at Brickside warehouses. He and Dozer pulled on the heavy chain until it began to lift. They stopped when it was about halfway ajar—just wide enough to allow the motley crew of humans and mutants to walk, crouch, and crawl their way through the opening. Moments later, they all found themselves outside on the loading dock, staring at the open air, a blue ceiling, and a vast, dark lake.

And a fleet of crow boats, stretching out as far as the eye could see.

Ollie's eyes widened. When Tera had said she'd "get help," he didn't know she meant an entire goddamn Navy.

There had to be fifteen, maybe twenty, of them: crow boats just like Tera's, with a massive bird at the stern and rows of bench seats in the middle. Each boat was piloted by a single, determined-looking driver. Some, he recognized; Derrin, Kuyu, and Ajanta were right in the front. Behind them, he saw some of his former Floor Five Labor Force colleagues from Herrick's End: Edouard, Alfred, and Martel. Others, he had never met. Tera's friends, no doubt. Down here, nearly everyone was Tera's friend. Which came in handy on days like this.

A flash of motion caught Ollie's eye. He looked down to see Meatball leaping from the hull of Derrin's boat and scampering across the dock. Seconds later, the trog had climbed up Ollie's torso and settled onto his shoulder. Ollie gave him a grateful scratch and let out a sigh of relief that he didn't know he'd been holding.

"Ok, boys, load 'em up," Tera said, gesturing toward the gathered crowd of creatures on the dock. "We've still got a ways to go."

A ways to go. That was one way to put it.

With a jolt, Ollie heard his mother's voice in his head. *The woods are lovely, dark and deep,* she said, quoting her favorite poet. *But I have promises to keep, and miles to go before I sleep... And miles to go before I sleep.*

Me, too, Mama, he answered. *But I think I'm getting close.*

Nineteen

The fleet of boats sped as one over the surface of the lake, nearly silent in the blue-tinged darkness. Even the mutants seemed to understand that quiet was best. Above their heads, Mrs. Paget flapped in a steady rhythm, freed from her fishy, multicolored paint disguise after a cleansing dip in the water.

Ollie, Tera, and Dozer—each seated in a different boat—shared triumphant grins. They had done it. They had freed an entire bunkerful of victimized, captive creatures. Not some of them, but *all* of them. Granted, the mutants had pretty much rescued themselves in the end, but potato-potahto. All that mattered was that it was done. And now, they were about to come to Laszlo's rescue and bring two soul mates together. It was a win-win-win.

As the wind blew through his curls, Ollie felt positively formidable, like a Greenpeace protester who had just managed to foil an entire fleet of tankers with nothing but a can-do attitude and an inflatable raft. Nothing was going to dim his shine.

Well, almost nothing.

Remarkably, not a single one of them realized their miscalculation until they had reached the end of their speedy voyage. It was, Ollie assumed, the same spot in the lake they had jumped off from before. Tera motioned for all the crow boats to slow down, and they did. Then she stood in the hull, ready to orchestrate the mass exodus of creatures to Howerbout's cave.

She smiled, Ollie smiled, and Dozer smiled. Everyone else smiled with them.

And then, Tera's smile drooped. "Wait," she said. A look of panicked confusion crossed her face. "How...?"

Ollie saw it, then. What they had all missed.

Idiot! he thought, slapping the side of his own head. What the hell was the matter with him? Why didn't he think of this before now?

Hows and abouts, souls and mates.

How? How, how, how were they supposed to get these creatures to a cave *under* the lake? Ollie and Tera had been given the ability to breathe underwater, but no one else had. Most of the Unnatural Wonders were mammals. Or part mammals, anyway. They wouldn't get more than a few feet under the surface before having to rise up again for air. Assuming they even got that far.

Dozer had realized it, too, Ollie saw. And Ajanta, and Derrin, and Kuyu. It hit them all at once like a thunderous strike on a gong. The humans stared at each other, and at their unsuspecting passengers, with wide-eyed expressions of embarrassed dismay.

"Uh, oh," Kuyu said, climbing to her feet.

Tera held a hand over her mouth.

"How will you...?" Ajanta began, looking down at the lake as if an instructional manual might suddenly appear out of the depths.

"I don't know! Krite! I didn't even think—"

"How far is it?"

"It's too far! It's way too goddamn far!"

"C'mon, now," Dozer interrupted, holding up a hand. "No need to get ours tails up." He pointed to the Garabarnacle, which looked like a miniature seal, or a sea lion, perhaps, completely covered by a thick coating of barnacles. "That one can go in, right? And that one? The fish-eel thingy? Hell, that one's already in water. Just need to pour it out."

Ollie found himself nodding dumbly.

"And these!" Derrin added, gesturing to the brain-coraled Ceecilfeet waddling their blue flippers around her boat. "Look. They've got the, uh, coral...heads. So they'll probably be fine."

More creatures—the Gerstysnake, the Kimmerswimmers, the Hilligator, and the Hoopdeedoop, which was at least partially a frog—were pointed out as possible candidates, followed by an uneasy silence. Then Ajanta asked what all of them were thinking, but no one wanted to say: "But...what about the others?"

There was no way the Cassavacat was built for aquatic exploration. Or the White-Tailed Woodyworth, or the Llarsonllama, or the Screechwhits. And definitely not the knock-kneed Janedoe. Others, like the Salamandovers and the Blumbat, seemed to be more of a toss-up. Half-bat, half walrus? Could either half breathe under water? And for how long?

Tera slumped into the hull of her boat. She covered her head with her arms.

All was quiet until Dozer's voice boomed once again over the fleet. "Look here," he said. "This ain't no disaster. You said you was looking for a soul mate, ain't that right?"

Tera didn't lift her head. Ollie and the others nodded.

"A soul mate for the crab guy?"

More nods.

"Well, then, I don't see no problem," he said, pulling up his shoulders. "This crab guy lives under the water, don't he? So his soul mate must be able to do that, too. If they can't live in the same place, then they ain't very good soul mates, I'd say."

Slowly, Tera lowered her arms.

"He's right," Ajanta nodded. She flipped her long braid over her shoulder. "It only makes sense. So that means..." She looked around her boat, then pointed to the Stumeleon, which seemed to be nothing more than a color-changing fox. In the time it took her to turn, the animal's fur had already transitioned from pink to green. "This one is out."

"This one, too," said Kuyu, tapping the back of the Lonepayone beside her. It was, as far as Ollie could tell, a dog-sized forest beetle with a glittering shell. In response to the tap, the creature waved its serrated antennae cheerily.

"All right, all right," Tera stood, apparently having regathered her wits. "That's what we'll do, then. Anything that's aquatic, or part-aquatic, comes with me and Ollie. And the rest..." She paused, the uncertainty returning.

"The rest will come with us," Ajanta finished. "We'll take them to the nesting witches. Maybe something can be done."

Ollie had no idea what that "something" could possibly be, but he found himself fervently hoping that it was something good. "They can't go back to that place," he said, his voice firm. That was the one thing he knew for sure.

"They won't," Derrin assured him.

And because it was Derrin, he believed it.

Meatball, Ollie decided, would stay with him. Come what may, he wasn't going to risk losing his trog again.

The group began to shuffle its passengers and drivers, grouping the non-aquatic creatures together in the other boats for their journey to Elisha, Bert, and Lizbeth's nest. *Three on high.*

After brief goodbyes—too rapid and confused to be tearful—Derrin, Kuyu, Ajanta, and the others sailed away on the wind power of an entire flock of crows. Dozer, leaning against the railing at the stern of Kuyu's boat, gave a sad smile and a two-fingered salute to Ollie before disappearing into the fog.

Ollie found himself waving feebly, his heart sinking. He wished that Dozer could stay. What would become of the Screechwhits, the Blumbat, the Lonepayone, and all the others? What if the witches wouldn't, or couldn't, help? Where else could the Unnaturals find a home, if not in an underground sideshow of horrors? And what would Carmichael do once he woke up and found them gone?

Tera was talking, he suddenly realized. To him.

"Hmm?" he asked.

She smiled patiently. "I said, are you ready?"

Ollie hesitated. He looked down at the remaining mutants in the hull of the boat, impossible in their multitude. He looked at Tera, radiant as always, even now. He looked at the wide, somber, aquatic expanse all around them, beckoning and threatening at the same time.

Would they still be able to breathe under there, or had their chance already passed? Only one way to find out.

Moments later, air became water. Thought became delirium. And all of Ollie's worries dissipated into the swift, spellbinding currents below the surface of his lake.

The first one they lost was the Champerchomper.

They had poured the fish-slash-eel out of its bowl and into the lake, instructing it to stay with them.

Instead, the suction-mouthed mutant promptly swam away.

The Hilligator was the next to go, its incongruous long hair swirling in the currents as it circled the group, explored its surroundings, and took off for greener waters. That was followed by the rapid disappearance of the Gerstysnake, the Hoopdeedoop, all of the Kimmerswimmers, and three or four others whose names he couldn't recall. Just...gone. Were they seeking out solitary freedom in the depths? Were they just confused? He supposed he'd never know.

As Ollie watched them leave, he sensed that their departures should have made him upset. But it didn't, probably because nothing could make him upset while he drank in the enchanting, sparkling world below the now-distant surface. The Novas' gift, as always, had left him enraptured. And tipsy. And profoundly lacking in any kind of sound judgement whatsoever. He actually waved a happy goodbye to each creature as it swam away.

And so it was that they arrived at Howerbout's cave some untold amount of time later with just one, pathetic passenger. One, out of all the dozens they had rescued and tried to transport.

Its name, as far as Ollie could remember, was Whipper-snapper: a snapping turtle with a long, dinosaur-like tail and an easygoing countenance. Instead of a normal turtle shell, however, the animal sported an oversized clam shell on its back. The replacement shell was pearly and clean, opening and closing at irregular intervals. The turtle's face, meanwhile, chewed languidly on a long string of kelp, looking altogether unconcerned about where it was or what it was doing.

Ollie sighed. He stood in the cave entrance, dripping, feeling the euphoric effects of the miraculous underwater breathing trick wear off. The result was a thudding and thoroughly depressing sense of failure. And dread.

One creature. One? That's all they could manage, in the end?

Meatball emerged from the water. Tera followed soon after and pulled herself up onto the ledge. She wrung out her jumpsuit and gave her hair a quick shake.

"Damn," she said, looking at the Whippersnapper.

"Yeah," he agreed glumly. Meatball had toddled to Ollie's side and started to climb his leg.

Tera chewed her bottom lip. If she was nursing similar thoughts of defeat and distress, she kept them to herself. After a few seconds of contemplation, she said only, "Well, we might as well get this over with."

He nodded.

They trudged like condemned prisoners through the crack in the wall and into Howerbout's cave. This time, the reunion with Laszlo wasn't quite as effusive: He had only to catch sight of their posture and expressions to know that all was not well. Instead of rushing to embrace them, the acrobat merely rose to his feet and regarded his friends warily.

"Hey, Laz," Tera said. Her smile was half-hearted. "We're back!"

Howerbout had been polishing the far wall; at the sound of her voice, he spun. "Hello!" he squealed, clacking over to greet them. "Hello and hello! Oh my goodness, you're back and back and back! I am so happy to see you! Look, Laszlo! Look! Our friends are back to see us!"

"Yes, I see that," Laszlo said, folding his arms. "You are alone?"

"Uh, no," Ollie said. "Not exactly." He turned, bent his knees, and patted his thighs. "Here, turtle, turtle," he said, feeling foolish.

The Whippersnapper ambled out into the light. Its white clam shell gleamed; its wide, scaled feet padded silently against the hard floor. The creature gave a lazy look around the cave, still gnawing the clump of kelp with an almost imperceptible, side-to-side chew. Then it curled up its legs and plopped unceremoniously onto the ground.

Howerbout's eyes widened. "It is...for me?"

Tera glanced at Ollie. She cleared her throat and clasped her hands behind her back. "Uh, yeah. This is it! One soul mate, as promised."

"But it is..." Howerbout, for once, seemed at a loss for words.

Laszlo, Tera, and Ollie exchanged furtive glances. Ollie could feel his heart thudding in his throat.

"It is...wonderful!" the crab-man exclaimed. A wide smile spread across his face, revealing his fangs at their full, terrifying length. Each one of his six legs seemed to suddenly have a mind of its own, *clack-clack-clacking* in a kind of frenzied crustacean dance.

"Oh!" Tera said. She quickly wiped the surprise from her expression. "Great. Yeah, of course. We knew you'd love it. Didn't we?" She looked at Ollie with raised eyebrows.

He straightened. "Of course! The minute we saw it, we said, that's it! I mean, everything about it screams soul mate. The, uh, long tail, there, and the turtle...ness. Don't you think, Laz?"

Laszlo was staring at them in open confusion. Then he said, "Yes. I think all these things the first moment I see this, uh..."

"It's called a Whippersnapper," Tera provided helpfully. "See? It's got a clam shell on its back. A shell, just like you, Howerbout!"

"Ah," Laszlo nodded. "Is nice one."

The crab-man circled closer. He lifted one claw, slowly, and tapped the Whippersnapper's head. The creature glanced up—looking not quite curious, exactly, but maybe something close—and rose to its feet. Then it walked a few steps, stopped next to Howerbout's massive, swirled shell, and sat down.

Howerbout regarded the new visitor with open, obvious delight. And then he began to talk. And talk, and talk, and talk. He talked about the polishing procedure of the cave walls. He talked about the greenies, and his preferred sand-sleeping positions, and the best way to keep the fire burning. He talked about the new songs that Laszlo had taught him, and about the glowing lures in his back that allowed him to catch fish. And people.

Throughout it all, the Whippersnapper merely listened. And chewed. And blinked the lashes on its small, turtle eyes in a slow-motion sweep of dispassionate lethargy.

"Look," Ollie whispered. "Their shells are touching."

Tera gave him a wide-eyed, happy nod. "It's meant to be, I think," she whispered back. Then she reached out to grasp his hand and squeezed it tight.

Meant to be.

Ollie glanced down at Tera's hand in his own and felt a skittering in his chest.

Were Howerbout and this crazy turtle-thing really soul mates? Despite all the bungling, did he and Tera somehow manage to bring the right creature—the *only* right creature—back with them? Was it luck, or destiny, or something else?

He supposed he'd never know. More than that, he supposed it didn't matter. As long as Howerbout and the Whippersnapper wanted to be soul mates, then they were. Wasn't it really as simple as that?

He looked at Tera. Her face was glowing. Her brown eyes reflected the flickering firelight. She was happy. Happy that this zany plan of hers had succeeded, yes, but also happy to be holding his hand. Just...happy. It was so clear to him, suddenly. So undeniable. He could see the truth of it pouring and firming all around them, like the glaze on a lemon-drop cookie.

"I love you," Ollie said. The words had wings, floating up to ride the smoke. He hadn't expected to say it. But now that he had, nothing else seemed possible. He loved her with every blink, with every step, with every inhalation.

Tera's eyes widened, then crinkled. "I love you, too," she answered.

The feeling that flooded him was better, even, than the elation of an underwater breath. This was no illusion. No temporary, borrowed trick. This was real wonderment, real oxygen.

Real magic.

He was grinning like an idiot, he knew. And he didn't care.

"What, now, no love for Laszlo?"

They turned to find the acrobat facing them with open arms. Tera laughed and ran into his chest. Ollie followed behind to give his friend a hearty thump on the back.

"There! Is better!" Laszlo said. "So much love to go around, yes?"

"Yes," Tera agreed, pinching his bony cheek.

"I have soul mate, too, you know," Laszlo told them.

"You do?" Ollie asked in surprise.

"Yes! Different one every week!" The acrobat threw his head back with a belly laugh. "Now. As much as I love all this love, and I love listening to my friend Howerbout do the talking and talking...

Can we leave, now? I am running out of the days to get back to Brickside. Drip, drip, drip. I think it is ready time to say my goodbye."

Ollie nodded and turned on his heel. "Hey, Howerbout, buddy. How's it going over there?"

"It's going good, my other friend! So, so good! I think it likes me! What do you think?"

Ollie looked down at the languid Whippersnapper. The strand of kelp had shortened, but was still poking out of its mouth. "Oh, yeah. Definitely."

"I have even named it!"

"Awesome, buddy! That's a big step. What did you pick?"

Howerbout's expression grew serious. "Name."

"Right," Ollie nodded. "But what name?"

"Name."

Tera took a small step forward. "But what *is* its name?" she asked.

Howerbout tilted his head to one side. "That's it."

"Its name is...Name?"

"Yes."

The three friends shared a glance. "All...rightee," Ollie finally said.

"Name is great name," Laszlo piped in. He tucked a long hair behind his ear. "You are happy, yes?"

"Yes," Howerbout nodded. *Clack, clack, clack.*

"Then it's time to keep your promise," Tera said, her words coming slowly. Carefully.

The crab-man's face began to pout.

"Now, now, none of that," Laszlo said, holding up a finger. "You and...Name have much fun to do. We will only get in way."

The pout lingered.

"Remember, you promised," Ollie reminded him.

"The promise doesn't matter though, does it?" Tera asked, stepping forward to touch Howerbout's shell. "For the wish to work, it has to be real. Do you wish to make a new life here with...uh, Name? And to be happy?"

"I do!" he said.

"Great," she smiled. "And do you wish for us, your friends, to be happy, too?"

Howerbout considered this. "I do," he said again.

She nodded. "We don't belong here, Howerbout. You and Name do. So if you really wish for us to be happy, then you also have to wish for us to leave."

"But that makes me sad," the crab-man whispered.

"I know. Me, too. But sometimes the right thing does feel sad."

"It does?"

"It does. But that doesn't make it any less right."

Howerbout heaved a deep sigh. "We will still be friends? Forever and ever?"

Tera touched her chest. "Forever and ever."

He gave her the barest of nods. When he spoke again, his voice was barely audible. "I will miss you. And..." His eyes went to the floor. "And I wish for you to leave."

The air in the room went still. Meatball shifted on Ollie's shoulder. The three humans stared at each other, then started walking backwards toward the opening. Slowly, at first, then faster. Then faster still. They crashed into each other as all of them tried to fit through the crack in the wall at the same time.

"Goodbye, Howerbout!"

"Goodbye!"

"We'll miss you! We'll visit!"

Would they visit? Ollie doubted it. Still, it was clearly the right thing to say in the moment. He let Laszlo leave ahead of him—it seemed only fair—and then scooted out to join him and Tera at the water's edge.

"Where are we going?" Ollie asked.

"Let's just get to the surface," Tera answered. "Then Laz can head back, and you and I can find the lab."

How? he wanted to ask. *Hows and abouts.* But that was a problem for Future Ollie. Current Ollie, he knew, just had to get the hell out of that cavern before Howerbout changed his mind. So he kept all follow-up questions to himself.

They dove in together. Meatball, as usual, freed himself to dart and spin through the water like he was born to it. Which he probably was. The trog's webbed feet were part rudders, part paddles, and part flippers, allowing him a precision that the humans beside him could only dream of.

Ollie watched his furry friend frolic, smiling as he inhaled the intoxicating brew of hydrogen and oxygen molecules; delicious and heady. He followed Tera and Laszlo down through the tunnel and out into the open lake, marveling, as always, at the beauty and majesty all around them. He saw some familiar creatures, along with new ones whose names appeared like flashcards in his head: wavery grasselores, winding through the waves like ribbon candy. Pink-cheeked frogfish, hopscotching over each other's backs. And his new favorites, the pyrocods, which looked like honest-to-God swimming slices of cherry pie. With long, darting tongues.

Already, Ollie was forgetting: Where were they going? And why? He did a back somersault, then another, and would probably have started giggling like a kindergartener if the watery environs would have allowed it. He blew bubbles at the pyrocods, who stuck out their tongues in response. He reached for Tera's hand, intertwining her fingers in his. *Love,* he thought. *Lovety, lovety, love.* She loved him. And he loved her. And he loved this place. This marvelous, alien place. The bliss was all-encompassing.

Lovety, lovety, lovety, love. Ollie was humming it to himself, dancing with a silly swish of his arms, when something began to distract him. Something mildly unpleasant, at first, then increasingly urgent. His first emotion was surprise: What could possibly be unpleasant, down here in the depths? Nothing. Nothing at all.

Oh, wait. There was one thing.

By the time he put it together, the sensation had moved well past urgent to something closer to horrific.

He couldn't breathe.

He looked at Tera and Laszlo, and could see it in their eyes: They felt it, too. Whatever gift the Novas had given them, it was gone. The time had run out. The breath had run out. And all that was left was millions of gallons of lake water, pressing in from all sides in an unforgiving, drowning crush.

Ollie looked up, trying to see the surface. Nothing but more dark. More green. From the corner of his eye he saw Tera and Laszlo frantically pulling, kicking, clawing...up, up, up. He followed. His vision, so clear just seconds before, went murky.

Bubbles. Shadows. *Tera!*

Not now! Please, God, not now!

His brain told him not to inhale. But his body was begging; his lungs were burning. He looked up again, desperate to catch sight of a glimmer of light. A ripple. Anything.

Just one quick breath.

What could it hurt?

He had no choice. The surface was too far, too impossible. Ollie tilted his head back and opened his mouth into an aching oval. With sick clarity, he inhaled the lake water into lungs made for air. He felt his body flail and twitch. Watched the green fade to black.

His last thoughts were about brown-butter gnocchi. And the Egyptian statue of King Menkaura, so haunting and imperious, at the Museum of Fine Arts. And acorn caps crunching under his feet in the fall. And the smooth granite benches at Rachel Revere Square, which was actually not a square at all, but a triangle. How very, very peculiar.

And Tera's face.

Ollie let the images buoy him in those final, desperate moments. Then, they were gone, and he was gone, and all of it was gone—all that once was, all that would ever be, sinking in silence to the bottom of a bottomless lake.

Twenty

Flashes of red.

Burgundy, at first. Then a brighter ruby.

He was dead. Ollie knew he had died; he had felt the water invade his body. Saw the darkness come. He was definitely dead.

Wasn't he?

So much red.

Blood?

No, not blood. It was...fur? But longer.

Hair.

Auburn and maroon and pale rose. Curling and straight. Tied around his arm and legs. Pulling him with a speed he could barely register.

Hauling him through the water. Faster, faster, faster. Too fast.

Is this what happened when you were dead?

The air came like a sugar-coated slap: hard and magnificent. Ollie gulped and wheezed. No more water. Instead, he found himself inexplicably on his hands and knees. Coughing up a bubbling stream of liquid from the depths of his gut.

His vision was returning in uneven, blurry spurts. Dark brown sand. Lake-wrinkled skin.

And still, so much red. All around him; above, left, and right.

Ollie fell onto his side and looked up. He blinked, struggling to resolve the fractured shapes of his kaleidoscopic eyesight.

Novas?

Yes. There had to be a dozen of them, standing over him on a beach, looking down. Their wild and wavy hair had somehow already dried, though it seemed to Ollie that they had only been out of the water for a few seconds. Nearby, other Novas remained mostly submerged at the shoreline; Ollie could see their bobbing heads and still more shades of red hair. For a moment, he could swear he also saw tails, wide and scaled, flipping in and out of the lapping waves.

More coughing nearby. To his right.

He blinked again and turned. Another Nova? No, someone else. Curled up, bent over, hacking...

Tera! He tried to say her name, but found that he couldn't speak.

And next to her? Was that...? Ollie felt another surge of relief as he recognized Laszlo's hunched over body, struggling to stand.

What the hell happened? Where were they? Last he remembered, he was accepting his horrible fate. Dying. Hundreds of feet under the water.

He tried to ask. Only coughs came out.

One of the Nova Scotian Water Nymphs was talking. "Yes, I know," she said. Was she talking to him?

He remembered her, from before. She was the leader. Tight, auburn afro. Silver eyes. Boss-lady attitude. Her name was...Eelia? Yes. Eelia. But who was she talking to? Not to him. She seemed to be talking to a spot on the sand nearby. With effort, Ollie turned his head, but saw no one there. Only Meatball.

The trog was shaking out his fur. Droplets sprayed into the air and hit Ollie directly in the face. After the last shake, Meatball looked up. It seemed as though he was looking directly at Eelia.

"Well, what else would you have us do?" the silver-eyed Nova said, now sounding cross. "We had no way of knowing they would take so long. And they're alive, aren't they? I would think we're due some gratitude, not complaints."

Meatball continued to stare at her.

After a moment, she laughed. "Yes, I suppose that's true." The other Novas joined in the mirth. Meatball gave another, smaller shake, took a few steps closer, and settled into the sand next to Ollie's leg.

What was happening, here?

A few feet away, Laszlo had managed to stand up. He gave one final, powerful cough, wiped his mouth with the back of his hand, and croaked, "You saved us!"

The Novas twittered their pleasure. "Yes, we did," one of them said, sidling closer and resting her delicate hand on Laszlo's shoulder. She had long, straight hair and yellowish skin. Ollie remembered her, too, from their first meeting; he thought her name was Nerida.

"But how did you find us?" Laszlo asked.

"Oh, you can thank your friend, here, for that," Eelia said. "He called us."

Finally, Ollie managed to speak. "Who called you?"

"This little guy," Nerida said, pointing at Meatball.

Ollie felt a wave of disorientation wash over him. He looked at Meatball, who was poking at the sand with his long tongue. "But...he's a trog."

"Yes, he is," Eelia responded. She was now looking at Ollie the way a doctor might examine a patient who had bumped his head. As though she was starting to worry about his sanity. "Anyway, you're all in a bit of a hurry, I take it."

Tera climbed to her feet, hacked loudly, and asked, "Did the trog tell you that, too?"

"As a matter of fact, he did." Eelia looked from face to face. "What? You didn't know he could talk?"

"He has never talked to us," Laszlo pointed out.

"Well, of course not!" said another nymph with short-cropped hair. At this, the others giggled.

Ollie listened to the laughter fall around him as he got his bearings. Hands and feet, check. Lungs working, check. Tera, Laz, and Meatball, all here. All together. He would not have thought such a thing could be possible just a few minutes before, as he had watched all light and life melt away like vanilla ice cream in the sun.

"Thank you," he rasped, stepping forward.

As Eelia folded her arms, her freakishly long, webbed fingers came to rest on each elbow. "You're welcome."

"No, I mean it," he insisted. "Thank you. You didn't have to do that. I don't know *how* you did it, but...thank you. Really."

Eelia gave a noncommittal shrug.

"She got a note!" squealed a nearby nymph. "That's why she did it!"

A note? The word made Ollie freeze, then turn his attention back to the interrupting Nova. Her red hair was brighter than all the others'—closer to orange. Her name, if he remembered right, was Potamedes. She was the one who had asked him if people on the Brickside talked about the Novas' "many victories" in battle.

"What kind of a note?" he asked.

Potamedes clapped her hands together. "A secret note!"

Eelia sent her a cold glare. "That's right. Secret. And secret means what, exactly?"

The younger nymph ignored the comment. "We don't even know who it was from!" she said. Her webbed fingers and toes wiggled with barely suppressed glee. "The note told Eelia to listen for a call, and to come as soon as she heard it! We all came, too!"

The nymphs around her murmured in excited agreement while the blue light from above made their tiny skin-scales shimmer. As before, they wore wrapped "clothes" that seemed to be made from kelp. Down in the water, the still-submerged Novas splashed and spun. All of them seemed to be enjoying the hullabaloo.

"Wait." Ollie held up a hand. "What did it say, exactly?"

Eelia sighed in resignation. The cat, clearly, was out of the bag. "It said, 'Nova red, Nova true, fate of three, rests with you.'" She pointed. "I guess that's you three."

"And? And?" Nerida said. She spun her finger in a prompting circle.

Rolling her eyes, Eelia continued. "And then it said, 'Listen well, heed the call, speed like wind, save them all.' That's it. That's all it said."

"And here you are!" Potamedes added, spreading her arms wide.

Tera touched Ollie's shoulder. They shared a look of unspoken understanding: Another Herrick note. It had to be.

George Herrick had known all of this would happen. He had known that Ollie would need rescue, and that the Novas would provide it. Of course, he did. That also meant that he probably knew they would end up here, on this very particular stretch of sandy lake beach, in this very particular moment.

He shivered. Was this what it felt like to be an ant in a farm? A fish in a bowl? Thinking you were in control of your life and your surroundings, only to find that some larger, looming face had been watching you the whole time?

No—it was more than that. *Worse* than that. George Herrick didn't just own an ant farm: He knew what was going to happen to the ants behind the glass. Which tunnels they would dig, and when. What they would eat, and why. He directed their actions. He left annoying little hints and riddles to drive the ants to distraction and prevent them from living normal ant lives. He was the Ant Nostradamus. The Ant King.

George Herrick is dead: Long live George Herrick. Cue the trumpets.

For the first time, Ollie looked past the Novas to take full measure of his surroundings. It didn't take long. They were standing on a small island—so small that he could cover every inch of it with a five-minute stroll. He saw a clump of three large fern trees, and not much else. Sand, sand, and more sand.

And probably ants.

"Where are we?" he asked.

"It's an island," Eelia answered.

Ollie bit back his first response, not wanting to seem ungrateful. "Yeah, I can, uh, see that," he said instead, trying to keep his tone even. "But I mean, what island? Why bring us here?"

"The note told her to!" Potamedes burst out.

Eelia gave the younger Nova more side-eye, then said, "Not exactly. Technically, it said I should bring you to 'isle fallow, round and dry.' Which was not very helpful. I mean, look around. This whole damn cavern is filled with islands. Hundreds, probably. And 'round and dry' pretty much describes every one of them. But..." She dragged out the syllable.

"But what?" Ollie asked.

Eelia stared at him, as though she was deciding whether or not to continue.

"But what?" he asked again.

"But you all had mentioned, when we first met, that you were looking for a lab."

"And?" Tera pressed.

"And... the humans used to come here, back in the day. To get to the lab. When it was still operational."

Tera looked at Eelia, then gave a quick glance around their barren, sandy surroundings. "But there's nothing here."

Eelia shrugged.

"It's under the lake!" one of the smaller Novas supplied, hopping up and down. "I remember!"

"So, it's not on the island?" Ollie asked.

Eelia shrugged again. "It used to be underwater."

"If it's under the water, then why did the people come to an island?" Tera asked. Her voice was starting to get an edge.

"I do not know," Eelia answered haughtily. "I long ago stopped wondering why the humans do what they do. Speaking of which..." She turned to look at her flock. "Let's go, ladies. We have spent enough time meddling in this foolishness."

A murmur of protest rippled through the gossamer crowd.

"No, no," Eelia said, lifting a hand. "Enough. Time to go."

"Wait!" Laszlo called out. "I can go with you, yes?"

At this, Eelia thawed. She took a languid step closer to him. "Of course," she purred. "You can come with us anytime."

"Ah. This is wonderful," Laszlo beamed. "I must get back to Brickside. I am, how do you say, sitting on a clock." He tapped his wrist and added, "Tick, tick, for me."

The buzz returned to the group. Several Novas moved closer, running their too-long fingers along his arms, back, and chest.

"Not to worry, ladies," Laszlo assured them. "I need only short time there, and then I come back. Yes? And I will visit again with my favorite redhairs?"

"Red*heads*," Nerida corrected with a giggle, sidling closer.

"Hairs, heads, what difference?" Laszlo said. "Either way, none more delighting. On either side of bricks!"

"Delight*ful*," said Potamedes.

"Yes!" he laughed. "Yes, you are!"

Tera, meanwhile, looked unamused. "So you can take Laz, then?" she asked, directing her question to Eelia.

"We can," Eelia nodded.

"Great, thank you." Tera stepped forward to give the acrobat a hug. "Go. Hurry. You don't have much time."

He returned the hug, lingering for a moment before turning and holding out his arms. "Shall we go, ladies?"

Laszlo didn't have to ask twice; they had swarmed him before he'd even finished the sentence. The Novas fussed, murmured, and preened as they led him toward the water.

Caught up in the wave, Laszlo looked over his shoulder. "Goodbye, Tera! Goodbye, Ollie Delgato of the North End Delgatos! Goodbye, little fuzz trog! I will see you all soon!"

"Bye, Laz!" Ollie called out. "Thanks, man! See you soon."

And that, it seemed, was that. The next thing Ollie knew, his friend was gone, ushered with head-snapping speed across the surface of the lake.

He and Tera stood on the sand, waving. Waving, waving, waving, until they were waving at nothing. For a long, horrible moment, all was still. And silent. Aside from a few lingering, popping bubbles on the water's surface, the world around them seemed to have stopped.

Ollie let his waving hand drop, feeling dazed. He was still surprised to be alive. Now, just like that, Laszlo was gone, the Novas were gone, and he and Tera were literally stranded on a desert island. It made him think of that age-old question: *If you could bring one food with you onto a desert island, what would it be?* The question used to plague him: How could someone pick just one? Back and forth he would waver between sweets and starches and grilled, seasoned meats, each seeming perfect until he thought of the next. But now, as his stomach growled piteously, Ollie realized that there was only one right answer to the question. *Any food,* he thought with a miserable sigh. *Any food at all.*

Tera was watching him with a smile. "It'll be okay, Oll."

"How?" He wasn't being snarky; he genuinely wanted to know.

"That Eelia's a sharp one. She knows what she's doing. She brought us here for a reason."

"But...she said she didn't know where the lab was."

"She said she didn't know how to *get* to it. But if this is where the other people came, back in the day, then there must be an entrance here. All we have to do is find it."

Oh, is that all? Ollie thought to himself, casting a look around their forlorn environs.

As Tera's hands went to her hips, Meatball rose from his sandy nest and began a slow, predictable climb up Ollie's legs.

Ollie looked at the trog with narrowed eyes. "Maybe we should just ask Meatball where the lab is. Apparently, he's got a lot to say."

The trog finished the journey up Ollie's torso and moved onto his shoulder. Once there, he spun in a slow circle, settled, and let out a grunt. His eyes resembled two barely visible raisins protruding above his flat, wide beak. He blinked them, twice, then closed them.

"I guess he's done talking," Tera said, sounding amused.

Was it really possible that Meatball had somehow saved them? That he had called out to the Novas for rescue across the aqueous ether? Every part of that story seemed completely implausible. And yet...here they were.

Listen well, heed the call. Speed like wind, save them all.

Ollie reached up to scratch the brown fur. "Thanks, buddy," he whispered, just in case.

———— ⌘ ————

Sand, sand, and more sand. The stuff was everywhere on the little island: packed onto the ground, swirling in the air, and, before long, crusting into the corners of Ollie's eyes and mouth. Almost immediately, he found himself pining for a tall glass of water.

Ironic, considering that he'd nearly drowned in the stuff less than an hour before.

The exploration, such as it was, lasted only minutes—mainly because there was almost nothing to find. Ollie felt a bit like a stage actor in a theater-in-the-round: Gently lapping waves caressed the sand on all sides. And at the center, Ollie and Tera found more sand, the three fern trees they had seen before, and two wide stumps. One of the trees, oddly, had a metal cooking pan affixed firmly to its side.

And that was it.

"What's with the pan?" Ollie wondered out loud.

"I don't know," Tera answered. "But check it out. There's another one just like it over there."

244

She pointed across the water, where he saw another, similarly small island in the distance. When he squinted, he could just make out another stand of trees, and another cooking pan mounted on one of the trunks.

"Well, that's weird," he said.

She nodded, hands on her hips.

Ollie glanced across the horizon, searching for more. But all he saw was the on-again, off-again blink of a lighthouse on the far shore.

"Damn," he said. "There's really nothing here."

"There has to be something," Tera insisted. "There just has to be. Come on, let's...push some stuff around."

They spent the next hour poking through fern leaves, tapping on tree bark, jumping up and down on the tree stumps, and digging holes in the sand. The pan was subjected to similar scrutiny: They tried pulling it off the tree, but it wouldn't budge. Then they tried hitting it. Drumming a little beat on its surface. Ollie even tried staring into his own haggard, bewildered reflection in the metal. Anything and everything they could think of.

Nothing happened. Nothing changed.

Ollie was getting thirstier, hungrier, and more frustrated by the second. What had they done, stranding themselves in such a barren place? How would they ever get home? And why didn't he think to ask the Novas for more underwater breathing capability while he had them? How far was that shore, anyway? It might as well be a million-and-a-half miles. There was no way he'd ever stay afloat long enough to reach it.

Ollie spat out another mouthful of sand and dropped his butt onto the stump. This was useless.

He looked out over the water as Tera continued to forage through the giant leaves. His gaze landed on the other island. The twin to this one. They'd have to try to reach it, he supposed. What else could they do? Maybe there was something there that could help them. Food, or a map. But the distance, he knew, would be a problem. Not a million-and-a-half miles, perhaps, but still pretty damn far.

Ollie was so tired. So, so sleepy. The thought of swimming anywhere exhausted him to the point of delirium. His thirst had been a mere annoyance earlier; now, it was making him wobbly.

His eyelids began to droop.

No food. No water. Two islands. Two cooking pans? Why have pans without food or fire? So much sand. Distant lighthouse, cutting through the fog.

Lighthouse.

Ollie's eyes opened.

For the second time that day, his thoughts turned to George Herrick's rhymes. Not the note Herrick had written to the Novas, but the one he had written to Ollie.

Hows and abouts, souls and mates... Air and breath, truth and lie...

And what else?

There had been another verse, further down.

Good is bad,
Beast will bite.
Steer the course,
Bend the light.

Ollie stood. He turned to look at Tera. "Bend the light!" he said.

She peered out from the foliage. "What?"

"Bend the light!" Ollie said excitedly. "In his note, Herrick told me to 'steer the course, bend the light.' Look! The lighthouse, over there! It keeps sending out beams across the water. We need to bend it. That must be what the shiny pans are for!"

Tera's eyebrows lifted. "Bend it...how?"

"Uh, I don't know." Ollie began to pace. He tried moving the pan again, just for the hell of it, but it wouldn't budge.

Ollie chewed his lower lip. There was no boat to steer. No car, no...nothing. *Steer the course.* Like, an obstacle course? The island didn't have one of those, either.

The lighthouse was still blinking in the distance. Ollie watched in concentration, learning the cadence of the beams: Two quick blinks, then a break. Then one long blink, then a break. Then three quick blinks before the sequence started all over again.

Two, one, three.

On the Brickside, he knew, each New England lighthouse had its own unique pattern of blinks. It was like a signature, allowing the sailors to learn their location on even the foggiest or snowiest of nights. He supposed the Neath lighthouses did the same, perhaps for the crow boat drivers.

"That lighthouse," he said to Tera. "The blink pattern is two, one, three. Does that mean anything to you?"

She thought for a moment, then nodded. "That's Worthylake Point. Stays pretty foggy over there, all the time. Some nasty critters in the caves, too. I usually steer clear."

He nodded. "And that's all it means to you?"

She gave him a puzzled look. "Well, I don't send it a Christmas card, if that's what you're asking."

"No, I mean..." Ollie shook his head in frustration. "It doesn't make you think of anything else?"

"It makes me think of a lighthouse. Because that's what it is." Her mouth was lifting into a half-smile.

Ollie wiped sand from his jaw. *Think, think, think.* Two, one, three. Was it a code? T.O.T. Maybe there were tater tots buried under the sand. If only. Ollie imagined for just a second: Baskets full of deep-fried, golden-brown deliciousness. Scooping them up in his hands. Crunching through the crispy outsides to reach the shredded, potato-y goodness in the middle. When his mouth began to water, he shook his head sharply and returned to the task at hand.

Maybe it was a ciphered sentence: the first word has two letters, the second word has one letter, and the third word has three letters.

In a pie.

On a bus.

Am I bad?

Krite, this was stupid. His gaze dropped, falling onto the stumps. He tilted his chin.

Why stumps? The other trees hadn't been cut down. Who had cut them? Did they use the wood to build something? Maybe. Still, the fern trees themselves didn't look particularly sturdy. The trunks bent at the slightest provocation. Ollie wouldn't use that wood to build anything important; and besides, there were no structures on the island at all. Why would someone go through all the trouble to cut down two trees and then just...cart them away?

Weird.

The stumps were, he suddenly noticed, unusually symmetrical. They were almost perfectly round. Like wheels.

Like...steering wheels.

"Those!" he said, pointing.

"What about them?" Tera asked.

"That's what we have to steer." He felt sure of it.

"Ollie, those are tree stumps."

It made no sense and perfect sense, all at the same time. Ollie gave a *what-the-hell* shrug and bent toward the closest stump, which reached almost up to his kneecaps. Meatball's claws pierced his shoulder for balance. With an odd flashback to his driver's ed class, he gripped the wood at 10-and-2. His fingertips dug into the bark. And then...he twisted it.

"What the—?" Tera gasped.

The stump was rotating. It seemed to move like a padlock, with a series of evenly spaced clicks. Ollie spun it clockwise and counterclockwise, enjoying the feel of the oscillation. He laughed out loud. "It's working!"

"Yes, it is!" she said, her voice awed.

"Is anything happening?"

Tera looked left, right, and behind her. She stared at the trees and the sand. After a minute, she said, "No."

"Nothing?"

"I don't think so," she said cautiously, darting her gaze as Ollie continued to turn the stump back-and-forth in wide, steady movements. "Wait!" she suddenly shouted. "Look! Over there!"

Ollie looked over his shoulder and followed her finger to the other island. What he saw beggared belief: When he turned the stump left, the island in the distance also...turned left. The entire island. The movement was subtle, but visible. When he turned the stump right, the island turned right. It was like playing foosball with actual topography.

"How is that possible?" Tera whispered.

"I...don't know."

"Try the other one!"

He did. This time, when he turned the stump, their own island rotated left and right in conjunction with Ollie's movements.

"This is insane," she said with obvious delight. "Now, what?"

"Now, we have to line it all up."

"With what?"

"With that." Ollie pointed at the blinking lighthouse in the distance. "The beam."

"How?" she asked.

He smiled. "We use the combination."

For years, he'd been having a recurring nightmare about standing naked in his high-school hallway, wanting to open his locker but forgetting the combination. This time, at least, the numbers were easy to remember. And he was wearing clothes.

He lined up two notches of wood on the first stump. That, he hoped, was the starting point. Then he spun it left for one click, then another. He stopped. Right for one click. Stop. Left again for one...two...three clicks. Stop.

"Oll! Look!"

He peered over his shoulder, then stood.

Even from this distance, he could see: The lighthouse's beam was hitting the pan on the tree on the other island. The light was bouncing off the shiny surface and redirecting itself in their general direction. Close, but not quite right.

"We have to turn ours, too," Tera said.

He nodded and got to work on the other steering stump. He repeated the motions of before: Two left, one right, three left.

Ollie and Tera looked out over the water. The beam of light was still escaping into the open air.

"It didn't work," he said, surprised.

"Try it backwards," Tera suggested. "They're sort of mirror images of each other, right?"

With a nod, Ollie reached out and spun the stump. This time, he went twice to the right, once to the left, and three times back to the right.

He looked up.

Three quick blinks. Two quick blinks. One long blink, and—

The beam bounced off the first pan, bent, and traveled straight towards them. It hit the mounted cooking pan on the nearby bendy fern tree, causing the metal to burst into a glorious, radiating glow.

For a moment, the flare was blinding, forcing Ollie and Tera to shield their eyes and look away.

By the time Ollie dropped his arm, blinked, and returned his gaze to the tree, the light had dimmed. The trunk had started to tremble. And the bark beneath the pan had begun to crack, groan, and separate. Like sliding doors at a department store. *Right this way.*

Ollie and Tera stared at the opening in the tree. They stared at each other.

"Are we supposed to...go in?"

He nodded dumbly. "I guess so."

"But it's so small!"

The tree trunk itself was only about as wide as Ollie's torso, and the newly formed gap was even narrower.

They took a few tentative steps forward. Tera stumbled, and he caught her arm.

"You okay?" Ollie asked.

"Yeah. I'm just...woozy, I guess."

"Me, too. I think we're dehydrated." The air around them felt unnaturally dry—a stark contrast to the cavern's typical muggy, underground conditions. The shifting sand drifts loomed in his peripheral vision. It was like someone had plucked a piece of the Sahara and dropped it into the loneliest corner of the Neath. Even Meatball was panting.

As if in agreement, Tera took a pained swallow. "Maybe we'll find something in there," she said, staring warily at the tree.

Krite, please, he thought. Visions of root beer danced in his head as he watched Tera turn her body sideways and inch through the trunk's opening. He followed behind, sucking in his stomach, holding his breath, and trying to ignore the sharp edges of the tree bark against his belly and back. Meatball climbed from his shoulder to the top of his head. And then, miraculously, Ollie was through.

Inside, the hollow of the tree was bigger than it should have been. Far bigger than the actual trunk itself. This space was about the size of a vestibule for a revolving door; plenty of room for both of them to stand comfortably. Ollie didn't understand how the inside could be larger than the outside—but he did understand that it was probably useless to wonder, or ask, or spend any brain power on the question at all. *It is what it is,* as Mr. Bonfiglio used to say, lamenting some difficult-to-grasp caffé conundrum. On the Brickside, Ollie had never really understood that expression. In the Neath, he did. In spades.

The fern tree vestibule had no revolving door, but it did have a set of short, dim stairs leading downward. Holding hands, Ollie and Tera descended. Meatball stayed on the top of Ollie's head like a stubborn, furry hat. It wasn't far; maybe 15 or 20 steps at most.

At the bottom, they found a tiny man in a tiny blue jumpsuit, sitting behind a tiny podium. He held a tiny clipboard and a tiny pencil in his hands. No tiny water bubbler, Ollie noticed with dismay. At this point, he would have welcomed even a thimbleful.

The man showed no surprise, or even interest, at their arrival. If anything, he looked like he might be stifling a yawn. "How many for entry?" he asked.

Ollie didn't answer. Instead, he stared at the space behind the tiny podium, where a not-so-tiny, elevator-like cage contraption waited for its passengers. The cage looked old, dilapidated, and dark. And the deep hole it hovered over? Even darker.

"How many? For entry?" the man asked again, holding his pencil in the air. His disinterest had started to morph into impatience.

Ollie swallowed and looked at Tera. She gave him an encouraging nod.

"Two," Ollie said. "No, wait…" Instinctively, he reached up to touch the trog on his head. "Three."

He liked the sound of that. He didn't like the sound of the cage elevator's creaking metal and wires, or the angry wind rushing up from unseen depths below. But he liked the sound of three.

Two, one, three. Click.

Twenty-One

As they stepped gingerly into the elevator, Ollie braced himself for a wild, stomach-dropping ride. He was remembering—with queasy clarity—the reverse-chairlift journey that had first carried him down to the Neath all those months ago: a harrowing, headlong plunge into the unknown, complete with whipping winds, sharp turns, and barely suppressed screams.

He had been astounded to make it to the end in one piece on that rickety contraption, and this one felt like it had come from the same ancient and probably condemned factory. It swayed over a narrow, utterly opaque shaft that was only inches wider than the cage itself. The chains holding it in place looked rusted, and too thin. Everything creaked. Would it drop like a bowling ball? How far down did the shaft go? Wherever the bottom was, Ollie feared that he was about to meet it at breakneck speed.

The diminutive, blue-suited attendant climbed a stepstool, reached for the handle on the accordion-style elevator door, and slid it shut with a snap. He was humming under his breath. Something fast and cheery, as though he was feeling especially pleased to send them to their doom. He returned to a nearby control panel and spoke into a wide, brass horn.

"Transport for three," he announced.

A crackle of static emitted from the tube. It sounded like someone talking, but Ollie couldn't be sure. The attendant looked pleased at the crackle. He gave one last, inspecting glance at the wrought-iron cage and at the passengers trapped inside, then pushed a button on the panel.

Ollie gripped Tera's palm with one hand and the bars of the elevator with the other. "Hold on," he muttered to Meatball, who complied by sinking his claws deeper into Ollie's scalp.

The chains above their heads gave a startled squeal, as though they hadn't budged in quite some time. Ollie slammed his eyes shut and squeezed Tera's hand hard enough to make her yelp. He flashed back to a memory of a Niagara Falls museum, where he had peered at pictures and videos of daredevils plunging over the falls in a barrel. The result, too often, was catastrophe. Shattered shards of wood floating at the bottom of the churning swells. Gasps of horror from the shore. *Kaboom.*

Somewhere in the back of his mind, Ollie heard the thundering water. He braced for the freefall.

Instead, he felt—a slight jerk. No more than a mild bump, really, as the cage elevator began to inch downward. Slowly, at first, and then...still slowly, after that. It was so slow, in fact, that Ollie began to wonder if it was actually moving at all. He opened one eye, then two.

Above, the chains clanked in steady rhythm. Ollie could see every pebble protruding from the stone wall as they passed. He could have reached through the bars to touch them, if he had wanted to, without any threat of injury. Hell, in the time it was taking to pass them, he could have cataloged and named each one.

This was no barrel drop. This was more like riding inside the New Year's Eve glitter ball in Time Square—tick, tick, tick. Counting down to a midnight that was a lot more than ten seconds away.

As the fear of breakneck speeds receded, a creeping sense of claustrophobia began to settle in its place. The cage was awfully small. Stiflingly so. And though Ollie knew very little about building codes, he was fairly certain that this particular elevator would not pass muster with the Boston Office of Public Safety and Inspections. Even if it didn't plunge to the ground, who was to say it wouldn't just...stop? And then they'd be trapped. Trapped and helpless, with nothing to do but name pebbles and hold hands and hope, foolishly, that the bored, blue-suited attendant would hear—or care—if they screamed.

Ollie's stomach growled in complaint—had been groaning, actually, for quite some time. How long had it been since he'd had a meal? Or a proper drink of water? His tongue felt thick and dry. He ran it over his lips, which had begun to crack and sting.

Meatball's weight on his head felt too heavy, suddenly. Smothering and hot. The air in the shaft was even drier than it had been back on the island, if that was possible. He tugged on collar. Started to pant. Hyperventilate?

And then: Tera's hand. Her fingers threaded his in a warm, easy squeeze. Her calm energy seemed to flow directly through his skin. Above their heads, the chains jangled steadily.

"It's okay," she murmured. When he didn't respond, she said, "Hey. Look at me."

He did.

"It's gonna be okay."

Ollie exhaled.

Five minutes elapsed, then ten, he would have guessed, before he sensed a muted glow coming from somewhere below them in the shaft. Eventually, excruciatingly, the cage lowered itself near the glowing opening and came to a stop. Another attendant, this one taller than the last, stared at them through the bars.

"How many for entry?" she asked.

Ollie sighed. One of these days, he was going to buy every last one of these people a second-grade addition workbook.

Tera gave his hand another squeeze and answered, "Three."

"Three for entry," the woman said. She opened a latch and yanked the accordion door open.

"Thank you," Tera said.

The attendant didn't answer.

Ollie peered over her shoulder and saw an unremarkable, unadorned hallway. Whitish walls. Rows of closed doors. No water bubbler, again. Was this it? Had they reached the lab?

He thought of the high-tech research laboratories on the Brickside, where everyone wore ID badges and pressed their thumbs against security scanners. What would Ollie and Tera do if this woman asked for identification? They had no valid reason for being down here, after all. Would they have to tackle her? Lock her up inside the cage elevator? And if they did, then how would they eventually get back up again?

These were all things that he probably should have thought about *before* descending hundreds of feet below the place that was already hundreds of feet below the other place. Ollie tried to run a hand through his hair, forgetting about his trog hat, and ended up giving Meatball a scratch instead.

"Let's go," Tera said, pulling him out of the cage.

The attendant stepped aside and watched them enter the hallway. Ollie waited for her to stop them, to ask some questions. To put her hands on her hips and bellow: "By whose authority do you enter this facility?" But the blue-suited woman said nothing. Did that mean this wasn't the lab, after all? Had they gotten it wrong?

Ollie and Tera began to walk. The hall was weirdly cone-shaped, wide at the start and shrinking down into a narrow point at the far end. Narrower than a normal visual perspective would allow. The walls were white, and sparkling in the torchlight.

Sparkling?

From Ollie's shoulder, Meatball shot out his long tongue and licked the closest wall. Then he licked it again.

Ollie touched the wall with his index finger and brought it to his lips.

"Salt!" he said.

Tera gave a slow nod. "Huh. This must have been a salt mine. Somebody carved the halls and rooms right out of the salt itself."

"That's...insane," he said, staring down the long hallway. The dab on his tongue had made his already severe thirst even more grievous. "Think Weelichka knows about this place?"

"I don't know. But I bet she'd pay a good price to find out." Tera's eyebrows waggled.

They continued walking, peering into doorways as they went. Ollie expected a musty smell, but instead found the odor to be oddly antiseptic and blank. Like a hospital, but less lemony. Doors lined both sides of the passageway, with thick glass windows installed on their top halves. Ollie peered into each room as they passed. Aside from a smattering of furniture and unidentifiable equipment, they all seemed to be empty.

"Maybe they're, like, trick windows," he said, pointing. "To convince you that the rooms are empty when they're not?"

The doors were unlocked; he opened the closest one, and the next, only to find that the rooms inside were exactly as empty as they had initially seemed. No tricks. Someone had been there, once. That much was clear from all the abandoned chairs, tables, bottles, and doohickies. But whoever they were, they were gone now. The silence was so complete that Ollie could still hear the echo of the attendant's nasal breathing behind them.

"Krite, what happened here?" Tera said. "This place is creepy."

Only one door in the salt-white corridor had a light emitting from its window. The last one. It lay not on either side of the hallway, but at its end. The narrowest point. The door was as tall as two men. One vertical window near its top betrayed the hint of activity—flickering and uneven—somewhere beyond.

"That must be the place," Tera said.

Neither of them moved. Meatball snuffled.

Ollie dug deep for something close to bravery. After all, their only chance to fix this mess might be waiting on the other side of that door. That creepy, towering, ominous door.

He rubbed his palms on his pants. Maybe it wouldn't be so bad. Maybe they'd step through the doorway to find a candy factory with a swirling chocolate lake and merry little helpers, all singing and dancing and beckoning Ollie and Tera into a world chock-full of sugary goodness. And tall glasses of ice water.

And shiny-new breathing devices, all packed up and ready for travel to the Brickside.

Maybe it would just be that easy.

Or maybe they'd open the door and find themselves face-to-face with a fire-breathing dragon—He Who Guards the Breathing Apparatus, last in a long line of scaly sentinels. The final thing they'd see before burning down to skeletal ash would be its nostrils, flaring. Its mouth, curled into a grin. *Stupid humans. Why did you open the door?*

Ollie looked at Tera. In response, she gave a determined nod.

Candy factory, he thought to himself, crossing his fingers. Then, he reached for the knob. It was mounted high—higher than Tera's head, but not as high as his—and resembled a hockey puck. He was surprised when it turned easily in his hand.

"Not locked," he whispered.

She gestured for him to keep moving.

Ollie continued to wheel the knob left and right, left and right, with the steady regularity of a hypnotist swinging a pocket watch.

"C'mon," she prodded.

Left and right. Left and right.

"Ollie! Hello? What are you waiting for?"

A knot was forming, growing, in his stomach. It roiled and kicked, as though he'd swallowed a bullfrog.

This is a mistake.

"Tera, I..." he managed, avoiding her eyes.

"What?"

He gestured at the angled hallway. Wider at the top and narrowest at the bottom, where they were standing now. "Look at this," he said. "Look at the shape. It's a literal funnel!"

"So?"

"It's like someone wants us here. Pulled us here. Like..." He let the sentence linger.

"Like what?"

"I don't know." Ollie shook his head, frustrated. "Like it was too easy."

"Too *easy?*" Her eyes bugged. "Are you insane? Babe, we almost died getting here. Twice."

"I know. Yeah, of course. But maybe..." The bullfrog hopped in his gut. Again. "Maybe we shouldn't go in."

She rubbed her forehead. She was trying to be patient, he could tell. Trying, and failing. "Ollie, I hope you brought a spare mind. Because you've lost the one you had."

"I know it sounds crazy. I can't explain it. I'm just... I have a bad feeling about this."

"Of course you do!" Tera was shout-whispering now, her hands waving in the air. "So do I! We almost drowned, for Krite sake. We're starving, and thirsty! We've been fighting clowns and stealing mutants and listening to goddamn Ukrainian traveling songs for days! And now we've been sent down here by a dead guy, looking for machines that probably don't even exist! And if they *don't* exist, or we can't find them, then people are probably going to die. Actual people. Lots of them. And it's going to be our fault! What about *any* of that would give you a good feeling?"

He blinked.

She was right, of course. And yet...

Despite all that, Ollie could not explain the new, strange foreboding that was suddenly seeping from his pores. Yes, it had been difficult. Yes, they just spent days surmounting a series of preposterous, fever-dream challenges: Bribing a top-hatted carnival barker. Playing cupid for a crab. Interrogating a salt-sorceress while she licked their arms. Fighting off face-painted security guards in a freak-of-nature zoo. Narrowly bouncing back from the brink with the help of beautiful finned-and-gilled creatures that were definitely, probably, *not* mermaids.

All of it, to get here. And here they were. But still, somehow, something felt wrong. Something about that damn door.

"You're telling me that nothing feels off to you?"

"This is the Neath," Tera answered, deadpan. "Everything is off."

"You know what I mean!"

"Ollie, that doesn't matter now. All that matters is that we figured it out, and we're here."

"I know, but..."

"But what?"

He didn't move.

"Ollie," she said again, more gently. "I know you're nervous. I am, too. But it will be fine."

Nope, the belly bullfrog answered. *Nope, nope, nope.* Nothing was fine—not here. And especially not beyond that door. And hadn't he known it from the start? From the moment he had peered into a glass dome and saw his name written on a Mirrormoth's wings? Ollie had felt the hopping in his gut all along, and he had ignored it.

And now, it seemed, he would ignore it again.

What choice did he have? Clenching his teeth, he thought about Mr. Bonfiglio in a hospital bed, battered and bruised. Of Nell, holding the paper sign, her face frozen in an expression of dismay. Of all the WRC women—Jennifer, Tracey, Claudette, and God only knew how many others—huddled together, somewhere dark and deep.

SEND OLLIE UP OR THEY ALL DIE

So much suffering. And all of it, because of him.

Ollie reached for the doorknob. "Saint Christopher, holy patron saint of travelers, protect me and lead me safely to my destiny," he muttered. His mother had invoked that one at the start of every journey. It occurred to him now that he probably could have invoked that one sooner. Then, with a deep breath, he turned the knob and pushed.

Ollie opened the door just wide enough to take a peek, and finally stepped through. Tera followed quickly behind.

No dragon. No candy factory. Instead, they found themselves standing in an enormous, white-walled room, much bigger than the others they had seen so far. The salty ceiling towered over their heads, glistening so brightly that Ollie found himself squinting. He saw lots of wooden tables, set up in rows with narrow aisles in between. He also saw two people—no, three, each wearing a long, black coat and black gloves. The people had not noticed Ollie and Tera. Not yet. They were too busy pouring. Measuring. Weighing. Scribbling notes. All around them, small fires burned through metal grates, heating bubbling liquids and melting blobs of goo. Beakers held colorful potions. Clay pots—some lidded, some not— rested on top of each other in precarious piles. Clear glass jars offered views of jagged, smooth, and vibrating ingredients that Ollie couldn't begin to identify.

The smell wafted over him: something like melted plastic, decomposition, and onion, all blended together in a distinctly unsavory stew. He covered his face with a hand.

"I think we found the lab," Tera whispered, leaning close.

They stood quietly for another minute, taking it all in. Rising ringlets of purple smoke. Small explosions inside suspended, glass flasks. Acids sizzling and burning through heavy fabrics. Pellets rolling through long tubes, dropping onto mats, and piling into mounds. Color. Spark. Flame.

Eventually, Ollie noticed the fourth person in the room. A man, way in the back, hunched over in a chair next to a set of huge, closed, red doors. The man was looking at the floor. He wasn't wearing a black lab coat or bustling around like the rest. He was just...sitting there. Looking dejected. Wearing a small, dark hat. Something about him made Ollie's hair stand on end.

It wasn't until the man raised his head that Ollie realized who it was.

Michael Carmichael?

The Fancy Man himself.

They all saw each other, recognized each other, in the same instant. Carmichael's handsome face first reflected shock—then quickly twisted into blind, bottomless fury. He rose from his chair fast enough to make it topple. Walking. Then running. Coming straight for them. His hands balled into fists.

Not fire-breathing, technically, but something close.

"Uh, oh," said Tera.

Ollie's thoughts exactly.

⸙

It all happened so fast.

For the first few seconds, Ollie found himself frozen, watching in sick fascination as Carmichael advanced like a rabid wolf—all zigzags and spittle. He tripped and stumbled. He knocked into one of the lab techs. He gnashed those perfect, pearly teeth. And all the while, his eyes stayed locked on Tera.

"You're dead, Martinez!" he shouted as he ran. "You hear me? Dead!"

Carmichael rounded the corner of a nearby table, arms outstretched. He was just a few feet away. Reaching for Tera. She stared at his bedazzled suit coat and lunging, polished fingernails with wide-eyed shock, pressing her back up against the salty wall.

Finally, Ollie snapped out of his stupor. He lurched forward and hip-checked the big man, sending him sprawling along the dirt floor.

Carmichael stared up in a daze. Confused, at first, then furious again. He jumped to his feet and let out a guttural scream as he tackled Ollie to the ground. They grappled and wrestled in a mess of grunts, roars, and wild swings, neither getting enough traction to cause any damage. Then Carmichael found an opening: He pinned Ollie's shoulders, straddled his torso, and raised his fist, poised for a blow.

A snarl from behind stopped his hand in midair.

Both men paused their brawling just long enough to catch the gleam of multi-layered, razor-sharp fangs. A flash of fur. A bill that was open wider than seemed physically possible. Meatball snarled again, flung himself onto Carmichael's back, and sunk his teeth into the man's shoulder.

Carmichael yowled. Blood spurted in every direction. He climbed off of Ollie and pressed his hand against the wound. When he lifted it again, his fingers were dripping red. He looked down at the trog in shocked indignation. "What the fuck? You little—" He lunged again, this time for Meatball.

"Don't touch him!" Tera yelled. She grabbed a wide-bottomed empty flask, smashed it against the edge of the table, and held it up threateningly.

Carmichael looked at Tera, then at the pint-sized tube of broken glass. He gave a derisive laugh and started advancing.

Ollie scrambled to get to his feet. But before he could, Meatball was airborne again. The trog landed on the Fancy Man's thigh, tearing furiously at the pantleg and the skin that hid below. Bits of fabric and flesh flew through the air as Carmichael screamed and tried, fruitlessly, to push the furry creature away.

"Get it off me!" he yelled. "Krite, get it off me!"

Ollie, now back on his feet, was watching Meatball with an awed mix of repulsion and wonder. At length, he gathered himself enough to ask: "You going to calm down?"

"Yes! Yes, goddammit! Get it off me!"

Ollie looked at Tera, who nodded. "Fine," he said. "Meatball, that's enough."

The trog paused mid-chomp and looked up.

"That's enough, buddy. Thanks. It's all right."

Meatball let out a grunt that sounded an awful lot like disappointment. A long swath of bloodied, black silk hung from his mouth.

Carmichael looked down at his leg with dismay. "Krite on a cracker, they're ruined! Do you know what those pants cost me?" Before anyone could answer, he continued: "You've ruined everything, you know that? My pants, my business, my whole friggin' life. I could kill you. I *should* kill you!"

She held up both hands. "You're pissed. I get it. But if you'd let me exp—"

"Let you explain?" Carmichael let out a short laugh. "Last time I let you explain, it didn't work out so well for me, now did it?"

Tera's expression was a blend of acknowledgement and apology.

"You waltz in, all friendly, all nice, and you tell me what I want to hear. That was the plan, right? To make a fool of me? To ruin me, and ruin my show? For what? What the hell did I ever do to you?"

"No," Tera said, still holding up her hands. "That was not the plan. Look, Mikey, I know we've had our problems—"

He interrupted with a snort.

"I know we've had our problems," she again, louder. "But I never wanted to ruin you. You have to believe me. If I could just—"

"I'm fucking bankrupt, you know that? You took everything! And now the Doc is pissed, and I'll be lucky if he ever trusts me again. How am I supposed to run a House of Unnatural Wonders *with no Unnatural Wonders?*" His voice was booming now. He stepped closer, stopping only when Meatball hissed and bared his teeth again.

Ollie stole a glance at the lab techs, who had stopped their work to watch the commotion. They looked unnerved.

Tera sighed. "I'm sorry. I really am. We had no choice."

Carmichael snorted again. He looked at Ollie. "You helping her with this? Is that why you wanted Jinx?"

Ollie nodded.

"Great. Just great. What are you, starting a gang now, Martinez?"

"She's looking for some missing people. *Kidnapped* people," Ollie interjected. "People who helped her. Helped both of us. And now they need our help, up on the Brickside. And there was an... Unnatural Wonder, I guess, in a cave, and we had to find his—" Ollie stopped, shook his head. "It doesn't matter. We needed the creatures. Well, one of them, anyway. And we knew you wouldn't give them to us, so we...took them. If you want to blame somebody, blame me."

"Where are they?" Carmichael demanded.

"They're gone," Tera said. Her lips pressed together in a firm line.

"What do you mean, gone?"

"I mean, gone, gone," she said. "You can't have them back. That was horrible, what you were doing down there. They didn't deserve that."

"Jesus, Tera. Get over yourself. They're mutants."

"They're living creatures," she retorted. "And they deserve better than you."

The two of them stayed locked in a staring contest until Ollie cleared his throat. "Look, we're kind of on a clock, here. Can we maybe continue this later?"

Carmichael turned to Ollie in disbelief. "Oh, I'm sorry. Am I keeping you?"

"Kind of, yeah," Ollie said, choosing to ignore the sarcasm. "Like I said, we need to get to the Brickside. ASAP."

Carmichael's hands landed on his hips. Blood trickled down his shoulder and dripped onto his coat, adding spots of red to the already colorful array of rhinestones. He looked amused. "And how exactly do you two losers plan to do that?"

"We heard there's a device here, in the lab. To let you breathe up there."

At this, a strange expression crossed Carmichael's face.

"What?" Ollie asked, stepping closer. "You've heard of it?"

"Of course I've heard of it," Carmichael said smugly. He flipped a thick, black lock of hair from his forehead. "I know about everything down here. But you'll never get it. It belongs to the Doc, and he's not giving it away. Especially not to you two. So...I guess that means you're screwed." This seemed to make Carmichael exceedingly happy. He leaned his butt against the table and grinned.

Tera and Ollie shared an uneasy look. Nearby, the lab techs had resumed their work, apparently no longer interested in the newcomers' squabbles.

"Where does he keep it?" Tera asked. "Is it down here?"

"Why the hell would I tell you?"

"Because, Michael. I need help. I'm begging you."

"So let me get this straight," he said, starting a count on his fingers. "First, you lie to me and get me black-out drunk. You steal my property. You destroy my livelihood. You have your little monster here bite me, twice, and tear up my Versace. And then you ask me for a favor? Am I getting that right? Am I forgetting anything?"

"Mikey, I—"

"Don't call me that," he growled.

"Dude, it wasn't her idea," Ollie interrupted. "It was mine, okay? She was just doing what I told her to do."

"That's not true," Tera said.

Ollie flashed her a look that said *help me out, here.*

"No," she insisted, shaking her head. "It was my idea, and I'd do it again. And you should help me now because it's the right thing to do." She dropped the broken flask, letting it fall to the floor. The glass shattered with an almost gentle, tinkling sound. "C'mon, Michael. You can do another job. You can start another business. Hell, you can do anything you want to do. You always could. Everyone knows that. You live a charmed life."

His expression didn't change.

"How about this," Tera suggested, taking a small step closer. "You just point us in the general direction. We won't tell anybody, I swear. My lips are sealed."

Carmichael shook his head, his arms still folded.

"How about if *we* point," Ollie suggested. "And then you just, uh, tell us if we're getting hot or cold."

Carmichael shook his head again.

Tera sighed. "Krite almighty. What do you want from me?"

"I want you to get what you deserve," he sneered. "And believe me, Martinez, you will. You have no idea what you're dealing with, here. *Who* you're dealing with. But you'll find out soon enough."

Tera ran a hand through her purple hair and opened her mouth to respond. But before she could speak, another voice rumbled into the open air. It came from somewhere behind them.

"Good heavens. Is that any way to treat our guests, Mr. Carmichael?"

Startled, Ollie turned. The man had appeared seemingly out of nowhere. He wore a black lab coat, a pleasant expression, and a pair of wire-rimmed glasses on his nose. In his right hand, he clutched a cane.

"Who are you?" Tera asked.

Ollie flashed her another look of warning. *Be nice,* his look said.

The man appraised them with a lopsided grin. "From what I can gather, I think I'm the one you're looking for," he answered. "They call me the Doc. And this—" he waved the cane—"is Grimshawe Laboratory. My pride and joy, you could say. Innovative, unparalleled, and, usually, impossible to find."

Tera shrugged and folded her arms. "Not so impossible," she said.

"So it would seem," the Doc answered, lifting his brows in admiration. "So it would seem."

Twenty-Two

"Would you care for a tour?"

The Doc spoke in a formal, slightly British accent. A pointy brown beard hung like an arrowhead from his chin, accompanied by a sharp-edged moustache. His thick, dark hair had a streak of white running down the side. Calloused hands. Terrible teeth. Massive earlobes. His eyes—hazel, perhaps—hid behind a pair of lenses that were perfectly round, like the bottoms of jars. The glass was so wavy, Ollie wondered how the man could see anything at all.

All of it combined to give the Doc an outdated, throwback aura. Ollie guessed he had been down here long enough to miss a few decades of trends up on the Brickside.

"A tour? Uh, sure, thanks," Ollie said. He cast a tentative glance at Tera.

She raised a finger. "But first, if it's not too much trouble... Could we get a drink?"

At the mention of it, Ollie's mouth began to water. His stomach twisted in desperate longing.

"Of course!" The Doc said. "Where are my manners? You must be thirsty from your travels."

"But, Doc—" Carmichael stammered, anger still glowing on his face. "These are the ones! The ones who took everything!"

The black-coated man gave him a smooth smile. "You would do well to remember the first rule of hospitality, Mr. Carmichael," he said. "Always make your guests feel at home."

"But, Sir—"

The Doc raised a hand. It wasn't overt or threatening. Just a slight upswing of his fingers. But it was enough to stop Carmichael mid-sentence.

As Ollie watched the exchange, he understood the power balance at play. This man, this doctor, apparently, had some kind of hold on Carmichael. Which was odd, because Carmichael didn't seem like the type to hover under anyone's thumb.

Ollie expected the older man to relay the order to one of the lab techs, or perhaps to tell Carmichael to fetch the drinks. Instead, the Doc walked to a table against the wall and began pouring and stirring. He returned moments later with two tall glasses and a smaller bowl on a tray.

"For your friend," he said, holding up the bowl to Meatball's mouth. The trog shot out a tongue and lapped up the liquid with fervor.

Ollie and Tera followed his lead. Ollie tried not to chug but found he couldn't help himself. When he finally came up for air, he said, "Wow. That's...*really* good." Granted, he was so insanely thirsty that asphalt-puddle water probably would have sufficed. But that had to be hands-down the best drink he'd had since dropping through the Freedom Trail months before. Maybe he was going to like this lab, after all.

Tera nodded in agreement, still gulping.

The Doc looked pleased. "Yes? I'm so glad you like it."

"Is that fruit? It almost tastes like...peach."

"My special blend," the man nodded, holding a finger against his lips. "I'll never tell."

Ollie couldn't imagine where the man had found peaches in an underground cavern, but he also couldn't seem to tear the glass away from his lips long enough to ask.

"Speaking of special blends..." the man said, gesturing with a wide black sleeve. "Shall we?"

They nodded, swallowing the last of the liquid before dropping the empty glasses onto a nearby table. Their host started to walk down the closest aisle, and Ollie and Tera gave each other cautious, relieved smiles as they followed behind.

If Ollie had to guess, this Doc was a perpetually distracted and probably brilliant scientist, like so many others Ollie had seen riding the T to the universities and medical labs strewn throughout Boston. A tinkerer. A bit feeble, leaning on his cane. A bit full of himself. Stuck in his own head, most likely, and completely removed from the real world—though Ollie had to admit that "real world" had a different meaning to him now than it used to.

Ollie took in the whole package and chewed the inside of his cheek. The Doc was an odd character, to be sure. And a complete stranger. So why, then, did he seem so familiar?

"Have we met before?" Ollie asked, the words tumbling out before he could stop them.

The Doc smiled through his facial hair. "My goodness, I don't think so, young man. Though you'll have to forgive that my memory is not what it used to be."

"Sorry. Right. Of course not," Ollie dropped his hands into his pockets.

Next to him, Tera cleared her throat. "We're hoping you can help us," she said. "We're looking for—"

"All in good time, Miss," he interrupted genially. "All in good time."

Tera's mouth closed into a tight frown.

Ollie could read the frustration on her features. Afraid she might burst into an argument, or a speech, or perhaps a fist fight, he interjected: "So, uh, what do you do here in...uh, was it Griswald?"

"Grimshawe," the Doc corrected. "Silly, I know. A laboratory doesn't really need a name, does it?" He pronounced "laboratory" in the British style, accenting each syllable. "But I must admit, I do enjoy such things. And when you get to be my age, you must take your pleasures where you can find them." He chuckled.

"Sure," Ollie agreed. They needed this daft old man to like them, to tell them what he knew. *You catch more flies with honey than with vinegar,* his mother had always told him. Ollie had never understood why someone would want to attract flies at all, but he got the gist of her advice. And if honey was all he had to work with, then he damned well planned to pour it on thick.

The Doc walked past a toppled stack of scrolls, a steaming, fat furnace, and buckets full of shovels and pitchforks. He stopped, finally, at a messy workstation, where a lab tach was face-deep inside a clump of potted plants.

"Hummingtails!" Ollie exclaimed, strangely excited to see something he recognized. Like the others he had seen in the Neath, these resembled Brickside cattails, with fat, brown tops and green stems.

The Doc's mouth curled into a smile. "In a sense, yes."

At the sound of voices, the tech spun. "Sir! Hello. And...hello," she added. That second greeting seemed intended for Ollie and Tera, though the woman's subservient, lowered gaze made it hard to tell.

"This is one of our newer innovations," the Doc said proudly. "Might we give our guests a demonstration?"

Nervousness flashed in the woman's eyes. "Uh, this one is still in the testing phase, Sir."

He waved a hand. Ollie noticed that his fingernails were yellowed and caked with a thin film of dirt. "Pish," the Doc said. "Everything is in the testing phase at Grimshawe. We will all agree to keep an open mind, won't we?"

Ollie felt himself nodding.

"They're not hummingtails?" Tera asked dubiously.

"They *were* hummingtails," answered the Doc. "Now, they are something more. Something better." His eyebrows waggled.

Ollie nodded again. It was becoming more of an automated movement than an actual, considered response. Like someone had shoved the back of his head into motion and now he couldn't seem to make it stop.

"Well?" the Doc asked his tech. "Let's see what we have!"

The young woman gave a wan smile and straightened. "Of course. I'm going to ask you all to step back... Just there... Yes, that should be fine."

Warily, Ollie stepped backwards, then again, until the tech was satisfied.

She joined them, standing three or four feet away from the plants, then uttered a guttural expletive. The word might have been *"Fass!"* or possibly *"Fiss!"* Ollie couldn't be sure. Whatever it was, it caused a quick and obvious reaction in the hummingtails. The stalks shimmered and shook in a jittery little dance; seconds later, the furry brown pods along the tops began to shrink and expand in the same steady, accordion-like movements he had observed at the lakeshore. Ollie waited for the music to begin.

Instead, the plants erupted in pain-inducing, earsplitting shrieks. It was the worst sound Ollie had ever heard: nails on a chalkboard and spoons on Styrofoam and a toddler's tantrum all rolled up into one, nightmarish blare.

Ollie and Tera reacted with startled alarm, crouching and covering their ears with their hands. Meatball tumbled to the ground and curled himself up into a ball. The technician and the Doc merely winced.

"That's phase one," the Doc shouted above the din, looking exceedingly pleased. "The stun phase."

Ollie glanced up from his crouched position just in time to see the start of phase two. Still emitting the hideous wail, the brown pods began to shoot tiny, white spores in every direction. As the spores landed, they sizzled and burned through the surface of whatever lay below: the wood, the dirt, the pots. Now, Ollie could see why the technician had asked them to step back. Meatball raced into sudden action, darting between the falling spores to hide behind Ollie's leg.

Beside them, Tera yelped.

One of the spores had landed on her jumpsuit sleeve. Ollie rushed to help her brush it away; seconds later, all that remained was a hole in the fabric.

"You okay?" he asked.

She nodded numbly.

The spores, he now noticed, had stopped flying. The horrible noise died down into a whimper, then went silent.

The Doc stepped forward to survey the damage. Tiny holes scattered every surface nearby, like polka dots strewn about the scenery.

"Hmm," he said, touching a still-sizzling pockmark on the wooden table. "We'll need to work on the targeting."

"Yes, Sir."

"And the damage."

The lab tech nodded. "Too much?"

"Too much?" he asked her, looking aghast. "For heaven's sake, girl, no! Not enough. Look at this!" He pointed at Tera's damaged sleeve. "Are you even bleeding?" he asked her.

Tera's mouth fell open a little. Then she peered down through the hole. "Um, no. I don't think so."

"See?" the Doc told his employee, snapping his fingers. "Let's keep working on it."

"Yes, Sir," the young woman answered. Chagrined, she turned and began wiping up the mess with her gloved hands.

Ollie and Tera stared at each other in utter confusion. Meatball clambered up Ollie's torso and settled onto his shoulder, letting out an annoyed grunt.

Carmichael, meanwhile, didn't seem much interested in the mutant hummingtails. Or the tour. When Ollie looked around for him, he saw that the Fancy Man had returned to his chair beside the large red doors. He was sulking, hunching, and just generally glaring in Ollie's direction. If their host noticed the absence, he didn't say; the Doc had already spun on his heel and started moving toward their next stop with an uneven, cane-assisted gait. *Step, tap, lean. Step, tap, lean.*

Ollie and Tera followed, doing their best not to trip on the various odds and ends that littered the aisles. In less than a minute, Ollie had sidestepped a fallen container of coils, hopped over a stack of ancient-looking textbooks, and made a wide berth to avoid a row of steaming tea pots. Steaming, *singing* teapots, if he wasn't mistaken. Not whistling, but actually singing. Harmonizing with each other in breathy, ethereal exhalations from their spouts. For one unnerving moment, Ollie was reminded of the row of singing insects back at the witch's nest. They had harmonized, too, in much the same way. Come to think of it...had they been singing the same song? He stared at the pots. They were coppery and only slightly tarnished, giving him a glimpse of his own reflection as he drifted past.

The tea pots glowed. His reflection glowed. Everything in the laboratory glowed in the ceaseless rays of firelight. The candles were everywhere: on tables, on shelves, and even on the floor. There were so many—big and small, skinny and fat, dripping and flickering and towering over wide, waxy puddles—that Ollie wondered how it was possible that the place hadn't already accidentally burned to the ground.

The Doc was talking again. Ollie hurried to catch up.

"...is something special," the Doc was saying. His face, of course, glowed. He was standing in front of another lab tech, this one a young man, and a table that held an array of wooden, pointed objects. Each doohickey had a bag stretched between two handles—like fireplace bellows, Ollie realized. Squeeze the two handles together to expel oxygen from the bag. Fuel to a flame.

"What do these do?" Tera asked.

"Well, that all depends on what you put in the bag. Doesn't it, son?" He pounded the lab tech on the back. The young man coughed and nodded. "That little beauty, there?" the Doc continued, pointing to the nearest bellow. "That one holds what we like to call 'Created Memories.' Ready for insertion. The target simply needs to inhale."

"What, like, false memories?" Tera asked.

The Doc held up a finger pleasantly. "We prefer the term 'created.'"

I'll bet you do, Ollie thought. This guy was starting to give him the creeps. How long were they going to have to ogle his stuff before he started getting useful? "Why would somebody need false memories?" he asked.

"Ah, my friend," the man answered, resting a hand on Ollie's arm. "You are perhaps too young to understand. In life, sometimes there are things that are too terrible to bear. Things we would rather forget, if given the chance. Would you blame a man for wanting to remember false pleasure over an all-too-real pain?"

Ollie didn't reply.

"So you do this...when people ask you to?" Tera interjected. "Like, a service? They *want* false memories?"

The Doc blinked. The question seemed to surprise him. "In some cases, yes."

She tilted her head. "And in other cases?"

"My goodness, you two certainly have a lot of questions!" The Doc wiped his hands on his black coat and barked a quick "Carry on!" to the young lab tech. Then he continued down the aisle, his mind apparently already on something new.

Ollie gave her a palms-up gesture, and she shrugged. They were already waist-deep in the creek, as Dozer would say. Nothing to do now but keep wading to the other side.

At the next stop, an elderly lab tech was adjusting a monocle on his eye as they approached. He seemed much too old to be working in a place like this. Much too old to be working anywhere. He tried to straighten his stooped posture as they approached but only partially succeeded.

"This magnificent device is one of our earlier prototypes," the Doc was saying. "Very successful. We call it the Doubler."

The contraption came in a variety of sizes. The smallest one looked like the bagel cutter Ollie had used back at Bonfiglio's Caffe: Drop the bagel into the slot, press the blade down, and remove two perfectly even halves, ready for the toaster.

"We have those!" Ollie said. "Had those, I mean. Back at home."

"Oh, I don't think you had one quite like this," the Doc said, his eyes glinting. Then he turned to face the tech. "How about a demonstration, old chap?"

The elderly man paused; Ollie could swear he saw him flinch. Then, with a newly hardened, blank expression, the lab tech reached into a box below the table, rummaged around, and used both hands to pull something out. Something…wiggling. Flailing. Alive.

A bat.

The tiny creature had a furry face and small, wide eyes. It was panicking, trapped inside the old man's hands. For a moment, the bat was the only thing moving; Ollie and Tera had frozen in place.

"Wait, what are you going to do?" Tera asked, a note of dismay in her voice.

The Doc waved a hand. "Nothing we haven't done a hundred times before. This one never fails us. Isn't that right, old friend?" He squeezed the tech's shoulder until the elderly man gave an almost imperceptible nod. "Go ahead, then. Let us show our guests the Grimshawe artistry."

With shaking hands, the technician placed the bat inside the slot. As the animal struggled and squealed, the man spread its body symmetrically and pinned its wings down with four clips.

"Wait, stop!" Tera called out, stepping forward. "What are you doing?"

But it was too late. Like a tiny guillotine, the blade dropped.

Ollie slammed his eyes shut, horrified. When he peeled them open a few seconds later, the tech was lifting and securing the blade. Unpinning the clips. Ollie expected to see bat blood and guts pouring out all over the table. Instead, he saw...

Two bats.

No—almost two. But not quite.

When Ollie dared to step closer, he saw two bat *halves*. Each half was alive and astoundingly wound-free. Each was lifting one wing in useless flaps. Blinking one eye. Pushing itself around with one foot. Moving in circles.

"Thing of beauty, isn't it?" the Doc asked. He was stroking his beard, looking like a proud papa.

"Jesus," Ollie said, turning away.

The Doc laughed. "It's fine, see? *They're* fine. One made into two."

"I wouldn't say fine," Tera retorted, watching the helpless, lopsided creatures with open disgust. "One made into two? You just cut it in half!"

The man shook his head and rested both hands on the tip of his cane. "You are missing the point, my dear girl," he said. "Let this be your first lesson in business. Whenever you have the chance to double your investment, always take it. Always." He looked across the room and raised his voice. "Isn't that right, Mr. Carmichael?"

From his chair in the corner, Carmichael gave a weary thumbs-up.

Tera was shaking her head. "Listen, Sir, this is all great, but we were hoping you could help with—"

"All in good time, my dear," the man interrupted, running two fingers through his beard with a pleasant smile. "All in good time."

How much good time? Ollie wondered. "Maybe we should take a break," he suggested to Tera in a whisper.

"No," she muttered. Her expression had gone grim. "Let's just finish this."

But finishing, it seemed, was not at the top of their guide's agenda. With a puffed chest, the Doc continued to lead them up and down the rows, using the tip of his cane to point out a dizzying array of potions, contraptions, widgets, elixirs, concoctions, and gizmos. Exhibit A: The Pocket Bomb. Exhibit B: Shoes that leave no footprints. Exhibit C: Ice that does not melt. Exhibit D: Alchemical transformations calculated to disguise gold as other, less valuable metals—"Wonderful camouflage," the Doc explained, tapping a gold bar as it shimmered into silver. "And easily reversed."

"What are they doing over there?" Tera asked, gesturing toward a monumental stack of wood, metal, and fabric rings.

The Doc followed her finger and shrugged with disinterest. "Oh, they're trying to reinvent the wheel. Been at that one for a while, now, I'm afraid."

His reply left her speechless. Ollie just blinked.

The assortment seemed infinite: Pointy things. Poison things. Misleading, alarming, and astonishing things. Before long, Ollie felt himself teetering from the sheer abundance. There was so much here, and yet nothing at all. It all seemed so needless, somehow. So hollow. And so...unfriendly.

The Doc was in the midst of yet another description of yet another thingamajig when Ollie interrupted him. "But why this stuff?" he asked, his voice coming out louder than he had intended it.

"Hmm?" The Doc turned and looked over the rim of his wavy glasses. "What do you mean?"

"I mean, you can do anything, right? Anything at all. This place is freakin' magic. So why not, I don't know...whip up world peace? Solve hunger? Take that thing, over there." Ollie pointed. "What's that one called again?"

"The Preserver?"

"Yeah, the Preserver. You could use that to make, like, everlasting rhizers that never rot. Right? That would be great. Instead, you're using it to..." Ollie searched his memory, trying to isolate this particular object's purpose from all the others in the vast, bizarre inventory of the previous thirty minutes. It had something to do with bad breath, maybe.

The Doc leaned on his cane and didn't respond.

"Anyway, you know what I mean," Ollie added in a rush. "You could, like, cure cancer in here!" *You could have cured my mom's cancer,* he thought, but kept that to himself. "Just look at this stuff! It's incredible."

Tera stepped forward. "You could even make a breathing device," she said, smiling sweetly. "You know, to help us breathe on the Brickside. Unless, of course, you've done that already."

The Doc leaned on his cane with a quiet laugh. "Alas, my dear, some things are out of even the Grimshawe's grasp."

"What, the cancer thing? Or the breathing thing?"

He gave another chuckle. But he did not, Ollie noticed, give an answer.

"Look, this is a great place. Really," Ollie said, doing his best to sound like he meant it. "You're doing great things. Very, very cool. But there's trouble, on the Brickside. Big trouble. And it involves me. There was a note, with my name on it..." He cleared his throat. "Anyway, I'm sure you don't want the whole story. But we really need to get up there. Can you help us? We heard you have the device, or the, uh, helmet, or whatever. We just need to borrow it. I swear, we'll bring it back. We don't want to stay up there. We only want to visit and come right back. What do you say?"

Tera slipped her hand into his; he squeezed it. Together, they waited for an answer.

The Doc licked his lips. He looked thoughtful. Then he said, "How rude of me. I didn't even offer you something to eat. You must be hungry."

"I—" Ollie paused, confused. He looked at Tera.

"Are you not hungry after your travels?"

"Uh, sure, we could eat," Tera said. "But—"

"Wonderful," the Doc said. He turned and gestured to Carmichael, who was still brooding in the corner. "Mr. Carmichael! Please fetch some refreshments for Oliver and Tera, won't you? Get the carawackers, in the tin. Not the overflow—the good stock, right at the front." He turned back around with a self-satisfied smile.

"Thank you," Tera said. She let go of Ollie's hand and began wringing hers together. "But seriously, we really need to—"

"Wait a sec," Ollie interrupted. He tilted his head to the right. "How did you know our names?"

The Doc blinked. His smile flitted away for just a moment, then returned. "I suppose Mr. Carmichael must have told me," he said. "You and he are old friends, are you not?" he asked Tera.

"Well, I wouldn't say friends, exactly," she muttered.

"Names have great power, don't they?" the Doc said, ignoring her comment. "The power to change everything. I suppose that's why I gave my laboratory a name. And why I name even the smallest of our inventions."

And all of the Unnatural Wonders, Ollie mused. His eyes narrowed as he recounted the mutants' varying degrees of discomfort and modification. All done under the Doc's watchful eye? Probably. Given what he had seen so far in the Grimshawe, it seemed the most likely explanation.

He gazed at the silver streak in the Doc's hair, meandering like a current. The pointy-bearded man was trying to change the subject. Why?

Something was making Ollie's stomach clench. Something too strong to be ignored. "No, wait," he pressed, holding up a hand. "Carmichael knew Tera's name, not mine. But you just said, 'Oliver and Tera.' Fetch some refreshments for Oliver and Tera."

Not even "Ollie." The Doc had called him "Oliver." No one called him that.

The older man didn't answer. Instead, he continued to fix them with an intense stare. Ollie didn't look away. That face... That damn beard. Those dirty fingernails. Why was it all so familiar? And how did this guy know his name?

"Who are you?" Ollie asked, taking a step back. "What's going on here? What is this place, really?" His hands went cold. His bowels felt dangerously and embarrassingly loose, like they always did when he faced confrontation. His fight-or-flight response was kicking in, and he didn't even know why.

"Ollie—" Tera said, touching his sleeve. She was trying to calm him down, trying to get their mission back on track.

"No!" he said, pulling her backwards with him. Whatever food this guy was offering, Ollie wasn't going to eat it. No matter how good it looked. The candlelight haze was dulling his vision. The smells of melting wax, soldering metal, and simmering compounds hit him in a sudden, retch-inducing wave. "You'd better tell us right now! What's really going on here?" *I have a trog, and I'm not afraid to use him!* he wanted to add, but didn't.

The Doc held his steady, pleasant expression for several more seconds, and then, finally, let it go. Like a facelift reversed, his skin began to droop. His welcoming smile tipped into a frown. The lines between his eyes deepened; his clench on the knob of his cane tightened.

"Oliver, Oliver, Oliver," he said, heaving a deep sigh. "You disappoint me. I was so hoping the next part of our tour could wait."

The Doc had started walking—*step, tap, lean; step, tap, lean*—toward the set of wide, crimson doors. Carmichael rose to his feet, looking suddenly gleeful. This, Ollie knew, was not a good sign.

Tera looked from face to face in bewilderment.

"Just as well. I suppose you've seen all there is to see here in the front room," the Doc continued, talking as he moved. He was not looking at them, but at the doors. "Time to see the back. Where the real magic happens, as they say." He chuckled, enjoying his own joke. Carmichael laughed with him, though his sounded less like a chuckle and more like a bootlicking snicker.

At a nod from the Doc, Carmichael rushed forward to grab the thick, wrought-iron handle. With a grunt and a heave, he began to yank on the right door, pulling it open. The left one automatically mirrored its movement in the opposite direction.

Like a wooden Red Sea, the doors began to part.

A trickle of yellow light filtered through the center crack, then a wider burst. It wasn't luster, exactly—more like radiation.

The sounds came next. Horrible howls. High-pitched cries. Rhythmic pounding. Growls. Clacking. Thumping.

"As I said," the Doc continued, "I do want you both to feel at home." His grin, once so amiable, had thinned into something sinister.

Ollie's thighs weakened.

You catch more flies with honey, his mother had said, and it was true. But flies, in reality, were attracted to all kinds of things. Decay. Feces. Fermenting fruit. Rotting meat. Carcasses. And worse.

Because there was worse, of course. Much worse.

Like the scene unfolding with sickening clarity behind every opened inch of the laboratory's formidable, blood-red doors.

Twenty-Three

The room was not square, or round, or rectangular.

As Ollie's glimpse of the space broadened into full view, he could see walls jutting and bending into uneven, indefinable contours. A whateverexagram. It looked as though the room had been somehow molded to fit its contents instead of the other way around.

The ceiling was high; so high that Ollie couldn't quite make it out in the dark distance. But he knew it must be up there, somewhere, because it supported the weight of dozens of candelabras. The hanging lights were festooned with hundreds of candles, and suspended at varying heights. They illuminated just enough of the space below to make him wish they didn't.

His eyes went next to the source of the beastly sounds. They emanated from the farthest wall, which supported a series of mounted shelves and cages. Ollie felt a wave of déjà vu when he realized that the creatures trapped inside the enclosures were freaks and amalgams: parts from one thing mixed gruesomely, cruelly, with parts from another. Like the Unnatural Wonders, but...worse. Angrier. More aggressive. More desperate. Even from a distance, he saw fangs, horns, and talons. Bared teeth. Flying spittle and drool. Swiping claws. Flapping wings and snapping beaks. Each one, no matter its size or shape, seemed hell-bent on tearing out its neighbor's eyeballs and snacking on the bloody, dangling remains.

The captives were repulsive—individually and as a group. Horrifying. And in any other room, in any other world, the gnashing, caged creatures on the back-wall shelves would have been the most terrible, most awe-inspiring, and most retch-inducing sight glimpsed in a lifetime. In this particular room, however, they were not. In this room, they were barely a bud on a twig on a branch on a tree in the vast wilderness of awfulness that surrounded them.

Ollie's gaze slid unwillingly to the left and right, seeing but not understanding.

He closed his lids, counted to five, and then opened them again. Nothing, unfortunately, had changed.

Huge, cylindrical structures filled the space in front of him. Each was perhaps as tall as three or four stacked dumpsters, and constructed of thick, clear glass.

The vessels made Ollie think of the massive fish tanks at Boston's aquarium. Oddly, they also reminded him of summer block parties in the North End, where one of the neighborhood *nonnas* had brought the same dessert each time: She called it Lemon Jiggly. It was popular with the kids, if not the adults, and usually consisted of chunks of fruit floating in a Bundt pan-shaped blob of yellow gelatin.

Ollie found himself temporarily transported back to his Lemon Jiggly past as he stared up at the looming tanks. They were filled to near-overflowing with a thick, gooey substance that looked a hell of a lot like gelatin, though the yellowish color in this case looked less like refreshing lemon and more like oozing pus.

Similarly, the contents floating inside looked less like fruit and more like ghastly affronts to all of humanity. And Mother Nature. And God. And maybe even the devil.

The closest tank held a wasp. And not just any wasp: It was a six-foot, gold-and-brown striped monstrosity, as big as a man, with too many legs. Sixteen, maybe, or twenty. The multitude of segmented limbs hung spread-eagled in the yellow gunk. Its razor-sharp wings were constructed, it seemed, of actual razors.

Hundreds of beady black eyeballs coated the creature's face and head. Each eye stared, unblinking, into Ollie's soul.

He spun around with a terrified shudder, only to come face-to-face with the next container's gelatin surprise: a two-headed hyena caught in mid-snarl. Teeth protruded from not only its mouth, but its entire face. The deformed hyena was motionless, suspended in the goo, and appeared to be dead, though a second glance revealed the tiniest, in-and-out movements of its chest. It was breathing, then. Alive. And yet somehow also encased in the thick ooze.

Next to that, Ollie saw an ice-blue box jellyfish—one of the most poisonous creatures on the planet, if he remembered right. Unlike most jellyfish, though, this one was the size of a compact car, with tendrils that seemed to curl in infinite loops. Each tendril ended in a shiny, sharp point, which Ollie finally realized were actual metal needles.

Ollie's eyes jumped, wide and aghast, from tank to tank.

A school of Piranha, mouths open, baring rows of pointed fangs. No—not a school. Many fish fused together into one, massive killing machine.

A cat-sized green scorpion with five barbed tails.

A bald, lithe creature that might have been a wolverine without the fur; its musculature strained against its exposed, pink skin.

And so many more—all of them entirely motionless inside their prisons of goop.

Ollie stumbled. It was too much. Too much malevolence, all staring down at him in a kind of hostile, suspended animation.

Only then did he understand what Dozer had been trying to tell him, back at Carmichael's carnival menagerie: The Unnatural Wonders hadn't been rejected because they were too grotesque. They had been rejected because they weren't grotesque *enough*. Or dangerous enough. Or vicious enough. This lab was not designed to make sideshow attractions—at least, not intentionally. It was designed to make weapons. And only the deadliest weapons would do.

Ollie was still gaping at the hairless carnivore when Tera clutched his arm and pointed.

Her finger was extended, shaking, directing his attention to the furthest row of tanks. Beyond the scorpion and the jellyfish and the bald wolverine. Beyond the nightmare of conjoined piranha. Beyond the killer wasp with razor-blade wings. Ollie felt his heart thud like a tribal drum in his chest.

Good God.

Tera wrapped her arm around his and squeezed. Her entire body was trembling.

Ollie's breath left him in a rush of revulsion and disbelief. He was looking at...people. One per tank. Women and men alike.

They were trapped, lifeless. Spread-eagled and open-eyed, preserved like mosquitoes in amber.

Tubes of all sizes protruded from the tops of their tanks. The tubes sucked away the yellow gel, ferried it into some kind of metal contraption, and then carried it back to the tank. To and fro, back and forth, in and out, like a deranged dialysis machine. The process created a steady, throbbing sound that Ollie only now noticed in the din. *Chunka, chunka. Chunka, chunka. Chunka, chunka.* And throughout it all, the submerged people never moved.

"What...the...hell?" Tera breathed.

Ollie lifted an arm over his eyes; on his shoulder, Meatball snuffled and spun.

He became aware of more sounds behind them. A whoosh of air. Crackling flames. The squeak of a crank. *Step, tap, lean.*

Ollie whirled around.

The Doc.

The old man was leaning on his cane, a knowing smile plastered on his face. Carmichael stood a few feet behind. Both men seemed to be enjoying watching Tera and Ollie's reaction to the laboratory's ghastly handiwork.

Between them, yet another lab tech tinkered with a row of fires and bubbling cauldrons on a work table. She kept her head down. Unlike the two men, she did not seem to be enjoying anything at all. She seemed, if Ollie was guessing correctly, to be there against her will.

Tera spoke first.

"What the hell's the matter with you?" she demanded. "What is this? Who are those people?"

The Doc's gaze traveled lovingly around the cavernous room. "This, my dear, is the result of many, many years of hard work. Hundreds of years, in fact." He waved a hand. "No need to worry about our guests. They're all just fine, I assure you."

"Fine?" Ollie sputtered. *"Fine?* Are you insane? What did you do to them? They're all...they're all..."

"They are all very much alive and feeling nothing," The Doc interrupted. "Not good, not bad. Simply...alive. And waiting."

Tera's voice shook with anger. "Waiting for what?"

"Waiting for me to revive them."

"And when are you planning to do that?"

The Doc shrugged. "When they are needed."

"For what?" Ollie asked. The thumping in his chest quickened.

Instead of answering, the Doc grinned. It spread like a snake through the deep folds of his face. He turned to the tech and dismissed her with a flick of his wrist; she scampered away.

"You're not going to help us, are you?" Tera asked.

The old man seemed to consider her question, or perhaps ignore it, as he peered inside one of the cauldrons on the table. It was filled with a thick, plum-colored paste. The fire below the bowl made its contents flop and gurgle like a mud-pot geyser, leaving messy splats on the table. The Doc turned a small crank to dampen the flame; as the temperature dropped, the splattering lessened with it. Satisfied, he returned his attention to Tera. "In a way, yes," he finally answered. "Yes, I am going to help you. But perhaps not in the way you suppose."

She looked up at Ollie. Stark fear was raking across her features. "I think we should go," she said. "Now."

Ollie nodded and took her hand. With his other hand, he tried to settle the now-restless trog on his shoulder. "We're leaving," he said. "Get out of our way."

"So soon?" Carmichael sneered.

Nobody moved.

Chunka, chunka. Chunka, chunka. Chunka, chunka.

The creatures on the back wall's shelves continued to scream. The cages rattled and shook. The humidity in the room seemed to rise with abnormal speed, thickening the air. Above their heads, accumulated condensation—or maybe something more sinister—

fell from the ceiling, the rusty, watery drops landing on and around them in tiny, explosive splats.

A drip landed on Ollie's nose, rolled along the skin like a tickle, and fell. He should have been moving, running. Escaping. But something made him ask a question, instead: "What is this place?"

Behind the beard, the Doc continued his maniacal grinning.

Ollie could feel the anxiety building in his throat. Meatball began to knead his claws like a cat, sending sharp jabs of pain into Ollie's shoulder blade. "Answer me!" he shouted. "What the hell is really going on down here? Who are those people back there, in the tanks? What are you doing to them? How do you know me? And who are you, really?"

He watched, exasperated, as the old man sauntered a bit further down the length of the table—*step, tap, lean; step, tap, lean*—and inspected a different splattering cauldron. This one was filled with something that looked like hot, wet cement. The Doc reached out to touch the paste, brought his finger to his lips, and tasted it. When he was done, he looked up at Ollie. The two locked eyes.

Ollie stared past the man's wavy, bottle-glass spectacles, trying to read something in the greenish irises that hid beyond. But all he could see was spinning swirls of distortion.

"Who am I?" the Doc asked, looking amused. "Is that what you want to know?"

Ollie nodded. He didn't trust himself to speak.

"Time means so little down here, I've found. Perhaps you should first ask who I *was*."

Ollie threw Tera a sideways glance. The frustration simmered between them. "Okay, fine," he said. "Who were you?"

The Doc leaned forward and blew into the fire below the table's nearest cauldron, causing the blaze to jump. Then he straightened and stared into the flames as he spoke. "I was, once, a journeyman. An old comer. I was born a gentleman, from a family of respectable means, turned by the new world into something else entirely. Something...low." He growled the last word, narrowing his eyes. "Despite all this, despite the injustices that I suffered, I did not buckle. I made the best of the circumstances I was given. I worked as a man should. I provided for my family and for my parish. I did what was asked of me, and I did it well. And for that, I was punished."

Ollie and Tera shared another side-eyed look. Neither spoke.

"But isn't that always the way?" the old man asked with an exaggerated sigh, fingering the quill pen in the ink pot absently. He turned to look at Carmichael. "You work, and you struggle, and you scrap, and in the end, it does not matter. They will never give you what you deserve."

Carmichael gave a short, hard nod.

"In the end, they will keep themselves at the top, and they will keep you at the bottom," the Doc continued, lifting a beaker from a metal rack to examine its contents. He swirled it, then took a sniff. "It was the way of things then, and it is the way of things now. Nothing changes but the sun on the dial. And so, one day I realized: If I want what is mine, I will have to take it." The smile returned. "And that, my young friend, is exactly what I did."

The words had a chill that made Ollie shiver. When he spoke, his voice was barely audible. "You know who I am," Ollie said. It was more of a statement than a question.

"I do," the man answered.

"How?"

"My dear boy, you continue to ask the wrong questions," the Doc said with a disappointed shake of his head. "The how is never as important as the what."

"All right then, *what* do you know about us?" Tera interjected, folding her arms.

The man stroked his mustache, seeming amused. Finally, he turned away from the worktable and pointed his cane in the air. "I know many things about you. Too many things, one might say."

Tera snorted. "Such as?"

The Doc pushed his glasses up the ridge of his nose. As several quiet seconds passed, Ollie thought for a moment that Tera had called the old man's bluff. That he was nothing more than an eccentric, power-mad octogenarian, hiding in a cave and playing God with whatever unfortunate creatures he could get his hands on. Delusion-spinner. Gaslighter. Lucky guesser.

Then he started to speak.

"Tera Martinez," he began. "Formerly Teresa. You fancy yourself a rescuer. You are looking for a poor, lost group of women, and you have come to believe that I can help you with that task." He gave a mocking pout and rubbed the corner of his eye with a knuckle. "So sad. What will happen to them? You left them all behind, yes? Up on the Brickside? Escaped to safety and left all those women to fight the battles all alone?"

Tera's face blanched.

He continued: "You drive a crow boat with a bird called Mrs. Paget, and you live in a house with other refugees like yourself. You adopted this one—" he paused, gesturing toward Ollie—"not too long ago. Thinking, perhaps, that you could save him. That you had some kind of duty to do so. But then your simple little mission became more complicated, and now you have...how do the kids say it nowadays...*feelings* for him. Big feelings. Isn't that right?"

Tera did not answer. Her eyes had gone wide.

"I know also that you both carry this vile creature with you everywhere you go," he said, shifting the cane in midair to point at the trog. "And that you call it 'Meatball,' correct?" He drew out each syllable to express his disdain.

Ollie and Tera looked at each other, mute. Meatball's kneading accelerated, leaving Ollie's shoulder feeling like a pincushion.

"An unfortunate name, to be sure. But there you have it. We don't always make the best decisions, do we?" He shrugged, then moved the tip of the cane to the right. "And I know that you, of course, are Ollie. Oliver Delgato. You have strange friends. The vagrant fellow, with the eye patch. And the acrobat, of course, traipsing around in that ridiculous, shiny suit." The man's British accent seemed to be getting thicker with each sentence. "You arrived in the Neath only a short time ago. Lured by a false mission, and then trapped by a real one. That was quite something you pulled off at Herrick's End, by the way. Quite something indeed."

Ollie's mouth hung open. His skin began to prickle. "How do you know all that?"

"I know everything I need to know, as soon as I need to know it," the man replied. All trace of joviality was gone. "And I know you."

I know you, too, Ollie wanted to say. He almost did: The words lingered on his tongue. But why?

Something about the way this man talked... the accent, the gruff tilts of the head. Sun dial? Journeyman? *From a family of respectable means. Quite something, indeed!* Who talked like that? Everything about him was foreign, and yet somehow eerily familiar.

It made Ollie think, suddenly, of his time in the witches' nest. Of the flashbacks they had subjected him to: the flickering, terrifying trips into the past. Bonfires. Hangings. Thumbscrews.

The irregularly shaped room began to close in around him. The humidity crushed like a hydraulic press.

I know you, too.

"You said they call you the Doc," Ollie heard himself say, the words tumbling out into the air between them. "But you never told us your name."

"Didn't I?"

Names have great power, the old man had said, just a few minutes before. *The power to change everything.*

The flashbacks returned in a surge, obscuring Ollie's vision. Fat, ancient books. Flames and screams. Swaying bodies on the gallows. Wooden tables and gravel roads. A cart. Two horses. Trapped prisoners.

"Who are you?" Ollie whispered. But of course, he already knew.

He heard the clopping of hooves. The wind in the leaves. A woman's cry, echoing across a long-ago, grassy hill: *You bring us to hell!*

The snap of the reins.

"Aye, but you have guessed already, have you not?" the old man asked. He tilted his head with a satisfied smile. "George Herrick, of the Salem Village Herricks. That is my name. And soon, the whole world shall speak it."

Twenty-Four

Vertigo swept Ollie off his feet. Leg muscles suddenly slack, he stumbled backwards and knocked the back of his head against the closest tank. Its inhabitant, the horrid, eyeball-covered wasp, bobbled inside the gelatinous vat.

He tried to speak, emitted only a series of croaks, and then tried again.

"No," Ollie rasped, head shaking. He reached for the tank, trying to regain his balance, but ended up on the ground when his sweaty palms slid uselessly along the smooth, clear glass. "George Herrick is dead! He died in Blackstone Park. I saw it!"

"Indeed, someone died in that park," the man agreed pleasantly. "But I can assure you, it was not me."

"Then...who?" Tera asked. She had shuffled closer to Ollie and was reaching for his arm, helping him stand.

"If memory serves, I believe it was someone from Thirty-Two."

Tera looked from face to face, puzzled.

Ollie stared into the old man's wavy glasses as recognition surfaced. "He means Floor Thirty-Two. In Herrick's End."

"Aye," the old man nodded. "It was a bit of a pickle. I needed a fellow with the same height, build, that sort of thing. And a dark heart, of course. But I knew that would be no problem on Thirty-

Two." He chuckled. "Dark hearts from end-to-end up there. But you already know that better than most, don't you, young man?"

"But...the Warden!" Ollie sputtered. "The Warden gave you the powder!"

"The Warden *thought* he gave me the powder," George Herrick said. "The Warden thinks a lot of things. Not the brightest torch in the wall, that one. You both met the man," he added, rolling his eyes. "Surely you know what I mean. All I had to do was fool him into giving the Dark Heart Powder to my...let's call him my *alternate*." He winked. "And then, trick my alternate into drinking it. Neither task was particularly difficult, truth to tell. And you know the rest. As they say, the darker the heart, the more damage the powder does. It didn't take long for my new friend to become permanently incapacitated up on that hill, and everyone thought it was me. They even carved a sign! With my name on it!" He chortled again and shook his head. "Can you imagine?"

"But, how?" Ollie asked. White pinwheels exploded in his peripheral vision. "The witches must have known it wasn't you."

"Witches," Herrick said, unfurling the word with scorn. "Idiots and harlots, every last one. They wanted to 'teach me a lesson.' What a joke." His mouth tightened. "So I let them think they had. I convinced them that I wanted to help. Convinced them to create this place. I even convinced them to share a bit of that damn magic they hold so tight. They gave me power, and I used it."

"To trap them at Herrick's End," Ollie breathed, remembering the circular, dismal cell where he had found Bert, Elisha, and Lizbeth languishing. A deep, dank hole, lost to the world for centuries. *The rightful ones tarry in the place that is not a place.*

"Ollie." Tera tugged his sleeve with urgency. "We have to go."

"Wait," Ollie said, once again trying to steady himself against the smooth tank, and once again slipping awkwardly. None of this was making any sense. "Wait. If it was you who imprisoned them, then why did you help me find them? Why did you help me set them free?"

Herrick's brow dropped. His lip curled in amusement. "Help you?"

"Yes! Why did you leave me all those notes?"

A flash of confusion registered across Herrick's face. He covered it almost instantly, but Ollie had seen it drift and pop. The old man turned to look at Carmichael, who shrugged.

"And if that was just some guy from Floor Thirty-Two, then why did he tell me all that stuff?" Ollie pressed. "The lion's feet, the place that is not a place... Tell Widow Hibbins Zero. All of that?"

Again: the confusion. Artfully disguised, but there nonetheless. The old man smiled thinly, then turned his attention to the closest cauldron. He lifted a wooden spoon from the table and started stirring.

For such a chatterbox, the guy had suddenly gone pretty quiet.

Tera straightened. She hoisted up her jumpsuit and looked at Ollie, then at George Herrick, curiously. Suspiciously.

Words resonated, unbidden, in Ollie's head: *Air and breath, truth and lie.*

Herrick continued stirring. His face had gone decidedly blank.

Ollie knew that look. It was the same look his mother had adopted the first time he had asked her about the birds and bees halfway through a plate of Puttanesca. The look Isabella Moretti had given him when he had stopped at her locker in an ill-fated attempt to ask her to the prom. The same look Mr. B had worn when Ollie had mustered the courage to ask for a raise that wasn't in the budget.

Herrick's careful blankness had betrayed him more than any expression ever could. It meant he was trying to come up with an answer. Or a lie.

"You don't know what we're talking about, do you?" Ollie asked.

The old man dropped the spoon into the bubbling pot. "Of course I do."

Behind him, Carmichael shifted his weight from foot to foot, looking at his boss with worried eyes.

"You don't," Ollie said, and the knowledge made him feel strangely gratified. Here was a man who thought he could control everything and everyone. Who had said, "I know everything I need to know, as soon as I need to know it."

But he didn't know this.

"I...don't understand," Tera said. "If George Herrick didn't write all those notes, then who did?"

She and Ollie stared at each other, dismay and confusion sliding back-and-forth between them like beads on an abacus in the humid, misty air.

The verses danced in his mind:

Good is bad, beast will bite. Steer the course, bend the light.

Hows and abouts, souls and mates, find him his, seal your fate.

And his favorite: *All will be mended. The waiting is done.*

"What are we doing here?" Ollie asked. "What do you want?"

Herrick had regained his composure. He tossed a handful of twigs onto one of the cauldron fires and said, "Again, you'll have to forgive me for rephrasing your question. It's not what I want, so much as what I need. And as it turns out, I need you."

"Need us for...what?" Ollie asked. He had no intention of helping this psychopath with anything, laboratory-related or otherwise, of course. But for now, he had to keep the guy talking. Had to buy some time. Then, he and Tera would figure a way out of this. Somehow.

He eyed the space around him nervously. Yes, the lab was overflowing with terrifying beasts that would rip his throat out for a nickel. But they were all either frozen or caged. All that stood between him and freedom was a feeble old man, a conceited dimwit, and a bunch of sniveling lab techs. He and Tera had gotten out of worse.

George Herrick wrapped his fingers around the knob of his cane. "You misunderstand, young man. I only need you. Your friends—" he gave a nod toward Tera and Meatball—"as charming as they are, are just in the way, I'm afraid."

Ollie could feel Tera's acrimony simmering up beside him. She started to retort, but he held up a hand to stop her.

"Fine," Ollie said. "Let them go, and I'll do whatever you want."

"Sadly, I don't believe you," said Herrick, who didn't look sad at all.

"I swear," Ollie said, crossing his heart like a third-grader. "You have my word. Let them go, and I'm yours. Do whatever you want with me."

The old man laughed softly. He had returned to the rack of beakers and lifted the largest one, on the end. It was full of something that looked like butterscotch candies. He shook it, watching the golden globules bounce. "Assurances aren't what they once were, it seems. I'm sure our friend Mr. Carmichael here would agree."

Behind him, Carmichael stretched his mouth into a hard, angry frown. He was still standing like a sentinel by the door.

"So you see, I'm going to need some collateral."

"Collateral?" Ollie repeated, perplexed. "Well, yeah. Okay. I mean, I don't have any money, but I can get whatev—"

He stopped mid-sentence, right after noticing that Herrick was staring at Tera. The man's focus and weird titillation made a tremor of dread run up his spine.

"Whatever you're thinking, you can forget it," Ollie said, his voice a low rumble. He stepped in front of Tera.

Herrick gave the barest jut of his chin; hardly noticeable. But the small gesture was enough to spur Carmichael into action. The Fancy Man in the fancy clothes finally left his post, removing his hands from his pockets and marching forward.

Tera clenched her fists into balls and strained to meet her nemesis halfway; Ollie held her back.

On Ollie's shoulder, Meatball opened his beak and began to hiss.

"Don't come any closer!" Ollie yelled. "I mean it! He's very protective! I don't know what he'll do!"

"Oh, Ollie," George Herrick said, shaking his head with a smile as though they were sharing a delightful joke. His hands reached out to touch Carmichael's arm, stopping the advance. "My goodness. So dramatic! You don't have to worry. I'm not going to hurt your paramour—or your strange little pet. And neither is Mr. Carmichael, I can assure you."

"You're...not?" Ollie asked warily.

"Of course not," Herrick said, flashing a row of teeth from the depths of the beard. "You're going to do it for us."

Ollie laughed then, an involuntary expulsion that made his chest jump. He looked down at Tera, who was leaning against him. Their eyes met. He expected her to laugh, too. But she didn't.

"Oh, shit," she said, panic flashing across her features.

"What?" Ollie asked.

"The drinks!" she said. "The fucking drinks!"

What drinks? And then he remembered: the delicious, peachy concoctions, served to them when they first arrived. The Doc—Herrick—had mixed each one himself. One for Meatball, one for Tera... And one made especially for Ollie.

My special blend, he had called it.

Ollie was staring into her brown eyes, dark and troubled, when he felt it.

A shift. The room seemed to jump around him, while he stayed perfectly still.

"Ollie?"

Ollie buckled. His head pitched forward.

Tera reached for him. "Oll! What is it? What's wrong?"

Meatball's claws dug in for balance.

The room was still drifting, veering, all around him. He attempted to speak. Garbled sounds traveled up his throat and lodged there; all that escaped was a moan.

"Ollie!"

A shutter fell over his vision, obscuring everything. It reminded him of the tiny guillotine on the Doubler—the precise, dropping blade that had sliced the squirming bat in half.

Just as quickly, the blackness slid away. Down, then up. There, then vanished. His vision cleared. The room went still once again.

Ollie unfurled. The moaning stopped.

He inhaled, hard, which felt remarkably satisfying. His whole body felt remarkably satisfying, suddenly, as though he'd been trying on tuxedos and finally found one that fit. He inhaled again.

Someone was calling his name. He turned his head to see a tiny young woman tugging on his arm.

This interested him.

She had short hair, shaved on the sides, with a silvery-purple swoop rising like an ocean wave from the top of her head. She was shaking him. Shouting something. Saying the same things, over and over again. She seemed very upset.

Ollie stared at her. She was fascinating, this odd little person. Very animated.

Something shifted on his shoulder. Turning, he saw an animal. Brown and round. A wide flat beak stuck out from its fur. Two black eyes blinked rapidly; Ollie blinked back. The creature, like the girl, seemed quite unsettled.

A voice echoed. This sound was different than all the others. It reverberated inside his skull, jumping and skittering across the synapses, making his entire body twitch.

The voice said, "Put them there."

Ollie turned to see a man, an old man. He had a white streak in his hair and a pointy beard. Thick glasses. The man was the voice. The voice was pointing at a big, empty tank nearby. Well, not entirely empty. It did seem to be filled with some kind of thick, yellowish gelatin. And a few scattered air bubbles.

"Put them there."

Ollie looked at the brown animal and the young woman. "Them?" he asked. Like the old man, he did not say the words out loud. He merely thought them, in his head, and the old man heard them nonetheless.

"Yes," the voice said. "Put them inside the tank."

Ollie gave a perfunctory nod. The creature was already resting on his shoulder and did not seem inclined to move. The girl, though, was not as cooperative. She struggled and yelled as he gripped her arm, yanking her toward the tank. When they reached it, Ollie found a set of curved stairs around the back. He climbed them, dragging the girl along. At one point, she bit his hand: Ollie paused and looked curiously at the deep mark she had left on his skin.

Put them inside the tank.

Ollie resumed the climb. The animal on his shoulder was making snuffling, wheezing noises, and spun in circles. Ollie ignored this. Once they reached the top of the staircase, he looked down to see that the tank was uncovered. There was no lid to open. The pale-yellow goo reached almost all the way to the lip.

The voice reverberated again: "Now," it said. "Do it."

Ollie's right hand was wrapped around the girl's forearm. She bucked and twisted, trying to escape him, but he held her easily enough. He was large; she was small. With his free left hand, Ollie reached for the creature on his shoulder. He lifted the round, furry body, and held it aloft for a moment. Unlike the girl, the animal didn't fight him. It seemed to trust him completely.

For a moment, they stared at each other. The creature's small, dark eyes widened. Blinked. A tiny shudder seemed to run through its body.

Put them inside the tank.

With an easy thrust, Ollie tossed the spherical body into the air. The animal squealed as it flew. It landed with a splat on the surface and began to sink almost immediately. Its feet disappeared first, then the round ball of fuzz. The beak was the last to submerge, opening wide at the top, gasping for air. And then, it was gone.

Ollie watched dispassionately as one last air bubble rose to the surface. And popped.

The girl was screaming; he knew this because the sound pierced his earlobes in a distinctly unpleasant way. She was pushing, crying. Propping her feet stubbornly against the lip of the tank. Yanking and grappling in an effort to free her arm from his grip. But Ollie was stronger than the purple-haired girl. And much bigger. She would not get away unless he let her. Unless the voice told him to.

He waited. Heard nothing. Remembered the last directive: *Now. Do it.*

He pulled the girl forward. The screaming was louder now; Ollie covered one ear with his free hand. She bit him, again. He tightened his grip and pulled harder. Water spilled from her eyes, creating streams along her cheeks. She was staring at him, shouting. The words dissipated uselessly around them.

He used both hands, now. Gripped her waist and her shoulders. She was facing him, still fighting. Still shouting. Staring directly into his eyes all the while. This fascinated him, too. Why did she stare so intently?

Ollie tilted his head.

He began to push her, then paused.

Something bright dawned in the girl's expression. For a moment, the water stopped falling from her eyes. She used her hand to grip his lower arm, shaking him. Nodding her head. Talking lower, quieter. Faster.

Something nagged at him; something distant.

What was it?

Something about this girl...and the furry round creature. What was it?

Ollie hesitated. He stared down into the sea of gelatin. At the stairs. At the vast, irregularly shaped room, filled with other tanks like this one. At the candelabras dangling above his head. At the old man standing on the ground, far below.

The voice came again: "Put her in the tank."

Yes.

Ollie nodded. *Put her in the tank.* That's why he was here.

He bent his arms slightly, and he shoved.

The girl's face registered something new, then. Her eyebrows lifted. The screaming stopped as her mouth opened into a wide O. She was airborne for several seconds, arms outstretched, before hitting the surface. It pulled her in, thick and greedy. She flailed her arms, spluttering. Searching for something to hold on to. But there was nothing. Only more goop.

Ollie wondered, briefly, why she had stopped making noises. Then he realized: She was under. The girl's face had sunk beneath the surface. Like the small, furry creature before her, she was gone.

He stood there, motionless, staring down. Breathing slowly. Then he spun on his heel. With the open tank at his back, he began to descend the stairs. Down, down, down, down.

The voice spoke again; Ollie strained to hear it, but could not. The voice, he realized, was growing dimmer. Hazier. Its sound no longer pulsated inside his skull. He found himself longing for it. Searching for it. He bent his head left and right.

Bent too far. Ollie swayed. His foot missed the step.

He tumbled, and then he began to fall. Down, down, down, down.

Six words danced somewhere in the recesses of his memory:

Hows and Abouts, souls and mates.

He tried to consider the words. But before he could grasp them, the blade of the guillotine fell again across his vision with a swift, sharp slice. He knew, on some level, what this meant.

Sounds, muted. Light, snuffed.

Ollie, erased.

Twenty-Five

Ollie woke to a sharp jab in his side.

Groggily, he rolled over. He struggled to open his eyes, but found that his lids were not cooperative. So...heavy.

"Wakey, wakey," someone said.

He managed to separate the top and bottom lids, just a crack. Through the veil of eyelashes, he saw a face peering. Leering. Only inches away.

Ollie pulled back in revulsion.

Michael Carmichael.

He groaned. "Where am I?"

Carmichael had borrowed Herrick's cane and was using it to poke Ollie repeatedly in his stomach.

"Ow! Shit! Knock it off!" Ollie moaned, shoving the cane away.

The Fancy Man laughed and took a step back. He swung the cane in wide, triumphant circles as his feet danced a two-step along the graveled ground. "Welcome back, coma boy. You know you snore, right?"

"That's enough, Mr. Carmichael," came a voice somewhere up and to the left. Ollie bent his neck back and squinted. There, silhouetted against the flickering light of the colossal candelabra above his head, stood George Herrick. He reached out for his cane, and Carmichael reluctantly handed it over.

"Where am I?" Ollie asked again.

"Wherever you go, there you are," Herrick answered. "Isn't that what they say?"

Krite on a cracker. Ollie was barely awake, and already he wanted to throttle the both of them. What was he doing with these two assholes, anyway? And why was he on the ground?

He struggled to sit up, leaning his back against something cold and hard. Behind Herrick, he saw a wooden worktable, strewn with various lab paraphernalia: test tubes, fires, an ink pot with a quill pen, long spoons, metal clamps, cranks, and bubbling basins that splattered thick, colored gunk in every direction.

Ollie turned his head, then swiveled it up, up, and up. He saw a huge tank to his left. A terrifying horde of conjoined piranha bobbed inside, their mouths agape.

Right.

The tanks. The lab. The creatures.

George Herrick was not dead.

Good is bad, beast will bite.

You have to think in opposites, down here.

Ollie's head began to throb. His hand went instinctually to his shoulder; then he pulled it away, confused. Meatball was not there. Where was Meatball?

"What's going on?" Ollie asked, rubbing both palms into his forehead. "Where's Tera?"

The two men stared down at him.

"See for yourself, young man," Herrick said. "Your Tera is right where you left her."

Something started to rumble in his abdomen. It felt like hunger, but darker. The hairs on his arms began to rise.

Ollie's back was leaning on something. It was smooth, and solid. Then, like a garage door ordered to open with the tap of a button, Ollie found himself pushing with his legs and sliding his body upward, slowly, along the hard surface behind him. He kept his eyes forward, on the men.

Once on his feet, Ollie stopped. He swallowed. Dread and fear had hijacked his nervous system, sending icy shots through his limbs.

Carmichael held his index finger upside down and twirled it in a happy little circle. *Turn around,* the finger said.

Ollie did.

He had heard the expression "bloodcurdling" before, of course. Up until that moment, he had always taken it to be metaphorical. Just a bit of dramatic license. But as Ollie pivoted and took in the unimaginable sight before him, he realized that it was, in fact, possible for a person's blood to curdle. Or at least, to feel like it was curdling. As it turns out, if you see something heinous enough, you will feel as though your entire vascular system is invaded, clogged, with rotting dairy. Putrid, runny cheese, perhaps—the orange kind they dispense at Fenway into little plastic cups—except older, and more congealed. This curdling will make your body want to reject the very blood in its veins. Reject all the organs that pump and filter and circulate. Reject and expel all the contents in its stomach, and reject the very premise that life as you now know it is worth living.

Ollie was staring into an abyss of mucus-yellow, gelatinous slop. A huge, glass tank, filled to the rim. Air bubbles were scattered throughout. And there, submerged, he saw them both. Meatball and Tera. Their mouths were open. They had been gasping when the ooze closed in around them, pouring down their throats, freezing each face into an eternal grimace.

All at once, he remembered.

The voice. The stairs. The screaming.

He saw himself dragging Tera. Shoving her. Watching her struggle and scream as the tears poured down her face. Begging him to stop.

He saw Meatball, so trusting to the very end, sailing through the air and landing on the surface with a splat. Then sinking, slow and steady. Sinking, and gone.

He saw himself watching them. Observing their terror with detached disinterest.

Feeling nothing as he hurled them both to their doom.

A wail escaped his throat. Ollie's head dropped, hit the glass. What had he done? What had he done? What had he done?

The voice.

Ollie spun. "What did you do?" he screamed.

Herrick lifted one hand. Casually. "Ah, but don't you remember, Ollie? You did this. With your own two hands."

"That's bullshit! It was that drink, wasn't it? That voice! That was you! You made me do this! You made me do—" He stopped, his voice choked. His head fell into his hands. And then he sobbed, deep and hard, falling to his knees. He had not sobbed like that since his mother died. He thought he would never sob like that again. The grief wracked and swallowed him. Grief for all that he did, and all that he had failed to do.

You did nothing, the Widow Hibbins had told him, back at Herrick's End. *You were nothing. And so, that is how you shall remain, within these walls, until the end of your days. As nothing.*

He was a scourge. A contagion. A curse on everyone he had ever met.

"I'll kill you," he growled, finally lifting his red, tear-soaked eyes. "I swear to God. I will fucking kill you for this."

"That may be," the old man said, looking unconcerned at the prospect. "I don't doubt your enthusiasm. But I'm afraid your plans will be delayed a bit. Quite a long time, in fact. And at the end of it... Well, who knows how you'll feel?"

Ollie lunged forward.

"Uh, uh, uh," came a voice.

Ollie stopped, slid his eyes to the right. Carmichael was standing behind Herrick, grinning. He was also holding one of those zapping rods—the same kind used by the guards at his House of Unnatural Wonders, and by the Reds at the prison. Ollie had felt its jolting sting more times than he could count during his days inside the crumbling walls of the tower. A cattle prod for people. He backed away.

"Oliver," Herrick said, rolling the name around on his tongue as though finding it distasteful. "You've proven to be quite a pain in my bollocks, I'm afraid. Running around, sticking your nose into places where it does not belong. I just can't have that. Not anymore. My work here is too important. *You* are too important." He leaned both hands on his cane. "And in time, I assure you, you will understand why."

Ollie said nothing.

"But I am not a cruel man, despite what you might think," Herrick continued amiably. "As I told you, all of my buoyant guests here at Grimshawe are only…suspended, we'll call it. Interrupted. And that includes these two." He waved his cane in the general direction of Tera and Meatball's tank. "All I have to do is say the word, and pop." He flicked out his fingers. "Out they come. Won't that be lovely?"

Hope glinted, distantly, in Ollie's chest. Still, he did not speak.

"And that goes for you, too, young man. For now, yes, you will be taking a rest." Herrick pointed to a large tank in the back of the cavern, near the others that contained the suspended, inanimate humans. The tank was empty. Waiting. It also seemed to be hooked up to one of the strange goop-dialysis machines. "But soon…who knows? When my work is complete, and if you prove to be useful, and cooperative… You and your friends will awaken and go along your merry ways. Until then, however, you will be my guests. On that, I really must insist."

Carmichael took a step closer and jutted his weapon. "Let's go," he growled.

And with that, the small flicker of hope was snuffed. Ollie looked at the two men, and at the prod in Carmichael's hand, and at the gelatinous tank that awaited him. He waited for the despair to overtake him. Instead, strangely, he felt nothing at all.

His body had gone as rigid as biscotti on a cappuccino saucer. He had never felt anything quite like it: the coldness, the utter emptiness. It was as if his normal emotions had been siphoned away to make room for…what, exactly?

He turned again to look at Tera, his feet pivoting with an abrasive scrape along the dirt floor. She had somehow managed to swim, or crawl, or claw her way to the outer edge of the glass before she succumbed. Her hand was lifted, fingers splayed. Like a palm reader, he squinted to make out the gently curved creases he saw on her skin: Heart line. Fate line. Life line.

Even now, he could hear her voice. Feel her small fingers on his cheek.

In a world full of dandelions, Ollie Delgato, you are a sunflower.

Ollie stepped forward, lifting his own hand in a mirror-image of hers. He pressed it against the glass, imagining that their palms were touching. The emotional chill began to thaw and crack.

Whatever else was coming, it was coming fast. Salty tears blurred his vision.

He closed his eyes, seeing the other Tera. The real Tera.

Running her hands absently along the shaved sides of her hair. Reaching up to pin the laundry on the line. Adjusting the miner's lamp on her forehead while navigating the crow boat through the fog. Tossing Rat-a-Tat pegs at him in the middle of a game. Sharing her lunch. Terrorizing miscreants down at the Tea Party. Scrunching her face in concentration at the easel, paint splattered across her nose. Tossing back her head in loud, unbridled laughter. Holding his hand. Gazing up into his eyes. Standing on her tiptoes to kiss his lips.

Filling him. Lifting him. Fixing all of his broken pieces.

Agony rattled through him with almost audible thunder.

What came next felt peculiar, and yet as familiar to Ollie as the lyrics of a favorite song. It was white and hot—a surge with unimaginable force. Not anger, exactly, but something more. Something worse.

Your rage will show you, the Salt Witch had said.

Ollie looked down at his hands. They seemed, suddenly, to belong to someone else. The skin on his palms looked thinner, and brighter. A burnish glowed within. He pushed up a sleeve, knowing what he would see: the crimson flush. The red freckles, rising to blisters, growing and spreading until they covered his epidermis from scalp to toes. He could feel them all there, under his clothes. Burning. Eager. Impatient. Like greyhounds catching sight of the rabbit.

Your rage will show you who you are.

Ollie's lip curled into a snarl.

Show me now, he thought.

The light was traveling. Mutating. It heated him, incited him, and surrounded him. The blisters on his skin thinned into transparency as they grew, letting the light escape from within— each one shining a thin, bright beam through the fabric of his jumpsuit and out into the darkness all around. Hundreds of beacons, bursting in every direction, bouncing against the walls, the worktables, the men, the tanks. A primal scream of illumination. When the beams hit the ground below him, they lifted Ollie's body several inches into the air.

He threw back his head, swallowing the light and the anger. Recognizing them. Harnessing them into something savage, and hideous, and extraordinary.

Then he opened his eyes and saw his surroundings clearly for the first time.

The room was cavernous and yet somehow claustrophobic: Ollie could sense every crack in the distant ceiling and hear the rodents and insects scurrying behind the walls. The two men, Herrick and Carmichael, were watching him. Their expressions were startled, frightened. Carmichael was gripping his weapon, rivulets of sweat dripping down his face. George Herrick had gone as still as stone. As still as the petrified, ancient man he had pretended to be on the hill at Blackstone Park. Pretended to be, but wasn't.

And still, the fury rose. Ollie relived it all: Forcing Tera up the stairs. Listening to her cries. Condemning them both to a suffocating, tormented end.

He could feel the fire glowing ever hotter; the beams lifting him higher off the ground. His eyes flitted around the space as everything came into clear, sharp focus. Ollie saw not only the massive tanks, but also the individual molecules of silicon dioxide that made up the thick glass. The pathetic electric charge inside Carmichael's weapon. The air was thick with microscopic creatures; he inhaled, sucking them into his sinuses like kindling to the flame. He saw the table, not too far away, scattered with bubbling cauldrons. Spoons. Tubes. Scattered papers.

The pufferpine quill, resting inside the pot of ink.

Ollie titled his head to the side.

The two men were panicked, and shouting. Carmichael was waving his weapon foolishly.

Ollie ignored them both. Instead, he focused on the quill, black and motionless in its pot. The words formed like thunderclouds in his head.

Come to me.

The glow inside his hands grew hotter. It felt painless and natural, this summoning. Like running into an old friend and falling back into easy, effortless conversation. The beams of light radiating from his body began to redirect themselves like search beacons, clustering in the direction of his gaze. One after another, they swooped, spun, and landed on the table. On the ink pot. On the quill.

Come to me.

The pufferpine quill gleamed in the glare of the spotlights. It jiggled in its jar. It swayed from side to side. And then, finally, it rose into the air, dripping fat globs of black ink from its tip as it moved slowly across the table and over the ground.

Ollie inhaled. Exhaled. *Come to me.*

The two men had not seen it. They were still shouting at each other, and at him. Dodging the beams of light. Their words reached Ollie's ears and burned up in the flare, unheard.

The quill was traveling in an upright position, its tip pointing toward the ground. Ollie watched it move and he thought about Tera, half-dead in a gelatinous hell. He thought about his trog. He thought about what this man, this place, had made him do. He thought about his dismal, hopeless cell at Herrick's End. He thought about his father's abuse, his mother's cancer, and every thug who had ever slammed his head into the side of a bathroom sink. And as the rage welled and thickened, the quill changed direction. No longer moving toward Ollie; no longer floating upright.

With a sudden, violent snap, the quill flipped onto its side. It veered sharply, traveling like a silent torpedo through the air. Seconds later, the pointed tip of the pufferpine quill found its target, plunging deep into the side of George Herrick's neck.

For a moment, Herrick only stared. Wobbled. Then his hand went to his throat as he touched the protrusion, tried to make sense of this sudden, unwelcome development. Finally, he dropped his cane. He staggered left and right. He pulled at the embedded quill, yanking in desperation.

Ollie narrowed his eyes. The quill stayed put.

And then, like a balloon filling with air, Herrick began to...expand.

Ollie stared, unmoving, as the transformation began. He had seen pufferpines, lots of them, down in the depths of the lake; the species was more or less a strange, Neathian cross between a pufferfish and a porcupine. Furry and quilly and fishy, all at the same time. He remembered the way they had ballooned themselves up into barbed spheres in order to deter predators. Now, it seemed, the same thing was happening to Herrick—minus the barbs. With head-snapping speed, the aquatic creature's latent poison was seeping into his bloodstream, morphing the menacing old man into something that more closely resembled a doltish, bearded eight-ball. And all the while, Herrick gurgled and groaned as he struggled, fruitlessly, to stay upright.

Instead of rushing to Herrick's aid, Carmichael took a few stunned steps backward. He looked at his boss, and then at Ollie, with open alarm.

On and on it went until, at last, Herrick's body reached the limits of its expansion. The end result was shocking, and comical—a honeydew-melon of a man, with two pitiful arms and two pitiful legs poking out like toothpicks.

Herrick was still gurgling. It was an awful sound; Ollie enjoyed it immensely.

Stepping closer, he reached out to squeeze a bit of Herrick's bloated shoulder flesh between his fingers and grimaced. Then he gave a little shove. It was barely a tap, really, but enough to send Herrick rolling: With a series of wheezes and panicked snorts, the once spry old man went bumping and spinning along the dirt floor, changing direction haphazardly as his flailing limbs made contact with the ground. He came to rest against the giant blue jellyfish's tank. Head to the side, legs splayed. His fingers waved desperately, uselessly, in the air.

"What did you do?" came a shocked whisper. Carmichael.

Ollie turned to face him. His anger was ebbing. The loss of it made him lightheaded. He searched his consciousness, trying to regain his hold on it, but found that he could not. The rage was just...tumbling. He looked down at his hands: The glow was fading. The raised red freckles, and their blinding rays of light, were gone.

Carmichael held out his prod shakily. "Wh...who are you?"

The candelabras continued to glow overhead. The musty, rancid smells continued to permeate the air. The caged creatures on the back wall continued to shriek. And the answer, when it came, was surprisingly easy: "I am Ollie Delgato, of the North End Delgatos."

"What does that mean?"

Ollie didn't know, exactly. But the words had somehow taken on a strange sort of weight, like pebbles congealing into strong, heavy cement.

"Krite... You're a...witch!"

Ollie felt dazed; he took the deepest of breaths and tried to steady himself, to return to himself, as the room swam around him in a coppery, spinning smudge. What had just happened?

Ink pot. Quill. *Come to me.*

Exposed neck, bulging vein. Deep, perfect puncture.

After several slow blinks, Ollie righted his posture. He stood firmly, evenly, on both feet and considered the weapon pointed at his chest. Could he somehow summon the same, strange energy to make the sparking rod levitate? Or malfunction? Probably. But as he took in the full picture of the top-hatted, ridiculous man standing before him—unsteady grip, shallow breaths, sweaty brow—he realized that no extraordinary means would be necessary. Instead, he just yanked the prod out of Carmichael's hands and tossed it. Carmichael, for his part, seemed too unnerved to resist, and they both watched the weapon land on the ground with a clatter.

"I'm not a witch," Ollie said. Despite all evidence to the contrary, the thought was preposterous. Obviously, one of the witches had bestowed some kind of temporary power onto him. But when? And how? And...why? His mind raced with implausible possibilities.

Carmichael's head titled. "No..." he said, sounding thoughtful. "You can't be. Herrick has a shell around this place. Like, a block, for protection. Witches can't get in." He suddenly looked more curious than scared. "So, what are you, then?"

Ollie had no reply. Moreover, whatever power he had managed to harness, and however he had managed to harness it, it had already drained away like the last bit of stormwater down a sewer grate.

But Michael Carmichael didn't need to know that. At the moment, there was only one question that Ollie cared about answering. "How do I get them out of there?" he asked, pointing to Tera and Meatball's tank.

Carmichael held out his now-empty hands. "You can't."

"What do you mean, I can't? There has to be some way."

"He told you, man," Carmichael said, gesturing toward Herrick's flailing body. "Only he can do it. It looks open, but it's locked up with a spell. That's how he designed it. How he designs everything. He's a control freak, you know?" Now that his boss was incapacitated, Carmichael seemed a lot more open to constructive criticism.

Ollie took off running, heading toward the stairs at the back of the tank. He took them two at a time. Once at the top, he reached out, leaning over the open vat—and hit his hand against something hard. And invisible. He grimaced, banging his fists against the radiating field. He could see them there, below...floating beneath the surface of the goo. So close, and yet so mind-bogglingly far. Tera and Meatball were out of his reach. George Herrick had seen to that.

He roared again, then rebounded down the steps and ran back to Carmichael, who was watching the scene with an *I-told-you-so* look on his face.

"Okay, fine," Ollie said, panting. "Fine. He has to do it. So how do I make him do it?"

"That might have been helpful to ask *before* you blew him up like a water balloon," the Fancy Man answered wryly. "He's got to speak the words. Say them clearly. And now..." His voice trailed off as they both glanced over at Herrick, whose mouth and neck had been almost completely consumed by his billowing chest.

Ollie sighed. "How long until he can speak?"

"It's a pufferpine quill, dude! He's going to be like that for days! Maybe weeks. I don't know. And even if he could talk, he has to want to do it, you know? He has to be, like, a willing participant. That's how it works. And now..."

As he watched the man shrug his bejeweled shoulders, Ollie thought back to the curse of Howerbout's cave. *Wishes only work when they're true.*

Goddammit. Ollie cringed as the painful realization dawned: He may have acted a bit...rashly. "Stab a Man's Neck with a Poisonous Quill" probably wasn't a chapter heading in *How to Win Friends and Influence People.* And if he really did need Herrick to willingly participate in releasing Tera and Meatball from their captivity, as Carmichael insisted... Was it too late? Had he just screwed up his one opportunity to free them?

No. Ollie lifted his chin, feeling the last of the tingling warmth linger in his fingertips. There had to be another way. There always was, down here. And whatever it was, he would find it.

He turned back to look at Carmichael, who had collapsed into a chair near the cluttered table.

"Why them?" Ollie asked, pointing to Tera and Meatball. "Why did Herrick want them in there?"

Carmichael looked exhausted—just a rumpled, vague echo of the dapper "proprietor" Ollie had met on his first visit to the House of Unnatural Wonders. The façade had all but vanished. "You're asking the wrong questions," he finally said.

"What do you mean?"

"I mean, why are any of you here at all?" Carmichael asked. "Why did you come to Grimshawe?"

"Because we needed to get to the Brickside."

"Uh huh. And why is that?"

"Because of...the people. The women, who were taken. And my friends, who were hurt. And..." He paused, then continued. "There was a note. It had to be me. I was supposed to go up. 'Send Ollie up or they all die,' it said." He stopped. Carmichael was staring at him. "What?"

"Think about it, man."

"Think about what?"

Carmichael shifted, looking like the unwilling bearer of bad news. "He needed you to come here. He needed you to *want* to come here, to the lab."

"What are you saying?" Ollie asked, a knot of anxiety already starting to twist in his abdomen. "Are you saying...Herrick was behind all that? He took those people, just to make me want to get the Brickside? To make me want to go searching for this stupid, goddamn lab? That's why my name was on the note?"

Michael Carmichael raised a hand wearily and snapped his fingers. "Bingo."

"But...but...why?" Ollie sputtered. "If he wanted me so bad, why not just come get me?"

"Herrick can't leave," Carmichael said. With a sigh, he removed the small top hat and ran his fingers through the patch of flattened, dark hair. "He's got that shield around the place, like I told you, to keep the witches out. But also to keep them from finding him. He's supposed to be dead, remember? Martyred up on that stupid hill? The second he leaves this lab, the witches will sense him. They'll know it. And they'll know he lied."

Hundreds of follow-up queries swirled in Ollie's head. He asked the one that rose to the top. "But why *me?*"

"He needed you. Well, more accurately, he needed to get you out of the way. Dude's got plans, big plans, and he thought you were the one person who could stop him."

"Why the hell would he think that?"

"Somebody told him so."

"Who told him?"

"I don't know! He doesn't, like, confide in me. All I know is what I hear. Or overhear. Someone gave him a warning, or whatever you want to call it. Ollie was the guy who was going to screw him. To foil all his big plans. And so, he decided to remove the threat. So to speak." He gave an apologetic half-smile.

Ollie's throat went dry. He remembered Weelichka pointing a shaky finger at him in her salty, mountaintop cabin. *You!* She had looked frightened, as if she had seen something awful behind his eyes. *Soon, your rage will show us all.*

He thought about the nesting witch named Bert, slamming his palm against Ollie's forehead. Hovering so close that Ollie could smell his breath. *It is no accident you are here, our dear young giant. It is your kismet. Kizzee, kizzee, kismet!*

He swallowed. "What kinds of plans are we talking about? What's he going to do?"

Carmichael shrugged. "I'm just the help, man."

Ollie glared at him. Funny how people were suddenly "just the help" when the shit starts to hit the fan. He shook his head and began to pace. "None of this makes any sense. Why would anyone think I could stop anything? Why me?"

"Well, I think we know the answer to that now, don't we? Mister Make Shit Fly Across the Room?" Carmichael waved a hand. "Herrick said he needed you out of the way. That's all I know."

"So why not just toss me into the tank with those two, then? Or kill me?"

Carmichael shifted again. He passed the hat from one hand to the other.

"What?" Ollie asked.

The Fancy Man cast a quick glance at Ollie's clenched fists. "I think he also wants...whatever you've got. He wants to take it. Use it. He's done that before."

"Done what?"

Carmichael's voice dropped to a frightened whisper. "He...steals magic." His eyes traveled to the tanks in the back of the room. To the humans, dormant and floating, and the long tubes sucking the gel back and forth, in and out, of the strange metal devices. *Chunka, chunka. Chunka, chunka. Chunka, chunka.* And Ollie, at once, understood.

"They're all...witches?"

Carmichael nodded.

"And they're here because...he's...siphoning their powers?" The thought made his skin crawl.

Carmichael nodded again, as though afraid to speak.

Ollie's legs went weak with disgust. How long had these poor, spread-eagled, hibernating people been trapped here? What kind of horrors had they been subjected to? Had the old man already bled them dry? Ollie never thought he'd see anything worse than Herrick's End. He would not have believed it was possible. But this... This was worse.

"Carmichael, you need to tell me now," Ollie said, his voice hard. "What is that psycho doing down here? Why does he need all...this?" He gestured to the grim surroundings. "What's he planning?"

All Ollie heard was a sibilant mumble. "Speak up!" he snapped.

Carmichael raised his gaze, and his voice. "Something big," he said, reluctantly. The shoulder wound caused by Meatball's bite was still trickling blood down his shirt.

"Like what, exactly?"

"I don't know, man. I don't want to know. I do what the guy tells me. That's it."

Ollie got the sense that he was telling the truth. Carmichael was a hired gun, weak and weaselly. He would go, happily, to the highest bidder. Or give in to the most threatening threatener. And in this case, he seemed smart enough to understand that Ollie was currently both.

He looked back at Herrick; the poisoned man was still flailing like a swollen tick. Useless. *Krite.* "So you're telling me he won't shrink down for days?"

"I'd say a week, yeah. At least."

"But he'll survive?"

"Sure, he'll survive." Carmichael waited a beat, then added: "Maybe."

Ollie stepped closer and leaned forward, nose-to-nose with the slumped man. "You'd better hope he does," Ollie hissed. "Because if I come back here and he's dead, then you're going to wish you were dead, too. Got it?"

"What do you mean, come back?" Carmichael asked, uncurling his spine. "Where are you going?"

Ollie didn't *want* to go anywhere. All he wanted to do was sit there, around the clock, and glare at the whole damn lot of them until the balloon man shrunk back down to normal size. Then he would summon back the rage—that delicious, disturbing rage— that had made him light up like Chernobyl. Then he would hold George Herrick's face against an open flame and force him to speak whatever words were needed to free Tera and Meatball from the vat of yellow Jell-O. Then, and only then, he would burn this whole place, and everything in it, to ash.

Easier than rolling off a log, as Dozer would say.

But nothing was easy in the Neath. Not logs, not rolling, and definitely not this.

"I'm going to the Brickside," Ollie finally answered. "And you're going to show me how."

The infamous "device," as it turned out, really did exist. But it wasn't a helmet, or a mechanical lung, or any of the other things Ollie had imagined it to be.

Carmichael didn't have to go far to fetch it. He didn't even have to leave the room. He simply jumped out of his chair, scurried past the worktable, and approached a closed, iron-grate basket sitting on the dirt floor. As he opened the lid, a piercing, metal-on-metal squeal erupted and echoed against the walls. He winced at the sound, then reached inside and removed something rubbery and black. It looked like an old peashooter, with a barrel at one end and a long, clear tube at the other. Holding it by the handle, Carmichael crossed the room and held it out to Ollie.

"What is it?" Ollie asked, eyeing the contraption dubiously.

"It reacclimates your lungs to the Brickside," Carmichael said, though he didn't sound convinced. "Everything's in the one pellet. You use this to inject it under your skin."

"What's in the pellet?"

Carmichael shrugged and readjusted the tiny top hat on his head. "Dunno. I do know it's just a short-term thing, though. So you can't stay up there for long."

"I'm not planning on it."

A short-term thing.

Carmichael's time-limit warning was an eerie echo of Laszlo's, way back on the Brickside. *You must come back in time.* Then, Laszlo had been standing on the Boston Common, ready to send Ollie down. Now, Ollie was standing in the Neath, ready to send himself up. Opposite legs of the same journey along the Freedom Trail, though neither one, it seemed, would make him free.

"How long do I have?" Ollie asked.

"I'm, uh, not exactly sure," Carmichael answered.

"Why not? Hasn't anyone used it before?"

"Well, yeah. But..."

As Carmichael avoided his eyes, Ollie's heart began to patter. "But what?"

"But we haven't documented a...round trip. Yet."

"What the hell are you talking about? No one has ever come back?"

"Not that I know of. But like I said, man, they don't tell me everything."

"So what happened to those other people?"

Carmichael's palms rose in a helpless gesture.

Ollie rubbed his forehead and squeezed his eyes shut.

"Look, you told me to get the stupid thing, so I got it," Carmichael said. "But I didn't say I recommend it. I don't even know if it will work. I'm just—"

"Yeah, yeah, I know," Ollie interrupted. "You're just the help."

What was he doing? This was crazy. He should just stay here. Keep an eye on Tera, and Meatball. Watch Herrick shrink back down to size. Return the damn injector to its squeaky box and forget he had ever seen it.

But the inconvenient truth remained, gnawing like a starving rat at his conscience: All the hostages were still missing on the Brickside. Because of him. Mr. B was probably still sitting in a hospital bed, and Nell was God-knows-where doing God-knows-what. Because of him. Even if they'd all been taken as bait to lure him to the lab, even if it had all been a ruse, that didn't change the fact that they were still in danger.

Because of him.

Worse, he still didn't know *why* they were in danger, or what Herrick was planning. That's what troubled him the most.

The deranged old guy, clearly, was up to no good. It only took one quick glance around his Laboratory of Horrors to put together the pieces of that puzzle. Mutants, weapons, captive witches, stolen magic... Whatever he wanted, and whatever he wanted it for, the end result was bound to be nefarious.

George Herrick, of the Salem Village Herricks. That is my name. And soon, the whole world shall speak it.

Sure, Ollie could probably stab a few more quills into a few more necks as needed to help himself and his friends escape the lab. But until he knew what Herrick was planning—and what he had already accomplished—they would remain in danger. All of them. The people that Ollie had grown to love, and the place that he had begun to call home.

And then, of course, there was the small matter of his sudden, mystifying ability to levitate several inches off the ground and commandeer inanimate objects. Had the strange gift been a one-time loan, like the underwater-breathing aptitude from the Novas, or was it something else? Something more...permanent? Someone had told Herrick that Ollie was the "one person" who could keep him from his goal, whatever that meant. For now, unfortunately, Ollie thought it meant that spending the next week with his feet propped up in a La-Z-Boy recliner was probably not on the agenda.

But...

Ollie turned slowly, painfully, to look inside the tank. To peer at her distorted, frozen, beautiful face.

How could he leave her?

The thought of walking away, even for a few days, made Ollie want to peel off his own skin. And the thought of going up there alone, without Tera by his side, felt even worse.

But...

If he didn't go to help the hostages on the Brickside, their blood would be on his hands, forever. And if he didn't figure out what was really going on in this lab, no temporary solutions would matter. And, most importantly, if he didn't somehow convince Herrick to say the necessary release spell, then Tera would never leave her grim, otherworldly confinement. She and Meatball would be stuck in that goddamn torturous tank forever. Not dead, not alive, but some horrible state in between.

And what of the notes? The "Herrick notes," as he had come to think of them. If George Herrick hadn't written them, then who did? And why?

Like drops of oil separating from water, the final lines of the most recent missive bubbled to the surface of his consciousness.

Soon, you choose:
All
    or
      one?

Ollie stared at Tera's lifeless, floating body. His breath came in ragged spurts. He knew what Tera would have wanted him to do: If she could speak, she would have told him to do what was best for the majority. For the Neath. For the hostages. For Mrs. Paget, and Ajanta, and Derrin, and Kuyu, and Dozer, and Laszlo, and everyone else they cared about. She would have told him to give George Herrick the finger and run out the door, and to leave her and Meatball behind to their fate. She would have been okay with that, he was sure. That was just the kind of person she was. Unselfish. Unafraid. Always thinking of others before herself.

Soon, you choose: All, or one?

Tera was the one. She always would be.

And still, he could not choose her. Not now.

Not yet.

The ache of it—the harsh, vicious reality—buckled him. He slumped forward, lost in the injustice, until a voice interrupted his stupor.

"I don't get it, dude," Carmichael said. "Where are you even going?"

Slowly, Ollie lifted his head. Through glazed eyes, he stared at the ridiculous man in the ridiculous bedazzled coat. It was, he realized, a good question. Where *was* he going? "The Brickside" was an awfully big place, after all. Even his little corner of Boston was home to endless shadowy alleys and darkened doors. He had no idea where the missing WRC people were, or who to ask. Or even where to start.

Or did he?

He heard the whispers, then, like swirling winds at his ear. Snippets of word and memory.

"Hold this," Ollie said suddenly, passing the injector gun to Carmichael. He turned and strode across the room to where George Herrick's inflated body sat propped against the tank. The Pufferpine quill still protruded from the old man's barely visible neck.

"Well, what do you know," he whispered into Herrick's ear. "It looks like the pen really is mightier than the sword."

Then, Ollie grasped the quill and yanked it free from the fleshy folds. A stream of blood spurted; Ollie ducked to avoid it. Did Herrick wince? It was hard to say, given the Shar-Pei level of furrows in his distended face.

Pen firmly in hand, Ollie walked to the worktable. He shuffled through the scattered stacks of papyrus papers until he found one that was blank. Then he dipped the pointed, still-bloody end into the pot and tapped the excess ink off the tip.

The witches' various pronouncements came back to him in a clear, terse rush.

A message for you, Bert had said, his face oddly enraptured. *From the one who wishes you to have it. Water, earth, air! He will need it, way up there!*

Ollie scratched the words onto the paper.

Then, he recalled Weelichka's more expansive chants: *I deliver a message. Three points. One key. Water, earth, air. Three points make one key. Not here, but there. Not down, but up. Up and up and up.*

Ollie wrote as much as he could remember, as fast as he could.

The old woman had moaned and slumped, then continued: *Water first. The water of your youth. From Myrtle to Coral, and then further still. Earth! Earth second. Herrick's home. The place of his sin. The remnants of the victims will guide you. Air! Air third. Two-twenty-one, two-ninety-four. Climb to fly. Walk the sky.*

Ollie scrunched his face as he wrote, struggling with the awkward quill. When he was done, he held out the yellowed parchment and surveyed his work. The scrawls of black ink were streaked with blood red. It was messy, but legible. A new kind of Herrick note. Or not-Herrick note. Either way, Ollie could only hope these words would work like the others had—guiding him and protecting him. Leading him to...something. Or somewhere. Or, God willing, to some*one* who could help. Ollie blew on the words to dry them, then folded the paper and tucked it into his pocket. He patted the bulge, feeling strangely comforted, as though he now carried a mighty shield instead of a delicate piece of paper covered with incoherent, chicken-scratched ramblings.

Ollie dropped the quill back into its pot and wiped his inky fingers on his pant legs. Walking back to Carmichael, he held out his hand.

The Fancy Man, who had been watching him curiously, handed over the injector. "I hear it hurts like hell," he said, not sounding particularly sorry about it.

Ollie stared at him. "You're an idiot," he whispered, and it was true. He almost pitied the man. If Carmichael had ever loved anyone like Ollie loved Tera... Hell, if Carmichael had ever loved anyone at all, then he would know: No pain could be worse than the one that was already stomping Ollie's guts into pulp. "Where do I do it?"

"In your arm, I think," Carmichael said, pointing. "You need to blow into the tube. It works on lung power."

Of course it did. What didn't, down here? *Air and breath, truth and lie.* Ollie grimaced, steeled himself, and pressed the muzzle against his forearm.

He looked one last time at Meatball's motionless body, and then at Tera's unseeing, opened eyes. *I will finish this,* he promised silently, trying to somehow send the thought through the thick glass and into her mind. *I swear it. And then I will come back for you. Please...* Tears stung his eyes, again. *Please, don't let go.*

Ollie took a deep, ragged breath. He blew into the tube with all the force of his desperation, pulling the trigger at the same time. He cried out when the capsule rocketed through his skin. The sudden, mind-blowing burn made him drop the gun to the ground. His forearm jerked and flopped with tremors. With one swift motion, he had stabbed himself, then electrocuted himself, then infected himself. The agony was absolute. The room spun around him in a nauseating, erratic orbit until, finally, it slammed to a stop.

The pellet had lodged—he did not have to touch the lump with his fingers to know it was there.

Ollie balled his hands into fists.

Then, like a fiddlehead finding the afternoon sun, his spine unfurled. His chin lifted. The shaking in his legs subsided. He did not look back at the tank. He had seen all there was to see, and said all there was to say.

He stepped closer to Carmichael, then closer still, until their faces nearly touched.

"Keep him alive," Ollie growled. "Keep them all alive. You got that?"

Carmichael's eyes widened. He nodded quickly.

Ollie turned toward the big red door. *Nothing left but the leaving.* The sooner he went, the sooner he could get back. And the sooner he got back, the sooner everything would change.

After all, they had trained him well at Herrick's End, hadn't they? They had wanted to punish him, to silence him, but they had trained him, instead. And here, in this laboratory, they had managed to do what even the prison could not—they had hardened him. His anger was a solid, living thing, rising up in revolt. And in the process, it had awakened something new within him.

Your rage will show us all.

Ollie looked down at his hands. He could still feel it there, waiting. Gone, but not gone. Trailing him like an eager, expectant shadow.

He felt the lingering spark, and he understood: George Herrick and his henchmen would suffer. They would weep while he watched. And they would come to lament, deeply, every decision they had ever made that had brought them all to this moment.

Someday very soon, Ollie would make them all pay what they owed.

The creatures in the cages screeched and snarled; condensation and candle wax fell like rain at his feet. He ignored it all.

Water, earth, air.

Three elements. One chance. Zero mistakes.

Ollie was going back to Boston.

Epilogue

The tunnel was exactly as long, dark, and steep as he'd expected it to be. It was also cold as hell.

The beam from his miner's helmet, weak and linear, wasn't much help. Ollie supposed it didn't matter. He knew where he was going: Up. Everything else was just details.

The rungs protruded from the carved stone, too far apart, forcing him to reach and pull himself up to each successive one like an orangutan. He was not the first person to grip them, of course; many, many others had already ascended this murky, narrow tunnel through the earth. Women. Men. Children. Even his own mother, so many years ago. A regular exodus of Neath visitors, all leaving their torment—and their tormentors—behind. The difference was, they had all been climbing toward their futures. Ollie was climbing toward his past.

He moved steadily, robotically. He searched his reserves for courage, or determination, but found only a dull, pained exhaustion. The passion and fury that had fueled his departure from Grimshawe Laboratory seemed to have fizzled under the damp weight of reality.

How would he do this? He had no plan, aside from some scribbled, vague hints on a parchment. And he had no allies. All he had was an overwhelming sense of distress and the constant, nagging reminder of what would happen, and who would suffer, if he failed.

He climbed and he worried and he brooded until, at last, his head hit something hard.

Cautiously, Ollie reached up. His hand touched cold metal. He patted around the surface and edges until he found a handle. He tried pushing, then pulling. Nothing happened. Finally, he twisted, and heard a click. It reminded him of another sound: one he had heard on a day long ago, when he had dropped to his knees in the alley at the Boston Massacre Site, turned a dial to spell out a coded word, and opened the Freedom Trail medallion on the ground. *Click.*

Had he now returned to the very same spot? Would he push open the heavy portal and discover that his head was sticking out of the ground in that shaded alley, staring up at the brick facade of the Old State House? Surrounded by the rush of clicking boot heels and bike wheels and pecking pigeons?

He pushed.

As the first rays of light crawled through the crack, he recoiled. After so long underground, the brilliance was almost unbearable. Ollie shielded his eyes and kept shoving.

Once the metal plate was open wide enough, he poked his face out into the air. He squinted, waiting for his vision to adjust to the onslaught of harsh radiance. Then he began, slowly, to make out vague shapes and colors, which coalesced, more slowly, into recognizable sights.

Ollie did not see a cement sidewalk. Or the Old State House. Or tires, or pigeons.

He saw...grass.

Overgrown grass. A long stalk of it tickled his chin.

The smell of wet dirt hit his nose. Exhaust fumes trickled in, too, but fainter. And flowers. Definitely flowers. Bright and sweet, like summer.

With the metal plate still hovering over his head, Ollie blinked again and scanned the immediate area. He saw tipping stones, all around. Old and fragile. Most were tinged with moss. Graves? Harbor waters sparkled in the distance. He saw a long length of wrought-iron fence. Brick walls. Windows and doors. He saw...the

Skinny House? Yes, definitely the famous Skinny House, standing in all its unmistakable, narrow glory in the shadow of the more normal residences on either side.

He was in Copp's Hill Burying Ground.

Ollie had emerged from the deepest depths into the highest point in the North End, surrounded by the decaying bodies of long-ago Bostonians. He was rising from the dead—or rising from among them, anyway. It would have been funny if it wasn't so gross.

Mud to brick, dark to sun.

More prophetic words come true.

Ollie inhaled...and waited. This was it. The true test of the Grimshawe's breathing-pellet-pea-shooter-injector thingy. Would it work? If it didn't, would he know instantly? Would he keel over in seconds to become yet another dead guy at Copp's Hill? Or would it be more of a drawn-out, days-long, slow suffocation? He wasn't sure which would be worse.

He suddenly realized he was holding his breath. Anxiously, he let it out. Then in, then out again.

Nothing happened.

He had made it. He was back on the Brickside, and he was breathing. The pellet lodged under his skin seemed to be doing its job—for the time being, anyway. The awareness filled Ollie with unexpected elation, followed by an equally powerful wave of dread. Now, what? He found himself suddenly frozen, his face poking out into the light and his body still in the dark. Half in the new world and half in the old. But which world was which?

It was too much. He couldn't do this. Any of it. He didn't even know how to start.

Ollie's legs and arms began to shake. His eyes darted in trepidation. He saw more grass. A distant boat. Lanterns in doorways. The tip of one iron fence post twisted in a different direction than all the others.

A shoe.

No, not a shoe. More like a grayish slipper.

"Is long climb, yes?" a voice asked. It was deep. Thickly accented. Then a chuckle.

A face appeared suddenly, blocking the view.

Ollie's eyes widened. "Laszlo?"

The acrobat smiled in response. Dark hair framed his sharp cheekbones and nose with long, swaying strands.

"Wh—what are you doing here?"

"What I am doing here?" Laszlo responded, sounding insulted. "Our friends tell me we have much to do, and not much time to do it. And so, here I am. Doing all of the waiting. Sitting on rock." He gestured toward a low mausoleum stone behind him. "And I tell you, I am glad you are finally here, because I have had enough of rock."

Ollie stared. "You've been waiting? For me?"

"What am I just saying? Yes, of course. What else? We will do this together. That is, how do you say it... That is what the friends are about."

A smile began to tug on Ollie's lips. "That's what friends are for," he corrected softly.

"Yes. Right. That is what the friends are for."

Ollie tried to respond, but found a lump blocking the words. The shaking in his limbs receded, replaced by a jellied flush of relief.

"So, we will go now?" the acrobat asked. "Unless, of course, you would rather stay down in hole all day."

Laszlo held out a hand, and Ollie took it.

The heavy plate opened. A rush of fresh salt air flooded his nose and lungs. He heard the full cacophony of the city, his city—a song that seemed at once both mundane and miraculous. He opened his eyes as wide as they would allow.

And then, for the first time in a second lifetime, Ollie stepped out into the sun.

Acknowledgements

Thank you first and foremost to the incredible team at Tiny Fox Press, especially Galen Surlak-Ramsey, whose editorial eye and supportive feedback gave this book exactly what it needed, exactly when it needed it. I'm also forever grateful to Natalie Day, Maya Sherlick, and Elizabeth Young for continuing to usher Ollie and his friends safely—well, mostly safely—through the Neath.

Thank you to Julie Gwinn and everyone at The Seymour Agency for your guidance and insights.

Thank you to my fellow Tall Poppy Writers for helping me navigate the ever-shifting sands of the writing and publishing worlds. It means more than you know to count myself among such an impressive and talented group of humans.

Thank you to the indefatigable team at Operation Delta Dog: Service Dogs for Veterans, where they have a mission to rescue shelter dogs and train them to work as service dogs for veterans who suffer from Traumatic Brain Injury (TBI), PTSD, and related challenges. The dogs get the homes they need, and the veterans get the help they deserve.

Thank you to my colleagues at A Mighty Blaze, where books are always front-and-center and everyone gets a chance to shine. Let's keep that Blaze burning!

Thank you, always, to my real-life menagerie of Unnatural Wonders, led by the incomparable Jenna Blum: Hillary Casavant, Mark Cecil, Tom Champoux, Jennifer De Leon, Catherine Elcik, Chuck Garabedian, Julie Gerstenblatt, Kimberly Hensle Lowrance, Edwin Hill, Alexandra Hoopes, Sonya Larson, Joseph Moldover, Jenna Paone, Kris Paull, Jane Roper, Whitney Scharer, and Adam Stumacher. You make this writing life—and life in general—grand.

Thank you to my fellow fantasy fanatic Mark Cecil for his insightful beta reads, suggestions, and edits on this manuscript.

Thank you to Mom and Dad for a lifetime of encouragement.

Thank you to Lucy for tolerating my incessant chatter about fictional people and places.

Thank you to Ian for listening to all my story ideas...and then coming up with much better story ideas.

And thank you to Scott for everything, everything, everything. I can breathe underwater as long as I have you.

———⁓———

If someone is trying to hurt you, isolate you, or control you, you are not alone: On average, 1 in 4 women and 1 in 9 men have experienced violence or abuse from someone they know well. If you're under 18, this is often called dating violence or parental abuse. If you're over 18, it's usually called domestic violence. No matter what your age or gender, no one else has the right to physically or mentally harm you.

If you want to seek help, you can reach out to the National Domestic Violence Hotline at thehotline.org or 1-800-799-SAFE (**United States**), the Ending Violence Association of Canada at endingviolencecanada.org or the Kids Help Phone at 1-800-668-6868 (**Canada**), the National Domestic Abuse Helpline at nationaldahelpline.org.uk or 0808-2000-247 (**U.K.**), and 1800Respect.org.au or 1-800-RESPECT (**Australia**). Resources are also available at sites like ncadv.org, womenshealth.gov, domesticshelters.org, and loveisrespect.org.

About The Author

T.M. Blanchet is a former reporter, editor, and award-winning humor columnist, as well as the founder of the nonprofit organization Operation Delta Dog: Service Dogs for Veterans. She's also the producer and host of A Mighty Blaze Podcast, which features weekly interviews with bestselling and debut authors. T.M. is a proud member of the Tall Poppy Writers, the Society of Children's Book Writers and Illustrators, and the Science Fiction & Fantasy Writers Association.

Website: tmblanchet.com

Instagram: t.m.blanchet
Tiktok: @tmblanchet
Twitter: @TM_Blanchet

About the Publisher

Tiny Fox Press LLC
5020 Kingsley Road
North Port, FL 34287

www.tinyfoxpress.com